Miracle on Regent Street

Ali Harris

W F HOWES LTD

This large print edition published in 2012 by
W F Howes Ltd
Unit 4, Rearsby Business Park, Gaddesby Lane,
Rearsby, Leicester LE7 4YH

1 3 5 7 9 10 8 6 4 2

First published in the Great Britain in 2011
by Simon & Schuster UK Ltd

ISBN 978 1 40749 561 3

Typeset by Palimpsest Book Production Limited,
Falkirk, Stirlingshire
Printed and bound in Great Britain
by MPG Books Ltd, Bodmin, Cornwall

MIX
Paper from
responsible sources
FSC
www.fsc.org   FSC® C018575

To Ben. With never-ending superlove . . .

THURSDAY 1 DECEMBER

24 Shopping Days Until Christmas

CHAPTER 1

I gaze out of my bedroom window into the dark winter morning as the snowflakes fall softly outside. Is this it? I wonder. It's not a sudden change in the wind, like the one that carried Mary Poppins to the Banks family, or the tornado that carried Dorothy to Oz, but maybe, just maybe, this downfall is the universe's way of telling me that my life is about to change. A flurry of snow to signal the flurry of action I've been waiting for so long.

I drop the curtains so that they fall back in place and dash over to my dressing table where my Advent calendar is propped up against the mirror. I smile as I open door number one and pop the chocolate in my mouth. The picture is of a snow globe. Another sign that things are about to be shaken up?

Half an hour later I slam the front door behind me, heave my bike down the front steps and hop on, feeling a thrill of anticipation. Today big things are going to happen, I just know it.

Today, like every work day, I'm wearing plain black trousers, a white shirt (with a thermal vest underneath) and flat brogues. I'm also wrapped in a cardigan, my sensible knee-length duffel coat, bobble hat, and a multicoloured striped scarf, which I've wound tightly around my neck and mouth. Not a great look but it's not like anyone is going to notice at this time of the morning. Or indeed at any time. It's been two years since anyone really looked at me. That was when Jamie broke up with me.

Obviously I've changed *massively* since then and I'm completely over him. Well, maybe not completely. But, you know, these things take time. Two years isn't that long to get over a five-year relationship, is it? I don't care what my sister says, it's perfectly understandable that I'm not quite there yet. Besides, since we broke up I've been focusing on other aspects of my life. I mean, I don't live with my parents any more, for a start. OK, so I do live with my big sister, Delilah, and her husband, Will, in the converted attic in their house overlooking a gorgeous square in Primrose Hill, but it's different because I'm independent. Like a 28-year-old woman should be. Well, independent apart from the fact that in exchange for my lodging I have to look after my 3-year-old niece, Lola, and 2-year-old nephew, Raffy, before and after work. It's not ideal, but I can't complain.

I inhale deeply and gaze around me wondrously. How could I fail to feel positive on a day like this? The roofs of the grand Regency houses on Chalcot Square are covered in white, as if a big scoop of vanilla ice cream has melted all over the pepper-mint, orange, raspberry and lemon sorbet-coloured houses. And the pretty garden that they surround looks like a Christmas cake that's just been covered with a thick layer of royal icing. I push off, wobbling a little as I weave round it and cycle on to Regent's Park Road.

I cross the road and head over to Primrose Hill, pedalling hard to break through the thick layer of snow that crunches under my wheels. Then I stop for a moment and just cruise downhill, feeling the wind whip against my cheeks, throwing my head back and closing my eyes so that I feel like I'm suspended in space and time. I open my eyes, grip the handlebars tightly and pedal furiously again. Because today, for once, I'm determined to go somewhere.

It feels as if I have been magically transported back in time as I cycle into Portland Place. No vehicles are on the streets and I can't help but imagine them when they were cobbled and filled with horses and carriages. I'm just picturing myself in full Victorian costume, when I swing off down New Cavendish Street and onto Great Titchfield Street, past the unlit pubs and restaur-ants, and then I swerve down a smaller road, skidding to a halt as I pull up in front of Hardy's department store: a place that has been my daytime home for the past two years and where, today, all my career dreams will finally come true.

CHAPTER 2

Hardy's sits elegantly on the corner of two streets just north (or, as many people say, 'the wrong side') of Regent Street. Over the other side is Soho, home to numerous famous theatres, legendary restaurants and cool, destination bars. But here, in 'Noho', we're like Soho's less famous but much prettier sibling. Officially classed as in Fitzrovia, Hardy's is too far from the big shops on Regent and Oxford Street for the crowds who flock there every day. Tourists don't know we're here, and Londoners would far rather visit salubrious Selfridges, quaint Liberty or just-plain-useful John Lewis than schlep all the way over to us.

The small but perfectly formed store seems to rise up before me now like a pop-up picture in a children's Christmas book. I sit back on my saddle and glance up at it fondly, panting a little from my uncharacteristic race to the store. I'm not usually this desperate to get to work but today is different: the Big Announcement is happening at 9 a.m. My manager, Sharon, came into the stockroom last week and told me that they're looking

6

to promote someone to be assistant manager of the shop floor. She said that they had their eye on someone who'd been with the company for a long time (hello! Two years!), who knew the stock inside out (I'm only the *stock*room manager) as well as the customers (I can name all of our regular customers off the cuff). Then she'd said they wanted someone who was passionate about the store. And if *that* wasn't the biggest ever hint in the universe, then I don't know what is. There isn't anything I don't know about Hardy's. And Sharon knows how much I'd love to be out there on the shop floor, talking to customers, selling, being part of it all.

The store itself has seen better days, it has barely any customers and the stock wouldn't look out of place in a museum, but I still love the old place. That's why I was so excited to get a job here two years ago – even if it was only in the stockroom. I thought I'd only be working there for a short while, until they saw my potential and moved me on to the shop floor. But that still hasn't happened. At least it hasn't until today . . .

I glance up at the clock on the front of the store. It's still only six thirty. I chain up my bike in the parking bay and find I can't tear my eyes away from the store façade. Hardy's is a beautiful four-storey Edwardian building with warm sandstone bricks that sit above the modern glass-fronted ground floor. Beautiful arched baroque windows line the entire first floor like a dozen eyes peering

7

down on the street. Above them, thin rectangular windows are poised like eyelashes to flutter at passers-by. The rooftop silhouette is dominated by ornate columned balconies and a central domed tower, which is now lightly covered in a layer of snow. At the front of this tower is a clock that has been telling the time to passing Londoners for a hundred years. But looking at it now, the hands seem to stay perfectly still, like they're frozen in time. Even the windows seem to stare blankly back at me. It's as if the store is in a deep sleep.

It might be the 1 December but you wouldn't know it here at Hardy's. It's supposed to be the busiest shopping period of the year, but each day the store is like a ghost town. And to make matters worse, the board of directors has decided to go minimal on the decorations this year. So they've got rid of Hardy's traditional, crowd-pleasing fifty-foot-high Norwegian spruce, which has stood next to the central staircase, dripping with decorations and proudly guarding its bounty of beautifully wrapped gift boxes each December for decades. Instead, in a fit of frugality, Rupert Hardy, the fourth generation Hardy family member to manage the store, suggested that we make use of the two dozen tacky silver artificial Christmas trees that his father, Sebastian, had bought back in the 1980s but never used. Rupert said that they are a nod to the new, trendy 'Christmas minimalism', but we all know that it's just a money-saving measure. But at what cost? I feel like asking. No one wants to shop at a place that is devoid of Christmas spirit. And customers only have to see the sorrowful-looking windows to conclude that Hardy's is severely lacking in yuletide cheer.

I sigh as I look at the spray-on snow framing the dozen small, sad trees, which are apparently meant to symbolize the Twelve Days of Christmas, three in each of the four big store windows. They look pathetic. And now the real snow that has settled on the pavements this morning is illuminating the sorry state of our half-hearted Christmas windows even more.

I walk into the staff entrance at the side of the building, swiping my card and smiling at Felix, the security guard, who is, as ever, utterly occupied by his Sudoku. Along the corridor, I pass the staff noticeboards featuring details of the latest 'Employee of the Month'. This month it's my good friend Carly. I'm really happy for her; she deserves it. She does a great job in the personal shopping department, with her gift for finding the right style for anyone, no matter what their size, shape, personality – or even proclivity. (She once had a pre-op transgender client who, after two hours with Carly, walked out of Hardy's looking like he no longer needed an operation. Amazing.) She says she's like a matchmaker, except with customers and clothes.

I can't pretend, though, that I'm not disappointed that it wasn't my turn to be given the accolade. I've never been awarded Employee of the Month, whereas Carly's received it twice in the six months she's worked here. But it's OK, I tell myself as I stand in front of her picture – noting how everything about her seems to sparkle with life: her eyes, teeth, skin, hair; she's practically iridescent – today it's my turn. Carly may have got the job in Personal Shopping, but a managerial role for someone who knows Hardy's inside out? That's *much* more me.

The noticeboard features a photograph of every staff member. I'm proud to say I know each one of them; I know their partners' names, their kids' names, ages and their (infinite) talents. I know where they live, what their worries are, their hopes, their dreams. There's Gwen, the beauty department manager; a bright, incredibly polished woman, who is hiding a terrible secret behind that beaming, painted-on smile: mountains of credit card debts. Then there's Jenny, Gwen's faithful assistant. She's thirty-five and has been trying for a baby without success. In the two years that I've worked here I've watched her go from a hopeful honeymooner to someone who believes she may never be a mother. She and her husband want to have IVF treatment and she is desperate to make sales in the store so she can earn more commission to pay for this. It's awful seeing her so despondent now the store is so quiet.

Then my gaze settles on the photo of Guy, who works in Menswear. I suspect he had his teeth whitened especially for the picture; I almost need sunglasses to look at it. He's fabulously camp but recently he's lost his sparkle. His long-term boyfriend, Paul, dumped him for a younger man and, with his fortieth fast approaching, Guy has been swathed in uncharacteristic melancholy for weeks. Everyone's rather worried about him.

Another staff member heading for forty and unhappy about it is my manager, Sharon. She lives with her elderly mother. I suspect that the only thing she has in her life is her job. I certainly know that she's besotted with Rupert Hardy, not because she's told me but because I've seen the way she looks at him as they do the rounds of the store together. Her brittle edges seem softer when she's with him; her body relaxes, her tongue isn't so sharp, her expression is warmer. I think she would soften even more if only he would show some reciprocal interest. But he doesn't, and so Sharon prowls round the store like a frustrated lioness, snarling at anyone who crosses her path and, as a result, is hugely unpopular.

I know all this because, while I'm unpacking stock, I listen to each and every one of the staff when they come into the stock-room, which they often do just to get away from the shop floor. I mean, it's not like they have many customers to keep them busy. So they come and talk to me about everything: their lives, loves, problems and their successes. They talk and I listen. It makes me feel special, rather than just an unpacker of boxes, I'm the in-store counsellor, the secret

11

problem solver of Hardy's. But not for much longer, I remind myself as I bounce down the corridor. My time in the stockroom is nearly up.

I make my way purposefully through the fire exit doors that lead from the staff corridor directly into the impressive ground-floor atrium, with its dark, wood-panelled walls and grand central staircase (no new-fangled technology such as escalators at Hardy's), connecting every floor, including the basement. The store is laid out in a traditional way. Well, that's putting it kindly. It currently looks like a fusty old department store you'd find in the dreary back end of a small market town. Its beautiful original features – impressive art deco chandeliers and old mahogany counters – were ripped out during Sebastian Hardy's tenure and replaced with neon strip lighting, horrible white plastic-coated units and shelf displays. It's now stuck in a 1980s time warp.

In terms of layout, on the ground floor are the beauty, handbags and jewellery departments. On the first floor is Designers (a misleading department name; there's nothing remotely fashionable or desirable there) as well as Lingerie and Shoes. On the second floor are the children's department, Haberdashery and Hats. The third floor used to have a beauty salon (where my mum worked back in the day) but that's now empty and there's just Rupert Hardy's office up there. Downstairs in the basement is Menswear, which includes the sportswear department and is mostly made up of dreary hunting, fishing, golf and shooting gear – oh, and the lovely little original tearoom. Because of the open-plan nature of the store, from here I can see all the way up to the domed roof. The beauty department is at the centre of this floor where I'm currently standing and I take a deep breath as I look around at the old-fashioned displays. I love the smell of Hardy's, a homely, fusty smell that takes me back to my childhood. I get lots of different scents: top notes of old leather and wood, base notes of musk and spices, resin and vanilla. But the most overpowering sense I have here is of the many stories and lives that have played out under this roof. Including mine.

Despite the early hour, the place is a hive of activity. The cleaners are buzzing around like worker bees, shining floors and polishing shelves. On the other side of Beauty I spot Jan Baptysta, the Polish head cleaner, who has worked here longer than I have.

'Ahhh, Evie-English-Wife!' He waves enthusiastically at me from behind his industrial floor cleaner and smiles his big, gap-toothed smile as I wave back.

This has been his nickname for me ever since we spoke about the fact that his parents named him after John the Baptist, and my mum mistakenly picked up the Bible instead of the baby name book when she had my big sister, Delilah, and loved the variety of names in it so much that she used it again when Noah, Jonah and I came along.

Jan said his mother would think me the perfect match for him because of it.

Anyway, Jan Baptysta doesn't really want me to be his wife. At least, I don't think he does. He's at least fifteen years older and fifty pounds heavier than I am. He's built like a tank, with a shaved head, thick arms that are covered in tattoos, and has heavy-set, penetrating dark eyes. But despite his intimidating appearance he leads the other cleaners with a gentle authority. And they reward him with a cheerful, dedicated work ethic. None of them apart from Jan is actually employed by Hardy's; they're all contract workers for a cleaning company and many of them have been working all night at various establishments around the city. Yet they always have this incredible energy and pride in their work, despite this being their last job at the end of a twelve-hour shift. Like Jan, several of them have worked here for years, but their pictures don't appear on the staff notice-boards. In fact, most of Hardy's employees wouldn't recognize them if they walked past them on the street, which is a shame as they're such lovely people.

There's Velna from Latvia, who is obsessed with the Eurovision Song Contest. She sings constantly as she works, which drives all the other cleaners mad. She even has all the winning entries on a playlist on her iPod. It's her dream to compete in the competition but no one has the heart to tell her she can't actually sing.

'Boomp bangh a BANG!' she trills, hopping on one leg and waving as I walk past. She's wearing a scarf over her bright red hair, her tortoiseshell spectacles, and a patchwork dress over a rollneck jumper, which she's teamed with Wellington boots. I join her in a little dance as I pass, laughing as she spins me around before she twirls off and I head towards the stockroom.

Then there's Justyna, who clearly has the hots for Jan Baptysta and is thus distinctly cool around me. She must be six-foot tall, with feet and hands the size of tennis rackets. I'm pretty scared of her, actually. As a result I tend to overcompensate by being superfriendly, usually without much response.

'HelloJustyna how are you today? Are you well isn't thes now wonderful?' I garble as she stares at me with an expression as icy as the pavement outside.

She nods curtly and continues mopping the floor with her back to me, her vast bottom swishing from side to side like an angry bullock's. I hastily move on, waving up at the cleaners working on the floors above.

Just as I reach the stockroom door I turn round to take one last glimpse of the store before I burrow myself away. I immediately feel my good mood falter as I know that the cleaners' hard work can't polish this beautiful old jewellery box of a building back to its former glory. Nothing can hide the fact that the paint on the walls is peeling, the mahogany panels are tarnished and the intricately patterned tapestry stair runner is discoloured and torn. Seeing Hardy's, a place I've loved for so many years, like this is like watching a beautiful old film star slowly fade and die.

Ever since I was a little girl Hardy's has been like my own personal Narnia; I honestly felt that magic could happen when I stepped through its glass doors. I used to get so excited by our annual visits to London to celebrate the anniversary of the day my parents met, not just because of the actual treats themselves – trips to the theatre and ballet, dinner at nice restaurants and afternoon tea at elegant hotels – but because we'd always pay a visit to Hardy's.

Every year on 12 December my parents and I would travel to London together and stay overnight in our Hampstead flat whilst my grandparents looked after Delilah and the boys. Even though my parents had long since left London, Dad still had the flat in town for work. I would look forward to the trip for months: some precious time alone with my parents, away from my overbearing siblings, who were all too old and therefore too cool to come along.

We would get dressed up, me in a party dress with a bow round my waist and a satin ribbon in my hair, a bright festive-coloured winter coat, white tights and patent Mary Janes. Mum would wear some glamorous dress with an elegant coat, and lashings of perfume and lipstick, and my dad

16

always looked dapper in a smart suit, cashmere scarf and overcoat.

We would get the train from Norwich into Liverpool Street and then a black taxi to Regent Street. Full of wonderment, I'd peer out of the window as the famous London sights whipped by, dreaming of the day when I could live there myself. We always ended up standing with our arms around each other in front of Hardy's doors, which were framed with greenery and fairy lights, the windows sparkling with Christmas delights, watching the customers weaving through into the brightly lit store as if they were explorers returning from their long travels to the place they would always call home. My mum and dad would share a lingering movie-style kiss outside the store as I looked up at them, bursting with happiness that these were my parents and that they were so in love. Then we'd walk in and I'd be swept up in the sounds of old-fashioned tills ringing, the staff beaming in Santa hats.

Unlike at snootier department stores, at Hardy's no one minded a little girl exploring the higgledy-piggledy departments on her own whilst her parents reminisced over a champagne tea in the basement tearoom. I felt as at home as I did in our house in Norfolk. Except here I didn't have to jostle for attention or fight to be heard. I was just welcomed with open arms by the friendly staff, taken behind counters, shown how to use the tills, dressed up in too-big-for-me hats and too-old-for-me make-up, and made to feel like I was the most special little girl in the world. The store became my own personal dressing-up box. After an hour I would emerge decked from head to toe in vintage garb, pretty mother-of-pearl brooches pinned to my coat, flamboyant scarves wrapped around my little shoulders, wearing a fur muffler and a matching hat, my face covered in iridescent shades of lipstick and blusher. Then I'd go downstairs to the basement to find my mum and dad, who would be holding hands, oblivious to everyone around them – including Lily, the glamorous old lady who ran the tearoom. But she'd always spot me hovering in the doorway and beckon me over to her, tie a little white frilly apron on me and send me over to my parents' table with some cakes that had been especially iced with their initials beautifully woven together.

Mum would get all teary and Dad would tell me once again the story of how they met in Hardy's, how he proposed and how he knew, as soon as he set eyes on my mother, who had been working as a hairdresser and beauty therapist on the third floor, that she was the only girl for him. Then Mum would dreamily recall how she'd been struck speechless as my dad had entered the salon, all dashing with his thick, demi-waved hair and strong Roman nose. They'd stared at each other for what felt like hours as the clients and staff all stopped and watched them both. Then my dad had walked slowly over to my mother, tilted her back in his arms and kissed her on the lips as the crowd that had gathered around them applauded ecstatically. Walter Hardy, junior, the owner of the store at that time, had even come up to the salon to see what all the fuss was about, at which point my dad had walked over to him, his arm still clasped tightly around my bewildered but utterly bewitched mother, and informed Walter that she no longer needed her job because she was going to be his wife. Walter had laughed and shaken his hand – luckily they were acquainted as Dad had been close friends with Walter's son, Sebastian, since their school days – and Dad had then whisked Mum off into his waiting car outside and to Claridge's, where they had had dinner and danced. They got married three months later at Chelsea Register office and Delilah arrived nine months later.

That was thirty-five years ago now. They don't make enduring romances like that any more. And I should know; I've been fruitlessly searching for one for as long as I can remember.

Their love-at-first-sight story is folklore in our house – not to mention at the store. Even now the older members of staff still talk about the beautiful blonde beauty therapist who met her very own Prince Charming within these sacred walls. I've often quizzed my father about what it was that made him act so out of character on that day. As a successful financier he's by nature incredibly considered and not at all spontaneous. He always gives the same reply: 'If you see something you want, you have to go for it, Eve,' he'll say. 'You won't get anywhere in this life otherwise.' Sometimes I wish some of his single-mindedness had rubbed off on me.

So you could say that it's thanks to my parents' love affair that I've had my own love affair with Hardy's and ended up working here for so long. Although sometimes I can't help but wonder what might have been. I love the place and there's no other store I'd rather work in, but when I was a little girl imagining what I'd be one day, the answer was never a stockroom manager. I wanted to be an artist or a fashion designer or a window dresser. I spent my childhood doing endless sketches of shop displays on the notepads I carried everywhere with me. I pored over glossy coffee-table books, and trawled shops and markets for vintage clothes that looked like the ones I imagined people wearing back when fashion meant enduring style. After doing a degree at art college I even got a place on a graduate training scheme in fashion merchandising in London. I was all set to go when I met Jamie at the Norfolk hotel where I'd been working all summer. It didn't take much on his part to convince me to stay. I was twenty-one, he was my first real boyfriend and I was in love. And I'd had my parents' romantic meeting as my inspiration my entire life. Mum had immediately given up her career for lasting love; is it any wonder that I was so quick to do the same? It felt like my destiny. I didn't expect or want anything more for myself.

Mum's always said that of her children I am the one most like her. I think this means I am the one most likely to make sacrifices for love. I can't think what else we have in common – Delilah inherited Mum's show-stopping beauty – but Mum's always had this romantic notion that my life will mirror hers. So when Jamie broke up with me not only was I utterly heartbroken, I felt like I'd disappointed her too. After all, we'd been together five years and she was all set for a wedding and more grandchildren. Unable to deal with her incessant but well-meant probing and mollycoddling, I realized that I needed space away from the life I'd had.

So I packed a small suitcase and went to London to stay with my sister, who was then on maternity leave. After a week of weeping and wailing on her shoulder and generally being a mess because I was twenty-six and had nothing to show for my life – no career, no boyfriend and what felt like no future – she told me firmly to get out of the house and face the world. I was shocked into action. So I had a shower, got dressed, brushed my hair and headed to Hardy's, the only other place that had ever felt like home.

I spent the morning wandering sadly around its hallowed halls and reminiscing. It had been at least ten years since I'd last visited with my parents, having grown out of the annual visits when I hit my teens. In that time the place had lost its sparkle – just like me. It, too, felt abandoned and unloved. The store was deathly quiet, the staff all had a lethargy about them, and even though I was the only customer they completely ignored me. Which is why I was surprised when I was tapped on the shoulder by supercilious-looking lady.

'I'm Sharon. You must be the new girl,' she barked. I opened my mouth to protest but she bulldozed on, 'You're late. I thought you weren't coming.'

'Oh, no . . .' I began.

But she had already turned and stalked off, snapping her fingers and saying, 'Well, don't dilly-dally, girl. Follow me!'

I didn't know what else to do so I obeyed.

'You'll be in the stockroom,' she said haughtily as she marched me to the darkest recess of the store, to a door tucked away far beyond the beauty department. 'It'll help you to get to know the extent of our range. Rupert thinks it's the best training ground for new staff.'

'B-but . . .' I stammered pathetically.

'Do you have a problem with that?' she asked, and stared at me pointedly, her thin pencilled eyebrows almost disappearing into her harshly scraped-back hairline.

'N-no, ma'am,' I muttered, glancing around for an escape route but also suddenly wondering if this could be just the thing I was looking for. A job, in London, in the one place I knew better than anywhere else? It felt almost serendipitous. Delilah had already suggested that I lodge with her and Will for a while for free in exchange for looking after the kids before and after nursery, when her maternity leave was over. I'd still need a paid job, though. And where better than here at Hardy's? It could be just the start of the career I'd always dreamed of. I was just contemplating telling the lady I wasn't who she thought I was but I'd like the job anyway, but before I could open my mouth she'd officiously tapped a code into the security lock and ushered me through. I told myself I had no choice but to obey her, whilst fervently hoping that the real new girl I'd been mistaken for didn't turn up.

My mouth dropped open as I looked around. It felt like being swallowed up in The Place That Time Forgot. Old stock, old paint job, old *air*, even. The woman didn't follow me. She'd just waved me in and then disappeared back onto the bright shop floor that, in comparison with the dirty old stockroom, looked practically swanky now, telling me, as she left, to take lunch at one o'clock. I gazed back in horror at the stockroom and I remember being surprised at its size. Despite the small door I'd entered through, the space stretched back more than fifty feet, and although it wasn't very wide, it seemed to hold more stuff than you could ever imagine, like Mary Poppins' carpet bag.

Looking around me I decided Hardy's probably

had a few of those in stock as well. There was row upon row of full-to-bursting boxes stacked up on top of each other like Leaning Tower of Pisas. Some were overflowing so that random soaps, shoes and 1950s-style hooped petticoats littered the floor, as well as stranger items, like shooting sticks and old seamstresses' mannequins. It felt like the walls were closing in on me. Everything was grey, for a start, and not that trendy Farrow and Ball dove grey. Prison grey. *Grey* grey. The walls, the metal shelving units, the floor, even the light. It would have felt cold were it not so musty and airless. I took a deep breath and wrinkled my nose in disgust.

As I walked down the stockroom, watching where I stepped, I found myself looking more closely at the shelves. I pulled out a packet of pre-war stockings from a battered box by my feet, complete with a seam down the back and a price marked in shillings and pence. I'd have laughed if I hadn't been so shocked. Instead I'd held my nose and veered down the first aisle to take a close inspection. Totally unrelated items lived side by side. Hockey sticks next to hideous pastel Mother-of-the-Bride outfits; Wellington boots and trench coats next to boxes upon boxes of boulder-sized bras and petticoats that should have been displayed in a museum. There were original 1940s trilbies tucked away at the back, as well as talcum powder, flat caps and brightly coloured braces spilling out all over the floor.

I was just wondering if anyone had worked in here for years when a small, timid-looking girl peered out from behind a box in the next aisle. Her hair was long and lank, her expression blank.

'You the new girl?' she asked quietly.

I nodded and smiled brightly at her.

'I'm Sarah,' she said, and then picked up her bag. 'Well, good luck,' she added unconvincingly, and pulled on her coat, clearly desperate to leave.

'Wait,' I said slightly desperately as she walked towards the door. 'Aren't you going to show me the ropes?'

She turned back and smiled kindly. 'There aren't any. No one will notice what you do in here anyway. I suggest you make a cup of tea and bring in some good books.' And then she left.

I stood on the same spot looking around in bewilderment for a good ten minutes. I didn't know where to begin. All I knew was that I wanted to do something. I've always hated disorder. Even as a child I'd put all my toys away at bedtime and shut every door behind me when I was leaving a room.

Once I got over the shock I started exploring the place from top to bottom, searching through every box, every shelf, every pile, getting to know the stock whilst trying to work out where it could logically go. It was a bit like doing convoluted mathematical equations in my head. I actually kind of liked it. Once I'd acquainted myself with everything I began systematically listing each piece of stock, from the sublime (original 1950s pillbox hats) to the ridiculous (multicoloured striped long johns). It felt like I was taking a step back into my childhood: each of the items I came across I could visualize on the shop floor I remembered so well from then. It made memorizing all the stock easy really.

The next day I brought in a kettle, pulled out some old 1950s chipped cups from a box, hung them on some hooks above the sink against the back wall and dragged the battered old sofa that had been groaning under the weight of the boxes of junk over to the back of the stockroom to create a little lounge area. If I was going to do this job properly, I may as well make the place look habitable. Then I flung open the delivery doors to let in some light and fresh air, made a cup of tea and arranged myself on the sofa with a pad and pen, to try to work out how the hell to organize the place.

It took me that entire first month to transform those piles of dusty goods into a fully operating stockroom. It was a massive job, only made easier by the fact that I didn't get many orders through on the creaky old printer to disrupt me. It didn't take long to work out that Hardy's was struggling to get customers through the door. I assigned each department its own aisle and alphabetized the stock accordingly. I even drew up an annotated stockroom plan for each department manager. I figured that once I started my proper job on the shop floor they'd need to be able to find things easily themselves. It was surprisingly fulfilling, and what was even more surprising was that while I was at work I didn't think about Jamie once. Hiding away in the stockroom for that first month was the perfect way to rehabilitate myself after our break-up. I had a brand-new career and a new home. Finally, I was ready to come out of my cocoon.

CHAPTER 3

I couldn't wait for Sharon to come and assess my work at the end of that month and to tell me what my new job would entail, but first she had to get over her astonishment at the newly arranged stockroom.

'I don't believe it,' she gasped, turning around on the spot. 'I can see the floor. Everything has a place! It's like you've worked magic!' She pulled at her cropped hair thoughtfully and I thought I saw her almost smile. Then she patted me on the back, told me I was born to work in the stockroom and that instead of giving me a job on the shop floor she wanted to make me stockroom manager. For a moment I didn't know whether to laugh or cry, but I thanked her and decided to make the best of it. So what if I was starting at the bottom? Sharon would soon see that I could be an asset to the store. For the first time in my life I'd found something I was good at.

Little did I know that by taking the job, I was effectively packing up my hopes and dreams and storing them away at the back of the stockroom, along with all the other unwanted goods at Hardy's.

Until today, I think, as I press the security code on the door and then push it open. The harsh neon strip lights flicker uncertainly as I switch them on and eventually the dark room lights up and the stockroom is revealed in all its grey glory. I may have managed to organize it meticulously so it no longer looks like some dead granny's attic, but I never did manage to give it the lick of white paint it really needs. Sharon looked at me like I was insane when I'd suggested it a couple of months after I started. She said that there was no budget for such fripperies. So instead I took some bright, kitsch 1960s and 1970s magazine covers that I'd found in a box, framed them and put them up on the walls, then I put a couple of old display-damaged Tiffany-style jewelled lamps by the sofa. Each year, in December, I hang strings of fairy lights around the shelves. I've even bought a real Christmas tree and it has perched gaily in my lounge area since the last week of November.

I flick the kettle on, just as the door buzzer sounds. I wander over and swing open the double doors at the back of the stockroom, which lead out to the store's loading bays, and smile as a friendly, freckled face greets me. It's Sam, the delivery guy, who comes every Monday and Thursday. I really look forward to his visits; sometimes he's the only person I see all day. In fact, he's the closest to a work colleague I've actually got. We've been friends ever since he brought a delivery during my first week when I was trying to organize the stockroom. I was completely bewildered by the enormity of the job, but once he'd unloaded everything he sat and helped me work out a plan. He even stayed so he could help me rearrange the room, moving the heavier boxes and bits of furniture I couldn't manage. I honestly couldn't have done it without him and our friendship has grown in strength ever since. Sam's one of those lovely, laid-back guys who's really easy to talk to. I feel like I've known him forever, which is weird because I've never had many male friends before. My brothers' mates always treated me like some stupid kid and were way too intimidating for me, and the boys in my year at school were only interested in being friends with the girls they fancied. I've found it a refreshing experience to meet a guy like Sam. We just seem to get each other, you know? We're the same age, both stuck in dead-end jobs that we don't know how to get out of, and we both lived with our parents way longer than is socially acceptable. He's the youngest of three siblings. They're all more successful than he is, although I don't know why, as he's clever, funny articulate, creative and cute – if you like boyish-looking guys with messy hair the colour of maple syrup, a smattering of stubble, and big, soulful eyes, that is. He's always wanted to be a photographer for magazines, but he's finding it hard to get into such a competitive industry, so for now he's a delivery guy at his dad's company. But he never complains, which I really like.

'You're late,' I admonish him now, waggling my finger at him.

'No I'm not,' he retorts as he huddles in the doorway, proffering a paper bag with his gloved hand. 'I went to get you a pastry. I know better than to turn up here without breakfast.'

He's right. Sam has been bringing me breakfast every week since I started here. Sometimes it's coffee and pastries, other times it's a bacon or sausage and egg sandwich, and he's even been known to bring takeaway pancakes, including blueberries and maple syrup. On special occasions he really goes to town. On my birthday he brought Buck's Fizz and a selection of gorgeous cakes from Patisserie Valerie. I add 'thoughtful' to my mental list of Reasons I Like Sam.

I peer inside the bag, suddenly aware that I'm starving. 'Mmm, cinnamon and raisin, my favourite.' I take a large bite, bigger than my mouth can actually manage, and begin frantically chewing, trying not to spit bits of flaky pastry at him.

He gazes at me in amusement. 'So I see.' Then he gestures at the van. 'Shall I start unloading?' I nod, still munching hungrily on the pastry and he lopes off towards the van. 'Pour us a cuppa,' he calls back. 'I'll just have time for one before my next delivery. I need to thaw out. It's bloody freezing out here.'

I trundle obediently over to the kettle, happy to be spending time with him on my Big Day. I've not breathed a word of it to anyone but I really want to tell Sam about my impending promotion; he'll be so happy for me.

'Hunfffff.' Sam heaves the last of the delivery boxes into the corner and I turn round, clutching his cup, to be greeted by a wall of cardboard.

'Great,' I grumble good-naturedly as I hand him his tea. '*More* stuff to unpack.'

Sam takes a long gulp of tea and glances over at the boxes. 'It's from the latest collections, apparently.'

I roll my eyes. 'Which were designed when, 1984?' Being on trend is not Hardy's strong point.

I walk over to the boxes, pick up a Stanley knife, swipe it down the centre of the first lid and then gasp as I pull out a shimmering sequined top with padded shoulders and slashed sleeves. 'Hang on, Sam, this is *gorgeous*.'

I may not be a fashion expert but even I can see that this is more than a cut above the stock we usually buy in. Under the plastic the gossamer material is so light to the touch it feels like liquid silk between my fingers and, oh my God, the way it *hangs* makes me think it could look good even with my curves. I'm almost overcome with an urge to try it on but, aware of Sam's indifference to it, I merely glance at the label instead.

'Florence Gainsbourg?' I read, and shrug my shoulders. 'Never heard of her. How come we're stocking stuff like this?' I glance at the front of the box in confusion. 'Are you sure this is my delivery, Sam?'

He looks affronted. 'Since when have I ever mixed them up? This job isn't exactly rocket science, you know.'

I flap my hand at him dismissively. 'Don't be so sensitive. I just can't believe that any of our managers would order this stuff. It's not exactly Hardy's usual style. Whereas this is.' I lean over to the shelf behind and pull out a massive pair of jodhpurs, stretching them to their full girth to emphasize my point. Sam laughs and I throw them back on the shelf before sitting down wearily on one of the crates. I've been trying to think of a way to tell him my news.

'Oh, Sam,' I sigh dramatically. 'How much longer am I going to be unpacking boxes?'

'About four hours, judging by this lot,' he says, slurping his tea and leaning against the shelves, seemingly oblivious to my hint. I hit him on the arm and a bit of tea dribbles out of his mouth. He pushes me back playfully. 'Ow! What did you do that for?'

'I don't mean how long am I going to be unpacking *these*. I mean working in *here*.' I look up at him, suddenly curious. 'I know you don't want to be doing deliveries for your dad forever either,' I probe. 'Don't you ever get frustrated by your job?'

'It's not so bad,' Sam shrugs. 'I quite enjoy it.

Plus there are perks.' He raises his cup at me and I laugh.

'Well, I just hope the new stockroom manager is as good a host as I am,' I say casually. I drop my eyes and then look up at Sam to gauge his reaction.

'You're not leaving are you?' He's clearly shocked.

'Not leaving Hardy's, no, but I *am* leaving the stockroom.' I pause before saying tentatively, 'You're looking at Hardy's new assistant manager. Well,' I add bashfully, 'it's not official yet but I think it's going to be announced this morning. I just couldn't wait any longer to tell you. You're the first person to know!'

Sam puts his tea down and before I know it his arms are wrapped around me. I'm surprised at just how warm he is, given how cold it is outside.

'That's FANTASTIC news!' he says as he squeezes me tightly.

'Oh, it's nothing.' I wriggle from his embrace, pleased but embarrassed by his reaction.

'Don't put yourself down,' he says softly, then he lifts his hands up dramatically as if he's making a declaration. 'Tomorrow Hardy's shop floor, next year, the entire fashion world!'

'Oh shush.' I'm blushing. 'Hardy's is good enough for me.' I shuffle my feet on the floor as I try to think of a way to deflect the attention back to him. 'But what about you? I know you want something more than this too . . .'

He shrugs and looks uncomfortable. 'Life isn't always about what you want, Evie.'

I tilt my head to encourage him to go on but he's too busy throwing the remains of his tea down his neck to continue. He wipes his mouth and then grins at me. His tawny-brown eyes are the colour of one-pence pieces, I notice. That's probably why they always shine so brightly.

'Gotta go, I'm afraid, or I'll be late for my next delivery.' He pauses. 'Maybe we should . . . go for a drink to celebrate your promotion? I mean, we won't get to have our morning chats any more now, will we? Not when you're "One of Them".'

'Oh. No. I hadn't thought of that. Well, yes, let's definitely do that.' I suddenly think of other people I could invite. We could make a night of it.

'Just let me know where and when.' And then Sam's gone, waving his hand without looking back.

For once, time passes quickly. It's unusually interesting seeing what surprises lie in store for me in the new delivery. There's a short, shimmering silk dress that looks like it's been dipped in the Indian Ocean because of the way the bright aquamarine wash cascades down the swathes of silky white material. My jaw gaping, I pick out another. It's a Park Avenue princess's dream made in frothy white tulle embroidered with tiny gold cobwebs of sequins. I gently put it on a padded hanger, worried the delicate material will disintegrate at my touch. I pull out another garment, a scoop-backed, sculpted black dress, the skirt finished with hundreds of tiny beads. I've never been in such close contact with so many beautiful clothes and I'm almost too scared to touch them. To be honest, I imagine our customers will be as well. I mean, I know Hardy's needs a serious fashion update, but this is way too ambitious for the kind of customers we actually have. But it isn't my place to say anything . . . yet.

As the clock hands inch towards nine I begin to get a fluttery feeling in my belly. I'm excited by the thought that once everyone knows about my promotion they'll start to treat me like an equal. A shiver of anticipation comes over me as the staff begin filing into the stockroom, the new place for staff meetings. Rupert decided it was bad for business for potential customers passing the store on the way to work to see us all slumped lethargically around the till point on the ground floor during our meetings. He thought it put them off coming in the store.

'Hello there, Sarah dear!'

My heart sinks as Susan and Bernie, the silver-haired Irish sisters who've worked in Haberdashery for forty years, walk in and greet me. Even *they* haven't noticed I've replaced the old stockroom girl, though as a child I used to spend hours helping them sort through the old buttons and fabric swatches. Each time I see them I hope that they'll suddenly put two and two together. Maybe I'll tell them now, start afresh with my promotion. I open my mouth to correct them just as Gwen and Jenny from Beauty walk in.

'Hellooo, Sarah!' they chime simultaneously.

'Hi,' I mutter, defeated again. I brighten up when Carly appears, flanked by Paula and Tamsin, her colleagues from Personal Shopping. All three look immaculate. Carly is stylish and naturally sexy; Paula is austere in a 1980s throwback kind of a way, with frosted lips, blue eyeshadow and big backcombed hair, like a latter-day Mrs Slocombe from *Are You Being Served?* Tamsin is pure Essex thoroughbred, complete with fake nails, fake tan, dyed platinum hair and suspiciously perky-looking boobs.

The staff gather round Carly, gasping at her outfit and giggling as she regales them with yet another anecdote about one of her notoriously crazy and fun nights out.

'Oh, Carly,' Gwen wheezes, clutching her sides, 'you are a card. Tell us what you said to those football fellas again?'

After finishing her story Carly inches through the adoring staff members towards me.

'Hiya, babe, how are you doing?' she says warmly. I smile up at her. She looks radiant as ever in a futuristic-looking gold sequined top with fierce shoulders that protrude at right angles, in contrast to the rest of the top, which hangs against her body like a sheath. I recognize it as the

Gainsbourg immediately. She must have pre-ordered one for herself to wear on the shop floor. It helps to sell the clothes, though they've never before had such a tempting selection as today's delivery.

'What do you think this announcement is all about?' Carly asks me excitedly.

I look at her curiously. It was only last week that I told her all about my hopes for promotion. To be fair, I *did* say it was top secret and she wasn't allowed to tell anyone but she's obviously forgotten. It's understandable, though. Carly has such a busy social life she probably doesn't have space in her brain to remember the things I tell her about mine. Every night she's either going on a date, or to a fabulous party, or being invited to some opening of a cool new bar. Our lives couldn't be more different.

I glance up at her as she shakes her wavy brown hair off her shoulders. I say 'brown', but it isn't brown like mine is brown. It's intricately woven with gold, copper and auburn tones that make it glimmer and shine like a crown. She also has these cute, perky freckles all over her nose, and her eyelashes, which are long and perfectly frame her pale green eyes, giving her a wide-eyed look, as if even she is surprised at how beautiful she is.

I still remember seeing her on her first day. I'd just left the stockroom to go on a break and she walked past me, followed by a trail of fawning staff members. She was telling an hilarious anecdote about a date she'd been on that had everyone – even grumpy Elaine from Designers – in hysterics. She was so confident and at home with everyone that I felt intimidated by her and didn't introduce myself, but the next day, she turned up in the stockroom with a cup of coffee for me.

'Mind if I come in?' she grinned, and passed the cup to me. 'I thought you could do with one of these. Someone told me you start at 7 a.m. every day. How do you manage that? I can barely drag myself here by nine! I'm Carly, by the way. Your name's Sarah, isn't it?'

I took the coffee and opened my mouth to tell her otherwise, but I was too shy to explain that my colleagues were still getting my name wrong and I was also worried about drawing attention to the fact that I'd hijacked someone else's job. It was just so embarrassing. Instead I asked her how she came to be working here. We sat for half an hour while she told me all about her year spent living and working in Sydney, her bijou Clapham flat where she lived with her best friend from university, and what it was like being newly single again. I heard about good dates and bad dates, girls' nights in and big nights out. And I listened, completely intrigued by her colourful life, which seemed so different from mine.

Then she asked me about Hardy's and I was happy to oblige her with my knowledge. She was so grateful she offered to buy me a drink after work. Buoyed by the thought of having made my first proper friend at work, I phoned Delilah and asked her if she wouldn't mind picking the kids up from nursery. Then I spent the rest of the afternoon shopping in town ahead of my 'date' with Carly.

I met her when she finished at 6 p.m. and we went for cocktails at a cool hotel bar in Soho. It was the best night out I'd had in ages. OK, make that the *only* night out I'd had in ages. We got tipsy and talked about bad boyfriends and good sex, like all girlfriends inevitably do. Well, she did most of the talking, to be honest, but that suited me fine. I went home that night feeling happy and young, and like someone had *seen* me for the first time in ages. And so what if she didn't know my actual name?

Since then we've spent lots of time together at work. Carly's always hanging around here and we've had the occasional night out too; Mondays usually, as she's always got something on the rest of the week. But we have hilarious conversations about the dates she's been on, the latest clothes she's bought and the nights out she's had with her best girl mates. I love listening to her stories. It gives me a taste of the kind of life I'd love to lead.

Now she turns, winks and motions at me for a cup of tea just as Sharon opens the door. I sidestep towards the kitchenette to pour Carly a cup from the pot I made earlier. Actually, I'm quite happy to be tucked away in the corner as I don't want to draw attention to myself before the Big Moment. I imagine Sharon will spot my absence and wait for me to emerge. Or she'll ask where I am and Carly will tell her. Then I'll step into the cheering crowd as Sharon announces my promotion. Maybe Carly and her colleagues from Personal Shopping will even elevate me above people's heads, like fans do in rock concerts.

I smile at the thought as I top up the teapot and hear Sharon announce other notices. I've just poured Carly's cup when Sharon's thin, sharp voice rises in volume and she claps her hands. I swirl the teabags quickly when I realize she is about to make the Big Announcement.

'And now,' I hear her say, 'I want you all to join me in giving our congratulations to the member of staff who has been given a long-overdue promotion . . .'

I clutch Carly's tea, partly in fear, partly in excitement. I can imagine Sharon's eyes working the room like searchlights to find me.

'This young woman has worked tirelessly to prove her commitment to Hardy's, often in difficult circumstances, and over recent months she has consistently amazed me with her work ethic, her ability to transform her department and her unique vision for the store . . .'

I can feel myself blush. All my hard work has finally paid off.

'She is a credit to the store,' Sharon continues,

'so I'm sure you will all join me in congratulating her on her promotion. She is an irreplaceable team member and I know that Hardy's will be a better place with her on-board the management team. Now, where is our new assistant manager? I can't see her?'

Oh my God, this is it, I think. This is my moment.

I peer out and see Sharon searching amongst the sea of staff. I step out into the crowd just as she says, 'Ah, there she is! Don't be shy, step forward!' Blushing, I take another step, and then Sharon enthuses, 'Everyone, please give Carly a big round of applause.'

CHAPTER 4

I freeze. Discordant clapping echoes around the room and I slowly reverse back into the kitchenette and lean my head against the cool, tiled wall above the sink and close my eyes. I want to cry with frustration. How can I have got it so wrong?

Once I've gathered myself I wander back out into the crowd and immediately spot Carly holding court. I *want* to congratulate her, *want* to feel happy for her but I can't help but feel like pounding my fists on the floor like Delilah's daughter, Lola, does when she's having a tantrum. But of course I do nothing of the kind. Instead I wait for more people to leave, take a deep breath, paint a bright smile on my face and walk over to her.

'Congratulations, Carly. You really deserve it,' I say warmly, but my words sound hollow, like an echo of all the congratulations that have gone before. I wonder if she'll be sympathetic once she remembers that I was expecting to get a promotion myself. But she doesn't seem to recall.

Once everyone leaves I slump against some

shelves. I pull out my mobile and dial Sam's number, desperately wanting the sympathy only a good friend can give. But it goes straight to voicemail. I put the phone back in my pocket and look miserably out of the small window at the plump flakes of snow still falling. Much as I wish I had someone to share my disappointment with, part of me is relieved to be left alone in my prison. Because at this precise moment that's what it feels like. I've served nearly two years here, and now my sentence has just been extended; and with no parole. I groan as I think of how I boasted about my impending promotion to Sam this morning. Why didn't I keep my stupid mouth shut? He's going to think I'm such a loser when I tell him what happened. And he'll be right.

I hear a shuffling noise, peer through the shelves and see that Sharon is still here, flicking through delivery reports. For a moment I'm tempted to ask her why she's overlooked me for promotion again but I get the feeling she doesn't want to be disturbed.

I sigh and settle down, busying myself by colour-grouping some deerstalkers. I put a soft brown one aside for Sam as an early Christmas gift from me. It cheers me up momentarily, but as I continue sorting I gaze down at myself in my grubby white shirt, plain black trousers and then I stand up and look in the mirror above the sink at my unwashed hair hanging limply around my face, my features devoid of make-up. My eyes fill with tears and I gulp them back, not wanting Sharon to hear me. I must be deluded to think anyone would ever consider me for a job that involves being in public. I'm a complete mess. Ever since Jamie broke up with me I've let myself go; I've lost my confidence and most of all, my*self*. Suddenly an image of Carly – laughing, smiling, looking stylish – pops into my mind. If only I could be more like her, then maybe I wouldn't be so . . . invisible.

I hear Sharon walk out and the stockroom door slams shut. Just then I spot something winking at me temptingly from amongst the pile of clothes. It's the Florence Gainsbourg that came in this morning. The same top Carly is wearing. I look down again at my plain white shirt and bite my lip as my arm, unbidden, stretches towards the glittering prize. My hand shakes as it touches the plastic it's encased in, and with a sudden movement I pull it out from the pile and find myself studying it with wonder.

As I hold it up it occurs to me that this top embodies everything I'd like to be. It is stand-out-from-the-crowd, forget-me-not fabulous; edgy and bright and exciting. Every sequin seems to hold a promise of what life could be like if I just slip it on. I glance behind me nervously. Perhaps if I put this on, just for a moment, maybe some of that magic will rub off on me. Before I know what I'm doing I tear off my shirt and stuff it down the back of a radiator. It can burn, for all I care. I shiver as much with anticipation as cold as I pull the top tentatively over my head, closing my eyes as I relish the feel of the expensive fabric against my skin, the coarseness of the tiny, intricately sewn sequins on the outside contrasting with the smooth, satin finish of the material underneath. I panic as the expensive garment gets stuck as I try to pull it over my head. And then one of my arms won't go through. For a moment, I stagger about like a headless one-armed zombie, banging into boxes and cursing my clumsiness, feeling the tears spring back into my eyes. At last I get the precious top on and I look in the mirror. My eyes are bright with tears, my cheeks flushed from exertion and crying, and much as I'm tempted to hide behind my long, straight hair, like I usually do, instead I pull it into a loose, messy bun at the side of my neck, the way Carly sometimes wears hers, securing it with an elastic band I find on the floor. Then I go to the beauty department's aisle and pull out a powder compact, some mascara and a clear lip gloss and apply them using the compact's mirror. Finally, I wander back to the cracked, full-length mirror in the corner of the stockroom, close my eyes and open them again.

It's like looking at a different girl.

I study myself, comparing this reflection to the one I see every morning. With uncharacteristic pluck, I decide to try it out on the public, the people who brush past me on the street every single day, when I'm on my lunch break, seemingly oblivious to my presence. After one last look in the mirror I walk determinedly out of the stockroom and hurry through the empty beauty department. I reach the safety of the staff exit, where Dave, the day security guard, has taken over from Felix. His feet are propped up on the desk and he looks like he might be asleep. I turn and see the staff photo roll call in the corridor that I was studying this morning, where Carly's beaming 'Employee of the Month' picture is displayed.

My gaze falls to the bottom of the board, where my picture is. My long, straight hair looks nice, I note with some surprise, like I've taken the time to blow-dry it properly. I had make-up on that day too. I tilt my head appraisingly. Maybe I *should* make the effort more often. It *can* actually make a difference, although no amount of lipstick, powder and paint can hide the wistful expression I am wearing.

I glance down further and see with horror that underneath my picture is printed my job title and name. Except it isn't my name. It says 'Sarah Evans'. Then as I gaze back at the picture it suddenly hits me. The girl in the picture isn't me at all. It's my predecessor. Suddenly my memory of meeting Sarah on my first day comes flooding back: a plain girl with no distinguishing features other than the palpable air of disappointment surrounding her. Now even I can't tell the difference between us.

Clearly there's a distinctive 'type' of person

who's blessed with the stockroom manager's job, I think miserably.

With that soul-destroying thought I lurch over to the security office, open the door and grab the pen that Felix was doing Sudoku with earlier.

Dave doesn't even look up. With unflinching determination I slash an angry line through the photo and the name below it and write 'EVIE TAYLOR' in thick black capitals, vowing to get a passport photo taken at the tube station on my way home. I may not have been promoted to the shop floor, but it's time for everyone finally to get to know the real me.

CHAPTER 5

I was only going to wear the top for a while. I just wanted to have a few short minutes of feeling that I could be someone other than me. But a few minutes has crept into half an hour and then an hour, and now I've become so used to the soft material brushing against my skin that I've almost forgotten I'm wearing it at all. I glance in the mirror in the stockroom again and lift my hand up to my face tentatively. For the first time ever, I'm unable to resist looking at my reflection. Maybe it's the gold sequins that are giving me this new glow. It must be the way they reflect against my skin that make it look creamier and less pallid than normal, and my hair less mousy. Even my irises seem to have turned from opaque chocolate pools into bright tiger eyes.

I jump as an order comes out of the old, noisy stockroom printer. I glance at the ticket. One peacock-feather fascinator. I head straight to aisle nine and climb up the ladder, stretching to reach the shelf where I quickly find the item. We still have three left. No need to order any more for a while. Mrs Fawsley is the only customer who buys them. She's brought one every December for the past ten years, according to stockroom records. I wonder what she does with so many. Maybe she's trying to put the peacock's tail back together again.

I smile despite myself, and put one on my head. I go to look in the mirror and laugh. Combined with the glittery, showy top the headdress makes me I look like I'm about to go on stage at the Folies-Bergère. I do a high kick – well, to be honest, it's more of a low kick – and then sigh as I hear another order noisily start to print.

Two orders in five minutes? Then the machine makes a loud grunt of protest and stops mid-print. Bloody thing, I think, and give it a whack. Like everything else in the store, the order machine is knackered. I give it another hearty smack but feel safe in the knowledge that I don't actually need to see the ticket anyway. I look at my watch. By my calculations, an order at 10.15 a.m. on the first Thursday morning of the month can mean only one thing: Iris Jackson and her lavender soap. I glance at the ticket and nod with satisfaction as I go to the necessary aisle to retrieve a bar of Iris's special soap.

As I crouch to dig out the order I think about Iris Jackson. Hardy's has been stocking her soap for years, in fact I'm pretty sure we're the only store that sells it any more. According to her, it's handmade in Somerset by a group of WI women who started in business after the war, making and selling toiletries. They needed something to do to keep their enterprising spirits up when their husbands returned and claimed back the jobs the women had been doing in their absence. Apparently Iris grew up in the village. All these years later, she still wants to support this local enterprise, even though those women are probably long gone. I often wonder why she doesn't just buy the soap in bulk to save her coming in, but I sense her trip to Hardy's is the highlight of her month.

I pop a bar in my pocket and glance at my watch to see if it's time for my break. I always go and deliver the soap personally to Iris. It's been a ritual of mine since I met her shortly after I started at Hardy's. Jenny, who was relatively new to the store, didn't recognize Iris and said they didn't sell her soap. Iris asked Jenny to check in the stockroom, but when Jenny came in she got caught up in telling me how she and her husband were trying for a baby. I spent half an hour listening to her excitedly talk about what being pregnant would be like, and the merits of religiously following Gina Ford versus the Baby Whisperer once the baby was born. She talked for so long that she forgot why she'd come to the stockroom in the first place until she suddenly recalled the old lady who was asking about some lavender soap. When I explained that Iris was the only person who actually bought it so we kept it in the stockroom for her rather than take up space on the shop floor, Jenny shrugged.

'Well, she's probably long gone now,' she said, then looked at her watch and exclaimed, 'Ooh, it's time for my lunch break! I'm going to Topshop to look at their maternity range.'

After she'd gone I went straight to the shelves where I'd stacked hundreds of the delicate little parcels that were individually wrapped in parchment paper and tied with string. I grabbed one and decided to try to find the customer myself. It didn't take long, to be honest; Iris was the only person wandering aimlessly round the ground floor. She looked delighted when I handed her the soap.

'Thank you, dear,' she said. 'I was just about to give up and go for an Earl Grey. Would you like to join me? My treat. Not many shop assistants give such a personal shopping service these days.'

I accepted her invitation and ever since then, on the first Thursday of the month, at approximately half-past ten, I've delivered her soap to her in Lily's tearoom in the basement, where, without fail, she'll be sitting at 'her' table, sipping Earl Grey and delicately popping pieces of Victoria sponge into her mouth.

My tummy rumbles. I'm looking forward to my monthly catch-up with Iris. I've just grabbed my rucksack and duffel coat and am making my way out when the stockroom door swings open and Carly appears. I immediately pull my coat up to my chest.

'Babe!' she gasps, her face shining with excitement.

She pauses, tilts her head and looks at me strangely. I self-consciously pull my coat closer around me. 'I'm so glad you're here,' she goes on. 'You'll never *believe* what just happened!'

I try to look interested but am more concerned with ensuring that my coat is covering the top. I don't want her to think I'm some style stalker. But she's so caught up in her own excitement that she doesn't even notice.

'I have just seen the hottest man EVER.' She fans her face, panting a little as she leans against the door. 'He's out there,' she hisses, and clutches her hands to her heart. 'We made eye contact – and I mean *serious* eye contact – on the stairs. I was coming down, he was going up, and I've just seen him down here in the beauty department too. I mean,' she laughs, 'how obvious is that? He must have run back down to try and catch up with me! Honestly, babes, he's so dreamy, you'll die! He's got dark hair and really brooding, big eyes and he's tall and he's got these broad shoulders and, oh, he's just GORGEOUS.'

She turns round and presses her ear to the door, and whilst she has her back turned I quickly pull my coat on properly and do it up over the sequined top.

'I wonder if he's still out there?' she says, her face still squashed to the door.

'Why don't you just go and have a look?' I ask, glancing at my watch surreptitiously. I'll be late for Iris if I'm not careful. 'If he wants to ask you out he's not going to do it through a closed door.'

'I know *that*.' She turns round and rolls her eyes despairingly at me. 'I'm playing hard to get. Honestly, hon, don't you know anything about men?'

I consider her question. The truth is I actually only know a lot about one man. Jamie. And he dumped me for being 'too predictable'. So no, I've never mastered the 'hard-to-get' game.

'So what are you going to do?' I ask her, feigning interest but unable to stop thinking about my tea break. I'm desperate for caffeine, and even more desperate to get out of this stifling stockroom.

'I'm going to wait here until I know he's gone. If he wants me that much, he'll find me,' Carly says confidently. 'Put the kettle on, will you, hon?'

'Um, I was just about to go on my break, actually,' I say timidly.

'Oh.' Her face falls for a moment, then immediately brightens. 'Can't you have your break here, with me? Then we can wait here together!'

It's tempting, but Iris is waiting for me and I don't want to let her down.

'Can we chat later?' I say as I head for the door. 'I've got to deliver this to someone.' I wave the bar of soap. 'You can stay in here if you want. Make yourself a cup of tea and wait till he's gone.'

'OK.' Carly looks down, disappointed. She smiles up again. 'My new job is cool, don't you think? I never expected to make assistant manager so soon!'

'You must be really thrilled,' I say, edging towards the door as a subtle hint.

'I guess,' she replies, wanders over to my 'lounge and listen' area and throws herself onto the sofa as if preparing to embark on a lengthy conversation. I stare at her and then at the door. I really need to go.

'Have you heard that Rumors are looking for a central London flagship store?' she continues. I have my hand on the door but turn politely and look interested. 'I'd *kill* to work there. I went to the New York store on Fifth Avenue once and it was so cool. All the staff wear couture and the whole shop façade is made of glass – even the changing rooms face on to the street and have frosted glass to cover your body up to your neck but you can see everyone's faces as they're getting changed!'

I shrug. I've never been to New York but I have heard of Rumors. It sounds like my idea of shopping hell. 'Hardy's isn't so bad,' I say, feeling defensive. 'It just needs a bit of love and attention and some . . . direction.'

'I know, that's what I think too,' she says, and crosses her impossibly long legs. I can't help but look at the gorgeous stacked patent heels she's wearing, then compare them unfavourably to my own sensible, scuffed brogues. 'That's why I spoke to Sharon and suggested we use some new designers. I think that's what swung me the promotion, you know. I told her, I said: "Sharon,

55

we need to be more modern, appeal to the younger clients, clients like me. They want shops to be more exclusive, more *fashion forward.*"'

'I guess,' I say tentatively. 'But they also want somewhere they can relax and feel at home—'

But Carly cuts me off and carries on recounting word for word her promotion monologue.

'. . . They want glamour and excitement and fabulousness, not some safe, staid boring old shop that just stays the same for, like, a hundred years. I mean ya-aawn. Now,' she claps her hands, 'tell me what's been going on with you. Is there any gossip from the stockroom today? Other than my promotion, of course!' She throws her head back and laughs so that the tinkling sound reverberates around the room like wind chimes.

I honestly think I'll suffocate if I don't get out in the next thirty seconds and somehow I manage to make my excuses and leave. I wander despondently out into the store.

'God, where is everybody today? I am *so* bored.' I turn to see Becky from Handbags slouched against one of the beauty counters, staring at her face in the mirror. She's in her early twenties but she says she thinks that she's starting to look leathery because she spends her days dealing with horrible old bags (I'm presuming she means her stock and not Hardy's customers, but I can't be sure).

'Well, it's still early, I guess,' I reply.

Becky puts her hand up to heart. 'Christ . . . er,

Sarah, isn't it? You made me jump! I didn't see you there. What are you doing creeping round the store? Shouldn't you be in the stockroom?' Having dismissed me she turns and continues examining her pores.

I sigh and look out at the street beyond. Lots of people are milling around but they all walk straight past Hardy's, utterly oblivious to its presence. I want to jump into the barely dressed windows and wave at them, do star jumps, shout, scream, anything to get their attention.

As I walk down the staircase to the basement, I envision myself, as I always do, as a beautiful woman of the 1940s, in a two-piece Chanel suit, with red lips and short, pin-curled hair, about to meet my American GI lover.

I increase my pace as I go through Menswear and towards the tearoom, tucked away at the far end. It's always a welcome retreat when I want some peace from the comings and goings of the stockroom. None of the staff ever comes here; they prefer the buzzy Starbucks opposite the store, or they go to Oxford Street on their breaks.

Lily has worked here ever since I was a child, and then some. She's a tiny slip of a woman who must be in her late seventies but looks at least ten years younger. She won't tell me her exact age; she just tells me she's old enough to know better and young enough not to care. She has dyed black hair, which she wears pulled back into a tight bun with wispy strands that frame her heart-shaped face. Her lips are painted red and her eyes are cobalt blue and dazzle against her pale skin ('a tan is so ageing, darling'), and she always smells of face powder and Chanel No. 5. She used to be a professional dancer. Among many other things, she was one of the Windmill Girls at the famous theatre in Great Windmill Street, which remained open throughout the war and which was famous for its nude *tableaux vivants*. I've never really understood exactly what that means, though. Lily just says it was 'art'. She always wears black and white ('you can't go wrong, darling') and is never to be seen without a double string of real pearls around her neck. When I look at her I am reminded that real style transcends time. She tells the most wonderful stories of London in the fifties. She's utterly fabulous and I love spending time with her.

Her customers enter Lily's tearoom just a few steps down from the basement shop floor where there's a sign saying 'Please wait to be seated'. I know Londoners hate to be kept waiting for anything, but you need this moment to take in the wonderful surroundings. The tearoom hasn't been decorated since the 1930s; somehow it escaped Sebastian's dire makeover back in the late 1980s. Black and white tiles cover the floor and the little round tables all have claret-coloured vintage table lamps with faded, tasselled shades that glow invitingly. It makes me think of the film *Brief Encounter*, even though there isn't a railway carriage in sight. It has a warmth and intimacy I adore, and when I'm there I always imagine the hundreds of love affairs that must have played out here over the past century. The old walls are painted a deep, rich burgundy and along each side of the room brass lights glimmer merrily beneath faded gold lampshades. Vintage tea cups are laid at every place and original, framed black-and-white movie stills from the thirties and forties hang on the walls, with signatures from stars like Cary Grant, Clark Gable and Bette Davis, all of whom visited the store at some point.

I grin as I notice that since my last visit Lily has put two real Christmas trees either side of the sign and has adorned them with gorgeous vintage decorations and fairy lights shaped like candles, as well as hanging old-fashioned paper chains around the room. She clearly disapproves of the store's Christmas decorations as much as I do. She waves at me from behind the counter, which displays a number of china cake stands filled with the most delicious homemade cakes, pastries and desserts. None of them is baked by her, though. Lily won't mind me saying this, but she can't cook to save her life. She says it's because she was too busy having dinner dates every night in her youth to learn. And I don't doubt it.

'Darling Evie,' she calls, 'I almost didn't recognize you! You look like you could have been a Windmill Girl!'

I touch my hair and realize I still have the

peacock-feather fascinator on from earlier. No wonder Carly looked at me strangely when she came in. I tug it off my head and try not to blush.

'Come and sit down!' Lily ushers me into the tearoom, twirling around me with her dancer's grace. 'Iris, look who it is!' she calls merrily. I turn to wave at Iris, who beams at me as she lifts a piece of Victoria sponge to her lips.

'Sit down, dearheart!' Iris says, and she dabs the corner of her mouth delicately with her napkin. 'Lily, dear, stop gabbling at her and get this girl a cup of tea. She looks like she needs it.'

Mrs Jackson is in her late sixties but, like Lily, she looks more like a movie star than an OAP; Jane Fonda springs to mind. Iris's dyed and highlighted hair is perfectly straightened in a sharp, flicky style around her face, and her eyes shine brightly from within her carefully painted gold and tawny-brown powdered eyelids. Her lips are always covered in a bronze lip gloss. She always wears a polo neck – today it's cream with a big brooch pinned at her throat – teamed this morning with high-waisted black trousers and a cream seventies-style safari jacket. She has mid-heel black pumps and a large cream leather handbag with a gold clasp. She looks fabulous in a glossy, retro kind of way.

I sit down and hand her the bar of soap and she claps her hands and puts it straight into her handbag. 'That'll keep the wrinkles at bay,' she says with a wink. 'Now, darling girl, how's it going in that dusty old stockroom? Any chance of them putting you on the shopfloor where you belong?'

'No. The opposite, in fact. I think I'm going to be in the stockroom for a long time to come.' I tell her briefly about this morning's disappointment, then smile weakly at Lily as she hands me my tea and pulls out a chair. She's clearly overheard our conversation.

'Well, they're even bigger fools than I took them for,' Lily tuts, and throws her arms in the air, somehow creating a perfect *port de bras*. ('Years of ballet training,' she once answered when I remarked on her expressive arm movements. 'It never leaves you.') 'No wonder this store is falling apart if this is how they use their best staff. I've said it before and I'll say it again, that Sebastian Hardy ripped its heart and soul out. Hardy's has never been the same since he got his hands on it and that young upstart, Rupert, is no better.'

She shakes her head disapprovingly as she pours me a cup of tea through a silver strainer ('you'll get no horrible teabags here, darling').

'Have you seen their pathetic excuse of a Christmas window? Minimal schminimal,' she sniffs haughtily. 'If I get my hands on that Rupert Hardy I'll tell him what he should do with this store to make it shine again. His grandfather would be turning in his grave.'

'What was he like?' I ask, resting my elbow on the table and cupping my chin with my hand towards her. Iris and Lily both remember the late

61

Walter Hardy, junior, son of the founder, who successfully and passionately steered the store through the post-war years and ran a highly successful empire until he passed away in 1987, which is when Sebastian took over.

'Walter junior was the reason most of us girls shopped here. He was one of London's most eligible bachelors; we all held out the hope that if he spotted us shopping in the store he'd fall in love with us instantly. Imagine what a catch he was; a gorgeous man who would one day inherit his own magnificent department store! It was that age-old heady combination,' Lily adds sagely. 'Shopping and sex.'

'Lily!' I exclaim, and the ladies both giggle naughtily.

'What?' Lily says, holding her hands up innocently. 'You think just because we're old we don't think about sex? We're not dead yet, eh, Iris?'

'Too right,' Iris chortles, and raises her tea cup in a toast. 'Personally I'd love to get stuck in a lift with that Brad Clooney. He reminds me of Clark Gable.' She nods at a movie still on the wall and sighs. 'I adored Clark, the old sexpot.'

'You mean George . . .' I offer helpfully.

'Eh?'

'George Clooney, not Brad.'

'George, Brad, whatever. Who the hell cares what they're called when the lights are off?'

'Iris!' I splutter through a mouthful of tea. 'Honestly, you two are worse than teenagers.'

'Teenagers, hmpfff,' Lily says derisively. 'They know nothing about love and romance. None of you young folk do. Speaking of love, young lady, what's going on with you?'

'Nothing,' I say as I shrug off my coat, extracting my mobile phone from my pocket and putting it on the table. It's reached Sahara temperatures in the tearoom. Lily will never admit it, but she feels the cold.

'Well, clearly you're trying to impress someone . . .'

Lily and Iris look at each other knowingly, then back at me. I follow their eyeline and realize they're looking at my Florence Gainsbourg top. Instantly I feel self-conscious. I shouldn't be wearing it in public. If Sharon sees me I'll be in big trouble.

My phone buzzes and I welcome the distraction. 'Sorry, I'd better just get this,' I say, and open my message.

'*How did it go SG?*'

It's from Sam. He calls me SG, short for 'Stockroom Girl', as a joke. He knows my name but he's aware that none of the shop-floor staff does. In return I call him DG ('Delivery Guy'). I close the message down; I don't want to deal with the embarrassment of telling him right now.

'Sooo?' Lily says, raising one perfectly pencilled eyebrow at me and nodding at my phone. 'Was that him?'

'Who?' I ask, utterly lost.

'The one you're trying to impress?' She points at my sparkly top then winks at me.

'What? No,' I splutter defensively. 'That was just Sam, and this?' I look down at the Florence Gainsbourg and feel faintly ridiculous. 'This is just an . . . experiment.'

'In what?' Lily sniffs. 'Wearing clothes that look like they belong on an astronaut?' She sees my face fall. 'Oh, don't get me wrong, darling, I just find these modern clothes so . . . baffling. Coco Chanel would turn in her grave if she saw that.'

Reluctantly I concede Lily is right. This top is for a person far more glamorous and daring than I'll ever be. It's for someone like . . . well, like Carly.

'So who is it for, then?' Lily asks impatiently.

'Sorry, what?' I've drifted off again.

'That!' She gestures at my top. 'Keep up, darling!'

'Oh,' I shrug, feeling bashful all of a sudden, 'I . . . I don't know really. I just wondered what it'd look like. I guess I'm a bit fed up of looking like me.' I note their concerned faces and I know I can always tell them how I really feel and that, most importantly, they'll listen to me. 'The truth is, I don't want to be invisible any longer. I'm sick of being overlooked and fed up of waiting for things to change, because they never ever do.'

'I've never heard such nonsense!' Lily exclaims. 'So what if you didn't get that promotion? Something else will come up. You just need to put some positive energy out there. And as for the way you usually dress, well,' she nudges me and winks, 'you're a beautiful girl but you could do with a *leetle* sprucing. Have you ever thought of trying a rouge lippy?'

I giggle as I imagine myself as a mini-Lily, fifty years younger but nowhere near as fabulous. 'I would if I thought I could look as wonderful as you,' I laugh.

'You know, darling,' she says conspiratorially, 'the best thing to do if you want to impress someone is be yourself.'

'But, Lily, I told you I've got no one I need to impress.' I drain my tea, grab my coat and stand up.

'Aha!' She waggles a finger at me. 'Then for the time being just focus on being happy with yourself. You're perfect just the way you are.'

I smile at them both gratefully. 'You have cheered me up enormously, much more than this silly top ever could. Thank you, ladies.'

'Bye-bye, dear girl,' Iris says, and waves regally. 'See you next month!'

I'm lost in thought as I head back towards the stairs. I decide to go up to Personal Shopping on the first floor to see Carly and find out what happened with the dashing bloke she saw earlier. The store is, as usual, totally empty. I pass through the ground floor and spot Gwen and Jenny standing at opposite ends of their department, bored-but-desperate smiles painted on their faces, atomizers in hand ready to spritz the first person that comes along. I glance over at Handbags and see that Becky is still examining her pores. Up on the first floor I can just see poor Jane in Lingerie, slumped against the balcony, eating a cake whilst sorting beige bras into piles, and Barbara in Shoes is sitting on her little measuring stool, staring into the distance. I pop my head into Personal Shopping, but there is no one on the desk. I call out, but no one answers. Maybe Carly is still waiting for me in the stockroom.

I'm so busy trying to imagine the place back in Walter Hardy, junior's day that I don't notice that there's someone behind me until I feel a gentle tap on my shoulder. My heart races as I glance down and realize I haven't put my coat back on. I close my eyes and turn round slowly, waiting to be berated by Sharon.

'Don't worry, I'm going to take the top off now. I was only going to wear if for a while anywa . . .' I open my eyes, expecting to see Sharon's disapproving face, but what I see instead is a tall, movie-star-handsome, dark-haired man with broad shoulders, a jaw you could crack brazil nuts on, and bright, searching blue eyes that are looking at me in amusement.

'Shit!' I splutter, and attempt to cover my body with my hands as though I were actually naked. 'I thought you were someone else. I'm sorry.'

'Don't be,' he says flirtatiously, his unmistakable

American accent ringing out around the first floor. That's the best offer I've had for ages . . .'

Feeling uncharacteristically brave, I fix my eyes on his and allow a half-smile to hover over my lips. 'Do you mean to say the department stores you usually frequent don't train their staff immediately to offer to strip off for you? How strange. It's the done thing here in Hardy's, you know. We find it's the best way to get our customers to spend money.'

'It's certainly the best sales technique I've come across,' he drawls sexily. His accent is as smooth and delicious as golden syrup being poured over freshly baked scones.

'Well, we aim to . . . tease,' I shoot back, and he laughs, a great, infectious booming sound that echoes round the department. I'd be embarrassed, but I feel like I'm in this weird vortex and no one else can see or hear us.

'You're funny! Carly, right?' he says with a knowing smile. I blink at him, noticing how his mouth tilts deliciously in the corners causing two lines like punctuation marks to appear either side of his lips. His thick eyebrows lift expectantly, which makes another two lines appear in his forehead, like old-fashioned tramlines. I don't understand how he can possibly mistake me for Carly and I'm just about to point out his mistake when it suddenly hits me. The top. It's because I'm wearing this blasted top. Now it all makes sense. *This* is the guy Carly was talking about. Somehow, he's mistaken me for her. Well, I *have* just walked out of Carly's personal shopping department. But even so, he should know with one glance that I am not her. Perhaps there's something wrong with his eyesight. I look at him through narrowed eyes.

'Are you OK?' he asks, and I realize I'm still peering at him.

'Oh, yes . . . yes, I'm fine. I was just thinking that you need glasses.'

He laughs and nudges me. A crackle of electricity shoots down my arm and straight between my legs. He leans in and I blush as he murmurs, 'Is that a style tip?'

'That depends . . .' I answer, trying to rack my brain for another, more clever response. He raises his eyebrows questioningly and tilts his head as he waits for me to continue. My mind goes blank. I can't stop looking into his eyes; they're utterly hypnotic. I blink and shake my head. '. . . Er, that depends on whether you value fashion over flirtation. After all,' I add flippantly, 'girls don't make passes at boys who wear glasses.'

'Really? That's interesting.' He looks amused, then puts his hand into his jacket pocket, pulls out a pair of black-rimmed spectacles and puts them on.

My mouth goes dry and I swallow quickly. Jesus, he looks even hotter, if that were possible.

'I've always wondered why I've been single for so long,' he laughs, and I swear I hear church bells ringing in my head.

'Well,' I squeak, then clear my throat and try again. 'Now you know.' I point at his frames then pull an agonized face, feeling terrible for lying to him.

Still laughing, he shakes his head as he slips them back into his pocket. 'So that's where I've been going wrong. I've always thought they made me look more intelligent.'

'You're American; it'll take more than that, love,' I blurt out, wondering why I suddenly sound like a character from Coronation Street and why I'm intent on insulting him.

Luckily, he throws his head back and roars with laughter. 'I love the British sense of humour. You guys are so dry!' He shakes his head and looks at me. 'You know, I've heard a lot about you, Carly, but no one said how funny you are. Beautiful and stylish and intelligent, yes, but funny . . . ?'

He touches me gently on the arm again and I gulp as I look at him. He smiles at me and this time it's the big reveal; a perfect chorus line of straight, white teeth are high-kicking their way across his mouth. I want to tell him he's made a mistake, that I'm not Carly, but all the saliva has disappeared from my mouth (along with my voice, and the strength in my knees). Luckily I am saved because he speaks first.

'I'd really like to take you out. If you'll allow me, that is. I've heard so much about you. And you're just how I imagined.'

I feel my heart plummet to my toes. I have to tell him.

'I think you've got the wrong girl,' I say softly, sounding much calmer than I feel, and I turn to go.

'Surely that's for me to decide?' he replies quickly, his hand pulling me back to him. I stop, immobilized by his touch. 'After all, isn't that what dates are for? To find the right person?' I gaze up at him and he looks meaningfully back at me.

I should walk away now, I know I should. This is Carly's date, not mine. But he is looking at me so intently and my heart is thumping so wildly under this sparkly top that it looks like a glitter ball is bouncing out of my chest. And then I think to myself, so what if this cute guy thought I was Carly when he stopped me? He seems pretty determined now he's met me to take *me* on a date.

I think about Carly and her life: the endless parties and dates, the trail of men who've lost their hearts to her, and the promotion she's just got. She doesn't need any more good fortune, surely? Would it be so wrong for me to grab this opportunity that's been handed to me? After all, it isn't like they've ever actually met. I'm not doing anything wrong. I can't even be sure this is *definitely* the man she saw. I mean, he could be someone completely different. This could be another heart-stoppingly gorgeous man who's just walked into Hardy's this morning. Because obviously we get them *all the time* in here.

Sod it, I think. Why not chance my arm? The

opportunity has presented itself and, as Dad would say, surely I should just 'go for it'.

'Do you want to try asking again?' I say bravely, fixing my eyes determinedly on his. I wanted my life to change today, so maybe I have to force its hand a little. It's not like working hard or waiting for good things to happen to me has worked so far. Maybe it's time to try a different tack. The sequins on the Gainsbourg top prickle my skin like a conscience, but I ignore them. He smiles and adjusts the collar of the impeccably starched white shirt he's wearing.

'O . . . K,' he drawls, and takes a step closer. He clears his throat. 'Would you care to allow me to take you on a date to remember?'

'And what if I don't?' I shoot back.

'Don't think I'll hold it against you,' he replies quickly, just like Clark Gable in *Gone With the Wind*. I think of Lily's movie-star photos in her tearoom and suddenly feel like they have come to life and this is all happening in monochrome.

I teeter on the brink of doing The Right Thing. I should just say, 'Actually, Mr Handsome American Man, I'm Evie, the stockroom girl,' and then wait for him to retreat. I can then dream about what it might have been like to kiss those *really* nice lips of his.

'Well . . . ?' He smiles and his eyes crinkle at the corners. 'Are you going to make my day?' Oh heavens, now he's Clint bloody Eastwood. 'Will you go out with me, Carleen, I mean Carly?' He brushes the palm of his hand against his temple and looks at me expectantly, vulnerably almost.

Just tell him the truth, Evie, I think as I open my mouth and then, before I can stop myself I blurt out my response.

'I'd like that very much,' I reply.

CHAPTER 6

I'*d like that very much?*
What the bloody hell just possessed me to say that?

'Wunnerful,' says Mr Wonderful in front of me. I look at him aghast, then smile dumbly and edge away, hoping to retreat before I get myself in any more trouble.

'Well,' I begin politely, 'it was nice to meet you . . .'

'Joel,' he interjects. 'Parker.'

'It was nice to meet you, Joel Parker.' I turn round and make for the staircase.

'Just Joel is fine.' He turns and starts walking alongside me. I have a sudden urge to say, 'Well, *just Joel*, you can call me Evie.' But I don't. I pick up my pace. So does he.

'You live in Clapham, right?' he drawls. I swivel my head to look at him, even more aghast than before. That's where Carly lives. How does he know that? Is he some sort of a stalker? What have I got involved in here?

He catches my horrified expression and laughs. 'Oh God, that makes me sound like a weirdo,

73

doesn't it? I only know because I've been looking at the personnel files – for work reasons.'

I edge away, unconvinced.

'I work in retail?' he adds, his accent turning everything into a question. 'As a consultant? For big department stores? Mainly in the US but I'm over here temporarily so I can work on a couple of projects in the UK. Actually my friend Rupert invited me here to show me around his store.' I open my mouth to ask a question but just then his phone rings and he makes a face. 'I'm sorry, I have to take this call but shall we do something this weekend?' He looks bashful for a moment. 'Could I take your number and I'll give you a call tomorrow to make arrangements?'

I don't know where to look or what to say. I can't look him in the eyes, so I find myself looking at his arms, which are bulging under his suit. There is some serious muscle under there. Hypnotized by his biceps, I say yes, and I give him my mobile number.

After our brief encounter I head back down the stairs towards the stockroom. At least I think that's where I'm going. I'm not entirely sure as my legs don't appear to belong to my body any more and my head is floating somewhere above the grand central staircase. I can't think straight, let alone see. What possessed me to pretend to be Carly? I have no idea what came over me. But . . .

I've got a date.

I can't believe it.

This guy, this tall, handsome, erudite, well-dressed, drop-dead GORGEOUS American guy just asked ME out.

I slip on my coat and do it up so as not to get myself into any more trouble as I make my way back to the stockroom.

Suddenly someone jumps out in front of me brandishing a brush and a broad smile.

'Can I interest you in a makeover, dear?' says Gwen, who is the pushiest of salespeople. 'You have beautiful skin, but you look like you could do with some help applying your foundation – and, gosh,' her perfectly painted lips curl slightly, 'is that meant to be blusher?' Then she points at my face. I rub my cheeks self-consciously, aware that it's just me blushing because of my encounter with Joel.

'Er, no thanks, Gwen. I'm just going back from my tea break.'

She stares at me and a flicker of recognition crosses her face. 'Oh, I'm sorry, I thought you were a customer.'

'No,' I say quietly. 'I've been here two years. You talk to me all the time.' She looks at me blankly and shakes her head so I lean in and whisper conspiratorially, 'You have credit card debts that you don't want your husband to find out about . . .'

'Hush!' Her hand flutters to her chest in panic. 'How do you know about that?'

I take a deep breath. 'You told me when you

came into the stockroom for a cup of tea. Last week?' I pause and look at her. Still nothing. 'I work in there,' I add despairingly.

'Oh!' She heaves a sigh of relief. 'You're wotsit, um, oh, yes! Sarah the stockroom girl!'

'Anyway, gotta go.' I nod resignedly and edge away.

'Righty-oh,' she says, her smile painted on her face like a clown's. 'Er, Sarah love,' she grabs me by the arm and her long, cerise-painted nails pierce my skin slightly, 'You won't . . . tell anyone about my little, er, problem will you?' She laughs forcefully and I can hear the fear in her voice rise up and threaten to choke her. The thousands of pounds' worth of credit card debt she's secretly amassed over the past couple of years has become a massive burden to her. I'm no expert, but when she opened up to me last week I told her she needed to tell her husband and deal with the consequences. It would be far less stressful for her in the long run.

'Of course not,' I say gently. 'What's said in the stockroom stays in the stockroom.' She nods in relief and I walk on through the store.

When I reach the stockroom, I punch in the security code, open the door, step inside and shut it.

'Carly?' I call.

No answer. I peer over to the sofa, but she's gone. I do a double-check around the stockroom and then, when I'm sure I'm alone, I scream. And squeal. And jump up and down. Then I clasp my hand over my mouth as it hits me.

I'm a really bad person. Terrible, in fact. I've lied to someone really nice by pretending to be someone *I* really like and who *I* know likes the person that *I* think is nice. If that makes any sense. I need to rectify it. I need to find him and tell him the truth.

But you don't want to, whispers a voice inside my head.

I do, I really do.

No, you don't.

I squeeze my eyes shut and lean against the door. Yes, I do.

You don't want to because you deserve this. You deserve it more than her. You've been waiting for something like this for so long. It's your turn for some excitement.

Is it?

Yes.

I open my eyes and look down at the top I'm still wearing. The yellowy-gold sequins glimmer at me brightly as if they're winking at me.

Go on, they seem to be saying. *Go on . . .*

I shake my head, trying to get the voice out of my head and the devil off my shoulder. I dash past the aisles of stock, past the boxes waiting to be unpacked and the stack of order sheets waiting to be filed. When I get to the back of the stockroom I pull the top over my head and fling it down. I stand there, panting for a second in my faded white bra, gazing at the sequined Gainsbourg number like it's Carly's shroud. It may as well be. It has her face, her figure, her personality stamped all over it. I just happened to take them all on when I wore it. Now it's off I'm back to boring old me. I can feel the excitement drain from my body, like water going down a plughole. I grab my shirt from behind the radiator and pull it on. Then I scurry to the corner of the back aisle, doing up the buttons as I go, ready to begin working on the latest stockroom report. I don't want to be seen by anyone again today. And I don't want to be anywhere near that top. It's got me into enough trouble as it is. There's no way I can keep this pretence up, no way.

Joel will be so disappointed when he realizes who I really am.

CHAPTER 7

The hours trickle by but I'm finding the slow, methodical process of doing the stocktake to be very calming. I've even managed to convince myself it doesn't matter that I failed to tell Joel who I really am, he'll probably never call anyway. The 'flurry' of customers this morning was a one-off. I haven't had an order through the printer for hours. And, weirdly, none of the staff has popped by. I don't mind, though; I'm happy to be left alone. I clearly can't be trusted around people. Especially handsome American men with tranquil blue eyes who, when they look at me, make me feel like I'm swimming naked in a sparkling pool warmed by a glowing, Mediterranean sun.

I shake my head and chastize myself. Get a *grip*, Evie.

I stiffen as the door creaks open. It's two forty-five, fifteen minutes till my clocking-off time. I stand up, brushing my dusty hands down my legs. I'm about to go and see who it is when I hear the sound of muffled conversation.

'Is anyone in here?' says a reedy male voice.

I peer out from the aisle and see Sharon – who has her back to me – and Rupert Hardy. He has wiry, oatmeal-coloured hair, which he wears with a centre parting and which hangs down into his pale, watery eyes, and slightly too many teeth for his mouth. His cheeks are the colour of Russet apples, with lots of thin broken veins, which make him look like a child has drawn on him with a red Biro. I always think he has a look of perpetual surprise about him, like he can't quite believe he's running the place. He's somewhere in his mid-thirties but appears younger, due to his diminutive stature. And he looks even shorter standing next to Sharon. I duck back behind the aisle as she walks through the door.

'We're all alone,' she answers huskily. 'The stock-room girl probably sneaked out a few minutes early, thinking no one would notice!'

I gasp and then clamp my hand over my mouth in case they hear me. The cheek of her! She knows I'd never do that. I press my body against the shelves and desperately look for a way out. They clearly want to have some sort of private rendezvous and I don't want to be here during it, but if I reveal myself now they'll think I was hiding. Which I sort of am, but that's not the point. And if I *don't* come out, Sharon will think I've skived off. I hear rustling. Maybe I should just saunter out now, grab my coat and say goodbye nonchalantly?

Just then, Rupert speaks and my opportunity for a sneaky getaway vanishes.

'The figures are down again, Sharon,' he says gravely.

Sharon drops her head. 'I know. I've told the departmental managers what they need to do to improve their takings. We've tried remerchandising, retraining the staff with new sales techniques, but we can't do anything about the fact that the customers just aren't coming in.'

'W-w-well, i-it's not good enough,' Rupert stutters. He's a sweet guy but his management skills are shaky, to say the least. No one at Hardy's seems to have any respect for his authority. Maybe it's because he has no retail experience. Prior to this he was running the family's farm in Gloucestershire. The poor bloke's used to lovingly tending cattle, not dealing with argumentative, moaning shop workers. 'We need to try harder to entice them into the store with some canny moves and gentle encouragement,' he adds unconvincingly.

'You're not on your farm now, Rupert.' Sharon treats him like he's beneath her, probably because she *wants* him to be beneath her. Ever since he started here she's been on a mission to snare him. 'Customers aren't like *sheep*: you can't just *herd* them in,' she finishes huffily.

'But of course you can!' Rupert blusters. 'That's the point! You need to woo them, encourage them gently but firmly into the pen . . . I mean, store . . . and then shut the gate . . . I mean, door behind them. You should be like a sheepdog, Sharon!'

'And you're barking mad,' she grumbles. I stifle a giggle. They're like a comedy double act. Little and Large? I bite my lip to stop myself laughing.

Rupert sighs loudly. 'Look, Sharon, I understand that my lack of retail experience makes it hard for you to understand where I'm coming from, but I just want you to see that we have to do something. I care about this store, and the truth is, if we don't drastically improve our takings it won't be here much longer.'

Fleetingly I wonder if this is what Joel was talking about earlier. Rupert has obviously called his old friend in to help advise him on the store's financial situation.

'But Hardy's won't close,' Sharon replies quickly. 'It's been here forever.'

'And some people would say that's too long,' Rupert replies. 'Look, I shouldn't be telling you this but we've had interest from another store to acquire the site. My father is putting pressure on me to accept the offer. He thinks the store has had its day, that we should get out while we can and pour the money into other investments. He doesn't care about Hardy's any more, he just wants to ensure he has a hefty retirement fund,' he adds bitterly.

'But you can't sell Hardy's!' Sharon exclaims. 'What about our jobs?'

Rupert's voice is strained. 'I'm doing all I can to save as many jobs as possible right now. But the truth is, if the store's takings don't go up drastically, we'll all be out of work. Including me.'

I shake my head in disbelief. This can't be happening. Hardy's can't close. It's been here for one hundred years, survived two World Wars. What about Gwen's debts, Jenny's IVF, Becky's rent? Where will Iris get her soap? What about Mrs Fawsley's peacock fascinators? What about me? It's Christmas in three weeks. They can't lay people off before then, can they? Can they?

I peer through the shelves. Sharon has stepped closer to Rupert.

'What about you, what do *you* want?' She brushes her match-stick-like body against his, like a chicken bone propped against a side of pork. I have a sudden mental image of them as animals – with Rupert as a disgruntled pig and Sharon a clucking hen, pecking at him continuously. Her advances are clearly lost on Rupert. He steps away and turns his back on her, and Sharon staggers forward awkwardly. She quickly assumes a new position, this time with one hand on her hip, the other arm stretched up against the shelves. She looks like she's about to launch into the 'I'm a little teapot' routine. Poor Sharon, even *I* can do sexy better than this.

'I want to give this wonderful old place one last chance,' Rupert says with quiet determination. He seems to be talking to himself more than to her but I'm impressed by the passion in his voice. 'It's my family heritage,' he goes on, his voice now choked with emotion. 'My great-grandfather founded it; it was his and my grandfather's whole life. I grew up here and I know how great it once was. I want more than anything to turn it's fortunes around.'

Sharon's arm has tired during his speech and has dropped back to her waist. She flings it back up in the air as he turns to face her.

'But I can't do it without your help.'

'You know I'll do anything to help you, Rupert,' Sharon purrs. She takes a step closer to him again and runs a finger down his arm. 'Just tell me what you . . . need.'

Rupert gulps. 'I need you to triple our sales over the Christmas period,' he says nervously.

'WHAT!' Sharon exclaims, taking a step back. 'That's impossible!'

'W-W-well then,' he stutters, 'perhaps I need to find a general manager who believes it *is*. Um, possible, I mean.'

'You don't mean that,' she gasps. 'You wouldn't get rid of me. You couldn't.'

Rupert sighs and visibly deflates. I'm pretty sure he's wishing he was on his farm tending his cattle right now.

'Sharon, I don't think you understand the gravity of this situation. If we don't at least double our takings by Boxing Day the store will be sold. *Rumors* has been trying to find a prime location for their London flagship store and they think this is it. They have made a lucrative offer and the board is seriously considering it. We have less than a month to instigate a major turnaround. If we fail, Hardy's will be sold and my family's business will be gone. Forever,' he adds sadly.

There is silence.

'So what's the plan?' Sharon says eventually in a subdued tone.

He shrugs wearily. 'I was hoping you'd have one. All I know is that for now, staff cuts have to be made in the most underperforming departments. Menswear is a shambles. It hasn't taken more than a hundred pounds a day in months. Guy has to go. Then there's Gwen . . .'

As I walk out of the store at the end of my shift it feels like I'm leaving an old friend to its terrible fate. Poor thing, I think tearfully as I gaze up at the Edwardian façade. Suddenly I notice that there are two letters missing from the store's sign. The Y and S that were hanging loose have fallen off completely, so the sign above the door now just reads 'Hard'.

I choke back a tear. It truly is hard times for Hardy's. And what's worse is that none of my colleagues are aware of what we're facing. I can't help but feel the enormity of the store's loss, not just to me but to all of them, too. This place has been a sanctuary for so many people for so long. The thought of anyone losing his or her job so close to Christmas makes me feel sick.

As does something else. Rupert wants to rebrand

Hardy's as a high-end fashion-focused store. Apparently he wants a bright, young talent to help take the store in this new designer-led direction. He wants to start showcasing the best of young, breakthrough talent hot off the catwalk so Hardy's becomes known as a real player in the high-fashion world. This will bring in celebrities and PR, and then, he hopes, customers. But as he knows more about farming than he does fashion he needs help. And the person he is pinning all his hopes on to help him do this?

Carly.

I plunge my hands into my coat pockets. The sharp winter wind whips around me as a trickle of passers-by stagger past. Not one of them looks over at Hardy's. I glance up at the clock at the front of the store and I can't help but think that after nearly a century, it looks like Hardy's time is up.

CHAPTER 8

'Vino?' Delilah opens the enormous stain-less steel fridge-freezer and pulls out a bottle of Pouilly Fumé.

I lift my head off the island unit, nod glumly and then bury my face back in my arms. It's several hours after my stockroom eaves-dropping and, to be honest, if Delilah had offered me a bottle of Tramps Pee I'd drink it.

'What am I going to *dooo*?' I whine, as Delilah pours me a large glass.

'About what?' she answers. 'The Hot American Dude or the fact that Hardy's needs a miracle to save it from closing?'

'Both,' I groan.

She hops up onto the barstool next to me and places the baby monitor in front of us, making a sign of a cross on her chest as she does so. She's not religious, just desperate for a child-free evening. And so am I. Not just because of the day I've had, but because I've always loved it when it's just me and Delilah. Maybe it's the six-year age gap, but when I was growing up she was always more like a celebrity to me than an older sister, and I was in awe of her. She'd left home and gone to university by the time I was old enough to realize how cool she was, and when she came home for holidays she was like a beautiful breath of fresh air in a house dominated by testosterone-fuelled Alpha males. When I went to high school I became even more aware of her power. 'Ahhh, Delilah . . .' the teachers would sigh when they realized I was related to her. Their eyes would go all cloudy and distant, and for a moment they would imagine me to be a super-pupil just like her. Then class would begin, the realization that I wasn't like her would hit them and I'd fade into the background again. I understood completely; I was disappointed I wasn't like Delilah too.

Delilah and I have been looking forward to this night in for ages. Even though we live together, it's rare we get time on our own. She is either working on pitches for new business, out at client dinners, trying to spend quality time with Will, or seeing to Lola and Raffy. And I'm often . . . well, to be honest I'm always here. But most of the time I hang out upstairs as I like to give them as much family time together as possible. Which isn't much, given the long hours both she and Will work.

Tonight, though, I'm going to enjoy the one-on-one time with my big sister. More than anything, I really need her advice. She steered me through my break-up with Jamie, took me under her wing and helped piece me back together after the split. I guess I've relied on her ever since.

'So,' I press impatiently, 'what do you think I should do?'

'It's a no brainer!' Delilah replies. 'Date the Hot American Dude, what's his name – Joel.' She pauses and then grins. 'Hey there, *Joel*,' she drawls in a bad American accent, and I can't help but laugh. Then her face falls. '*God*, what I wouldn't give for a hot date,' she sighs dramatically.

I stare at her quizzically and wonder if this is the beginning of the seven-year itch. It's how long she and Will have been together but they've always seemed so happy. Or maybe it's the beginning of a mid-life crisis. She is thirty-four, after all. I study her intensely as if doing so will highlight other signs. No, it's just a silly throwaway comment; she and Will are the perfect couple. Everybody knows that.

'Seriously, sis,' I continue, 'you don't think I'm a terrible person for pretending to be Carly?'

'Not terrible, nooo,' she says carefully, and takes another sip of wine. 'Just a bit . . . desperate.' She catches my shocked expression. 'Oh, I don't mean that nastily,' she says as she goes to check on the pizza. A glorious waft of rich tomato, creamy mozzarella and fragrant basil wafts out of the oven as she opens it and my stomach rumbles. I realize I haven't eaten since this morning, apart from a couple of mouthfuls of the children's organic lentil stew to try to encourage them to put the food in their mouths instead of flinging it at the walls. To be honest, I felt like doing the same after tasting it. 'I just mean that if anyone had waited as long as *you* have for a date, they'd have done exactly the same.'

She smiles and takes a sip of wine, happy to have placated me, not realizing that she's failed miserably. She's usually much more sensitive than this. She knows how hurt I was after Jamie and I split up.

I met him in the Michelin-starred hotel in Norfolk I was working in while I finished my art degree. He was an ambitious trainee commis chef; I was doing bar and waitressing shifts to earn money before starting my graduate course at the London College of Fashion that September. Jamie was everything you'd expect a talented young chef to be: brooding, passionate, creative and wildly exciting, I'd never met anyone like him before. The attraction between us sizzled over the hotplate and during long, late post-shift drinks. Within a matter of weeks we were inseparable, so when August rolled around and my date to move to London drew ever closer we tried to come up with ways that we could make a long-distance rela- tionship work. After all, I reasoned, we'd only be a couple of hours away. But Jamie was adamant it wouldn't work. I loved his intensity; it was all or nothing for him. It made me feel needed, but I also wanted to go to London.

Two weeks before I was due to leave he turned

up late at my house and begged me not to go. He told me he couldn't live without me, and why couldn't I see the distance would ruin us? He told me he loved me and couldn't be away from me, and that if I left that would be it for us. I told him I loved him too. He grasped my hand and said if I'd just stay and support him while he finished his training he'd do the same for me and move to London with me so I could do my course. We'd both be following our dreams and, better yet, we'd be doing it together. Tearfully, I agreed. I loved that he loved me so much he couldn't let me go. It reminded me of my parents' relationship, the benchmark from which I'd always measured True Love. And look at them, I reasoned to myself. They're still happily married after twenty-eight years. So I decided my career could wait and I'd throw myself into supporting Jamie's, knowing that one day that support would be returned. It was a compromise, not a sacrifice, and it was one I was willing to make to have my happily-ever-after.

But a year turned into two years, which turned into three, and just as Jamie became a fully-fledged head chef and agreed to move to London, I was offered a place on that year's graduate scheme. It was perfect. But then out of the blue Jamie got the chance of the job of a lifetime at a restaurant in Paris. What could be better, he said. I could study out there instead. I was thrilled at the thought. It appealed to all my romantic sensibilities. I imagined us living in some pretty little studio apartment in Montmartre, wandering down the Seine, drinking strong coffee at bijou little pavement cafés. Jamie would work and pay the rent, and I'd study and maybe get some experience in fashion merchandising. And where better than the fashion capital of the world?

So I turned down my place again and Jamie and I began talking about the big move. Jamie was due to start in May, so I applied for graduate fashion courses beginning in September and said I'd spend the summer waitressing to help pay the rent. But Jamie argued that it made more sense for me to stay working at the hotel, wait for him to get settled in, find an apartment, then for me to move at the end of the summer. He said the time would fly by. That summer was interminably long. He was working seventy-hour weeks and there was never a good time to visit him. It wasn't until August that we finally co-ordinated a weekend together and I hopped on the Eurostar to visit him and to see the city that I would soon call home. We spent a wonderful weekend together, sight-seeing, drinking coffee and shopping in cute Parisienne brocantes, only for Jamie to tell me at the end of the weekend, while we were waiting at the Gare du Nord for my train, that it was over. He said there was no one else, he still loved me and he always would. I was his best friend, first love, blah blah blah. He just wanted to feel that there was more to life than what we'd planned. He said that being in Paris had made him realize that he wanted to enjoy life while he was young and everything in the future could still be a question mark. And then came the real killer. He told me that life had been too predictable with me. I was devastated. It felt like my entire future had been pulled from under me. I didn't know who I was without him and I was too scared to find out. I just wanted to hide from the world and be invisible.

Which is what I've been doing ever since.

Delilah turns round now, and I deliberately stare in another direction. 'OK, what's up?' she says, and tilts her head to look at me.

'Nothing,' I mumble, and try not to look at her as she tries to get my attention. She bobs down in front of me and her golden hair floats up and falls perfectly back into place, bouncing around above her shoulders. I pull self-consciously at my own brown locks. That pretty much defines the differences between us. Delilah is an exquisitely wrapped present tied with gold ribbon, whereas I'm a brown package tied with string.

'Ee-vie,' she pleads. 'What is it? Have I upset you? I have, haven't I?' She rushes over and covers my forehead with kisses. She always used to do this when I was little and mid-tantrum. It never failed to make me laugh and it has the same effect on me now. I giggle despite myself, and wipe my face.

'You just made me feel like a right loser,' I say petulantly.

Delilah's face drops. 'Oh God, I didn't mean to,' she murmurs. She puts her perfectly manicured hands on my knees. Her engagement ring and platinum wedding band glint magnificently as they catch the light and she's pulled me so that my stool has twisted round towards her. She looks at me intensely and her blue eyes darken for a moment. 'Evie, I have never, nor will I ever, think you're a loser. I'm so sorry if what I said came across the wrong way. I'm just a bit . . . I don't know . . .' she trails off. She seems to be struggling to express herself, '. . . disappointed with my own lot,' she admits shamefacedly.

'You?' I gape, and Delilah nods miserably. I'm shocked because whilst I feel like that most days, I have honestly never thought my big sister felt the same. Not with everything she has. I mean, her life's *perfect*. I focus back on Delilah, who is still apologizing profusely.

'. . . But I shouldn't take it out on you, Evie. You, more than anyone, deserve some excitement.' She cups my face with her hands. 'Date Joel, have fun, you deserve it. And don't worry about this Carly girl. It sounds like she's got more than enough to occupy her trying to save Hardy's from closure in the next few weeks, without a gorgeous man to distract her. In fact . . .' Delilah snaps her fingers and grins at me, '. . . what you are doing is positively *charitable*. You're probably saving

Hardy's by dating him. Here . . .' She lifts her wine glass and motions at me to do the same. I cradle my wine glass protectively to my chest and look at her like she's a madwoman. She continues regardless. 'Here's to you and the Hot American Dude! A match made in retail heaven.'

We clink glasses but I eye her suspiciously. She must be drunk she's acting so weirdly.

'Oh, Evie!' she exclaims wildly. 'All I'm saying is maybe this is karma. Carly got your promotion – you got her man.' She nudges me. 'This is what you've been waiting for, isn't it, Evie? A bit of romance and sparkle in your life?'

Buoyed by her enthusiasm, I nod and smile, feeling excitement bubble in my chest, despite myself. Whatever Delilah's got must be catching.

Maybe my meeting Joel *was* meant to be. And if that's the case I have to do everything I can to make him believe that he's dating Carly. Because if *I'm* being Carly, she can concentrate on saving the store and I can concentrate on saving my love life. Everyone's a winner. At least, that's what I'm going to tell myself.

It feels a lot better than admitting I'm just a fraud.

I suddenly know just what I have to do to help me become Carly. I slip off my stool.

'Will you come and help me choose an outfit for my date?' I ask breathlessly. I look at her meaningfully. 'I think it's time I opened The Wardrobe.'

Delilah's mouth forms an oval shape and she

claps her hands excitedly. 'Let me just grab the wine bottle,' she says, and dashes to the fridge. 'I've been waiting for this moment for a long, long time.'

Me too, I think. *Me too*.

CHAPTER 9

'You are *such* a freak, OCD-Evie,' Delilah says, using her old nickname for me as I swing open my bedroom door. I was the only child of my parents who inherited my mum's neat-freak gene. Delilah, Jonah and Noah are all self-confessed slobs. Delilah puts the plate of pizza on the floor, grabs a slice and leans against the doorframe, alternating little bites with large sips of wine. 'How are we related again?' she laughs. 'It looks like Mary Poppins lives here!'

I glance around the room, trying to see it through Delilah's eyes. I guess it is pretty tidy. At the far end under the eaves there's my bed covered with a silvery-white flocked quilt folded back carefully to reveal a cloud of plumped pillows underneath. I can't help being annoyed to notice that there is a large crease over the left-hand side of the bed. I resist the urge to go and smooth it. My white bedside tables are devoid of anything other than matching white lamps and a copy of Charles Dickens's *The Old Curiosity Shop*, which I am rereading for about the zillionth time. The pale, blond floorboards practically squeak underfoot they have been so well polished, and in the middle of the floor is a soft cream sheep-skin rug that Delilah bought for me when I moved in.

At the opposite end of the room, on the left-hand wall underneath one of the three large dormer windows, is a squishy cream sofa, and a flat screen TV in the corner, which sits in front of the white fitted wardrobes. But these aren't The Wardrobe; they just house my everyday clothes as well as Delilah's out-of-season clothes and piles of things Lola and Raffy have grown out of. I have only half a rail and two shelves and a drawer in here. But I don't need much space, just room for my four pairs of black work trousers (Topshop) four white shirts (Gap) and a drawer for my white, black and nude underwear (all M&S). Then there's a collection of hooded jumpers, T-shirts, long-sleeved tops and jeans (also Gap), which I wear when I'm looking after the kids. All are perfectly folded and either carefully hung or stacked on the shelves in the wardrobe, as if they're displayed on a shop floor. Force of habit, I guess.

But The Wardrobe is what Delilah and I are drawn to now. We pad across the room and perch on the side of the bed, clutching our wine glasses, munching on pizza and staring at the beautiful distressed white Provençal double armoire that stands grandly against the wall to the right of my bed. It looks almost regal with its distinguished hand-carved body sitting on its ornate feet. It seems to gaze down at me imperiously as if it's annoyed that its mistress is such a plain, dowdy character. I bought it from Porte de Clignancourt in Paris, the weekend that Jamie dumped me. It was our five-year anniversary and it was meant to be my first piece of grown-up furniture for our Parisienne flat together. I remember thinking when I bought it that the armoire would have the power to change my life, I just didn't realize it was about to change for the worse.

Despite my love of fashion, after Jamie and I broke up I couldn't face trying to look nice. I comfort ate and cried and lay around in my jogging bottoms, feeling unloved. So when I got the job at Hardy's and moved to Delilah's, the empty wardrobe became a reminder of the person I was before: a happy, positive, loved but horribly impressionable young woman. And I realized that it was time to fill it with a new me: the person I wanted to be. Independent, ambitious, unpredictable, unforgettable even. But I didn't have the confidence to be that person. So instead I filled it with the clothes of my dreams, waiting for the day when I'd feel ready to wear them.

'So, you're really ready to do this, then?' Delilah says at last.

I nod slowly. But the truth is I'm not ready. I'm not ready at all. I probably never will be. I'm just doing this in a desperate attempt to be different because I'm sick of being myself. I remind myself of this as I take a deep breath, stand up and walk towards The Wardrobe. I place my hand gently on the key in the lock and turn it slowly. I close my eyes, open the door and then open my eyes again.

Inside is a row of immaculate vintage pieces that I've painstakingly collected over the past two years, all unworn and covered in plastic, each one an embodiment of the girl I want to be. Vintage clothes are different: they're original. They have history, a sense of magic about them. Besides all that, I love the fact that these clothes have lived a life before. I feel that simply by having them in my wardrobe, that life might just rub off on me. I don't need to wear them. Once I buy them I immediately have them all dry-cleaned – a little luxury – and then they get locked away in the wardrobe. It's not like I can wear them in my day-to-day life. My job in the stockroom and evenings spent looking after Delilah's kids puts paid to that. But I've carried on purchasing them anyway. There's something from every decade of fashion that I adore: 1920s silvery-white flapper-style beaded dresses; shimmering nude, pale-pink and oyster-coloured bias-cut satin floor-length gowns from the 1930s, which I've accessorized by wrapping faux fur shrugs and strings of pearls carefully round the necks of the hangers. There are gorgeous 1940s floral print tea dresses; pastel 1950s prom gowns with corsages and layers of tulle; pencil skirts and beautifully tailored trousers, silk shirts in fabulous jewel colours and armfuls of gorgeous brightly coloured 1960s mini shift dresses.

Over the past two years these clothes have

become like my own personal priceless art collection. They hang in my wardrobe, perfectly curated in order of colour, style and length, but they never get taken off their hangers, or out of their plastic. They're just there for my viewing pleasure.

'Wow,' Delilah breathes as she takes in the row of glistening transparent plastic before us. 'Can I see some of them?'

I inhale sharply. Even though Delilah has always known about The Wardrobe, I've never shown her any of the clothes. I've always locked them away as soon as I bought them, before she had a chance to sneak a peek. She'd beg and plead, but I've always been adamant about keeping them private. Showing them felt akin to telling someone your dreams after you wake up; to you they're deeply meaningful and personal but they probably seem boring or bizarre to anyone else.

But today is different. I realize that if I'm going to pretend to be a stylish, beautiful personal shopper, these clothes are my only chance. I can't afford Carly's designer clothes, and besides, they just wouldn't suit me like these do. I love the way that each garment feels like it's been made especially for me, accentuating my waist, hiding my hips and making the most of every curve I've got. I may be pretending to be Carly, but deep down, I still want Joel to be attracted to *me*.

I step forward and lift a hanger off the rail, holding the plastic against my body for a moment, hoping that it will be enough. Fat chance.

Delilah shakes her head. 'Put it on.'

'I can't,' I reply, shaking my head vehemently.

'Why not?'

'I swore to myself I'd only wear these clothes for an Occasion.'

'Well,' she says patiently as she throws her pizza crust on her plate before stretching out on the bed, 'this is the "Trying on Outfits for the First Date you've had in a Very Long Time" Occasion. Come on, Evie, you've got to do it some time, and who better to do it with than me?' She smiles encouragingly and I bite my lip. She's right. If I'm going to do this, I need a practice run.

'But I don't know where Joel might take me or what we might do!' I protest, trying to buy myself more time. And part of me is still scared that he'll never call. That our delicious meeting will forever languish in my memory of Things That Might Have Been. 'Why don't I just take some of them out of the plastic to show you, and leave it at that?' I add hopefully.

Delilah grins. 'No chance. You've brought me this far, you can't back out now. This is better than a night at the movies. I wish I had popcorn,' and she snuggles down into my bed. I can't help but be thankful that her kitchen is on the bottom floor so there's little chance of her bothering to go back down to get snacks. The thought of her munching messy popcorn on my bed is horrifying. I'm having a hard time as it is ignoring the pizza crust.

'But I don't know which one to try on!' I wail pathetically.

'So try them all,' Delilah shrugs. 'I've got all night. Will's out with the boys and won't be back till the early hours. Again,' she adds, leaning over to take a sip of wine. She throws her arms above her head. 'Come on, sis. Let the show begin!'

Reluctantly I head for the bathroom. I should be excited about this, but I can't help but feel I'm about to disappoint Delilah and let these beautiful clothes down, even though each one of these garments was bought because I knew instinctively when I saw it that it would make me feel different, special, beautiful, *visible* for once in my life. But suddenly the thought of putting something on that could make me stand out is petrifying. I have faded into the background for so long I'm not sure I can handle the spot-light. Even one in my own bedroom with just my sister as an audience. How pathetic is that? I glance down at the dress I'm holding and notice that I'm shaking a little. Here in my hand is the fabric of a life I've only ever dreamed of stepping into. Each stitch is a story of what could have been.

Then I remember the unyielding feeling I had that something special could happen to me when I put on the Gainsbourg. And it did. I met Joel. And I know that when Joel saw me in that top, he really saw me as an effervescent, lively, attractive girl who was worth getting to know. That top saved me from the obscurity I've become so used to. And I want – no, I *need* – to have that feeling again.

I strip off my jeans and hoodie quickly before I change my mind, and lift the plastic delicately over the garment and off the hanger. It is one of my best vintage finds, a beautiful 1950s Larry Aldrich dress, which I discovered after trawling through endless American vintage clothing websites one rainy Sunday afternoon whilst I was trying to give Delilah, Will and the kids some 'family time'. It is beautiful, soft, sage-green silk chiffon with shoulders that can be gathered or fanned out over the tops of your arms, and a plunging neckline that is softened at the bust by a delicate corsage. There is a ruched satin waistband that accentuates that particular part of my figure well, and then the skirt itself is full and sweeping and falls to a flattering mid-calf length. It is demure yet sexy, classic yet different, simple but with exquisite extras. It is perfect.

I feel nervous as I unhook my bra and step into the dress. The chiffon brushes against my skin and I get goosebumps all over my body as I wriggle it up over my hips and bust. There is no need for my normal slimming underwear as the dress is internally structured to support and disguise, simultaneously lifting and hiding any (or, in my case, many) lumps and bumps. I pull my hair off my neck and twist it into a bun, holding it against the back of my head as I step over to the mirror that hangs over the basin. I stand on tiptoes to try to get a better look of the whole effect. I don't want to show Delilah until I'm sure I don't look ridiculous. The chiffon overlay hides a multitude of sins, drawing the eye to the natural curve of my waist that I am actually proud of, whilst hiding my hips and thighs, which I am not. Then the chiffon cascades down towards my knees in a stream of sensuously soft material, and with it, the eye heads down to my calves and ankles, bypassing my most unflattering bits. I slip my feet into a pair of peep-toed vintage silver Gina heels and take a deep breath as I look at myself in the mirror.

Not bad.

I step out of the bathroom. Delilah has her head buried in the latest issue of *Vogue*. I clear my throat to get her attention and she lifts her eyes and stares at me unblinkingly. Her mouth opens and shuts, but no words come out. I am not sure if this is a good or a bad thing.

'Lila?' I squeak. 'Say something . . . please?'

She just shakes her head silently. Then she clambers off the bed and steps towards me. She holds my arms and stares at me from my head to my toes, which are in need of a lick of nail polish, I realize. I try and scrunch them in my shoes to hide them.

'It's too much, isn't it?' I mumble. 'I mean, I wouldn't wear this on a first date, obviously. It's more for if I ever get invited to a big event, you know, like, like . . . the Oscars or something,

105

which, you know, obviously could *totally* happen because that's how my life rolls . . .' I force a laugh. Delilah is still staring. 'Anyway, I'm going to get changed now . . .'

'Will you just SHUSH for a moment?' Delilah says impatiently, and a smile bobs over the corners of her lips. 'I am trying to savour the moment when my little sister turned into a woman. Look at you, Evie!' She twizzles me around and pushes me in front of the full-length mirror on the inside of the armoire door. 'You look beautiful!'

'I wouldn't go that far,' I say bashfully. I look passable, yes, pretty even, but beautiful? Never. I love my sister and all, but even I know she's over-exaggerating. But that's OK. I realize that what she's trying to say is that I look better than I've ever looked before, which frankly, is all I'm aiming for.

I gaze at my reflection with the same eye I use on our shop-floor displays every morning when I'm assessing what I'd do to make them better, if someone would just let me. I try to be critical but even I have to admit that this is probably the best I've ever looked. The sage colour of the dress enhances my pale skin so it looks soft and creamy, and does the same for my mousy hair. It has a really lovely sheen to it this evening. My ankles look small and delicate, my thighs are well hidden under the full skirt, as are the tops of my arms. And my boobs – well, frankly, this dress makes them look fabulous. Usually I hide them under baggy clothes, but the hidden corsetry has lifted them, which forces me to stand tall and throw my shoulders back.

'Oh, Evie, it's so nice to see you happy with the way you look,' Delilah says. 'I hate the fact that you're always so hard on yourself. So,' she claps her hands, 'are we decided?'

'Decided on what?'

'Your outfit, of course.'

'Um, no,' I reply in horror.

'Evie, you have to wear this for your date, you just *have* to. It's PERFECT.'

I stare at her in horror. 'But I don't know where we're going. I'll look a right fool turning up to a pub or somewhere in this.'

'Oh.' She looks downcast for a moment and then her eyes light up again. 'Well, let's try an outfit on for every possible scenario then!' She claps her hands in delight, then dives into my wardrobe, peers under some of the plastic and pulls out a blush-spotted chiffon blouse and hands it to me. 'Try this with those navy cigarette pants, Evie. Go, GO!'

I skulk off to the ensuite. I know not to argue with Delilah when she's like this.

An hour later and I've tried on four more outfits for four very different dates: a black ruched long-sleeved wrap dress with a plunging neckline for a chic city dinner date; a 1940s fur-trimmed tweed jacket with a soft, cream cowl-neck jumper, denim skirt and knee-length brown 1970s boots for a Sunday afternoon countryside amble; a gorgeous horse-printed wrap dress with heeled brogues and a camel cape for a trip on the London Eye ('He's American,' Delilah exclaimed. 'He's bound to choose somewhere like that!'); and lastly, and because Delilah begged me to, I also tried on one of the 1930s bias-cut satin gowns for a sexy night in a hotel in Paris. Even though it brought back memories of Jamie. Delilah sighed and said she hasn't been to Paris, or had sex, for a long, long time and she needed to live vicariously, so I relented.

Another hour later and we're officially drunk. I've put *It's a Wonderful Life* on DVD and we're snuggled up in bed, simultaneously sniffing and swooning over Jimmy Stewart.

'The thing nobody tells you,' slurs Delilah as she stretches out next to me on my bed, 'is that once you're married and have got kids, you never go on dates any more or do any of the fun, exciting things that made you fall in love with each other. It's just endless monotony. Work, kids, dinner, tidying up, more work, bed.'

She rolls on her side and leans up on one arm. 'Do you want to know a secret, Evie?' I turn my head to face her and see a faraway gaze in her eyes. 'Sometimes, I wish I was you. You've got it all ahead of you, haven't you? Your dream job, buying your first flat, falling in love, getting engaged, travelling, marriage, first baby – all those

108

exciting firsts! Whereas me, I've just got this. For. The. Rest. Of. My. Life.' She sighs and turns her face towards the ceiling again. 'I know it sounds really awful, but I just can't help thinking, is this it?'

'It doesn't sound awful, Lila,' I say gently. 'It's normal. Lots of women feel the same. But look at you! You're beautiful, clever, you've got an amazing, successful career, a wonderful husband, two great kids and this incredible house. People would *kill* for your life. Whereas, you know, if they got offered mine they'd probably say, "Er, no thanks, I'll stick with what I've got." It's just the wine making you maudlin.'

'I know, I know,' Delilah says shamefully. 'I know I'm lucky, but I can't help how I feel. Maybe it's because I'm about to turn thirty-five. I mean, God how de*pressing*.'

I rub her shoulder soothingly. 'Would it help if I told you that you look younger than I do?' I reply. Delilah smiles weakly and I sit up and cross my legs. I over-exaggerate a frown and point out my forehead speech marks to her. 'Look. Now, tell me truthfully, wouldn't you be *more* depressed if you were twenty-eight and had these? Joan Collins has fewer wrinkles than I do!'

She laughs and I notice her brush away a solitary tear.

'Age means nothing these days, Lila,' I say, rubbing her knee. 'Look at Kate Moss! And now look at me. I may be six years younger than you but I work in a fuddy-duddy shop, I never go out and I haven't had sex since Jamie dumped me! That was two years ago, Lila. I mean, I'm practically a born-again virgin!' I force a laugh and Delilah joins me but I'm not laughing inside. Right now I'm focusing on distracting Delilah from her weird wine-induced mid-life crisis. I can focus on my less-than-average life later.

'Now,' I say, clapping my hands as I think of the perfect way to cheer her up, 'it's your turn for the fashion parade. So, let's just say that you were going on a date that could end in hot sex, what would you wear?' I indicate The Wardrobe, wordlessly granting her access to its priceless garments, despite feeling a little nauseous at the thought.

'Oh, I couldn't possibly Evie,' Delilah smiles at me. Her tears have separated her eyelashes so that she suddenly looks like a young Twiggy from the sixties, all thick, spidery lashes and wide-eyed innocence.

She looks towards The Wardrobe and then back at me before leaning across the bed and fanning my hair over my shoulders like she does with Lola. 'These clothes, well, they're the essence of you, aren't they? I couldn't possibly try them on. No one would do them justice like you can.'

I swallow, overcome by my sister's sensitivity. It's moments like this that I realize just how much I love and need her.

I honestly don't know what I'd do without her.

FRIDAY 2 DECEMBER

23 Shopping Days Until Christmas

CHAPTER 10

'Morning, Felix,' I say, brandishing a strong Starbucks Americano in front of his security office window.

It's Friday, thank God, but Felix doesn't look like he's got that Friday feeling at all. He smiles wearily at me and reaches out for his coffee. He looks almost grey with fatigue, but then again if I'd been up all night I'd look like crap, too. Felix is here every morning when I come in. He's in his mid-seventies, and he's what you'd call a rough diamond. He's lean for his years, with sharp blue eyes, messy dark-grey hair and matching stubble. He looks slightly unkempt, like a man who doesn't have a woman in his life. Maisie, his wife of nearly forty years, died almost three years ago. But before she died, Maisie left him a list of things she wanted him to do after she'd gone. The first was go back to his old employers and to ask for a job. The last was find a companion. Felix complied with the first, but has told me he's too long in the tooth to be meeting any new woman. 'Dating? At my age? She was a clever old bird, my Maisie, but she wasn't always right. Nope, having a job is good enough – I don't need anything else.'

I know when he came here that being a security guard wasn't exactly what he'd had in mind, but he says it suits him as he hates being at home on his own at night. Until Maisie's death they had never spent a night apart. Can you imagine that? After Jamie, I thought I knew what it was like to lose the love of my life. Now, since I've met Felix, I can only wonder what it would be like to find it.

I hand him his coffee and nod at the newspaper in front of him, which is, as ever, turned to the puzzle page. 'How are you getting on with that?' I ask, pointing at the Sudoku.

He shakes his head ruefully and flicks his pen between his teeth. 'I'm well and truly stuck, Evie. Feel like I've been on the same bloody square forever.'

'You and me both,' I laugh ruefully. 'May I?' I tilt my head towards the pen and he smiles at me.

'Go for your life, love,' he replies warmly and leans back in his chair, sipping his coffee with satisfaction.

I bite the lid of the pen as I stare at the puzzle. Figures have never been my strong point, but I love the certainty of knowing that every one of the nine numbers in a Sudoku has a place, and when they're in the right one every other number falls into place around them. I scribble a seven in the top left-hand corner of the box and then quickly fill in the rest of the missing numbers across the line.

'There,' I say, and hand the pen back to him. 'That should help.'

Felix leans forward and squints at the puzzle, then back at me. 'Whooo,' he whistles. 'You are on form.'

'Pity no one else thinks so,' I say, and before I can stop myself my chin is wobbling and I'm sitting in his office telling him about the promotion that never was. Felix shakes his head and pats my shoulder as I reel off my feelings of disappointment and failure.

'It's not right,' he mutters. 'It's just not right. Why can't they see what's in front of them? Walter would never have overlooked such obvious talent, that's for sure.' I smile at his loyalty to me and his old boss, whom he respected enormously. Felix used to be a manager here back in the days when Hardy's was a real destination store, and I love hearing his stories. Just like me he started in the stockroom, back in the late 1950s, working hard until Walter Hardy junior spotted his potential and moved him on to the shop floor. He's convinced the same will happen to me.

'It's crazy that you're stuck in that stockroom when you could be such an asset on the floor,' he says, and I resist the urge to smile. 'The customers would love you. I know,' he adds gruffly, 'because you're a little ray of sunshine for me.' I feel my eyes fill up and I can see he's embarrassed and doesn't know where to look. I don't know what's up with me today. I'm not usually this emotional.

'Sorry, Felix,' I say, swiping at my eyes.

He reaches out across his desk and squeezes my hand with his liver-spotted one.

'Don't worry about it, love. You have a good cry if you need to.' He smiles. 'Do you know I've just realized you're the only staff member who ever calls me by my name? Everyone else just says "Hey" or "Hi" or "Excuse me, mister!" or sometimes . . .' he shakes his head, '. . . they don't acknowledge me at all. It's like I'm invisible,' he adds indignantly. He pulls out a Father Christmas beard and hat from under his desk. 'I'm thinking of wearing this for the rest of the month to see if anyone notices.'

'Maybe I should do that too,' I laugh as Felix pulls on the beard. 'Everyone calls me Sarah, the last stockroom girl's name, or – worse – the Stockroom Girl. It's like I'm not allowed a personality of my own.' I feel my mood swing upwards like a pendulum as I share my frustrations with someone who understands. 'The other day I even answered my landline at home: "Hello, Sarah speaking." My mum was most confused.'

Felix roars with laughter and suddenly I feel better. It *is* pretty ridiculous. I keep promising myself I'll tell everyone at work my actual name one day, but, well, it's been two years now and I don't see the point any more. It's not like Sarah is a *bad* name, and besides, plenty of great people go by different names. Norma Jean Mortenson became Marilyn Monroe, for example, and Judy Garland was actually Frances Ethel Gumm. So I'm in good company with the whole name-change thing. I just wish I'd had a say in it.

I think back to my glorious encounter with Joel and realize that I can't really complain. After all, pretending to be someone I'm not seems to be my new thing. First Sarah, now Carly. I can't help but wonder if I'll ever have the confidence to be myself again at all. Perhaps I'll tell him the mix-up when he phones. Not that he probably will, but I live in hope.

Felix smiles at me quizzically. 'So who is he?'

'Who?' I reply innocently, wondering what it is about the elderly and their spot-on intuition. Felix and Lily always seem to know exactly what I'm thinking.

'You've got the glow of a girl who's just met someone.'

I blush and think about the pink silk pussybow blouse and tight, black fifties pencil skirt in my rucksack, and I can't help but smile. I couldn't bring myself to put the outfit on this morning, not for a day spent in the stockroom, but I never know when I might need it. Or, more to the point, when Joel might come into the store again.

'So come on, who is he?'

'Oh, no one,' I reply bashfully, and take a sip of coffee. I pause and look up at Felix, suddenly wanting to share my news with him. 'OK, he's just someone who came into the store yesterday . . .'

'Ah, good ol' Hardy's playing Cupid again,' Felix laughs gruffly. 'She's always been good at that.'

'You sound just like my mum,' I laugh. 'She met my dad when she worked here and has always told me I'd fall in love with someone at the store. I've never believed her, though.'

'Well, maybe you should,' Felix says. 'Hang on, you said she used to work here, would I know her?'

It suddenly occurs to me that he might. As Felix worked here when Walter junior managed the place, he would have been here at the same time as Mum. I can't believe I've never thought of it before.

'Maybe. Her name's Grace Taylor, but she worked here as Grace Samson,' I say, referring to my mother's maiden name. 'She worked in the salon from about 1971 till she met my da—'

Felix snaps his fingers. 'Bleedin' hell, of course!' he exclaims. 'I knew you reminded me of someone! How is she? She was such a wonderful stylist, you know. The best Hardy's ever had. Everyone thought so. We were all devastated when that posh bloke came and took her away from us. Charles, wasn't it?'

I nod. Everyone always remembers my father. He's hard to forget. He's got what people call a dominating personality. But I'm far more interested in hearing about my mum. I had no idea she was so well respected at Hardy's. She's always told us she was just a simple junior stylist who no one ever took any notice of until Dad came along and swept her off her feet. I genuinely had no idea that Mum had been considered a talent.

'She was really that good?' I say, slightly bewildered that Felix is a fount of knowledge on my mother.

He raises his eyebrows at me, clearly surprised by my lack of knowledge. 'Yeah, love. I mean, Princess Anne once requested that your mother style her hair for a big royal occasion. It don't get bigger than that.'

'Wow!' I rest my head on my hands, wanting Felix to tell me more. My mother's clearly been way too modest. 'Did Mum do it?'

'Grace turned the offer down. Said she wasn't confident enough. Everyone thought she was mad.'

I shake my head in disbelief. 'It's like hearing about a woman I don't know. God, I wish I'd been here back in those days.'

I stare at the monitor in front of Felix, which is flicking through all the different departments. They all look so sad and desolate and I suddenly remember Rupert and Sharon's conversation. I get up to go; I don't want to burden Felix with the store's problems. He's got enough on his plate. Besides, I know how much this job means to Felix and I can't bear to think of him losing it. Who else would employ a security guard in his seventies? I think of him sitting day in, day out at home, doing his puzzles, with no one to talk to, and it makes me feel awfully sad. I make my excuses, leave him to his Sudoku and head for the stockroom.

I walk down the corridor, past the staff notice-boards and suddenly remember the passport photo lurking in my rucksack. I had it taken yesterday at the tube station, after I picked Lola and Raffy up from nursery. I unzip my rucksack, extract the photo, then I put a bit of Blu-Tack on the back and, with a hearty thump, stick it over Sarah's old picture. I stand back and study it. I look awful and I'm tempted to pull it back down but then I remember it doesn't matter any more. None of us will be here for much longer anyway.

The lights are on and the cleaners are still here as I walk into the ground-floor hall.

'Hi, guys,' I call, and various heads pop up from different parts of the store. The cleaners wave at me, 'Hi, Evie,' they say in discordant unison, and then immediately get back to work. They're always so busy and have such a strong work ethic. The other staff could learn a lot from them. I am reminded of Guy, Gwen and Jenny, whose jobs are on the line, and wonder if I can somehow warn them about their fate, but I don't know how.

I decide to do a quick round of the shop floor before I head to the stockroom, making notes of the stock that needs to be replenished. I've always found it really easy to recall where everything is meant to go better than anyone else – even the department managers. And it gives me a chance to feel, for a short part of the day, that the shop floor is my territory. It's around this time that I play the game in which I remerchandise the whole place in my head, imagining how I'd make each department look, how I'd display the stock and what props I'd use to best enhance the shop-floor displays. It sounds weird but I know I'm good at it.

Today I decide to go first to Menswear, which seems to consist mainly of a wall of denim. Row upon row of pairs of jeans in blue, dark blue, faded blue, navy, indigo, black, faded black, dark grey. In the centre of the department is a display of socks. Then belts. Then a row of suits. Then come the endless racks of green, black and beige Barbour jackets, rain macs, and other drab outer-wear. It's the most uninspiring shop floor I've ever seen.

Guy is continuing to be the most miserable-looking department manager since his boyfriend left him. They'd just bought a flat together, too. And now Guy is heading for the milestone birthday that, in gay years, is akin to death. I haven't been able to stop thinking about him since I heard Rupert say that he's going to let him go. I just don't know what that would do to him. I feel particularly protective towards Guy because I understand what he's going through. He was besotted with Paul and when they broke up Paul told Guy that he felt 'indifferent' to him. After three years. I mean, what the hell is it with men and their ability to not just break your heart but to trample on your confidence and smash your spirit too? Since it happened I've noticed Guy disappearing within himself. His clothes have become plainer, his voice quieter, his demeanour apologetic. And this from the brightest, funniest, most extroverted person I know.

Boyfriend or no boyfriend, it's no wonder Guy always looks so miserable, staring at that uninspiring view of denim every day. There is no colour, no life, no energy here. Sometimes I wonder where all the glamour went in the world. Then I gaze down at my own drab black trousers and white shirt, my open coat over them, and feel the urge to laugh. Who am I to talk?

Across the dark shopfloor, the sparkle of the old-fashioned lights from the Christmas trees in Lily's tearoom catch my eye and I find myself drawn like a magpie towards them. I half expect to see Humphrey Bogart sitting in the corner, his legs stretched out in front of him, wearing his trademark trilby and trench coat and pulling lazily on a cigarette. Why don't men dress like that any more? Surely they want suave and sophisticated as much as I want sparkle?

Suddenly I hear a male voice and I dart into the tearoom. I've only met him once before but I'd recognize that accent anywhere. I'm completely panicked by Joel's presence, but also excited. What the hell is he doing here at this time of the morning? It's barely seven o'clock. I know he said he knows Rupert, but I've never seen a Hardy here at this hour. Things must be really bad.

I tentatively peer back out. He's wearing a sharp-tailored suit that hangs off his lean body perfectly. God, he's gorgeous. A smile hovers over my lips as I recall our conversation, which was right up there in the Best Flirt Of My Life scale.

Then I lean back against the wall as a thought hits me. What if Joel's come back especially to find me? I mean, we never actually set a date – he took my number, sure, but he hasn't called. I've been religiously checking my phone since yesterday. What if he came back to ask me out *in person?* Wow, I – I mean Carly – must really have made an impression.

He's murmuring to someone on the phone and I strain to hear him.

'Hello? Ah, Rupert,' he drawls. 'Hi . . . uh huh. I'm here. Just looking around. What time are you coming in? . . . OK, well, yeah I guess I'll see you then.'

Right. He's here to see Rupert. That makes much more sense.

Joel rings off and continues browsing, making notes as he does so. I am intrigued. Is he trying to work out a way to save Hardy's, just like I am? Could he be the hero Hardy's is waiting for? Rupert obviously thinks so. Joel couldn't look more like a store Superman if he tried. Oh God, I'm actually salivating.

I press my body up against the wall and hold my breath as I hear his footsteps approaching. On the opposite wall, Clark Gable appears to be smirking at me from inside the picture frame, as if to say, 'You are so busted, lady.' And he's right. I'm standing in the dark, still wearing my coat, crappy clothes and rucksack, looking the exact opposite of a sexy, stylish personal shopper. Joel can't see me like this, he just can't. There's only one thing for it.

'Carly?' Joel raises his eyebrows in surprise as I saunter out from behind a display. 'We must stop meeting like this!'

'Mr Parker?' As I say his name I realize that my top lip has attached itself to my teeth. I run my tongue around my mouth and swallow. I'm holding an armful of men's clothes, which I grabbed from the changing-room rail next to the tearoom. I clutch them to my body and wait expectantly for his response.

'Please, Carly, call me Joel,' he says, and I feel myself blush. I have a desperate urge to tell him my real name but I don't know how to do it without sounding crazy. And what is he doing here anyway?

Did I just say that out loud?

'Oh, you know,' he laughs, and dimples swing from his cheeks like anchors. 'I'm just doing some shopping.'

'It's 7 a.m.,' I reply evenly. 'We're not even open yet.'

'Is it?' He looks sheepish, but only for a second. 'Well, Rupert is an old friend. He said I could browse before the store opens. I think I'm still on Pacific time.'

He glances at his watch. He has good hands, I can't help but note. Our hands would be the perfect match. Mine would definitely like to be held by his. They could make sweet hand love. People would say how good our hands look together. I'm just not sure about the rest of us.

Seeing him again has made me realize he is way out of my league. Even with the mini-makeover I gave myself in the tearoom just now I know I'm still batting way below par on the looks front compared to him. I'm just glad I had the pale pink silk blouse and pencil skirt in my bag this morning. When I saw Joel was coming my way and I had no chance of escaping, I knew I had to change fast. So I did a superhero act of my own and quickly stripped off my grubby trousers and shirt and slipped on my 'Wardrobe' clothes. Then I hastily pinned my hair up, pinched my cheeks to make them rosy and pressed my eyelashes back with my fingers to make them curl, before rubbing on some lip balm that I found lurking in the bottom of my rucksack. The only thing I didn't have with me was tights or high heels. I completely panicked as I heard Joel coming closer, and quickly decided that my

125

battered old brogues were a no-no for a personal shopper so I whipped off my socks and shoes and put them behind Lily's counter, thanking God that I'd had the foresight to shave my legs in the shower and that Delilah had painted my toenails cranberry red last night after I'd paraded around in my Larry Aldrich dress. Then, when Joel's back was turned, I nipped out of the darkened tearoom and hid behind a display. I decided Joel wouldn't notice my bare feet as men never look beneath chest level when talking to women. Everyone knows that.

'Um, why aren't you wearing any shoes?' he asks as he glances at my bare feet.

Oh. Damn.

'We-ell,' I begin, trying quickly to think of a valid reason when it's approximately minus two degrees outside. And about the same in here. Hardy's old heating system is a tad temperamental. 'You know, Joel, I just find I . . . work better like this,' I say, prancing on my toes to demonstrate the freedom of being barefoot. 'I like to be free to dash around the store, you know, collecting clothes for people. I find I'm more in tune with what is comfortable and, um, chic . . .' I have no idea what I'm talking about. 'Um, so, anyway, is there anything I can help you with? I *am* a personal shopper, you know,' I add grandly. Just in case he was doubting me. I proffer my armful of clothes by way of example. 'These are for a client.' Is 'client' the right word? Or is that just a term prostitutes use? Shit, it's

126

customer. Of *course* it's customer. Oh well, maybe he won't notice my slip-up.

'A client,' Joel replies, his mouth twitching a little. 'Is that what you call them over here? And how would an experienced personal shopper dress the average Hardy's male . . . *client*?' He raises an eyebrow at me.

I glance at the clothes, racking my brain for something suitably insightful to say. 'Well, of course they are a high-class and *very* choosy type of person. They like style . . .' I pull out at disgusting pale pink long-sleeve gingham shirt with a white collar. It's vile. I gulp. 'But they are not afraid to push the boundaries of taste. They like casual, too. For when they're, you know, going to the polo or something.' I hold up a pair of pale lemon chinos the colour of cupcake icing and realize that they are also vile. '*But*,' I add hurriedly, 'they do *not* want to fade into the crowd.'

I put my hand into my armful of clothes and pull out some bright pink braces. Joel bursts out laughing and I try to appear offended. 'Are you laughing at my client's outfit?' I ask pompously.

He shakes his head and he touches my arm gently and a shot of adrenalin courses through my body. 'No, I'm laughing at you. You're very funny. I love the British sense of humour.'

'But being American you're not supposed to have one,' I reply quickly. 'Everyone always says you don't get irony . . . which is ironic.' I pause and smile. 'Are you being ironic?'

Joel laughs again and shakes his head. 'Not ironic. Honest. I like you. I'm glad you're here, actually. I was hoping to see you this morning so I could arrange that date in person.' He glances at his watch again and I take another sneaky peek at him whilst his eyes are averted. His thick, black eyelashes brush against his cheeks. There is the beginning of stubble on his chin which, against his American tan, looks like a heavy shadow cast over a sandstone rock. 'Is 7.30 a.m. too early for a date, do you think?' he says, raising his eyebrows a little.

'Some of us have work to do, you know,' I say with a hint of a smile.

'Ah, yes,' he nods. 'Your *client*. I forgot. So when *is* this polo match he's going to?'

'Oh. Um, very soon,' I reply, nodding vigorously.

'How about tomorrow?'

'Not *that* soon,' I say incredulously. '*Obviously* he needs to approve his outfit first.'

Joel laughs and I suddenly feel like the funniest girl in the world.

'No, I mean are you free to go for a drink tomorrow?' he asks.

I resist the urge to shout, 'YESYESYESYEEEES!'

'Yes, I think I am, actually,' I reply coolly, suddenly very thankful for my weird working hours that led me to bump into Joel again. 'I finish at— I mean my last appointment finishes at 3 p.m.' I mentally praise myself for my quick thinking.

'Fantastic,' he smiles. 'I'll meet you outside the store tomorrow at three.'

'Great, Joel, it's a, er, date.' I realize too late that sounds truly ridiculous.

Thankfully he's already wandered off.

I have a date. Oh My God, I have a date. I have a date I have a date I have a date, is all I can think as I wander around the still silent menswear department. I pull out my notebook and draw a quick but detailed picture of Joel, his sharp suit, his crisp shirt, his nice hands. I kiss it, then I scribble a quick sketch from memory of the picture in the tearoom, of Clark Gable. They look remarkably similar, apart from the cut of their clothes.

I've always loved drawing and I'm totally absorbed in sketching the sharp lines of Clark's trilby when I suddenly have an idea. I snap my fingers.

'That's it!' I say out loud.

I feel a bubble of excitement expand in my belly as I turn and run up the staircase, taking the steps two at a time. I have to get to the stockroom where I know there's a box filled with exactly what I need in the fourth aisle, in the middle of the third shelf, next to the 1970s polyester kipper ties and the dual-purpose shooting-stick seat umbrellas (which you can sit on *and* use as umbrellas, although not at the same time, obviously).

My idea probably won't work, but it's worth a shot. I can still hear Rupert's words in my head.

. . . Staff cuts have to be made in the most under-performing departments. Menswear is a shambles. It hasn't taken more than a hundred pounds a day in months. Guy has to go.

My idea may be crazy but it may just work. Guy's never going to improve his takings with his current display. I've got some serious planning to do.

SATURDAY 3 DECEMBER

22 Shopping Days Until Christmas

CHAPTER 11

The next day I'm relaxing on the stockroom sofa, having a much-needed cup of tea and daydreaming about my forthcoming date with Joel, when the door bursts open. I am exhausted. It isn't even 10 a.m. yet. It's Saturday and according to my Advent calendar (Door 3: chocolate church bells) there are exactly twenty-two shopping days left till Christmas, so we may even have a handful of customers today.

'You'll never guess what, Sarah!' Carly exclaims as she springs into the stockroom. She has somehow managed to make impossibly tight grey skinny jeans, black Ugg boots and a black, bum-skimming puffa jacket worn open to reveal a silver satin cowl-necked top, look both seasonal and stylish. Her chestnut hair is pulled back into a tight ponytail with flicky layers framing her features and her face is shining with excitement.

'What?' I say, and sit up. Carly bounds over and sits next to me and I feel a sharp stab of guilt penetrate my stomach.

'I've just had a phone call from some Human Resources lady from Rumors,' she gasps. 'They've heard all about me and want to invite me for an interview!' She squeals and hugs me. Then she slips off her coat and boots and opens her soft, black slouchy handbag. 'I mean, it's AMAZING. It's my dream job,' she says, popping her Uggs in her bag and takes out a pair of gorgeous silver high heels. 'It's just,' she continues, 'I feel like I'd be really landing Rupert in it if I left before Christmas. I mean, it's the busiest time of the year. Well,' she adds as an afterthought, 'maybe not here . . .' She looks at me. 'What would you do, Sarah? Go for something that you really want, or stay loyal to your friends?' She tilts her head and looks at me, and it feels like her green eyes can see right into my soul.

I cough and stand up. 'Stay loyal, I guess. But that's just me. I love Hardy's and couldn't imagine working anywhere else. But you, well, you have to do what's right for you.'

But she's not listening, she's busy burrowing in her gigantic bag, trying to find her ringing phone.

'Hello?' she says, resting it between her ear and her shoulder as she holds a finger up to silence me, then spends the next five minutes chatting while I wait patiently for her to finish.

'Sorry about that, hon,' she says at last. 'It was just my flatmate organizing the guest list for tonight. We're going for cocktails at this cool new club that's just opened. Last time we had the most hilarious night. This super-rich guy sent over a magnum of champagne to our table. I mean, it was clear he just wanted to get into our knickers, you know how it is . . .' I am nodding like one of those dogs people have in the back of their cars, but the truth is I don't know. I don't know at all. Being with Carly feels like I'm watching reruns of *Sex and the City*. Carly is now talking about not wanting to date anyone until she sees Mr Eye Contact Guy again. I feel a stab of guilt . . . Suddenly I realize Carly has asked me a question. Thinking about Joel had made me drift off.

'Are you OK, honey? You don't seem with it today.' Carly says kindly. 'You look a bit under the weather, actually. A bit pale.' She snaps her fingers and delves into her handbag. 'You should go to this amazing woman who does spray tans. I'll give you her number. She does all the celebrities. She'll even give you a discount if you mention my name.' Carly pulls a card out from her bag and gives it to me. 'She's just round the corner. We all need a glow in these winter months, hey!' She smiles at me. 'And it'd mean you'd be able to carry off that pretty top even better. It's gorgeous, by the way. I've been meaning to ask you where you got it. I haven't seen it before.'

I can't help but feel a rush of pleasure that Carly is complimenting *me*. It must mean I'm doing something right. It took me ages to choose what to wear for my date with Joel this afternoon and I finally settled on a 1940s delicate lace, cream blouse with billowing sleeves and a round collar with a rust-coloured 1960s tunic dress over the top. It's quite short for me, but I think the blouse, cream tights and the little string of pearls that sits just under the blouse collar makes it looks cute and chic. At least, I hope it does. I tell Carly about the little vintage shop I know in Islington but she wrinkles her nose.

'Vintage? As in some old dead granny's? No thanks. But I have to admit cemetery chic looks good on you.' She takes a sip of the tea I've passed to her. 'Now, talk me through the whole "no shoe" thing you're sporting right now.'

I glance down at my feet and blush. Ever since my quick transformation yesterday morning, I haven't wanted to wear my battered old brogues; they're like a symbol of the old me, the me I want to forget.

'Are you starting a new trend with that and that granny chic top?' She smiles at me and tilts her head comically, and I can't help but laugh. Obviously I can't tell her the truth. Besides, she'd never believe me.

'Oh, you know, I'm just bored of my boring old brogues,' I say, waving a hand in their direction. They have spilled out of my rucksack, which is lying in the corner of the stockroom. 'And they didn't seem to go with this outfit.'

'You're right there, hon. But then again they don't really go with *anything*, do they?' She giggles playfully. I should be offended, but I know she's right. 'You know what?' she says thoughtfully. 'I've got the perfect pair of shoes upstairs in the personal shopping department. I'd actually put them aside for me, but I need to wait till January now to get them. Shall I bring them down later? I think they'd look *fierce* with that outfit.'

'You'd do that?' I gasp, unable to believe my luck. 'Would you be able to bring them down before three o'clock? It's just I'm going out . . . um, later.'

'*Really?*' she says, and gives me a nudge. 'Hot date?'

'Sort of,' I reply quietly, feeling the cold grip of my treachery.

'Well, I'll give you the shoes if you'll be sure to tell me all about it on Monday. Every single detail. Promise?'

I nod and cross my fingers behind my back. 'Promise.'

As the hands inch closer to three o'clock I feel the nerves and excitement building. I can't keep still. I feel like I've got motion sickness and my stomach is in knots. I'm wearing the shoes Carly kindly brought down for me. I can't stop looking at the gorgeous black stacked heels and peep-toes. They're taking some getting used to, mind. But admittedly they make my legs look ridiculously long. I've spent the last hour practising walking in them up and down the stockroom as I went to collect orders. There were quite a few this after-noon, which was strange.

I glance down again as I pick up the vintage

chequered cape I've borrowed from the stockroom knowing that no one will notice. I throw it round my shoulders and pick up the soft black clutch handbag Carly lent me to go with the shoes. And thank God she did. I can't exactly turn up all dolled up and carrying a rucksack.

I take a deep breath to steady my nerves and walk out of the stockroom. I stumble a little, glance down and make a face. These shoes are nothing like anything I usually wear. But then again, I suppose that's the point. And *this* is what Joel is expecting. A stylish, sexy, high-heel-wearing personal shopper to swoosh out of the store. So that's what he's going to get.

As I walk out onto the shop floor I hope that my colleagues notice me for once. My hair has been brushed and is hanging loosely around my shoulders; I even have make-up on! Sam would be in fits if he saw me. He knows how much I scoff at girls who trowel on the cosmetics. This is way more make-up than I'm entirely comfortable with, to be honest, but Carly insisted on giving me a masterclass when she bought down the shoes and bag.

'You can't go on a date tonight looking like *that*,' she said, waving her finger at my face. Then she pushed me in front of the mirror. My face was blotchy and shiny, my hair was its usual dull, lacklustre self.

I muttered, 'I can't do this,' and tried to move away, but she begged and pleaded for me to let her help, which made me feel even *more* like going home. If I hadn't been doing such a terrible, unsisterly thing by stealing her date, I would have been overjoyed at the attention she was paying me. As it was, I felt horribly guilty. But in the end, her cajoling worked and she got to work on my face.

After what felt like a lifetime of pulling funny expressions so she could prod me in the eyes, pull at my cheeks and hair and lips, she pushed me in front of the mirror and clapped her hands excitedly.

'What do you think?' she said expectantly.

I gazed at myself with my mouth agape, hardly recognizing my reflection. She had done my make-up exactly like hers, using the same golden, honey-hued shades on my eyes. Then she'd applied a thick layer of black mascara and a delicate Bardot-esque sweep of liquid eyeliner over the top of my lids. I'd also been furiously bronzed with the biggest make-up brush I've ever seen, and attacked with a shimmering, toffee-coloured lip gloss, which makes my lips feel as if they have got glue on them. But unlike Carly, who always seems to look effortlessly glossy and beautiful, I thought I just looked, well, a bit . . . *overdone*.

'It'll take a bit of getting used to,' she said confidently, noticing my uncertain expression. 'But this is exactly what you need for a night out. Just imagine it in low candlelight at a restaurant, or in a cool, trendy bar.'

Obviously I couldn't tell her my rendezvous is

now. I didn't want her to risk trying to sneak a peek at my date. Her date. But then, I rationalized, the whole point is that I'm meant to be glamorous and shimmering and glowing. And that's exactly what I am. I'm just not used to it, that's all.

So with all this work I am hoping that someone in the store will turn round and say, 'Hey, look at Sarah!' (I'm not expecting them to use my actual name or anything. I mean, let's not hope for miracles.) I've even left my cape open so they can get the full effect of my 'look' (that's what personal shoppers call 'outfits', I think). But as I walk out I realize that most of the staff are all huddled by the stairs, gazing down into the menswear department and chattering excitedly. I tentatively take a few steps closer and a big, resounding 'Ooh' makes me jump, quickly followed by several 'Aaahs'.

Then I hear someone bellow: 'What's happening now? I can't see!'

It sounds as though there's some big, dramatic scene unfolding. And that's what worries me. My heart pounds as I take my place behind Gwen, who is herself straining to see over someone else's head. I don't want to get any closer. I'm terrified of what is happening down there. What if Guy is having some awful tantrum, or worse, is being fired by Rupert? I try to peer down into the basement to see what the hell is happening. What was I *thinking* earlier? I should've just left well alone.

'What's going on?' I whisper to Gwen, who doesn't even look round at me.

'Guy's got customers down there,' she whispers with glee. 'Lots of them! He's running around his department like a lunatic! Honestly, I've never seen anything like it.'

I squeeze into a small space by the banisters and peer down. I'm amazed to see that there is a huddle of male customers surrounding Guy, all holding up items of clothing that they want to try on or buy. He is holding court like he's Sir Philip Green, and is clearly in his element.

He glances up and gestures grandly at us. 'Well, don't just stand there you lot,' he trills. '*Some*one come and help me. I've got customers waiting to be served!'

Becky from Handbags rushes down the stairs to assist him, leaving the rest of us up here admiring the view.

'It looks like a scene from a 1940s movie,' sighs Gwen, and I feel a swell of pride as I look down and see that my little idea has worked.

Yesterday morning I spent a couple of hours designing a whole new display for the department. I wanted to show the best of Hardy's stock in a cool, classic way. So I imagined how Hardy's might have displayed the stock back in its heyday. I wanted to recreate that old image of London businessmen in sharp suits, trench coats, hats and umbrellas. I knew I could make a display of mannequins look cool and modern in Hardy's old-fashioned Menswear stock if I just presented them in the right way. Drawing the picture of Clark

Gable made me think about the pictures of classic film stars on the walls in Lily's tearoom and suddenly I knew just how to make it all come to life.

This morning I came in extra early, dragged the box of trilbies down to menswear, then collected all the other props I'd dug out of the stockroom. I stripped four mannequins of their denim, pulled them into a line in the middle of the department, put them in sharp suits and gave each of them a cool, tilted trilby. For some reason I just knew it would look good. As a final touch, I gave one an umbrella, another one was holding last night's copy of the Evening Standard, which I nipped out to get from Brian, the friendly newsagent across the road, the next one was holding a vintage brief-case, and the final one had his hand up as if hailing a cab. I was pleased with the first stage of my idea. But I had more work to do.

'Those trilbies looks so cool,' breathes Jenny.

'Why don't you see blokes dressed like that any more?' Paula from Personal Shopping says. 'It's all baggy jeans and bums out, these days. So not classy.'

'It's very *old-fashioned*,' ponders Carly, who is right at the front. 'I'm not sure the men I meet would ever want to wear a hat like that.'

I can't help but disagree. An image of Sam in a trilby pops into my head and I think, actually he could really pull it off, in a trendy pop star kind of way. And Joel, ooh, he'd look just like an old-fashioned matinée idol. And my dad would look just like a 1960s businessman, all sharply tailored suit, smart overcoat and umbrella.

'Well, *they* clearly do!' Paula exclaims, and points at the queue of customers forming round the paying point. More men are picking up trench coats and trilbies and heading to the changing rooms. I smile as I listen to my colleagues. The mannequins do look good, even if I say so myself. I've always felt it was a travesty that those vintage hats were hidden away in the stockroom. I watch as Guy rings through another one on the till for a young guy, who immediately puts it on. It feels nice to be proved right.

I've also created mini tableaux in the rest of the department. Over in the far corner, near Lily's tearoom, I've placed a mannequin in front of a table, sitting with one leg crossed over his thigh, leaning over as if talking to someone. He's wearing a crisp suit with dark-rimmed spectacles, and there's a packet of Lucky Strikes (also purchased from the newsagent) and a cocktail glass (which I found in the stockroom) in front of him.

In the other far corner, where rails of tracksuits and fishing gear used to hang, there's two mannequins dressed as golfers. One is wearing checked trousers, a polo shirt, a cool, jaunty cap and the red braces I picked up yesterday when I was talking to Joel. I've positioned him so he looks like he's just teed off. He was inspired by a picture of a popstar I saw looking super-cool in a celebrity magazine. The mannequin next to him is wearing the pastel lemon chinos I showed Joel, which I've teamed with a grey Pringle of Scotland diamond-patterned tank top over a white polo shirt, with a sharp, grey skinny tie underneath. I decided against the pink braces. I've re-merchandised the whole sportswear bit of the department by forward facing what I think is the coolest, most stylish of the old stock on the rails, and making it all look like outfits guys could wear, even if you weren't planning on playing golf, or going hunting, shooting and fishing. I've even done a display that is a homage to Guy Ritchie, with cool tweed jackets and trousers, and I've put out on display the deer-stalkers I was sorting through yesterday. I suddenly realized they're perfect for a cold, snowy December and should be properly displayed.

'Oh, *look*!' cries Bernie from Haberdashery. She and her sister, Susan, have been quiet up till now. They don't like change. They've never taken to Rupert and would love it if they could pretend it is still the 1950s. Which is why I was hoping they'd approve of my makeover. If they like it, it must be authentic. 'Look at the pictures in the frame!'

'They don't make men like that any more, sure they don't,' Susan adds whimsically.

'Who are they?' asks Carly as she strains to get a better view of the black-and-white pictures I've put up.

Susan and Bernie tut and roll their eyes. 'Only some of the greatest movie stars who ever lived.'

'They look so suave,' sighs Jane wistfully.

'Like proper gentlemen,' agrees Jenny.

I smile as I glance around the walls of Menswear, where I've hung the signed pictures from Lily's tearoom, in big, ornate gold frames that were languishing in the stockroom. I hope she doesn't mind.

I suddenly remember that Joel will be waiting for me. This is my perfect opportunity to leave without anyone – and by that I mean Carly – spotting us.

I slip past my colleagues and head unnoticed towards the front doors, deep in thought. My little idea has worked better than I could ever have imagined. Which makes me wonder: if I can do it for Guy's department, why can't I do it for everyone else's? Especially those who are also about to lose their jobs, like Gwen and Jenny. It's got to be worth a shot, hasn't it? No one need know it was me who did the makeover. Guy can take all the credit and then Rupert won't fire him.

As I push the doors open and step outside I am hit by a wave of cold air. I shiver and turn back to the store. Everyone is still huddled around the stairs, chattering and pointing excitedly. Smiling again, I walk round the side of the building and stand in front of one of the windows. I decided when doing the makeover this morning that I had to do something in the window to try to draw new customers inside. So in one window, I've replaced the horrid, fake silver Christmas trees with a mannequin looking exactly like a 1940s film star in his vintage trilby. He's kneeling on one knee and is proffering a small, beautifully wrapped gift box in Tiffany-blue wrapping paper out to the street, as if proposing to any woman that passes by. It's not particularly Christmassy, but then, I reasoned, nor was my other display. To the right of the mannequin, in another old-fashioned gilt frame, is Lily's signed picture of a smouldering Clark Gable, looking for all the world like he's waiting for his Scarlett O'Hara.

And in front of the window, checking his phone, is another handsome, debonair American, who is waiting for me.

CHAPTER 12

Joel looks up from his phone and as I teeter over to him I feel a flutter of panic that I look ridiculous. But then he smiles and steps towards me.

'I was beginning to think you'd stood me up.' He puts his phone in the pocket of his thick camel coat and smiles before kissing me gently on the cheek. 'You look glowing,' he murmurs.

Clearly he is too much of a gentleman to say, 'You look a bit more done up than when I last saw you at the crack of dawn yesterday morning.' But I'm convinced it's what he's thinking. I knew all this make-up was too much on me.

'Yes, well, sorry I'm late. I just had some stuff to do before I could leave,' I reply, feeling overwhelmingly shy all of a sudden. I'm cold, my feet are already hurting in these stupid shoes and I've only been out here two minutes. How does Carly do this every day? I longingly think about how snuggy my toes would be right now wrapped up in my thick wool socks and sensible leather brogues. And my coat – what I wouldn't give for my trusty duffel coat. There are all sorts of draughts creeping through this silly cape.

'You look . . . gorgeous,' he says, stepping back to look at me. Suddenly his eyes are locked on mine and I forget all about my feet. 'Are you OK to walk awhile?' he says, turning up the collar of his coat and offering me his arm before glancing down at my heels.

'Sure, sure,' I reply brightly, trying to get into character. 'I wear shoes like this all the time. In fact, I'm so used to wearing high heels that I feel uncomfortable in flat shoes. These are like . . . like extensions of my feet.' I lift my foot, wiggle it a bit and then step towards him, but I stumble a little and have to grab his arm. I can feel my cheeks flush.

'I thought we'd go to my hotel . . .' he says as we turn in the direction of Oxford Street.

I extricate my arm from his immediately. 'I don't think that's appropriate, to be honest,' I say stiffly. 'I may be wearing high heels and a lot of make-up but that's not the kind of girl I am.'

'I meant for afternoon tea,' he adds hurriedly. 'I'm staying at Claridge's and haven't had a chance to sample this fine British tradition yet. Is that OK?' He looks worried.

I nod primly and slip my arm back through his. 'Well, yes, that does sound OK. Um, how far is it again?'

The answer to my question is clearly 'too bloody far', but Joel doesn't know that. Mainly because he doesn't have to walk in four-inch heels down Regent Street on one of the busiest shopping days

148

of the year. In the space of twenty minutes my feet are trampled on by more tourists than I ever thought possible.

It is only when we reach the relative sanctuary of Bond Street that I am able to relax a little, but only because I've lost all feeling in my feet. We wander slowly down the street, which is home to some of the most elegant and expensive shops in the capital, chatting amicably about our homes and our lives. I tell Joel about Delilah, Noah and Jonah, and am just about to reveal my mother's obsession with naming us all after people from the Bible when I remember I'm meant to be called Carly, and I have to backtrack. After all, even with my relative lack of religious knowledge I'm pretty sure there was never a Saint Carly.

After that I decide it's safer if I stop talking for a while.

We walk past decadent art and antique stores, exclusive designer shops and bank-breakingly expensive jewellers until we arrive outside the grand London hotel that is the destination for our date. Suddenly I am hit by a wave of excitement. It is nearly Christmas. And I am on a date with a Hot American Man. At Claridge's, no less.

'Well, shake me up and put me inside a snow globe,' I murmur as I gawp at the warm, red-brick exterior of the hotel, unable to believe this is all really happening.

Joel's laugh rings out. 'You do say the cutest things. Come on . . .' He pauses and a twinkle teeters on the edge of his pupils like a star hanging in the night sky. Not that I'm staring at him or anything. He clears his throat. 'Aim desperaite for ai cup of char.'

'Oh, no, no, no, don't do that,' I say, wincing and making a face at his terrible British accent.

'I've been told my accent's pretty good!' he says defensively.

'Who by?' I retort. 'Dick Van Dyke?'

He laughs. Again. 'Come on, Carly,' he says. 'Let's take tea,' and he ushers me inside.

Half an hour later and we are nestled in the refined warmth and grandeur of Claridge's dazzling art deco foyer. Above us Dale Chihuly's famous silver-white light sculpture hangs from the foyer's high ceiling like Medusa's hair in all its glittering glass-coiled magnificence. We sip from the pretty green and cream striped tea service and smile at each other, slightly inhibited by our surroundings. We nibble on delicate finger sandwiches and I resist the urge to plough right into the scones and clotted cream. Instead I think, what would Carly do? I quickly deduce that she would probably have a single solitary sandwich and nibble on a little pastry but would leave the rest to her handsome companion. Or hide it in her handbag when he goes to the loo. She doesn't get a figure like hers by troughing through a plate of cakes, that's for sure. I decide the handbag idea is a brilliant one. Mainly because I figure that Felix will enjoy having his very own Claridge's takeaway cream tea if I bring it to him in a doggy bag with his coffee on Monday morning.

'Excuse me a moment,' Joel says, and he strides over towards the toilets. I hastily open my napkin in my lap and slip a scone in it. I glance around to check no one is looking, then pop a delicious-looking chocolate truffle cake thing into my napkin too. I decide not to risk the creamy strawberry dessert that's in a glass; this isn't my handbag, after all.

A minute later two glasses of pink champagne are delivered by a gracious waiter and I smile guiltily at him and clutch my cake-filled bag tightly in case he happens to have X-ray vision and can see right through it. I take a sip of champagne just as Joel comes back and I watch him swagger over whilst luxuriating in the sensation of bubbles exploding in my mouth. I can't help but notice most of the women in the room are watching him too.

'Mmm, champagne,' he says as he lifts his glass. 'I do love your English tea but there's nothing better than a glass of bubbly, don't you think?'

I nod happily and take another sip.

'So, Joel,' I begin, keen to find out a bit more about him, 'you said you work in retail too. What exactly do you do?'

He pauses before answering. 'Well, I'm a retail consultant, which means I help department stores with the financial side of the business.'

'Oh, yes,' I nod as if I know exactly what he means. 'Is that what you're doing for Hardy's?'

He shifts on his seat. 'Er, kind of. Obviously, it's a pretty big job. Hardy's is kinda struggling at the moment.'

I nod sadly and the mood drops momentarily.

Joel leans towards me and his eyes shine brightly. 'But other than my day job I actually have my own family store, back in the little town in Pennsylvania where I'm from.' He looks off into the distance. 'That's where my heart lies.'

'Really?' I exclaim in delight. A guy who has his own store? I can't help but hear Lily and Iris's voices in my head: *It's that age-old heady combination: shopping and sex.* And to be honest, I'm more turned on by his passion for his family shop than anything else. He suddenly feels like a kindred spirit.

'Tell me about it,' I say, sitting back in my chair and taking another sip of champagne.

'It's called Parker's,' he says with a smile. 'It's a cute little place on Main Street in Willow Grove, Pennsylvania but unfortunately it's not doing so well these days. My father doesn't have the necessary retail vision to move it forward. It's my dream to go back there and help steer it in the right direction. But it's hard. Small businesses just aren't doing so well since the economic crash, everyone seems to go to the nearest Walmart for everything from food to clothes to homeware, and failing that, they'll head into Philadelphia or even

New York for all the big department stores. Parker's doesn't seem to have a purpose any more.'

'Just like Hardy's,' I murmur.

He glances up at me and for a second there is a fizzle of understanding between us. He nods and smiles wistfully. 'You know, Hardy's reminds me a lot of my family business. There is so much potential there, but people want something different these days. It feels like there's no room for our friendly family stores any more. It's so sad.'

I shake my head fervently and feel my hair fan out. Thanks to Carly it has wings today. 'I don't agree,' I say firmly.

Joel raises an eyebrow at me and sits back. 'You know, I've heard that you have some great forward-thinking ideas for the store,' he says as he takes a sip of tea. 'I'd love to hear them from a personal shopper extraordinaire.'

'And who exactly has been saying all these kind things about me?' I ask teasingly, but desperately wanting to know who Carly's big fan is.

'Rupert, if you must know. He has high hopes for you.'

I nod, suddenly realizing just how esteemed Carly is in Rupert's view.

'Tell me, Joel,' I say, trying to appear nonchalant, 'what was it that made you so sure I was Carly when we bumped into each other the other day? I mean, we've never spoken, never met, I could have been anyone.'

Ain't that the truth, I think but don't say.

Joel leans towards me, his eyes locking with mine, and I resist the urge to back away from him. But I badly want to know the answer so I fix my eyes firmly on his. 'You couldn't have been anyone,' he murmurs, then reaches his hand across the table and puts it over mine. 'You have this . . . aura about you. I can't explain it. Maybe it was confidence, maybe it was style, but whatever it was I knew I had to get to know you. That realization hit me instantly.'

'When you first saw me?' I press, wanting to find out if he felt those things when he saw the real Carly in the store, or when he met me.

'When I first saw you,' he drawls softly, obviously thinking he is paying me the highest compliment. But he's just confirmed what I already knew: he fell for Carly, not me. This is a serious case of mistaken identity.

'Now it's your turn to answer my questions,' he says, turning all serious. 'Tell me why you don't agree with me that stores like Hardy's have a place in the retail spectrum any more.'

I am flummoxed. When he said that earlier I was about to launch into a passionate speech about how I don't agree with him because I think there *is* a place for stores like Hardy's and Parker's. That people *do* still want the same friendly, informed, intimate shops where assistants know your name and personal shopping isn't a department it's an *experience*, it's just that we've been conditioned into thinking that we should prefer either superstores

154

where you can get everything under one roof, or haughty high-end shops and malls where you can get lost in a sea of swanky products and snooty staff, so that we've all become shopping sheep, buying what we're told to by magazines, models, celebrities and advertising campaigns, rather than shopping for what actually suits us.

But now I know he really does want Carly I feel compelled to be just like her. So what the hell would *she* say?

I stall for time by taking an extra long gulp of champagne. I accidentally down half the glass in one mouthful, the bubbles go up my nose and I cough and splutter. Joel gets up and pats me on the back.

'Sorry,' I gasp at last. 'That went down the wrong way.'

'So I can see,' he says as I hastily down the rest of the champagne.

By the time I've got to the end of the glass I've thought of a response.

I look at him but his eyes bore into me and I lose my confidence.

Channel Carly, I think. *Think fashion, think modern, think like her.*

I clear my throat. 'Well, um, I don't think it's sad because shopping and especially department stores need to look to the future. People are used to internet shopping now, they don't want overly fussy staff and cluttered stores, they want minimal, minimal, MINIMAL.' I bang my hand on the table

155

to emphasize my point and Joel jumps a little. 'Clean lines and a selective number of products displayed in a pure, white environment.' I pause. 'Fashion should be like art,' I breathe, into my Carly character now, but in my head thinking that's exactly what it shouldn't be. I suddenly visualize my poor Wardrobe with the clothes that have hung unloved in there for so long. I put them from my mind and refocus.

'I mean, take Rumors, for example,' I continue. 'How cool do all the staff look in their couture? And those transparent dressing rooms are just *amazing*. A place like that is the future of department stores, not Hardy's. That's what I told my manager just before she gave me my promotion,' I say proudly, as I remember Carly repeating her post-promotion monologue to me the other day. 'I said to her, I said, "Sharon, we need to be more modern, appeal to the younger clients, clients like me. They want shops to be more exclusive, more *fashion*. It is the future, after all."' I smile beatifically at the waiter as he refills my champagne glass, then I take another gulp. I feel warm and fuzzy, like Christmas has come early. This date is going brilliantly, even if I do say so myself. Being Carly is easy.

'Well,' Joel says eventually, 'I guess I agree that department stores need to have a new vision for the future, or they'll fall by the wayside.'

'And that's what's happened to Hardy's,' I say gravely, forgetting that I'm not meant to know about Rumors' potential takeover. 'I mean it *could* happen,' I quickly backtrack. 'We're so quiet, after all. Is that why you've been coming in? To try and help us?'

Joel pauses and his expression becomes a little strained. 'It's top secret, to be honest. I'd love to tell you, but it's more than my job's worth. All I can say is that all will be revealed soon. And from what you've just said, you'll be very pleased with the results.' I furrow my brow, trying to unravel what that means. What result would Carly want? What have I just said? I'm so confused, I feel like I could be getting essential inside information about Hardy's fate from Joel, but I can't ask him directly. He's made it clear it's not open for discussion. I'm just left wondering if it's what Carly would want, would I want it, too?

Joel smiles at me and skims his finger around the top of his china tea cup. 'You know, Carly, I hear you're very talented. Rupert raves about you. And,' he adds leaning closer, 'I don't blame him.'

I furrow my brow and look away because I know that in actual fact, Rupert doesn't even know my name. Come to think of it, nor does Joel. I take another sip of champagne. I'm feeling a little bit squiffy. And I'm exhausted by all this pretence. I realize that my brow is still furrowed and so I open my eyes really wide instead, put my elbows on the table and my face in my hands to give me an instant facelift. I smile but Joel appears slightly

157

alarmed so I let go of a bit of my face skin and he looks relieved.

'I'm so glad I bumped into you this morning, Carly,' he says softly. 'I have to confess, I haven't been able to stop thinking about you.'

I try not to gape at him. 'You haven't?'

'I felt a connection to you from the moment I first saw you in the store,' he says bashfully.

But that wasn't me.

I force a smile in return but suddenly I feel like a complete fraud. Here I am on a date with a gorgeous man who is giving me compliments, but I'm caked in make-up, have crippled feet, am giving him opinions that aren't my own and completely and utterly not being myself. Maybe I should confess now. He's just too nice to deceive like this. I should introduce him to the *real* Carly instead. They'll probably fall instantly in love and I could start a matchmaking service or something when I lose my job at Hardy's. I'd be quite good at that, I think. Or I could be a wedding planner. I mean, with my organizational skills . . .

I'm so lost in new career thoughts that I barely notice when Joel pulls me to my feet.

'Come on,' he says. 'Let's get out of here.' He grabs my coat and swings it over my shoulders, leaving his arm resting there as we walk out of the foyer. I can't help but feel smug as I see every single female jaw drop around us. Then I wonder if they're thinking, what's a guy like *him* doing with *her*? and I lose the reflected glow a little.

The doorman opens the door for us and smiles warmly as Joel escorts me out, saying 'Mr Parker' deferentially and tipping his hat at us as Joel slips some money in his hand. In my excitement I find myself responding to the doorman's gesture by simultaneously curtsying at him and saluting. The poor doorman looks mildly horrified but doesn't lose his professional smile, although I'm sure I see the corner of his mouth twitch. Luckily Joel doesn't notice and just leads me into the street. As I look back I see the doorman wink and salute back at me and I laugh and wave at him.

Our afternoon tea was so elegant and refined I feel like I'm living in another era, and I love it. It is snowing again as we walk together through the busy streets. But this time I don't notice any of the people. It's like everyone has melted away, and there is just Joel and me.

Joel is telling me about his shop, describing the old-fashioned white weatherboard façade, the Stars and Stripes flag forever flapping on the roof and the lovely old ladies who work there.

'It sounds perfect,' I say.

'It is,' he smiles 'although it's not to your taste. They definitely don't wear couture in my shop!'

I laugh albeit awkwardly. 'So, why did you leave there if you loved it so much?' I ask, wanting to know more about the handsome stranger who has just slid his arm gently around my waist. I gulp and try not to show my excitement but realize it's now an effort to string two words together. 'Um, just because, well, it seems to me that, you know, if your father can't steer it in the right direction, maybe you, er, could?'

Joel smiles sadly. 'That's what I've always thought, too. It was my plan to finish my business degree in New York and then go back home.' He pauses and stares straight ahead. 'I had a girlfriend back there. We were childhood sweethearts . . .' he trails off and I rub his arm to encourage him to keep talking. His face is tense, as if he's trying not to get upset. He takes a deep breath.

'We had our whole lives planned out,' he says quietly. 'We were together throughout the whole of high school, but knew that one day we'd need to experience life on our own. That's what everyone kept telling us, anyway. So we decided to go to different colleges, date other people, maybe, but then after we both graduated, we'd come back home to each other. We planned on running Parker's together. I thought it was her dream. It was definitely mine.' He sighs. 'Anyway, we kept in contact with letters and emails for the first few months but then they petered out. I knew we were both busy, but I always thought . . .' He pauses again. He smiles at me and lowers his eyes to the lightly glimmering ground.

'Well, anyway,' he continues. 'I finished my degree, left New York and made my way back home. On my first day back in Willow Grove, I

160

was walking down the Main Street and I was so happy when I saw her coming towards me. I thought everything would be OK. Then I realized that she was hand in hand with another guy. She could barely look at me when I stopped to talk to them. Apparently they were just back for the weekend. They'd gone to the same college, in Florida, started dating after the first year and had been together ever since. In fact, they'd just got engaged and she was busy planning the wedding. They were going to travel for a year before settling into the home his parents had bought for them in Florida. She said she couldn't imagine living in such a small town as Willow Grove. I didn't want to admit I'd come home to do everything we'd planned together. Instead I told her that neither could I, and that I was staying in New York because I loved the big city so much. And at that moment I resolved to stay in New York, get some experience of other big stores and get over her. All my memories in Willow Grove were of her and I didn't want to go back until I'd got over her completely.'

Suddenly I can't help but think about Jamie. I can relate to what Joel's saying completely. My life back at home in Norwich *was* Jamie. And he left me because he didn't want that life any more because it was too predictable. My God, Joel and I are the same.

Joel suddenly shakes his head, clearly embarrassed by his emotional outburst. 'Shit, Carly. I'm sorry, I didn't mean to dump all that on you.' He rubs his forehead and suddenly looks vulnerable, not the suave businessman he's appeared to be so far. I like him even more for it.

'Don't worry,' I say, rubbing his arm gently. 'I can handle it.'

He turns and fixes his forget-me-not eyes on me. 'Has anyone ever told you you're a great listener?'

I just smile. *All the time*, Joel, *all the time.*

We walk along the city's busy streets in comfortable silence. It could be the effects of the champagne, but I am melting in the warmth of Joel's arm around my shoulders, trying to focus on my breathing as we keep in step with each other. We pass shop after shop decorated gaily with Christmas decorations and it feels like we're gliding through an ever-changing glacier of breathtaking blue, silver and white lights. We turn onto Bond Street and I gasp a little as Joel suddenly pulls me into the entrance of a small jewellery shop that is empty of customers. The street's glorious Christmas lights drape over our heads like a star-spangled canopy, swathes of glittering fabric twinkling like diamonds above us and around us. I feel like I'm in a glass prism and all I can see is Joel reflected back at me. He is facing me now, his arms wrapped around my body and he gazes at me intently as he brushes his thumb over my bottom lip, which has long since lost its gloss. I look down, embarrassed by the intensity of the moment.

162

'May I kiss you?' he murmurs.

I nod wordlessly as he lowers his mouth to mine and I am filled with the warmth of his breath, the softness of his lips, the wetness of his tongue, and I am floating, floating like the flakes of snow that frame us. I am no longer Carly. I am just me. But this new, improved me is being kissed by a man who thinks I'm wonderful.

SUNDAY 4 DECEMBER

21 Shopping Days Until Christmas

CHAPTER 13

'So he says he thinks you're wonderful and then what?' Delilah is sitting in the front passenger seat of her and Will's Land Rover and has twisted herself round to face me. I am sitting in the back, sandwiched between Lola (who is shouting out the colour of each car we pass approximately every two seconds in my ear), and Raffy (who is squashing cream cheese sandwiches between his hands and then rubbing them on my jeans).

I have been trying to relive my date with Joel at Delilah's insistence but am struggling to compete with Lola's shouts and Raffy's maniacal laughs. It's a welcome distraction, to be honest; I'm not really comfortable discussing my date in such a public forum anyway. I'd planned to divulge every last detail to Delilah once we'd arrived at our parents', when we're on our own, obviously. Mum will be all over me like a rash otherwise, bless her.

'Yes, darling it *is* a red car, clever girl!' Delilah turns and smiles at Lola, then notices my cream cheese-encrusted legs. 'DON'T DO THAT, Raff!

Poor Auntie Teevee. Now give her a kiss and say sorry.'

'Hi Teevee hi, thorry Teevee mummy thorry,' he murmurs remorsefully, and gazes up at me innocently through his long eyelashes. Then he pouts his lips and leans over in his car seat to kiss me on my cheek, so now I have cream cheese on my face as well as on my legs.

Will – sensible man – is ignoring us all and concentrating on the road, probably wishing he was going anywhere but to his parents-in-law on this Sunday morning. We are doing one of our monthly pilgrimages to Norfolk for lunch. It is Clause 1 of the endless contract that Delilah, Noah, Jonah and I unwittingly signed as offspring, which keeps us tied to the familial home far more than any of us would like. But even Noah and Jonah wouldn't complain about it or dare to miss a visit. We are also expected to spend Christmas, Easter, Mother's Day, Father's Day and Mum and Dad's birthdays there.

'So come on!' Delilah says impatiently as she twists even further round in her seat, so much so that I am concerned she may snap. 'What happened next?'

'Nothing really,' I mumble, and busy myself with singing 'The Wheels on the Bus' to Raffy, who immediately claps his hands with glee and lisps 'Butth!' joyously, causing crumbs to fly out of his mouth and all over me. I don't want to share the details of my kiss with Joel in front of Will and the kids. And the truth is that's all there was to it: one delicious kiss, then Joel put me in a cab and promised to call me soon.

I pretend to ignore Delilah and start the song over again.

'BUTTH!' Raffy screams again in delight as if I haven't sung it for a year.

'RED CAR, Mummydaddyteevee, RED CAR!' squeals Lola wondrously as if she has just spotted a four-headed alien and not the seventy-seventh red car in the last half an hour.

Delilah ignores them both. 'Oh, come *on*, Evie,' she begs. 'You can't get that far in the story and then bail out! We're *desperate* to know what happens next, aren't we, Will?' He doesn't answer. 'Aren't we, Will?' she hisses, and nudges him.

'Mmm,' he replies unconvincingly.

'OK, well *he* might not be,' she says churlishly, 'but I am. It's the nearest I'm going to get to any romance these days,' she adds pointedly.

'What does that mean?' Will shoots back, glancing back at me in the mirror as if to say, 'Look what I have to put up with.' I immediately gaze out the window. I hate getting involved in their spats. Besides, he should know by now that I'll always side with Delilah, whether she's right or wrong. She's my sister, after all.

'Just what I say,' she retorts. 'It's not like you've whisked me off to, you know, Paris recently. Or *anywhere*, come to think of it.'

169

He shakes his head in bemusement. 'I wasn't aware you *wanted* to go to Paris again.'

'My point exactly.' She rolls her eyes at me and shoots him a dark look. Even I think she's being a bit unfair. But I wouldn't dare say so. No, best to keep quiet in these situations. Unless . . .

'The wipers on the bus go . . . swish swish swish,' I sing brightly, hoping I can break the tension that is building up and remind them who's in the car.

'Swithh swithh swithhh,' repeats Raff.

'Shwish swishy shwish,' sings Lola after him.

'The wipers on the bus go swish swish swish,' the three of us sing.

Then Will and Delilah suddenly join in. 'ALL DAY LONG!'

Suddenly we're all laughing and the argument is averted. For now.

Finally we pull into Mum and Dad's driveway and emerge from the car with Raffy shouting, 'Granmadad! Granmadad!' to announce our arrival.

My mother comes out, gliding effortlessly across the perfectly manicured front lawn, looking a vision of style and elegance in an ochre shift dress over cropped tights, which she has teamed with a statement necklace and bejewelled ballet pumps. Her blond hair sits in perfectly set waves over her shoulders, fanning across her eyes in the Farrah Fawcett flick that has been her signature style for years. There's not a sliver of silver to be seen on her head – despite the fact that she's nearing her sixtieth year. Her make-up is done to perfection: a hint of pale green eye shadow and brown mascara to bring out her chestnut-coloured eyes, and just a touch of coral lipstick. She spreads her arms wide as she walks towards us, as if to embrace every single one of us at once.

My mum lives for her family. She adores our visits and she'd love – more than anything, I think – to have every one of her children back at home, or at the very least, down the road. But this distance hasn't stopped her being a very 'hands-on' mother. Aside from the monthly Sunday meets and the many family occasions we come home for, my mother uses the two-bedroom flat in Hampstead as a pied-à-terre from which to regularly check up on all her children.

'My darlings!' she squeals with delight, and covers her grandchildren's heads with kisses as Lola and Raffy wrap themselves around her legs like koala bears. Then she looks up and smiles at us. 'Come inside! Your father's just finishing an important phone call but he'll be right with us. Now, what can I get you all? Gin and tonics all round?' We nod wearily as we head towards the front door. Neither Delilah, Will nor I can bring ourselves to speak yet. We're still recovering from the journey. That doesn't stop my mother, though.

'Noah and Jonah are already here, so make yourselves comfy and I'll bring you some drinks and nibbles out. We're having roast pheasant with all the trimmings for lunch! Oh, it is *so* good to have all my babies here! You all look so well. Although, Eve, darling, you could have made a bit more of an effort,' she chides.

I gaze down at my weekend uniform of jeans and a hoodie. My mum is a perfectionist about everything: the way she looks, her house, her children. There's never a hair out of place on her head and not a cushion unplumped in the house. I may have got her whole neat-freak gene but the way we look couldn't be more different. She would have hyperventilated at the sight of me dressed up for my date with Joel.

'Why you insist on wearing those drab clothes is beyond me,' she sighs wearily. She reaches over and tries to smooth down my hair, then pinches my cheeks to colour them.

I wriggle from beneath her grasp. 'Stoppit, Mum,' I grumble, flapping my hands at her like she's a persistent fly.

'But, darling,' she says, stroking my face, 'how are you ever going to meet a man dressed like that?'

There's a snort of laughter from the lounge; Jonah and Noah are obviously listening.

'Mu-um!' I exclaim, swatting her away. She shakes her head and scuttles off into the kitchen to clean the surfaces one more time, and arrange some flowers for the centrepiece of the table. The house is already laden with gorgeous Christmas decorations, greenery and festive touches that Martha Stewart would be proud of. There's Mum's annual homemade Christmas wreath on the front door. This year's is fashioned from dried oranges, holly and cranberries. I walk into the lounge to find Noah and Jonah sprawled over the two huge chesterfield sofas in front of a roaring fire (complete with stockings hung round the holly-and-ivy-laden mantelpiece), reading the business and property sections of the papers.

Jonah looks up first. 'E.T!' he says, and untangles his legs and arms to stand up and hug me. This was one of the (many) nick-names given to me as a child because, according to them, my pale complexion reminded them of the Extra-terrestrial when he gets ill and nearly dies. I punch Jonah on the arm and he pretends to wince. I know he's just pretending because Jonah is built like a New Zealand rugby player. He's all beef and bicep, with thick dark hair like Dad's, thighs like tree trunks, a big mouth and a big heart.

Noah turns from his newspaper before jumping up and giving me one of his bear hugs. He is Jonah's wingman. Just a year younger than he and three years older than me, he is a slighter version of our big brother; less beef, less hair, less impact. He's gentler in every way. I guess you could say I'm closer to him than Jonah, but they come as a pair. It's rare to see one without the other. I pull back and make a childish face at them but they just flop back down on the couch and pick up the papers whilst I arrange myself neatly on the end of the sofa, twiddling my toes in front of the roaring fire.

Mum and Dad's Grade II listed house is a big Regency-style pile on the outskirts of Norwich. It's beautifully decorated to Mum's – and Laura Ashley's – exacting standards. It's kind of twee, with lots of florals and pastels, but I don't think I appreciated it enough when I was a kid. I sometimes found it suffocating, surrounded by so much, well, perfection. And silent. Dad would always be working, and Mum was always busy doing the house up, or at various charitable events. Delilah had left home and gone to university by the time I was old enough to notice, and when I was a teenager, the boys were always out at football or rugby games, going to the pub, going out with girls, or revising for exams. Usually in that order. I was just a nuisance to them. Most of the time they barely even noticed I was around. I mean, they loved me – I always knew that; they were protective like only big brothers can be – but other than that I held no interest for them. Delilah was an entirely different matter. With her hot university friends, followed by her fancy media job and swanky lifestyle, she was always of interest. This dynamic has never changed. I'm still the baby sister who they dote on but who isn't worth listening to. But it's fine. I've accepted my position in the family hierarchy.

Delilah drifts in with Will, and the boys get up

174

and practically rugby tackle each other to get to him first. They are as much in awe of Will the Hotshot City Hedge Fund Manager as my sister. There is much hugging and backslapping. Will and the boys immediately start talking about rugby and Delilah and I roll our eyes at each other. It's at times like this that I'm so glad I've got Delilah. I'd be truly outnumbered otherwise. The testosterone in this house can get unbearable.

Mum drifts in and out of the room in her Cath Kidston apron, serving drinks and snacks and checking we're all happy and settled. Dad, apparently, is still on an important work call. As usual.

'Kids!' Dad smiles as he finally sweeps in with the force of a hurricane, filling the room with the power of his voice and presence. He is the master of the house and he knows it. He envelops Delilah and me and his grandchildren in big hugs and makes his way over to the boys for more back-slapping. Then he stands, hands on hips, grinning widely at us all, clad in his usual Sunday gear of checked shirt, V-neck jumper and cords. He is still movie-star handsome, if I can say that about my own father. He has the chiselled features and determined jaw that would look great on camera. In many ways he and Mum have barely changed in the years that they've been married. My mum can still fit her petite frame into her wedding dress and has the slightly nervous, girlish gait of a new lover around him, as if she can't quite believe that he's really her husband. She is standing in the doorway now, looking fondly in on us all, although no one else seems to have noticed her. Her eyes light up when they rest on my father, and she heads over to him and hands him his pre-lunch gin and tonic. He takes it and pats her on the bottom without looking at her, so engrossed is he in his conversation with Will about stocks and shares. She stands there for a moment, then picks up some empty glasses, straightens some cushions and goes back to the kitchen.

Delilah has cornered me and is trying to get me to impart the last details of my date with Joel. I, quite sensibly, am refusing. If my family gets wind of it I will never hear the end of it.

'Come on, Evie,' she whispers out of the corner of her mouth. 'This is killing me. I promise I won't make a fuss, but just nod once for yes if he kissed you. Pleeeease.'

I glance sideways at her, then look back into the room. Delilah's kids are jumping up and down to a song they've put on, Mum is busy brushing invisible dust off Jonah's shoulders and he, Will, Dad and Noah are standing in an impenetrable circle in front of the woodburner, arms folded. Delilah and I may as well not be here.

I speak quickly, carried away by Delilah's desperation to hear about my life.

'OH MY GOD HE KISSED YOU!' she screams when I get to the good bit, then slaps her hand over her mouth, aware that what she's just done is akin to throwing me into a lion's cage. The Taylor clan all turn to face us as if in slow motion.

'What?' says Mum, a combination of hope and confusion plastered over her face.

'Who?' says Dad, as if cross-examining me in court.

'WHY?' say Jonah and Noah in unison, and they burst out laughing.

Then everyone else joins in.

After the initial furore, Mum's timely announcement that lunch is ready means my news is quickly forgotten. The Taylor men (and Will), like most men, are governed by their stomachs. I am hopeful that I can get through the next couple of hours without anyone bringing up the kiss again.

No such luck.

If the male members of my family are like hungry lions when it comes to food, my mother is like a blood-sucking vampire when it comes to my love life. Or lack of it. She has spent the last five years waiting for me to announce that I have met The One and am about to settle down and give her lots more grandchildren.

I think any mother likes to see something of herself in her daughters, and whilst Delilah ticks all the boxes on the looks front, I know my mother feels slightly out of her depth when it comes to Delilah's career. She's never understood Delilah's dogged ambition to break the glass ceiling. Delilah has always been driven by her desire to succeed. I often catch Dad shooting Delilah admiring glances when she's telling us about another big pitch she's won, or an important event she's been invited to speak at. She's appeared on numerous lists of most influential women in the media, was one of the youngest MDs of an ad agency ever, and has consistently proven that she's as capable as any man in her industry.

No, Mum seems far more able to relate to me, which means I get far more hassle from her than my sister ever did. She also believes that because I have followed in her footsteps by working at Hardy's, that means I too am just waiting for the right man to come along so I can give it all up for a life of baking and babies. And no matter how much I try to tell her that I value my independence and that I have no intention of giving up my career dreams for a man again, she is utterly convinced that someone handsome will sweep into the store one day and take me away from the drudgery of having a job. And I just cannot cope with her thinking that is about to happen.

The usual high-octane Taylor talking-round-the-dinner-table ceases for a moment as everyone tucks into the delicious roast lunch. And, like a seasoned pro, that's when Mum seizes her moment to snare me.

'So come on, darling, tell us about this man you've met!' she coos, and all heads turn to face me, chewing like cows on cud. I rapidly stuff a forkful of food into my mouth to try to delay my answer, but quickly realize this is a rookie mistake.

'She met him at Hardy's, Mum! His name's Joel and he's *gorgeous*, apparently!' Delilah exclaims excitedly, and she and Mum squeal and clap their hands like teenagers. I don't know what's got into Delilah recently. She knows about Mum's obsession with my love life and usually she is sensitive to it. I feel like Tom Cruise in *Top Gun* when Goose croaks it: suddenly I'm flying solo. I shoot Delilah a warning glare but she doesn't see me. She just carries on sharing my private affairs. I'm clenching in embarrassment as Noah and Jonah roll about laughing.

'Oh, I knew it!' Mum breathes as Delilah finishes telling the story of how Joel and I met. 'It's just as I said it would be.'

'Mu-um,' I groan, but she doesn't seem to hear me either. 'Do you remember when we first met, Charles, darling?' she says, gazing at Dad adoringly.

'Of course, Grace,' he answers, stabbing at a piece of meat and then looking at Mum fondly. 'How could I forget the best day of my life?'

We kids all make gagging noises on cue and then burst out laughing. But the truth is we love that Mum and Dad are still in love with each other. We know how rare that is these days.

Just then Dad's mobile rings and he looks at it and then up at Mum apologetically. 'Sorry, darling, I have to take this. It's work.'

'But your lunch . . . the kids are here . . .' she protests without success as he puts his napkin on the table and stands up.

'I won't be a minute,' Dad replies, then leans over, kisses her on the forehead and strides purposefully out of the room.

There is silence for one minute and we all look at each other as Mum sighs and then picks up her knife and fork and slowly continues eating, the chink of her cutlery echoing around the otherwise silent room.

'Come on, everyone,' she says, swallowing a mouthful before smiling at us all stoically. 'Don't let it get cold.'

We all busy ourselves taking big mouthfuls and making lots of 'mmm' and 'ooh' and 'aah' sounds, it's like we've suddenly turned into the Bisto Kids. Even though she tries not to show it, we all know it is a constant source of annoyance to Mum when Dad's work interrupts precious family time. She's so patient, though, sometimes I wonder if all her frustrations just fester under the surface. I can't work out where else they go.

Mum puts down her knife and fork and smiles at me benevolently as she links her fingers. Oh no, this is her 'tell Mum all about it' position. She may as well have turned a spotlight on me and adopted a German accent. In Dad's absence it is now interrogation time for me.

'Come on, Eve, I want to hear all about this fine young man of yours,' Mum orders. It is purposely not phrased as a question.

'Yeah, Evie,' echoes Noah, and winks at me. 'Tell us all about this bloke of yours.'

'Like how much are you paying him?' snorts Jonah.

I stick my tongue out at him as he chortles childishly. 'Speaking of paying people, have you been to any more strip clubs recently?' I say sweetly, which shuts him up. Jonah hates the fact that I found out about an ill-advised stag night from some pictures posted on Facebook, and I've been waiting for a chance to use it against him, but Mum doesn't seem to hear me. She is still lost in her romantic imaginings for me.

'So when are you going on another date with him?' she asks, her green eyes softening as she looks at me. She may be a pain sometimes, but I know she's always on my side.

'I don't know,' I reply briskly.

'Aaah,' she waggles a finger at me, 'so there will be another date?'

'Yes. No. I don't know.' Oh God, make this stop.

'Maybe he'll take you to Paris,' Delilah says wistfully.

'What is this obsession of yours with Paris?' Will shoots across the table at her.

'It's romantic,' she snaps.

'And we've been loads of times,' he replies.

'Not for *years*,' Delilah says flippantly.

'That's because we have kids now,' Will replies defensively.

'Doesn't mean the romance has to go out of a marriage, though, does it?' she tinkles sweetly, stroking Lola's raven hair.

181

'What's that supposed to mean?' shoots back Will.

'Oh, nothing!' laughs Delilah. She turns to me, leaving Will looking frustrated and bemused. 'Go on, Evie, you never told us what happened after The Kiss.' She clasps her hands together and gazes at me as if I am about to tell her some wondrous fairytale. I wish she'd stop using me as a distraction. And I'm not the only one.

'Oh, for God's sake,' mutters Will, and he wipes his hands on his napkin, throws it on the table and says, 'I'm going out for a cigarette.'

'Disgusting habit,' Delilah snaps over her shoulder, and Noah and Jonah hastily get up to follow Will, ducking like they're avoiding low-flying female hormones.

'Thanks, Mum, that was lush,' Noah says, bobbing down and kissing her on the head before he and Jonah make a hasty retreat. There's no doubt they adore Mum, but even they treat her like a housekeeper. Probably because that's what Dad has always done. It annoys me that they can't even clear their own plates. And it annoys me even more that Mum lets them get away with it. Lola and Raffy have slipped off too and are playing in the lounge, sensible kids. They've clearly sensed the change in atmosphere.

'What was all that about, Delilah?' I ask with concern. She and Will have been arguing much more than usual recently. And from what I can tell, it's usually started by her.

182

'What?' she replies, her face a picture of innocence. 'That? Oh, nothing. Will and I are just having a petty row. That's what married couples do, you know.' She glances at Mum for affirmation. Sitting next to each other they could pass for sisters. They look so alike but they're worlds apart in other ways, which, if I'm not mistaken, Mum's about to demonstrate.

'You shouldn't speak to him like that, darling,' Mum says softly.

Delilah rolls her eyes at me. Mum's very old-fashioned, despite her youthful looks. She'd have us giving up our jobs, running a home and working hard to make things nice for our men before you could say '1950s throwback'.

'You know, darling,' Mum begins, and Delilah looks at me desperately for help, 'you really should treat Will with more respect. I know better than anyone that it's hard to maintain a balance in your marriage when you've got kids, but the main thing to remember is to look after your partner as much as your children. He needs you, darling. He's a good man, he works hard for his family and—'

'And I don't?' Delilah shoots back, her eyes darkening dangerously.

'Yes you do, darling, you work very hard indeed,' Mum placates. Then she pauses. I glance at her. Oh God, she's not going to say it, is she? 'Maybe that's the problem,' she adds, and begins stacking the plates.

Oh shit, now that's gone and done it.

'*Here* we go . . .' Delilah folds her arms and looks up at the ceiling like a petulant teenager.

'I'm just saying, darling, that you'd have more time for romance if you were at home more. You could do all the things involved with running a home and family during the day, and you and Will could go on dates regularly, or even go away for the weekend.' She gets up and smoothes her hands on her floral apron.

'I don't need to listen to this.' Delilah pushes her chair back just as Dad walks in.

'Where is everyone?' he says, looking around the emptied dining room. He pours himself another glass of red wine and I can see him racking his brains for a reason to find the boys.

'Outside,' Mum says, smoothing down her hair before picking up the stack of plates. 'Sit down, darling. I'm about to serve dessert. I've made your favourite: chocolate soufflé.' She touches him gently on the shoulder, but Dad is looking at his BlackBerry, which is flashing at him to signal yet another call. He answers it and I see Mum's face drop before she turns and hurries out of the kitchen.

Fifteen minutes later Mum serves dessert and peace reigns for a bit. In fact, it is oddly quiet. All that can be heard is the clinking of cutlery against the plates as everyone scrapes up the last bit of chocolate.

'Delicious as ever.' Dad smacks his lips and touches Mum on the hand and she smiles, having got her reward. 'And can I say how wonderful it is for us to have our family around our dinner table. It is a rare blessing . . .'

Delilah, Noah, Jonah and I all roll our eyes simultaneously at this comment. It's anything but rare, as well he knows.

'. . . but one your mother and I always appreciate. It's always so lovely for us to catch up on all your news. Especially yours, Eve . . .'

I blush and don't know where to look. I'm never usually singled out for attention like this.

'Your mother and I do worry about you, you know, especially in your line of work. Retail is so . . .' he searches for a suitably inoffensive word, '. . . precarious.' I know Dad is disappointed by my job and I don't blame him. I am, too. He wouldn't mind if I was married or in a relationship; in fact, he was almost as disappointed as I was when Jamie broke up with me. He'd always liked Jamie, said he liked his 'spirit'. I think he reminded Dad a little of himself. I've never thought about it before but he was probably right. They're both ambitious and sexist. But I guess that's partly to do with their chosen careers. In their industries men always get to the top, and women, well, they usually don't.

Dad takes a long sip of wine and looks at me. Uh-oh, the grilling isn't over.

'You know I've read that Hardy's is struggling.

There's been talk in the business pages of another store trying to acquire the site.'

'Oh, poor Hardy's,' Mum says, her hand fluttering to her chest. 'It's not going to close, is it?'

'It's inevitable in this economic climate,' Dad says matter-of-factly, ever the money man.

'Well, actually,' I say, suddenly buoyed by the excitement of what happened in Menswear yesterday and wanting to share it with my family, 'I've had this really good idea . . .'

Dad looks at Mum and then raises his eyebrows at me encouragingly. 'Really, darling, that's nice!' he says in the patronizing tone he reserves for me. I swallow my frustration. I know he wouldn't be so dismissive with Jonah or Noah or even Delilah, so I carry on regardless.

'Yes, I've had this idea for a makeover. And I really think that with my plans I could save the store.'

'Oh, Evie,' Dad sighs as he wipes his mouth and puts his napkin on the table, 'when will you stop dreaming? It's a sweet thought, but you just don't have the power. I mean, no offence, darling, but you're just the stockroom girl.' He taps me on my hand and beckons for the coffee pot before turning to Will. The conversation is apparently over.

On the journey home I sit in the back of the car idly drawing patterns in the condensation on the back window, while the kids sleep and Delilah and Will sit in stony silence.

Just the stockroom girl, Dad's voice echoes in my head over and over again. I blow on the glass and draw Hardy's impressive façade with my finger.

If I wasn't determined to save the store before, I bloody well am now.

MONDAY 5 DECEMBER

20 Shopping Days Until Christmas

CHAPTER 14

The streetlamps seem to blink in surprise as I shut the front door behind me and am immediately swallowed up by the dusty coal-black darkness of this dreary Monday morning. I'm up and out even earlier than usual as I want to get a head start on the shop floor. My dad's words have made me feel even more determined to make a difference.

I'm dressed for comfort and warmth again, not style, despite my new-found love of The Wardrobe's offerings. I can't help but be grateful for my old, thick jumper and coat. I have no plans to leave the stockroom today so there'll be no unexpected meetings with Joel.

I carry my bike quietly down the steps, put my heavier-than-usual rucksack on my back, climb aboard and start pedalling furiously. It's a freezing cold morning and dawn is still a long way from lifting its weary head. But I don't care. I'm not tired, I'm full of life and ideas and excitement. I want to get to work.

★   ★   ★

'What are you doing here?' Felix says in surprise, looking at his watch as I walk through the staff entrance. 'You're not due to start for over an hour and a half!'

'Oh, I couldn't sleep,' I lie, averting my eyes guiltily. I know I should tell him why I'm here at half-five in the morning but I want to see if my idea works before I involve anyone else. I'm worried that what happened in Menswear was just a fluke. This place is too important to Felix for me to give him false hope.

Anxious to get started, I hand him his Claridge's takeaway cream tea – which to be honest hasn't fared as well as I hoped after a day at home and the bike journey this morning – but he seems pleased. I feel bad about not stopping for a chat like normal, but I'm hoping the scones and cake will make up for it. I rush through the corridor and out through the doors that lead into the beauty department. I head straight to the central staircase where I lean over the banisters and look down into Menswear. My display of matinée idol-inspired mannequins are still there, but the shop floor looks severely depleted. Guy must have had a busy weekend. I make a mental note to start my list of replenishments there – clearly he didn't have much time to do it himself. But first, I have other work to do.

I run to the stockroom first to grab a few essentials, then I head back through the ground-floor atrium and into the beauty department with its various counters filled with rainbow palettes of eye shadows and rows of brightly coloured lipsticks, all standing to attention like soldiers in some multi-coloured army. It looks like the displays haven't been changed since the 1980s. It strikes me again just how stuck in a time warp Hardy's is. I can't help but wonder if it is age that has been its down-fall. Perhaps my hunch is wrong and we *do* need to move with the times, as Rupert thinks, and become the fashion-forward store that Carly is envisaging. Do we all need to become tougher, smarter, sexier in order to ensure our survival in a highly competitive market and a tough economic climate? I bite my lip as I imagine my entire plan backfiring.

What I'm doing could cost me my job. But then again, I counter, it's worth the risk if there's the smallest chance of saving Hardy's.

I continue walking through the department, running my fingers along the counters and resisting the urge to inspect my fingers. A bit of dust is the least of Hardy's problems and, besides, the cleaners do a sterling job. I wouldn't want to offend them with my freakish habits. I think of Mum, who can't cope with even a speck of dust or disorder in her house, and wonder if I am genet-ically predisposed to turn into her. I don't know whether to be grateful or aghast at the thought.

It feels strange but pleasant to not be accosted by a fleet of white-coated assistants spritzing at me furiously as I walk past. I think of Gwen, with her carefully painted smile, poised to pounce on any unsuspecting customer who happens to walk past. Perhaps people would be more inclined to buy from her if she adopted a gentler sales technique. I know she's desperate for extra commission in order to pay off all those debts her husband doesn't know about, but her sales patter just isn't working. And judging by their consistently low takings, I'm not the only person who wants to run a mile as soon as Gwen or Jenny waves a blusher brush in my direction.

I pause to have a look at the displays of face and body creams. They all look the same to me, in identikit sickly pastel and cream packaging, and I can't help but yearn for the gloriously classy and decadent make-up packaging of yesteryear: the beautiful vintage gold-plated compacts that we still have boxes of in the stockroom; the fat, fragrant powder puffs and glamorous gold lipstick cases that contrasted so beautifully against the crimson, carmine and coral products within; in fact, the very same things I have with me now.

I stand there for a few minutes with my battered box full of goodies and other vintage treasures that have been gathering dust in the stockroom. Then I set to work recreating the pictures in my head, happy that this time I've come fully prepared. I don't have long and there's a lot of work to be done.

It didn't take long for me to work out what's needed to give Beauty a serious facelift. I've been thinking about what I could do to entice women into Hardy's hundred-year-old department. I can't help but feel that what women want is the same as we've always wanted: simple but effective products, packaged beautifully; no science, no promises, no endlessly confusing colour spectrums or anodyne celebrity campaigns, just a sprinkling of magic that will convince us we can be transformed by the products. Maybe I am only speaking for myself, but I don't want to see images of naturally beautiful models with translucent skin, touching their faces reverentially and gazing up at the sky to emphasize just how effortlessly beautiful they are. I don't want barely-there make-up advertisements. I want lipstick, powder and paint in all its glory. I want Betty Grable and Rita Hayworth and Marilyn Monroe. I want Sophia Loren and Brigitte Bardot and Faye Dunaway. I want Farrah Fawcett and Joan bloody Collins, for Christ's sake. I want sweeping eyelashes and bold lips and perfectly executed eye make-up.

When I walk into a beauty department I want to feel that I can transform myself into any of these women with a flick of a make-up brush and the right products. But more than that, I want to enjoy doing it. I may not be a make-up maven but even I want to imagine sitting at a dressing table, wrapped in a silk dressing gown, wearing marabou slippers and applying creams from pretty little glass pots, and sweeping gloriously coloured lipstick over my lips as I prepare for a date.

Because that's the point, isn't it? Shouldn't all this be about fantasy, about playing 'dress-up'? I want to feel glamorous. I want to feel like a woman. I want it to be just like the old days. And I'm pretty sure that's what other women want too.

Maybe I'm even more my mother's daughter than I realize, I think as I fly around the shop floor, sweeping the current displays to the floor and working quickly and meticulously to recreate the vision in my head. Just like her I can have a room cleaned, tidied and perfectly organized by the time I get from one end of it to the other, and clearly, despite appearances to the contrary, I'm more of a beauty junkie than I realized. I've never felt the need for it before but wearing Carly's make-up made me feel like a different person. It was like wearing a mask. I felt protected, confident, untouchable, and because of that, for the first time in a very long time, I felt good about myself. I wish I'd tried it years ago.

I glance anxiously at my watch. I don't have much time. There are still boxes of props and products strewn all around me, the shop floor is in total chaos, but I am in heaven. I feel alive, energized. Watching the displays take shape in front of me is like putting together a jigsaw; with each piece I can see what the full picture is meant to be. It's a painstaking process, but incredibly satisfying.

I spend the next half an hour working furiously, only taking my eyes off the displays to check my watch. I am achingly aware of the time as I can't risk anyone seeing what I'm doing – well, apart from the cleaners, that is. They don't mix with any of the floor staff or management and I know they are too absorbed in their own work to worry about what I'm doing. Their only concern has been to see if I need any help. Jan Baptysta saw me dragging a large, heavy box and offered to carry it for me, which was sweet of him. Mind you, he did say it meant I had to marry him so I'm not sure it was purely a charitable offer.

At last I take a long breath and, wiping my grubby hands on my trousers, I take a step back and look at my work. Even I am amazed at the transformation.

The horrible lurid plastic displays are gone. Instead, over the bare counter Jan has hung from the ceiling several ex-display vintage 1920s tiered chandeliers after I'd remembered him telling me that he is a qualified electrician. On one of the white counters I've recreated a theatrical dressing room, by adding a vintage triple mirror I found, complete with bulbs, in the stockroom. Then I've pinned photos of the most glamorous female film stars of all time onto the mirror, and underneath each picture I've grouped together the products from all the different beauty counters that will help customers recreate that particular star's look. So whether you're looking for Elizabeth Taylor's arched beauty, Audrey Hepburn's elegant sophistication or Marilyn Monroe's dazzling sex appeal, there's something for everyone. Palettes of make-up lie open invitingly on the dressing table, just waiting to be used. I've even found a pair of marabou slippers in the depths of the stockroom and placed them under the footstool. Forget Gwen and her hovering make-up brush, I want to encourage the customers to test the products properly, to sit down here and play with the products themselves.

Against the back wall of the department, behind the till, I've made use of the wall-to-ceiling shelves that usually house endless white boxes of moisturizers, toners and cleansers. Instead, I've created a simple display of fifty vintage bottles that I found in boxes in the stockroom when I first started here. They are all in pristine condition with the labels still perfectly intact, if somewhat faded. Some are beautiful cut-glass perfume bottles, complete with atomizers; others are old-fashioned French bottles holding various creams and lotions. The products are all well past their sell-by date but I couldn't bear to throw them away so I took them home one weekend, emptied them out and carefully cleaned each one, making sure not to get the labels wet. I brought them back in, knowing that the bottles alone were probably worth a fortune, and have always hoped that one day we could do something with them.

It didn't take me long to line them up on the shelves. They look so elegant and refined standing there. The modern perfumes that customers can

198

buy are displayed on the counters as usual. I like to think they're basking in the reflected glow of their vintage friends, who are showing them just what they can do.

I bite my lip as I try to imagine what Gwen and, more importantly, Rupert and Sharon will think. None of this is exactly what you'd call 'modern'. But I can't help having a hunch that what I'm doing is right for the store and what Hardy's customers really want. What's left of them, anyway.

I turn round and my gaze falls on the display I'm most proud of. It has brought to life exactly what Hardy's should be about: a store that is proud of its heritage, that wants more than anything to serve its people, and that truly believes that its customers – the generations of British people who have shopped here for one hundred years – are its future because they are the true shareholders of the store. It is, at its heart, a stoic survivor, a place that can be relied upon not just to get through the worst of times but to come out fighting.

Then it came to me. Make *them* the centrepiece of the beauty department. So in the middle of the hall I've stacked the pale lilac-coloured bricks of lavender soap, which are wrapped in parchment paper and tied with string, in a pyramid, just as supermarkets used to display their canned goods years ago. To one side I've placed a large, blown-up black-and-white photo of the WI ladies who created the product. I found it on Google Images

199

over the weekend. It's not the best quality; it's a bit grainy up close. The women are all standing in a line with one arm outstretched towards my display as if presenting their product in an advert. They're all wearing wartime Land Girls' uniforms and looking at once proud, determined and full of hope. They are immaculately groomed, with pin curls and dark lips. Looking at it, I suddenly feel like I've been transported back in time. I imagine Joel dressed in a GI uniform, swirling me around a smoky dancefloor. We're braving the blitz and ignoring the bombs that are falling outside, completely lost in each other . . .

My phone beeps and takes me out of my fantasy; I glance at it and realize to my horror that it's nearly 8 a.m. I'm late for my real job and don't want to risk being spotted by any early arrivals. I dash through the dimly lit ground floor, hearing the whirr of the industrial floor cleaner echoing around the empty space and make my way through Accessories and Jewellery, passing Handbags as I go. I don't stop, as the sight of so many expensive leather totes bunched together like old women in a post office queue would just depress me. That's a job for another day. I wave at Velna as I pass, though. She's pushing the industrial floor cleaner around whilst practising what appear to be Brotherhood of Man-style dance steps and singing about saving 'all your kisses'.

I wave and make an apologetic face as I dive into the stockroom before she has a chance to engage me in conversation, or song. I'm now officially out of time.

'What time do you call this?'

Sam is leaning in the doorway as I open it, arms folded with a disgruntled expression on his face. He has cute pillow creases along his right cheek and some food stains on his shirt.

'What happened to you?' I say. 'You look like me after feeding time with the Primrose Hill monkeys.'

Sam doesn't raise a smile, despite the fact he knows all about my second job as Super-Auntie/Nanny. Instead he ignores me as he lugs some boxes in. I frown; it's not like Sam to be in such a grump. And where's my breakfast today?

'Clearly you just don't care about being on time for delivery guys now you've been promoted then,' he says grumpily.

I smack my forehead. The text Sam sent asking about the promotion. I never replied to it because I was busy talking to Lily and Iris. It completely slipped my mind till now.

'Oh, no, that, er, that didn't happen,' I admit, turning away to hide my embarrassment.

'What. Do. You *meeean*?' huffs Sam breathlessly as he carries more boxes in. He's clearly in a rush this morning. I've made him late for his other deliveries and I feel terrible.

'I mean I didn't get the promotion,' I say quietly.

'Oh.' I hear him take a step closer. 'I'm sorry,

Evie,' he says at last. He doesn't sound it. I'm slightly offended. Maybe he's annoyed about my boasting the other day. I should've just kept my mouth shut. 'Did they say why?' he asks.

I shrug dismissively and turn round. 'I'm just not good enough, I guess.'

'Don't be silly, Evie, you know that's not true. You'd be brilliant with the customers. You're so warm and friendly, and . . .' He coughs and I see from the corner of my eye that he's holding his hands on the base of his back. 'Oof, that last box was a heavy one,' he groans.

'Do you want to sit down?' I offer. 'I could make you tea . . .'

'Sorry, not this morning. I've got lots to do.' He smiles regretfully at me but I can't help feeling mildly put out. He's clearly punishing me for being late but I could do with his company this morning. He's the only person who can cheer me up. An awkward silence descends.

'Well,' we both say at once.

'You first,' I add.

'I was just going to say we should still do that thing we talked about,' he says, pulling at a rogue strand on his cosy Nordic jumper.

'Oh, yes, definitely,' I reply quickly, just to continue the conversation but then I realize I have no idea what he's talking about. 'Um, what thing?'

Sam shuffles on his feet. 'You know, go for that drink,' he mumbles. 'To cheer you up. We can celebrate your non-leaving the stockroom.'

'Ohh!' I realize he's talking about the promotion party he suggested last time he was here. Part of me thinks there's no point, but then I reconsider. Maybe a night out is just what I need right now. Maybe it's what we *all* need. 'You know, that isn't such a bad idea. For a Delivery Guy you're pretty clever, you know, Sam.'

He grins and his cheeks go all chipmunky for a moment. 'Same goes, SG,' he retorts. 'So when are you free and where do you fancy—'

I hold my hand up to stop him. 'Leave it with me,' I say briskly. 'I'll sort it all out.'

'Oh, well, OK,' he replies dubiously. 'I'm usually old-fashioned about these sorts of things, but if that's what you want, fine. Just let me know where to be and when. I'll be there. Now, I've got to . . .' he stabs his thumb over his shoulder to the open door where his van is waiting.

'No worries. See you!' I say brightly.

I'm already busy planning our big night out. It's going to be great.

CHAPTER 15

Nine o'clock comes around all too quickly and the floor staff soon start trooping into the stockroom for our weekly Monday morning meeting, yawning and clasping their take-away teas and coffees for dear life as they mumble incoherently to each other. Most of them have still got their coats on so they've clearly come straight through the staff entrance to here, which means they won't have seen the shop floor yet.

I finish putting away the delivery quietly while everyone chats amongst themselves.

'Urgh, I can't believe it's Monday again,' moans Becky to no one in particular as she launches herself towards the sofa in my lounge area. I whip away a pile of new stock that I'd put there before she squashes it all. She doesn't seem to notice. 'Can someone wake me up when Sharon's finished talking figures? I really don't need to have a lecture about how many bags I didn't sell last week.'

'At least you don't have to put up with her and Carly interfering with your department,' grumbles Elaine from Designers. 'I couldn't get rid of them over the weekend. They were constantly prowling round, sizing it up and scribbling things down on a clipboard. I didn't get to sit down and read my *Grazia* once. It was so annoying.'

'Can you believe what happened in Guy's department, though?' pipes up Becky. 'It's amazing what he's done; he's like a changed man. Suddenly he's all preeny and keeps saying things like, "My vision" and, "I know what customers want . . ." instead of moping around the place with a face like a slapped arse.'

I can't help but smile to myself. I knew Guy would throw himself into the success. And I'm happy for him. If it continues maybe he won't lose his job.

'And he didn't talk about the loneliness of being homosexual *once*,' adds Jenny. 'Or wonder if his ex was going to be out cruising along Old Compton Street on Saturday night. He was just . . . happy.'

'It was weird seeing new customers in the store, though,' adds Becky. 'I mean, the place felt kind of buzzy for the first time in ages. I liked it.'

'I hope my department doesn't end up like that,' grumbles Elaine. 'I'll never be able to read my mags if I'm as busy as Guy. Looks way too much like hard work for my liking.'

I laugh at this. Elaine is notoriously lazy. She thinks working at Hardy's is the best gig ever. She used to work at Selfridges and says Saturdays were hell. She took the job here for a quieter life. She likes the fact that she gets paid to do nothing. Although she does always moan that it feels like time stands still in Hardy's. And she's right. One hour can feel like ten in here sometimes. Half the time the staff don't know what to do with themselves. There's only so many times they can tidy shelves and adjust the way things look before their only option is to stand in their departments, gazing vacantly out, hoping for someone – anyone – to come and pass some time with them. I do feel sorry for them. Half of them have forgotten how to do their jobs and I'm not sure they'd know what to do if they were inundated with customers. But Guy really rose to the occasion and I'm so glad. Of course, he had no idea that his job depended on it.

'Oh my God!' Barbara from Shoes bursts through the stock-room door, nearly spilling her tea in the process. 'Have you seen the beauty department? It's had some sort of amazing makeover! Quick! Come and look!' She disappears again and I watch as the other staff members quickly get to their feet. I've never seen them move so fast. I follow behind them. I can't help grinning as I hear their exclamations.

'Wow!' breathes Becky.

'It looks so cool, doesn't it!' Barbara claps her hands in delight.

'Where did that gorgeous soap come from? I've never noticed that before? Is it some new brand?' Jenny says.

'I want one!'

'Oooh, look at the cool dressing table!'

'Who did this? It's amazing!'

'Maybe it was Guy again.'

'What about Carly? Isn't she meant to be trying to change the direction of the store? I bet it was her . . .'

I'm standing on tiptoes, trying to see over everyone's heads. Sharon and Gwen are in the middle of the displays, turning round in a circle and trying not to show their astonishment.

Sharon claps her hands briskly and turns to face us all. She is still in her outdoor attire, which shows how flummoxed she is. Normally she is immaculately dressed and ready for action by eight forty-five. But today she is still wearing her mackintosh over her work outfit of a sleek, deep red pencil skirt and black opaque tights. Her black high-heel court shoes are still clasped in her hands and her beige Ugg boots are on her feet. She looks more like a chicken than ever. I can just imagine her striding proudly around on Rupert's farm, pecking at all the farmhands to get them to work harder.

She focuses her beady eyes on each of us, one by one. 'Who is responsible for this?' she says sharply.

No one answers. Everyone just looks at the floor, inspects their fingernails or looks out of the windows. I bob down behind Barbara.

Sharon turns to Gwen. 'Have you taken it upon yourself to completely remerchandise the department without permission?' she barks.

I hold my breath and for a moment regret my actions. Poor old Gwen looks like she's about to burst into tears. Her flushed, well-powdered face clashes somewhat with her cerulean-blue eyeliner and matching mascara, and she looks at the floor.

'I have to admit—' she begins nervously.

'Well, it's good,' Sharon interrupts briskly. I peek out from my hiding place and am amazed to see Sharon smile at Gwen who, understandably, looks shocked. Sharon never smiles.

'Oh, I can't take the credit for this—' Gwen looks around desperately, trying to see if anyone looks guilty. I hide behind Barbara again.

'Oh, Gwen, shush now,' Sharon interrupts. 'Don't make such a fuss. I might think your shop floor looks good, but will the customers? That's the real test.' She ruffles the papers on her clipboard. 'Now, enough of this jibber-jabbering.' She raises her voice above the excited chattering. 'Ladies, let's start—'

'And gents!' interrupts Guy as he dashes into the department clutching a venti latte that looks almost as big as he is. He is wearing one of the vintage trilbys with a camel scarf tied jauntily round his neck over a beautifully cut chocolate-brown over-coat. He looks hot. The girls all wolf whistle and he curtsies. 'Sorry I'm late, Sharon, I didn't get out of here till well past closing time yesterday. I had so much clearing up to do before I went . . .' he pauses and pulls off his leather gloves delicately, finger by finger, '. . . ON MY DATE.'

'OOOH!' we all gasp, and he puts his hand up to stop us.

'Do not fear, treacles, all the juicy details will be revealed later. Suffice to say the date in question won't be complaining about the customer service at the store!' He winks as he shrugs his coat off and throws it over his arm, but leaves his hat on. He tilts it slightly and looks at us all. He is wearing a suit. He never wears suits. 'I'm here to work now.' And he nods reverentially at Sharon to let her know she can continue.

Sharon rolls her eyes; she's never had much patience for Guy. 'Thank you, Guy, I'm sure we'll all be *dying* to hear about your date later,' she says with sarcasm that is lost on him. He just nods in agreement.

'Quiet, please,' Sharon snaps. 'We've got some important things to discuss before the store opens. Now, first on my list is sales figures. It was a pretty poor week, even by our standards.' She glances down at her spreadsheet. 'I cannot emphasize how important it is for you all to raise the figures in your departments. Hardy's simply cannot go on as we are. You must all know that we are barely taking any money at all. Rupe—'

The staff's giggles undulate through the room like an ocean wave. We all know how much Sharon fancies Rupert. Sharon glares at us and continues, 'This is not a laughing matter, ladies.'

'And gents,' pipes up Guy pedantically.

Sharon ignores him. 'As I was saying, the Hardy

209

family are under a huge amount of pressure from the board to drastically improve the store's takings by Boxing Day. That gives us just over three weeks to make a marked improvement.'

'We can't help it if the customers don't want to come in,' grumbles Elaine.

'Yeah, we're all doing everything we can to make the sales. But no one bothers to come in here,' adds Carly's colleague Paula. 'They all go to Selfridges, or Liberty, or the big department stores on Oxford Street. And frankly, I don't blame them.'

'Then we must do something about it,' retorts Sharon crisply.

'Like what? Have us all marching round the West End with sandwich boards?' laughs Becky.

'Don't joke about it, Becks,' calls out Elaine.

'I don't think any of you understand the seriousness of what I'm saying,' Sharon snaps. She looks around at us all in irritation and I can suddenly see how much she cares about this place. She may not have the best management skills in the world but she's passionate about Hardy's and she can see that it needs to change. This place is her life, too. 'If we don't all drastically improve the takings in this store, we'll all be out of a job.' Her statement silences everyone.

'What are you going to do?' says Guy, 'Fire us all?'

Sharon sighs. 'No, you are all wonderful employees and I doubt anyone else could do a better job than you.' I raise my eyebrows. Sometimes Sharon surprises me. There is a trickle of approval through the group at her words. 'What I meant is, none of us will have jobs because Hardy's won't be here any more.'

'Hardy's is going to close?' gasps Guy, and clutches his hand to his heart, inadvertently trickling coffee down his slick suit. 'Fiddlesticks!' he exclaims, and brushes his hand manically down the stain. 'I just bought this on staff discount.'

'It is more than likely,' Sharon confirms.

A shocked hush descends upon the room, then the babbling begins again.

'We can't let that happen!' calls out Barbara.

'London *needs* Hardy's!' says Gwen passionately.

'We need Hardy's,' adds someone else tearfully.

'What can we do, Sharon?' calls out Jenny.

'Well, we can begin by following Guy's lead,' smiles Sharon thinly, waving a long till receipt. Guy looks up from where he is still furiously dabbing at the coffee stain on his suit. 'His takings were up a massive five hundred per cent over the weekend. I don't know what he did or how he did it, but he's proved that Hardy's still has a chance.'

Guy curtsies again and we all laugh. Even Sharon.

'We can do this, people. We just need a bit of vision and a lot of hard work. Are you all prepared for that?'

Everyone looks at each other as if waiting for someone to agree to the terms: work hard for a few weeks or lose their job for good in a climate where it's practically impossible to get a new one.

'We'll do it!' says Barbara, the unofficial spokesperson of the group.

'I hope we get a pay rise at the end of it, though,' grumbles Elaine. 'I didn't sign up for this when I took this job. I should've stayed at Selfridges.'

Sharon ignores her. 'Well done, ladies, I'm really proud of you. And well done, Gwen, for taking the initiative and following Guy's lead. It's a good start, but you and your team need to work hard today to follow through with sales. And I don't need to tell the rest of you that we all need to be thinking of the best ways to maximize sales in our departments and get customers through our doors. I'll be sending Carly round to each department to help you creatively. After all, she seems to have the right vision for the future of the store. Although, where is she this morning? Does anyone know?'

Everyone looks around as if noticing for the first time that Carly isn't here. Whilst she's not the best timekeeper in the world she doesn't usually miss the Monday morning meeting.

Sharon frowns and looks at her watch. 'Well, I'm sure she's got a good reason. Carly has been working very hard on her creative vision for the store. Rupert has put his faith in her that she is going to steer the store in the right direction and I want you all to support her. As assistant manager she is going to be working alongside Rupert to bring a fresh look and direction to Hardy's.'

'Good luck with that,' yells someone.

'She's got a tough few weeks ahead of her,' says Sharon, ignoring the heckler, 'so I want you all to support her – even if her ideas for your departments are not what you expect – although Guy and Gwen have obviously got there first and taken control of their own departments, which is wonderful to see.' She turns to them and nods her head. 'Rest assured I will be passing on news of your hard work to Rupert.'

Guy beams at everyone and Gwen smiles uncertainly. She is still battling over whether to take credit for the work or not. I want to catch her eye and telepathically translate to her that she should. Neither of them knows that their job is the first for the chop this week.

I just hope that what I've done is enough to turn that decision round. At least for now.

Sharon dismisses us, and the staff all scatter across the store like mice, squeaking excitedly and nibbling hungrily at the gossip they've just received like it's a particularly tasty bit of cheese. Whilst the threat of closure is obviously worrying, I know they're all trying to work out who the secret elf is who's making such big changes in the store. We all know Gwen well enough to presume it isn't her. Guy is more plausible. Everyone always thinks gay men have creative flair.

I wander back to the stockroom, feeling elated. It was so great hearing the staff come together to

213

fight for Hardy's survival. I just hope it continues. I don't think I can do this alone.

I've just popped the kettle on and am trying to think up ways to transform the next department when Carly bursts into the stockroom.

'Morning!' she gasps as she throws off her red coat and takes off her thick cream snood and cute matching beanie. She looks like a latter-day Ali MacGraw in her *Love Story*-style preppie winter clothes. She shakes her hair so it pours over her shoulders like melted caramel.

'What have I missed, babe?' she says as she throws herself onto the sofa.

'Just the morning meeting,' I reply quietly, suddenly regretting the fact that I didn't make an effort to wear something from The Wardrobe this morning. My old, shapeless Arran jumper was cosy at five o'clock this morning when I left the house, but now I just feel like a slob. I'm also worried she's going to ask about the date she helped get me ready for, and I don't know what to tell her. Luckily, she doesn't seem to have remembered.

'Oh shit, I com*pletely* forgot about that.' She looks worried for a moment. 'Did Sharon notice I wasn't there?' I nod. 'Damn.' I wave a mug in front of her. 'Ooh, tea? Yes, please, hon.' She bites on her lips and then waves her hand dismissively. 'I'll just tell Sharon my tube got stuck in the tunnel.'

She claps her hands and her eyes glisten with excitement. 'Now, you've got to promise not tell anyone what I'm about to tell you.' She pauses and waits for me to agree. I feel strangely honoured that she should choose me to confide in. But that's part of what I like about Carly. She makes you feel good purely by choosing you to be her friend. It makes you think you must be special.

'Of course,' I say. 'You know you can tell me anything.'

Carly smiles gratefully at me and I feel like singing.

'Well,' she begins carefully, looking around the stockroom before lowering her voice conspiratorially, 'the truth is I've just had a brilliant meeting with the CEO from Rumors. Apparently, they're just waiting to confirm the location of the store and then it'll be all systems go. Whoever they employ, they want them to be there right from the start, helping to set up the premises. They might even be sent to New York to be trained! I mean, imagine that!'

I smile and try to be excited for her, but I can't help but feel she needs to know what's happening with Hardy's. After all, it's more than likely to become Rumors, so her job won't be so different after all.

'So you've decided to take the job?' I ask.

Carly nods. 'I just can't let an opportunity like this pass me by. I mean, I'll miss everyone, but it's not like Hardy's is the best place to have on your CV, is it?'

I hand her a steaming cup of tea. 'Well, you deserve it. You're brilliant at your job, but we'll all really miss you. Not that it matters now anyway . . .' Carly looks at me questioningly. 'Hardy's is being threatened with closure,' I say dramatically.

Carly's eyes widen and her mouth forms a wide O. 'Really? Shit, that's awful.' She shakes her head sadly. 'Well, I'm just glad that I'll be able to walk out of here when it closes and straight into a job at Rumors. What about you, though? What will you do?'

I shrug. I honestly haven't thought about it. Mainly because I don't want to.

'Oh, I'm sure you'll be all right, hon,' she says as she settles down with her tea. 'You're the best stockroom girl we've ever had. Everyone says so. Sharon even says you were born to work in here.'

'So what are your plans for today?' I ask, faux brightly, feeling a sudden urge to change the subject.

She puts her cup of tea down and sits forward in her seat eagerly, clasping her hands together so I get full view of her perfectly varnished finger-nails, which are painted a gorgeous soft mink colour. I look at my own and decide that tonight I'll give them a polish.

'I've got a hard day in front of me, actually,' Carly says, 'in that I'm going to have to actually, you know, do some work! I had a meeting with Rupert on Friday and today's the day I'm going to introduce my ideas and concepts into Designers and then roll them out in the rest of the store. Actually, I meant to ask you, did you get the delivery of my stuff this morning?'

I nod and get up to show her what I've unpacked.

'Fabulous.' She waves her hands dismissively and makes to leave as I pull out the sexy, daring, slashed, thigh-skimming, cleavage-plunging items that came in Sam's delivery this morning. 'Can you bring them up for me? I'm going to need your help, if that's OK? I'll run it past Sharon. I'm sure she'll be fine with that. It's not like there's going to be many orders on a Monday morning, are there! Although, weirdly, the beauty department looked pretty busy when I walked through just now. Gwen was running around like a mad thing. Anyway, see you in a minute, hon!' She disappears out the door.

The beauty department looked pretty busy? I'm suddenly excited to have a chance to see what's happening on the shop floor, as well as to spend more time with Carly. It's a brilliant opportunity for me to allow her style and personality to rub off on me more. I feel like I subliminally need her help to guide me through the dating process with Joel. The more time I spend with her at the moment, the better. I know I should feel guilty about what I've done, but I don't. Carly's got a promotion and another brilliant job offer on the table, a brilliant social life with lots of friends, and, let's face it, she's not exactly lacking in male interest. The last thing she needs is my sympathy. The thought is actually quite laughable.

I pick up an armful of stock and push the stockroom open with my bum, letting it slam shut behind me as I step out onto the shop floor. I look up as I hear a commotion and nearly drop the entire pile of clothes I'm holding.

All around me, customers are weaving around the beauty department, grabbing perfume bottles, picking up lip glosses and cooing over the displays. They must have been drawn in by the vintage products I showcased in the window, held by the female mannequins that I dressed in vintage 1950s clothing, positioned as if they were looking in a mirror to reapply their make-up. It went well next to the window with the male mannequin proffering the Tiffany box. Anyway, now there are people sitting at the different counters, playing with make-up. Some are being followed by dutiful husbands, who are nodding robotically as they're shown yet another pretty product that looks the same as the last to them. I can see from the expression on their faces that they're desperate to find an excuse to slip off downstairs to Menswear.

And there is even a handful of customers who appear to be clamouring to buy the soaps from my pyramid display. Gwen and Jenny are run off their feet, but they look completely elated. They have managed to sort out a system between them, but they clearly need more help. I wave at Becky in Handbags, but she doesn't see me. I wave again and this time she spots me, puts away her phone and hurries over.

'Bloody hell!' she exclaims, and bombs over to help a customer who is looking around for assistance.

Sharon and Rupert appear in the corner, talking and pointing at Gwen, who is blissfully unaware of her precarious job position. Then Sharon and Rupert jump to help on the tills together, and for a moment there is a beautiful unity to the team, with everyone fighting hard to serve the customers and, ultimately, to help Hardy's live to serve another day.

I stand and watch on the sidelines, still grasping my armfuls of Carly's stock as the customers swarm around me like a fog, making me more invisible than ever. A wave of excitement and pride fills my body and I allow the startling realization to wash over me completely. I did this. Me. And I'm good at it. I'm really good at it.

CHAPTER 16

Despite the bustling beauty department downstairs, Designers is a veritable graveyard when I arrive there with the stock. Carly is standing in the middle of the department, seemingly oblivious to what is happening on the floor below, whilst a grumpy-looking Elaine wheels various rails to different parts of the shop floor. There appears to be tension in the air.

'But you've tried it over there already,' Elaine protests when Carly points to the space near the till point, by the far wall.

'No I haven't,' Carly says, rolling her eyes at me as if to say, 'You can't get the staff these days.'

'You bloody well have,' Elaine grumbles, and sits on the bottom rail stubbornly.

'What did you say?' Carly purses her lips and spins round to look at Elaine. I draw back in shock. Elaine folds her arms and sticks her chin in the air. Carly glances at me and her face softens as she turns back to Elaine. 'I hope you didn't swear at me, Elaine. Remember, I'm a manager. Now,' she clasps her hands and pulls them to her lips as she ponders for a moment, 'where was I? Oh, yes, we were going to put the rail over by the back wall, weren't we, Elaine?' The last part of the sentence is clearly an order, not a question.

Elaine stands up and pushes the rail over to the required position, muttering as she passes me. I don't think she's even noticed I'm there.

Carly turns to me. 'Hi, hon, can you put all that down and go and get me another load of stock, please? How much more is there to bring?'

I want to say, 'Too much for one person to carry and, more importantly, too much for this shop to sell,' but of course I don't. The delivery of clothes this morning was massive, and that was on top of everything that arrived on Thursday. I checked the stock sheets this morning after the meeting and we didn't sell one of the Florence Gainsbourgs over the weekend, despite Carly wearing it in the store. I have no idea how we found the money to order all this expensive new stock, or how Carly is planning to shift it.

'There's at least another three or four loads,' I say, and I look at the stairs beseechingly. 'We could do it in two runs if we both do it?' I add hopefully.

'Oh, no, hon.' Carly shakes her head. 'I can't possibly do that. I'm in the creative moment. I need to imagine it all and work out where every-thing is going to go. It's a long, difficult process; you wouldn't understand.' She smiles kindly at me. 'You'll be all right, though, won't you?'

I nod wearily and head back down the three

flights of stairs. It's at times like this that I wish Hardy's was more modern and had a bloody lift.

And that I knew how to say no.

I'm climbing the stairs to the first floor for the last time with the last massive armload of clothes. I can barely see where I'm going but instinct and an intricate knowledge of the footprint of the entire store appears to be leading me. Suddenly I hear a distinctive voice rising over the throng and I try to peer round the precariously balanced bundle that I'm clinging to. I look down.

There's a guy in the beauty department talking to Jenny. I can just see the top of his head. Maybe he's come into buy a perfume for his wife or girlfriend, drawn into the store by my beautiful bottle display? Then I hear his voice again and I know for certain it's not just some guy. It's Joel.

'What's he doing here?' I whisper under my breath, and press myself against the banisters in case he looks up and sees me. I hide my face behind the clothes and do my best to listen in to their conversation. I'm learning that being invisible can come in handy sometimes.

'Just come in to mumble mumble check out mumble mumble unit area mumble nice displays mumble who did them mumble . . .'

I want to shout, 'Speak up, Joel!' but realize that would be fool-hardy. Mostly because if he looks up he'll see that I am wearing the ugliest jumper you have ever seen in your life. The wool has caused an unattractive rash to work its way around my neck and up to my jaw. And I'm wearing my horrid rimmed glasses because I couldn't face putting in contact lenses when I got up at crazy o'clock this morning. My hair is unwashed and pulled back in a ponytail, and I have on my Worst Black Work Trousers. The ones that are tight in all the wrong places. I look like a Cornish fisherman who's been out trawling for fish all night. I can't let him see me like this. More importantly, I can't let me see him with Carly. I know I was going to come clean to him but I need to keep *some* dignity whilst doing it. Oh, why didn't I put on that cute sixties dogtooth miniskirt and black polo neck I pulled out this morning? Damn my natural comfort-over-style reflex. I need to try harder.

I dash up the stairs and am panting by the time I get back into Designers. Carly doesn't appear to have moved or made any sort of headway since I left. The department is a mess, the current stock is on the floor and the rails are empty. Elaine is prowling round with a face like thunder.

I put down the clothes and walk towards Carly but Elaine gets to me first. 'She doesn't have a clue what she's doing,' she hisses. 'She won't listen to me. She's going to put all this old stock in the stockroom and hang all her new stuff up. Even though the old dear who'll be choosing her selection of crushed velvet and tartan taffeta evening dresses for her Hogmanay celebration is due in today . . . what's she called?'

'Lady Fontescue,' I say, glancing behind me nervously to see if Joel is going to appear at the top of the stairs at any moment.

'And what about that mad woman who is obsessed with printed kaftans?' presses Elaine.

'Babs Buckley,' I reply automatically. It is no consolation to me right now that I can still win at my 'Match the Customer to the Random Item of Stock' game. I have to get out of here.

'That's her. Well, she's not going to like this either.' Elaine folds her arms and glares at me as if it's my problem. 'I can't see her swapping her kaftans for *this*!' She grabs a small, shimmering sheath of a dress at the top of my pile and I can't help but agree. These are not garments for Hardy's current clientele. Carly risks alienating the only customers we have. I hope she knows what she's doing. But looking at her now, her face furrowed into a frown of concentration, tongue sticking out slightly, I have a feeling she doesn't.

'Elaine, hon,' Carly calls, 'can you help, please? There's a lot to be done here.'

Elaine growls under her breath and I hastily intervene before she launches at Carly.

'Carly,' I say as I jump in between them, 'the new stock is all up here now. I'm going to get back to the stockroom, if that's OK? I've got stuff to get on wi—'

Carly widens her eyes at me in surprise. 'But

you can't leave now. Not with all this work still to do! Elaine and I need you, don't we?'

'But they need me more, Carly.' I point at the department below and walk towards the grand staircase before Carly has a chance to reply. I'm not usually this assertive but I can't risk Joel coming up and seeing me. Not dressed like this.

I peer over the banisters to see if I can spot him. A crowd of people has clustered around the various different counters. Gwen and Jenny are flitting busily between people like butterflies in their crisp uniforms, thrusting lipsticks and soaps and moisturizers into various hands. Joel is no longer anywhere to be seen, which is a good sign. If I can just get down the rest of the stairs and into the sanctuary of the stockroom I'll be all right.

I slam the stockroom door behind me, panting from my sprint down the stairs. There are now more than a dozen orders printed on the machine and I dash over, grab the long roll of tickets and set to work. I don't have time to breathe, let alone think.

Nearly two hours go by and I am starving and exhausted by the time 3 p.m. rolls round. But I can't leave for the day as I normally would. In fact, I have to phone Delilah to tell her I won't be able to pick the kids up from nursery today. And still the orders keep coming through. It is unprecedented for a Monday – no, make that *any* day – and I can't help but feel a wave of pleasure that my work has made a difference. Even if no one knows it but me.

Gwen dashes in at one point, her face bright and flushed with exertion, rather than blusher. She garbles something about lavender soaps selling out and when I point her down the right aisle she rushes out with a whole box without saying a word. I'm going to have to order some more, which is unheard of. I'm not even sure if they're made any more; I've been selling Iris's soaps from the same order for the past two years.

Sharon also comes in, her face crisscrossed with a mix of anxiety and hope. She grabs a box full of lipsticks and runs out. Everyone is too busy to speak today. Even Carly hasn't been down for her usual afternoon cup of tea and chinwag.

By five o'clock I am about to faint. When the stockroom door opens again I'm ready to pounce on whoever it might be to get them to cover for me whilst I go and grab a sandwich. It's Carly.

'Guess who I've just seen,' she squeals as she sashays into the room, and I know from the expression on her face that it can be only one person. 'Cute Eye Contact Guy!' she exclaims, confirming my fears.

Oh God. Joel. He's still here. She's met him. Well, that's it then. It's time to own up.

'God, he's gorgeous,' she breathes. 'Don't you think?' I gasp as she swings open the stockroom door and I see Joel standing just feet away from us, hovering around the beauty department, which is still full of customers. I jump behind Carly but I can just see his profile. He takes out an iPad and appears to be making notes. He looks up again, but luckily it's in the opposite direction. I jump over to the door and slam it shut.

'Hey, why did you do that?' she exclaims. 'You've spoiled my view! And *what* a view!'

I shrug and she turns back to open the door a crack and peer out. This is the moment that I should come clean. If Joel is working for Rupert he's clearly going to keep coming into Hardy's so he's bound to bump into the real Carly at some point, and I don't have the energy to keep up this stupid pretence any longer.

I take a deep breath. 'The thing is, Carly—' I begin.

'He totally checked me out on the way in here, you know,' she says, talking over me. 'I don't understand why he doesn't just come on over and ask me out. He clearly wants to. Why does he keep coming back to this shithole otherwise?'

I bristle at her words. Doesn't she have any sense of loyalty? I let it pass, though, as I'm determined to say what I need to say.

'Well,' I try again, lowering my eyes and taking a deep breath, 'the truth is . . . he's actually here to see me.'

'What!' She stares at me, her expression one of true disbelief, and the silence fills the room. Then she breaks into a broad smile and then a high-pitched laugh. 'Oh, heee heeee, oh, you are hilarious, hon, *really*.' She puts her hands on my shoulder. 'That was a good one. You really had me going there.'

Her words hit me in the chest like darts. Each one hurts more than the last because I know Carly doesn't mean it cruelly. It's just the thought of me and Joel is too laughable to be true. 'Now, do you fancy taking a break? You can be my wingwoman whilst I go and speak to the hottie out there. He's obviously just shy . . .'

I look away as another set of orders come through on the printer. Suddenly, I feel nauseous. The last thing I want to do now is eat. If she wants Joel she can go and get him. I'm not stupid enough to compete with her.

I busy myself with another order as I reply, not wanting to give her the benefit of my attention. 'No,' I say tightly. The word feels strange on my lips, alien almost. 'You go. I'm far too busy here.' I turn round to gauge her reaction, but the door is already swinging shut behind her.

CHAPTER 17

I stay in the stockroom for another hour, even though it is long past my clocking-off time. All normal rules that apply to my life seem to be going out of the window these days. I know I wanted things to change, but now everything is so different I genuinely don't know what I'm doing any more. I don't feel like me and I don't know how to be myself with anyone.

Part of me feels relieved that Joel is soon going to know the truth. Carly might have already introduced herself to him. And he'll realize that *of course* she's the personal shopper he's been told so much about. He'll only need to look at her to see that. And me? He'll just see me as a desperate girl willing to do anything for a bit of romance and excitement in her life. And he'll be right.

I pack up my rucksack slowly. Once I'm certain that Joel and Carly are long gone I head out of the stockroom, flicking off the lights behind me.

The beauty department is still heaving as I walk towards the front doors, and no one gives me a second glance.

I stumble out of the store and onto the

pavement, shivering as I wrap my big coat around my body. I take a step forward and turn and glance up at Hardy's clock. It is nearly 6.30 p.m. and pitch-black. A disgruntled passer-by swears and shunts me on the shoulder as he walks past me, as if I have inconvenienced him hugely simply by standing there. Then someone else coming in the opposite direction does the same. I mutter an apology and start walking, pulling my hood up, digging my hands deep into my pockets and nestling my chin into my coat. I'll come back for my bike after I've made a little detour.

Ahead of me I see a familiar figure rushing down the street. It looks just like Sam. I quicken my pace to catch up with him but then he stops, embraces someone, and starts walking slowly next to her. I'm not sure who it is, they're not holding hands or anything, but their heads are close together, it's like they're discussing something important. And he looks dressed up. Not in his usual checked shirts or hooded top, but in smart dark jeans and a tailored coat. He's not even wearing his cute beanie. They disappear around a corner and I shrug to myself, sad not to have been able to chat to him. I could've done with a friendly ear. I make a note to ask him who the girl was. He never mentioned that he's seeing anyone. Not that it's any of my business, but he usually fills me in on what's new in his life. Although weirdly, he doesn't talk about girlfriends much. I've always presumed he was single.

I sigh as I walk down the street. I can't help but think of the last time I took this route with Joel. I'd stepped into Carly's shoes – quite literally – and we were off on our date. I was so happy, so excited. But even then I knew that it couldn't last long. Girls like me don't date men like Joel, or get kissed like that. Well, maybe once in a lifetime.

And that should be enough, I tell myself sternly. *I should count myself lucky.*

Because my life may not be glamorous or exciting, but my shoes are *way* comfier than Carly's. And this jumper I'm wearing? It may look like something an old man would wear, but it's warm. It's me. And I like it. Just as I think Hardy's shouldn't try to be something it isn't, perhaps I should apply the same rules to myself.

That thought makes me feel a little better and as I turn on to Oxford Street, I stand and gaze at the glittering display around me: everywhere is lit up like a gigantic circuit board, with bright, brash, gawdy Christmas lights and decorations that sparkle magnificently over London's most famous shopping thoroughfare. Lola and Raffy would love them, I think, then wonder guiltily if I should phone Delilah to check she was OK picking the kids up from nursery. She knows that it's not often that I haven't managed to make it on time and I think she liked having an excuse to leave work early. But I do feel bad. Just then my phone buzzes and I open a text from Delilah.

231

'Got kids. Need you home by 7.30 as I have a client dinner. OK?'

I reply swiftly with a yes, pushing through a crowd of excitable, chattering Japanese tourists, taking photos with their fancy cameras. They look so happy to be here. And I know I should be too. I love London, particularly at this time of year. I honestly don't think there's anywhere I'd rather be. I love watching people, gazing in the store windows, pointing at the Christmas displays and gasping at the lights above them. I just wished I shared their enthusiasm for them. Don't get me wrong, I adore the decorations on Bond Street; the twinkling fairy lights, the elegant trees and the beautiful, delicate canopy cobweb lights that illuminate Regent Street. But the big Disney-film-inspired display over Oxford Circus all feels a bit . . . fake. Like Christmas is about marketing and the magic of making money, not the magic of making people happy, which is, surely, what it should be about?

Call me old-fashioned, but personally I don't want my city's main Christmas display to be a glorified advertisement. I want to see hundreds of old-fashioned lights and traditional decorations. I want a Christmas shopping experience in which people wear bright coats and smiles, hold each other's hands as they sip hot chocolate and carry armloads of perfectly wrapped parcels. I want candles and lanterns, cranberries, popcorn and eggnog, and crepe-paper crackers.

Maybe I'm alone in this, I think as I walk past department store after department store that have windows full of fancifully designed displays. I turn my back on Topshop, which still has customers streaming greedily in and out of it, and cross over at the Oxford Circus traffic lights. I walk down Argyll Street – past the London Palladium where I spent many a happy afternoon as a child with my parents – before coming to a standstill in front of Liberty. It's always been my favourite London store (after Hardy's, of course). But tonight I am left disappointed by what I see. Even this wonderful old store has gone with a 'modern' take of Christmas this year. In the window I'm standing in front of is a mannequin leaning against a brick wall that is spray-painted with Banksy-inspired graffiti, a load of fake snow and a plain park bench. I can't help but curl my lip in disgust. This is Liberty! With its exquisite Elizabethan aspect, Tudor beams and hand-carved mahogany staircase, it's a symbol of traditional old-fashioned English luxury in the heart of the West End. What is everyone's obsession with being modern?

I walk along Kingly Street looking at the rest of Liberty's treacherously non-traditional windows. In their next one they have replaced the mannequins' heads with fox heads. I shake my head and continue towards Regent Street, crossing over and bypassing it completely to head back on to Oxford Street, towards Marble Arch. I'm deeply

233

disappointed that my detour to Liberty didn't do anything to lift my Christmas spirit.

I stop and buy a bag of roasted chestnuts from a friendly street seller, hoping this will help me evoke the Christmas spirit. I crunch on several at once and the sweetness explodes in my mouth. I carry on down Oxford Street, my hand delving back into the bag as I throw chestnuts into my mouth hungrily; I realize I can't remember the last time I ate. I can't help studying each shop window as I pass, wondering what it is about them that draws the crowds in. What is the magic formula?

I suddenly find myself outside Selfridges, the elegant century-old store that beat Bloomingdale's in New York to be named the world's best department store, and gaze rapturously at its windows. I can immediately see that the fabulous window displays that have become synonymous with the store's success are everything Hardy's aren't: bold, adventurous, artistic, they constantly attract attention and praise from the public as well as the art, fashion, media and photography worlds.

The store itself is everything a modern department store should be: large and luxurious, slick and sexy, relevant and cutting edge. You feel its power as soon as you walk through the grand revolving doors at the front of the store. It doesn't have the quaint appeal of Liberty or the over-powering wealth and power of Harrods, or the homeliness of John Lewis, but it has something more: it has mass appeal. I have never met anyone who doesn't love Selfridges.

I stand outside the store for a while, still crunching on roasted chestnuts and sipping on a latte I picked up from a cute little Italian café I know nestled behind Selfridges on Duke Street.

I watch as vast swarms of people crowd through the doors. This, here, is the pinnacle of shopping power. It's what Hardy's has to tap into in order to survive. But *how?* I shake my head. It seems like an impossible task. Hardy's is never going to be like Selfridges. It just can't compete.

I edge along the street, tilting my head as I study the store's windows. This year, they have done a modern take on Pantomime, with each window framed by fairy-lit garlands depicting grandiose scenes from various shows. So in one window the Ugly Sisters as dressed by Matthew Williamson, another features Vivienne Westwood's Widow Twanky, then there's Santa Claus, who is graciously pulling Cinderella's carriage. Each window is also festooned with flashing slogans that say things like, 'He's behind you!', 'To the ball!' and 'Boo Hiss'. The overall look is completely kitsch, cool and chic. Small crowds are gathered in front of each window, pointing and smiling. The whole window display is modern, smart, witty but also completely Christmassy; totally right for the store's image.

But what about Hardy's? I think, biting my lip thoughtfully as I stare at the Selfridges display and then visualize our sad, stark windows. There has to be something we can do to make the store stand out, something we're just not seeing. I stare at the windows so that they blur into a mass of whirling kaleidoscopic colour in front of my eyes, trying to picture a scene that could work for Hardy's. But all I can see now is a rainbow snowstorm whirling in front of my eyes.

I blink and shake my head as I feel a buzzing in my pocket. I pull out my mobile phone and look at it. Joel's name flashes up on the screen and I feel sick as my stomach bungee jumps to my toes and then up to my mouth. *He knows.* I put the phone back in my pocket. I don't want to answer it. I can't speak to him.

I focus on the people going in and out of the store instead, trying to ignore the incessant ringing in my pocket. Suddenly I spot a familiar figure, carrying an unmissably bright yellow bag in one hand, the other pressing a phone to his ear. He pulls it away from his ear and looks at it, frowns, then puts it back to his ear as he steps away from the door and in front of the window. I dart back against the window where I'm standing. I'm only metres away from Joel and I want to hide, but there is literally nowhere to go. I can either go in the store and risk him seeing me or keep him occupied by answering the phone. I plunge my hand into my pocket and breathlessly answer.

'Hello?'

'Hey, stranger,' Joel drawls.

Stranger. Someone you don't know. A definite dig. I don't reply, I just watch as he tucks his phone under his ear, puts his bag between his legs and folds his arms. 'I thought you were never gonna answer. How are you?'

I press myself against the window and edge away from him, thankful for the constant stream of people walking by, blocking me from Joel's view.

'I'm OK,' I reply quietly.

Joel laughs. 'You don't sound so sure. I missed you today at Hardy's.'

I don't say anything.

'Carly? Are you still there?'

I freeze. Carly? That means . . . Suddenly the street seems devoid of people and I can just see Joel, leaning against the window, one foot crossed in front of the other. His dark hair has been whipped up into a quiff by the wind and his expression is sweet, vulnerable almost.

He doesn't know.

I feel elated, my stomach has been whipped like cake mix into a frenzy of excitement and my head feels sparkly. Then reality hits. Perhaps this is the moment for me to own up. All I have to say is, 'I'm not Carly.' Three simple words.

'I'm still here,' I reply instead as I feel the guilt stab at my stomach. The irony is lost on Joel. If he were just to look over his right shoulder now he couldn't fail to miss me.

'Sooo,' he says playfully, 'guess where I am right now?'

I am giddy with adrenalin and lies. 'Ooh I don't know,' I reply. 'How many guesses do I get?'

'As many as you want,' he replies with a sexy laugh.

'OK,' I say as I edge back along the window and then dive through the revolving doors. I step away from the entrance and turn round so I can still see him. This game is fun all of a sudden. It's nice to feel in control for a change. 'Completely random guess number one. Selfridges?' I peer out of a gap in the window and stifle a laugh as I see Joel look to the left and right and then shake his head.

'How did you know that?' he exclaims.

'Just a lucky guess.'

'Well, you're right.' He's still looking up and down the street. He turns slightly and I catch sight of his handsome profile. He turns even more so he is facing the doors and I dart further into the shop.

I hold up a big designer handbag to my face, pretending to study it closely, peering out after a minute to see if Joel's still looking. He's turned back to the street, thank goodness. I don't want him to think I'm a stalker as well as a fake.

'I've just bought you a present,' he murmurs in my ear, and I jump a little. I've been so focused on looking at him that I almost forgot we were on the phone.

'You didn't have to do that,' I reply, suddenly embarrassed.

'I wanted to,' he says. 'It is nearly Christmas, after all. And I probably won't be here for the holidays. I'll be going home to Pennsylvania on Boxing Day.'

I feel my heart plummet to my toes.

'I wanted to give you a gift, not for Christmas, but just because . . .'

I am gobsmacked. I lower the handbag and gaze at the back of Joel's head through the window.

'That's really nice of you,' I say quietly.

'So can I see you again tonight? We could go for a drink or something?'

'Oh, I can't,' I say remorsefully. 'I'm baby-sitting tonight.' Much as I'd love to, I've been up since 5 a.m. and look like shit. It will have to wait. Besides, it's true. It's quarter to seven now so I have to hurry in order to be home in time for Delilah to get to her client dinner.

'Oh,' Joel says, the disappointment clear in his voice. 'Well, never mind. It'll just have to wait. How about tomorrow? Are you free then?'

I smile and nod, and then remember he can't see me so I murmur an affirmative into the phone instead and feel myself blush as Joel replies, 'Till tomorrow, Carly.'

I press the End Call button and hug the phone to my chest. Then, as I'm barged in all directions by customers coming in and out the store, I creep back to the revolving doors and sneak outside. I peer out of the entrance just in time

239

to see Joel put his phone in his pocket and then punch the air.

I feel like doing the same because suddenly I don't care about anything other than seeing him again. At whatever cost.

CHAPTER 18

It is nearly midnight by the time Delilah comes home from her client dinner and I have spent the past few hours floating blissfully around the house, dreaming about my next date with Joel.

I'm up in my room when I hear the front door slam shut. I pause for a moment, then continue rummaging through The Wardrobe, trying to find another appropriate outfit from my treasure trove. I can't decide between two different outfits: a soft angora blush-beaded sweater that hugs my curves perfectly, with a short floaty black 1960s georgette miniskirt; or a gorgeous 1940s red belted shirt-dress with short sleeves and a collar, and with cream horses printed all over it. It's very Stella McCartney, apparently. Well, according to Delilah, anyway. Or did she say Chloé? I can't remember, all I know is that I love it.

I pull it out of the wardrobe and hold it up against me just as Delilah bursts into the room. Without knocking. She has clearly had a drink or several hundred. She is swaying, her choppy blond bobbed hair is standing up on end and her make-up is smeared.

'Hisssis . . .' she hisses and flops on my bed. 'Hesnoherethen,' she slurs, and a bit of her spittle lands on my hand. I wipe my hand on my trousers surreptitiously as I try to decipher what she's saying. Luckily I'm well practised in this art form, having seen Delilah drunk many times over the years. She's usually pretty funny, but tonight she appears to be harbouring a darker mood.

'No, Will's not here,' I say gently.

'Asstard.'

Delilah sits up suddenly and puts her hand over her mouth. Oh, Jesus, she's not, is she . . . ?

I sidestep quickly as Delilah pushes past me and dives into my ensuite, and just in time, judging by the grotesque sounds coming from in there.

'Are you all right?' I say, peering round the door.

She is hugging the toilet bowl and looks back at me pathetically. I go over and hold her hair back, smoothing it gently into a stubby ponytail at the nape of her neck as she continues to retch.

'Eurgh,' she says, wiping her mouth. She sits up, groans and then lies on the floor, her face pressed against the tiles. 'Mmm, tha' feels nice,' she murmurs as her eyes roll back and her lids flutter to a close. 'I'll just lie here for a lil' minute.'

'No, Lila,' I say firmly, pulling her up. 'Go to bed. You'll feel much better for it.'

'Won't feel better,' she says petulantly. I am alarmed to see her eyes are brimming with tears. She leans against the wall. 'I don't wanna to go to bed becaush I think . . . no, I *know*.' she shakes

her head vehemently. 'My hushband doesntlove-
meanymooooore.' She looks at me, shakes her head
and begins to cry.

I bend down and put my arms around her,
rubbing her back as she sobs into my chest. I'm
shocked and don't really know what to do. I have
never *ever* seen her like this.

'What makes you think that, Lila? Will idolizes
you,' I say reassuringly.

'He's never here,' she wails. 'He's always
"working late", he never notices me any more,
and a-a-a and . . .' She inhales and hiccups at the
same time. 'I read today in a magazine that more
affairs happen at this time of year than any other
because there are so many feezble . . .' she pauses
and tuts, trying to get her words out, 'fea-feas*ible*
alibis.' She pulls the magazine out of her designer
handbag and immediately flicks to the offending
article, stabbing her fingers at it to emphasize her
point. 'Work Christmas parties, client dinners,
working late to pull ahead before the Christmas
break . . . it all makes sense. Will wasn't home on
time all last week, Evie!' She shakes her head as
a fresh round of sobs rack her body.

'But you're late tonight, Lila,' I say reasonably
whilst secretly wondering if she's right. Will's a
good-looking guy, he works in the City and he's
always 'working late'. I mean, it's not beyond
the realms of possibility. Then I rationalize that
it's unfair to jump to conclusions without any
solid evidence. He's also a great dad and

husband, and has always been utterly besotted with my sister.

'You haven't got any proof that Will is having an affair so why get yourself in such a state? He loves you, Lila. And you know how hard he works. You both do,' I add quickly, knowing how sensitive Delilah is about her job being considered equal to his.

'But this is different,' she says doggedly, staring at the opposite wall. She shakes her head. 'I s'pose you're right, though. I don't have any proof.'

Just then we hear the front door open and shut quietly. Delilah stares at me but doesn't say anything, her plump bottom lip still quivering though her green eyes seem relieved.

'See? He's home, there's nothing to worry about,' I say, stroking her back soothingly. 'Are you going to go and see him?'

She shakes her head and wipes her mouth. 'No, let him come to me.' She pauses and listens for a moment. 'Shhh,' she hisses. We can hear Will climbing the stairs. He opens a door on the first floor, Raffy's or Lola's. Then the other. He closes each one quietly then climbs more stairs. Then he opens his and Delilah's bedroom door and shuts it firmly behind him. There is silence.

'SEE!' Delilah bursts into fresh tears and scrambles to her feet.

'See *what*?' I'm confused and, to be honest, a bit concerned about her sudden paranoia.

'Proof that he's having an affair!' she wails, and

a little more spit lands on my arm. 'If he wasn't,' she continues, 'he'd come and find me. But clearly he wants to just go to sleep so I don't smell perfume on him, or . . . or question him about what he's really been doing this evening or . . .'

'Oh, Delilah,' I say wearily, playing with her hair, 'I'm sure it's nothing. Why don't you just go and talk to him about it?'

'I'm going to do better than that . . .' she says ominously quietly.

She is still talking as I walk out of the ensuite and back into my bedroom. I pick up the red print dress and hold it against my body, turning from side to side as I imagine me wearing it tomorrow night.

'. . . give you proof,' Delilah mumbles as she walks through my room towards the door.

But I'm no longer listening to her. I'm already wrapped up in the early Christmas gift I've been given: my next date with Joel.

TUESDAY 6 DECEMBER

19 Shopping Days Until Christmas

CHAPTER 19

Felix glances up from his Sudoku as I walk towards his office and raises a thick, untamed eyebrow at me.

'Morning, Evie. You're in early again,' he says pointedly.

'You know me,' I reply quickly, averting my eyes so as not so betray their guilt. 'Diligent as always.' He tilts his head slightly and studies me, as if I might reveal something more. Instead I cough, lean over and hand him his coffee, glancing at his puzzle as I do so. 'You're doing well today, Felix! You're becoming quite the expert.'

'Hardly,' he snorts. 'It's the same one I was doing yesterday. Drive me up the bloody wall, they do. But they pass the time. Although,' he sighs, 'it feels like that's all I'm doing these days. Ever since Maisie . . .' He clears his throat, sits up and tries to pull himself together, which makes me want to cuddle him and cry all at once. I go for the cuddle.

'Thanks, love. Sorry for being maudlin.'

'You never have to apologize to me, Felix.' I pause. 'You know what?' I say, thinking about the party that Sam had suggested, 'I think I've got

249

something that will cheer you up. I'm working on having a little night out with a few people from here. I want to introduce you to a couple of people, like my friends Sam and Lily . . .'

Felix's face visibly brightens. 'Lily? I haven't spoken to her in ages. She's a wonderful lady . . .'

'You know her?'

'I employed her!' he says proudly.

I'm desperate to know more about the old days, but I glance at my watch and realize I've run out of time. I make an apologetic face. 'Hold that bit of information!' I exclaim. 'I have to go now. Got lots to do this morning, you know, er, deliveries to unpack for Christmas and everything . . . but we'll pick up on this chat tomorrow! Bye, Felix!'

I turn and flee, desperate to get to work. Part of me really wants to tell Felix what I've been doing with the shop floor – I know he'd support me but I don't want to implicate him in my deception. I have no idea if what I'm doing is right, or even if it'll really work. My last couple of makeovers could've been complete flukes for all I know.

That's why I've decided not to do another one for a day or two as I want to see how Menswear and Beauty get on first, and besides, I don't want to arouse too much suspicion that it isn't the departmental managers themselves doing the work. I've only come in early today to spend some time in other departments so I can plan the next big makeover properly.

★   ★   ★

The morning passes quickly, so ensconced am I in my new role as secret shop-floor remerchandiser. I spent the first couple of hours, before anyone came in, roaming through the store, sketching mock-up makeovers in my notepad and scribbling down ideas for props I could use from the stockroom before heading back there to get even more inspiration. I spot the group of oval gilt mirrors I've been thinking about, which have been stacked against a wall in the corner of the stockroom for ages because I didn't know where else I could put them. I've had this idea that I could use them in the shoe department to display some beautiful vintage shoes that have been gathering dust here. These pretty mirrors would look perfect dotted on the walls around the department, and I could ask Jan Baptysta to put a little shelf in front of each as the shoes would look great reflected there. There's so many beautiful pairs in the stockroom that deserve to be properly displayed: gold T-bar sandals with a cute little heels; cherry-red pumps, silver ballroom shoes and a beautiful pair of peacock-blue Yves Saint Laurent peep toes. It's utter sacrilege that they've all been hidden away in here for so many years. And then there's the boxes of beautiful ex-display evening shoes I've found; faded, stretched and, as a result, unsellable, but I have another idea for them. Something bigger than just a shop-floor prop. I'm thinking a festive shoe tree in the middle of the department, with these shoes hung like

251

precious, shiny decorations. It'll look amazing. Just because we can't sell them, doesn't mean we can't use them. They shouldn't be in here gathering dust, with only me to appreciate them.

I gaze around and smile. Suddenly my grey little stockroom has been transformed into a veritable Aladdin's cave, an endless treasure trove at my fingertips; every item seems to spark a new idea. All these forgotten vintage items have the power to turn Hardy's fortunes around, I'm sure of it. I just need to convince everyone else. I step back and look about, feeling as though I'm seeing the stockroom properly for the first time since I started working here. All you need to do is look beneath the surface to see how beautiful these things really are.

I blink, feeling overwhelmed for a moment. Maybe it's because it has dawned on me that this place feels more like my home than the beautiful converted attic I currently live in at my sister's multimillion-pound house. Right here in Hardy's stockroom was where my broken heart was slowly healed after my split from Jamie. It gave me a purpose in life again. Now, if I can just use its healing power to restore Hardy's fortunes then perhaps the store, in one capacity or another, will continue to be my home for a long time to come.

I don't want to work anywhere other than Hardy's. I love it here. It's the only thing in my life I'm certain about and I can't lose it, I just can't.

Suddenly the stockroom door swings open and Sharon marches in. Her usually pinched face is bright, her sharp eyes sparkling. I bob out from behind an aisle and she looked at me distractedly.

'Oh, hello, uh . . . um . . .' she stutters as she clearly struggles to remember my name.

I wait, resisting the urge to spell my name out with my arms YMCA style.

'. . . Sarah?' she says at last. I can see the relief in her face that she's remembered it. 'Working hard, I hope.'

'Yes, Sharon,' I mumble.

'Good.' She pauses and looks at me. I look back. She seems different today, softer somehow. Maybe it's because her hair, which she usually wears pulled back in a harsh bun, is loose around her face. And she's replaced her bright red lipstick with a caramel-coloured gloss. I suspect she's been experimenting in the all-new beauty hall. 'Stop whatever it is you're doing for the moment, you might as well come and see this too,' she says briskly. Clearly her manner hasn't softened. 'Carly is about to reveal her latest makeover.' I try not to feel offended; after all, Sharon doesn't know it's me who's responsible. Then Sharon smiles. This is very strange. 'Carly has been working really hard on the designers department and we want the staff to be the first people to see the incredible work she's done. I guess that includes you. So come on, chop chop!'

'Oh, yes, right, OK,' I say. I follow Sharon out

of the stockroom. As we walk on to the shop floor I see a train of staff filing up the central staircase, chattering excitedly. I join the end of the queue behind Sharon. When I arrive on the first floor I stand at the back of the semicircle of staff whose excitement has diminished to a quiet murmur.

I take this moment to have a proper look at Carly's work. To say the department is minimalistic is an understatement. The entire shop floor looks like it has been stripped bare. The gorgeous original wood-panelled walls have been covered with large white boards. Every single clothes rail and shelf has been removed. Strange, modernist glass prisms now hang desolately around the department from the atrium ceiling, like stalactites in an empty cave. Instead of endless rails tightly packed with garments there are now just four rails along each side of the department, each one holding only half a dozen or so items. All of them are in varying shades of grey, silver, black and white. In the centre of the room, four statement dresses are suspended from the ceiling with invisible thread, like pieces of modern art.

Carly is standing proudly in the centre of the department in between the four dresses/ installations, a disgruntled-looking Elaine next to her. Carly is wearing a tight white dress with capped sleeves and crazy-high white stiletto shoes. Her hair is pulled back into a tight ponytail and her eyes are glittering brightly. She looks like a pop star commanding a stage at a massive arena.

She raises her hands and silence immediately descends on the department. 'Welcome to the all-new designers department,' she announces proudly. She waves her hand and accidentally hits one of the scary looking installation dresses. Elaine rolls her eyes. Carly clears her throat and continues, 'As you can see, I've worked terribly hard . . .' Elaine coughs and clears her throat. Carly glances sideways at her, a flash of annoyance on her face. '. . . *we've* worked terribly hard to remodel the entire shop floor in a new, fresh, totally modern way. Hardy's has been stuck in the past for so many years and I truly believe this is the reason that has caused us to fall so far behind our competitors.'

In front of me, Sharon nods in agreement. I try not to pull a face. I glance around at the other staff members, who are all gazing awestruck at Carly. Except Elaine, who is picking her fingernails.

'This,' Carly waves her hand, indicating the department, 'this *redesign* is a symbol of what the store needs to do to survive.' She raises her voice and lifts her hands. 'We need to be modern, of the moment, fashion-forward and style savvy. This department,' she declares, 'is the future of Hardy's.'

There is silence as we all take in her words. I hope for her sake that she is right. At that moment, Rupert steps forward and begins to clap. Everyone swiftly follows suit and soon the sound of applause echoes around the minimalistic department, bouncing off the white boards, refracting back off the glass prisms.

So, clearly I'm wrong then.

Carly smiles and nods, bowing a little as she accepts the positive reception. She catches my eye and I give her the thumbs up, then I slip away unnoticed.

I head slowly downstairs, towards Lily's tearoom, feeling exhausted and defeated all of a sudden. I am desperate for a cup of tea and a chat with someone who is on the same wavelength as me. I could call Sam but what I really need now is some company. It is no consolation to me that the person I'm turning to now is an OAP. What does that say about me? That I'm an old-fashioned girl, stuck in the past who has no concept of what people want any more?

Judging by what just happened in Designers, this is obviously the case. My work in Beauty and Menswear was clearly a fluke.

For a moment, I am frightened about what this means. Then I rationalize that it just means that Carly will be its saviour, not me. Well, hopefully, anyway. She is far more qualified for the job. I should just go back to stacking shelves and doing delivery reports. Dad was right: I'm just a stockroom girl. I should forget about trying to be anything more.

'Darling!'

Lily breezes over to me. Today she is wearing a

chic black bouclé two-piece suit with white trim. Her hair is pulled back into a neat chignon and, as ever, her lips are painted a deep red colour. She hugs me warmly. A scent of fresh gardenia and fragrant face powder fills my lungs and Lily pulls back and looks at me appreciatively, turning me around in a circle so she can get a full look at the red print shirtdress I chose to wear for my date tonight, currently the only bright prospect in this depressing day.

'It's *wuuhnderrfull*, darling,' she purrs. 'That dress is perfection on you. Nineteen forties, isn't it? I always knew you had some glamour in you. This suits you way more than all that cheap modern tat you girls wear these days. Where did you find it?'

'Battersea Vintage Fair,' I reply, holding the skirt out with one hand. 'I've had it ages, just . . . never had an occasion to wear it before. Or the inclination,' I admit.

'And you have an occasion now, do you?' asks Lily, ushering me through the empty tearoom and to a table. 'I'm still listening,' she calls over her shoulder. 'Just making you a nice pot of Earl Grey. You look like you need it.' Lily glides back, clutching a tray filled with a gorgeous Clarice Cliff teapot, two matching tea cups and a little mini cake stand filled with pastries. 'You pick first,' she says, nodding at the stand and settling herself down in the chair opposite. 'I'm going to join you. I'm not exactly rushed off my feet.' She gestures around the empty room and smiles wistfully.

'Maybe you should get Carly to come down and give you a makeover,' I say, not without bitterness. 'Everyone seems to be raving about her right now.'

'Carly? Pshhh!' Lily snorts. 'She wouldn't know true style if it came up and bit her on her arse.' Her hand flutters up to her lips and she pulls a face. 'Oops. Potty mouth. Sorry. I mean, she's a beautiful girl but she has no imagination, no appreciation for art, or history or . . . or, *ensemble*. She simply copies catwalk looks she's seen on models or celebrities. That's not style, that's imitation. It may be the sincerest form of flattery, but it sure ain't fashion, Evie.'

Speech over, Lily takes a sip of her tea and looks at me. 'Now, more importantly, tell me about this date of yours . . .'

An hour later I head out of Lily's tearoom, my spirits lifted. I'd told her all about Joel, and she'd sighed and swooned in the appropriate places and clapped her hands, and did everything, in fact, that I hoped a good friend would do. I didn't tell her that I'm pretending to be Carly as I can barely admit it to myself. Lily has even lent me her vintage black Chanel handbag for this evening, which she says will go perfectly with my outfit. I put it over my shoulder, gazing wondrously at the beautiful soft, quilted bag with the distinctive emblem. Lily sat back in her chair, looked me up and down and told me that Coco would be proud in a way that made me think perhaps she knew her. Then she held up her finger, got up and went to scrabble behind the counter, and came back clutching a handful of hairgrips. Then in one swift motion, she scooped my hair back off my face and with a single twist had pulled it back into a 1940s style, which she told me was called the Victory Roll, popular during that decade to celebrate the Allies' victory in the Second World War. Then she stood back and nodded approvingly. 'Now Joel will see more of your pretty face.' Then she kissed me on each cheek and sent me off. But not before promising to come for a drink on Thursday night.

I've decided that instead of having a 'Promotion party', like Sam originally suggested, I'm going to invite my favourite people at Hardy's to a little gathering and introduce them to one another. It seems crazy that Lily has never met Sam and that Sam doesn't know Felix – they're all such a big part of the store and yet, like me, they work in 'invisible' jobs. All the shop-floor staff go for drinks together, so why shouldn't we? I know they'll all get on really well. I haven't told Sam yet, but I reckon he'll think it's a great idea. And Lily seemed uncharacteristically speechless, and a bit teary, actually, when I asked her. Then she'd clapped her hands and said she couldn't wait to 'step out' with me and my chums.

I tentatively put my hand up to my hair and pat it, feeling my fingers bounce off the smooth roll. I feel taller suddenly, more confident. According to Lily all I need now is a dash of red lipstick and I'll be ready to wow on my date. I didn't tell her that I planned to use my usual lip balm instead. I don't want to look like I've gone in fancy dress. Thankfully everything I'm wearing is so classic and stylish even now that I don't look like some 1940s throwback. But the stockings and red lipstick Lily expects me to wear would definitely tip me over the edge.

I wander back to the stockroom through Menswear, which is quieter than it was on Saturday, but still far busier than it has been for months. Today Guy is sporting a flat cap and classic Pringle jumper with a pink shirt and tie and straight black slacks. He looks very cool. He doesn't see me as I walk through his department. He's standing with his hand cupping his chin, head tilted to one side, studying the mannequin he is in the middle of dressing. He looks . . . happy. I feel a swell of pride that I have helped him in some small way. I'm still watching him when his mobile phone rings and he answers chirpily.

'Hellooo . . . Oh. Hello, Paul.'

I freeze. It's Guy's ex, the one who dumped him so cruelly the day they were meant to complete on their dream flat in Soho, leaving Guy homeless and hopeless.

'I'm faboosh, thanks, sweetie,' Guy says in a singsong voice. 'You? . . . Sorry, what? I wasn't listening . . . Oh, that's nice . . . Hang on, sorry, can I put you on hold a sec?'

He pulls the phone away from his ear, pops it down on the floor and continues dressing the mannequin for five minutes. I watch, totally entranced by this new Guy. Seeing him now, being so cool with the man who had broken his heart – and, worse, his spirit – is incredible. It's amazing what a self-esteem boost can do for a guy. Especially this particular Guy.

And this girl, I think, looking down at my outfit and thinking of Joel.

Just then, Guy picks up his phone again. This is better than any movie.

'Sorry about that,' he says flippantly. 'Now, what were you saying? Tonight? Oh, sorry, Paul darling, no I'm not free.' He pauses for just the right amount of time. 'I've got a date. It's with this real cutie who came in the shop over the weekend . . . What?' His expression hardens. 'Yes he is under seventy,' he snaps. 'I'll have you know Hardy's is having a turnaround.' Another pause. 'Well, you'd better believe it. Things are changing round here, and I like it. After all, a change is as good as a rest. Isn't that what you told me? Now, sorry but I have to go. Customers to serve. Ta-ra!' He stabs the Call End button and then claps his hands and squeals, 'Ohhh, that felt gooood!'

I give him a round of applause and he turns in surprise and then bows, sweeping an arm across the floor and up in a *port de bras* that Lily would be proud of. He whistles as he slowly walks over

261

to me. 'Woohooo, honey, you look hot! Who's the lucky fella?'

I shrug, embarrassed suddenly.

'Well, just you remember what someone once told me: that you're truly special and you deserve to be loved. You just need the courage and the heart and brains to find the right person.' He pauses and shakes his head. 'Can't remember who told me that, but it really helped me.' He snaps his fingers suddenly. 'It must've been Judy.' He clips his heels, makes a sign of the cross and looks heavenward. I clearly look confused as he sees fit to elaborate. 'Garland, sweetie. Keep up!' He snaps his fingers. 'The Wizard of Oz! Courage! Brain! Heart! Yes, it was definitely Judy.' Then he shakes his head ruefully at me as if he can't believe I didn't know he was talking about the great woman herself.

I don't have the heart to tell him it was actually *me* who gave him that advice during one of our many stockroom heart-to-hearts. But it doesn't matter that he doesn't remember. What's important is that my advice helped.

By the time I reach the stockroom I am ready to flop. My red stacked heels with little patent bows over the toes are killing me, and the last thing I feel like doing is running round the aisles collecting items for various departments. Judging from the ticket-roll that is spurting endlessly out of the printer, it is clearly proving to be another

262

busy day for the store. Curiously, I haven't had one single order from Designers. It is much more of a niche department, though, I rationalize.

Just then the stockroom door opens and a despondent-looking Carly comes in. Her sleek ponytail has sagged, her tight, white dress is ruched in all the wrong places and she immediately kicks off her heels and comes stomping into the stockroom.

'I need caffeine,' she growls, and then flops down onto the sofa and buries her head in her hands. This is most unlike Carly.

'Coming right up,' I say, and dash over to the kitchenette, glancing back over my shoulder as I pop the kettle on. Carly hasn't moved. Fleetingly, I notice her toenail polish is chipped. I look down at my own feet. I did my toenails last night especially for my date. They're painted ruby red. Lily would be proud of me. I wanted to make the effort even though my high-heeled pumps are not peep-toe.

'I am so over today,' Carly says through her hands.

'Why, what's happened?' I ask, intrigued.

'What's *not* happened, you mean.' She looks up and slumps back on the sofa, as if her body cannot support the weight of her head. Which to be honest, given her skinny frame, is highly likely. 'We haven't made one sale in Designers,' she says tearfully. 'Elaine says it's a total disaster. And Rupert and Sharon are probably saying the same.'

Her bottom lip quivers. She swallows and sticks her chin out defiantly. 'Not that I care what they think anyway.'

I sit down next to her, adopting my usual sympathetic expression. 'It's probably because none of the customers knew about the makeover. It's not like you're on the ground floor, like Beauty. Perhaps you should think about advertising the new look in the window tomorrow?' I add helpfully.

Carly looks at me, her green eyes sharpen for a second and then cloud. She shakes her head, her ponytail flopping lankly left and right, and frowns. 'Oh, we had customers all right. The bloody blue-rinse brigade. They walked in, around and then walked out again, swinging their granny handbags and muttering that it was "much better before" as they left.'

I raise my eyebrows sympathetically but inside I'm wondering if maybe I was right after all. Mrs Fawsley, Iris, Babs Buckley, Lady Fontescue – they don't want sculptured dresses by the hottest designers, they want wearable fashion that makes them feel comfortable but chic. Obviously we need to move on from their particular idea of style, which mostly seems to consist of flammable fabrics in pastels or in vomit-inducing patterns. But they just need to be educated gently; guided in a direction they don't even know they want to go in until they are there. Like Rupert's sheep back on his farm. Poor Carly, I think as I look at her now, sitting so dejectedly. It doesn't feel good to be right. I feel like I should help her. But I don't think she'd accept my help. Although there's no reason not to try.

'I think I know what the problem is,' I muse thoughtfully.

'You do?' She looks at me and smirks a little as she takes a sip of tea. 'Go on . . .'

'It's not that your idea isn't good, it's just not right for Hardy's current clientele,' I say breathlessly.

Carly rests her face on her hand and ponders this for a moment. 'I can accept that,' she says at last.

'And the truth is,' I continue, 'you're catering for a type of customer we haven't got yet . . .'

'Unfortunately,' Carly adds bitterly.

'What you need to do is straddle the old and the new. Bring in lines that our old customers will be drawn to, whilst incorporating stock that will appeal to people who have never shopped at Hardy's before . . .'

'Young, fashionable, cool people, you mean,' she laughs. 'You know what, Sarah?' she says, sitting forward on the sofa and thrusting her empty mug into my hand. 'I think you're right! It's not my fault the makeover hasn't worked. It's the customers!'

'Well, I didn't actually say that . . .' I protest, but she doesn't seem to hear me.

Instead she stands up until she is towering over

me. I can see straight up her nostrils, which are flared with excitement.

'So what I need to do is stop worrying about the fusty old fuddy-duddies who've shopped here for years. I don't care what they think anyway. Frankly, if they'd liked my shop floor I'd have been *offended*. No,' she nibbles on a fingernail and then looks into the distance as if realizing something for the first time, 'it's not *me* who has to change, it's *them*. And that's *exactly* what I'll tell Rupert. I'm a genius!' She smiles beatifically at me. 'No wonder they gave me this promotion. What would they do without me, hey?' And she bends down, squeezes me on the shoulder so that it burns a little, and then swans out the room. 'Thanks for listening, Sarah!' she calls back, as an afterthought.

As the door swings shut I flop back on the sofa and close my eyes. I've just made things worse. I turn my head, glance at my watch and suddenly I feel better. At least there are only a couple more hours till I see Joel. Then I can forget all about this mess.

Kind of.

CHAPTER 20

The evening darkness hugs the city like a blanket. I weave through the streets towards Charing Cross, where I'm due to meet Joel. I'm passing Hamleys and I pause to look at the cute carol-singing teddy bears that make up one of their windows when Sam comes out of the store.

'Evie!' he gasps in surprise and glances back at the store nervously. He looks really cute, all wrapped up in a big brown duffel coat and the faux-fur deerstalker hat I gave him when he came in yesterday. He's grown some stubble and looks like a big cuddly bear. I want to put him in Hamleys' window so everyone can walk past and admire his cuteness too.

'Sam!' I exclaim. 'What are you doing here? I didn't have you down as a Hamleys kind of guy.' He flushes and I wonder if I've hit a raw nerve. I nudge him playfully. 'Expanding your Star Wars figure collection, are you? Or no, hang on, are you more of a cuddly toy boy?'

He blushes and just at the moment a girl – the same girl I saw him with yesterday, I think – exits the store and stands by his side. She is pretty and a little older than he, I'd say, with short, pixie-cut hair and a harried, disgruntled expression. She looks at me, then at Sam, and hitches her handbag over her shoulder

'Ella, this is my *friend* Evie,' he says, emphasizing 'friend'. 'Evie, this is . . . Ella.' No emphatic use of 'friend' for her, I notice.

'Hi.' I smile warmly and hold out a gloved hand to Ella. She shakes it and looks away, distracted by something in the window, turning her back on us completely.

'We're just doing some Christmas shopping,' Sam says brightly, lifting up his bulging Hamleys bag.

'So I see! I haven't even started mine yet.' I pause and my eyes flicker to Ella, who still has her back to us. I wish she'd turn round so I can get another look at her. 'Well, brrr!' I say loudly, stamping my feet and clapping my hands like a kids' TV presenter demonstrating the cold. 'Can't stand here in the cold all night. I'd, er, best be off . . .' I flap my arms around my body and do a fake shiver, then point down the road in the direction I'm going, accidentally smacking a passer-by as I do. He tuts at me and I apologize profusely. Then I hurriedly turn, bumping into someone else, who staggers out of my way.

'Remind me to take you sale shopping with me,' Sam laughs. 'Those elbows of yours are lethal!'

I stop and step closer to the store window, afraid

of derailing any more shoppers. Ella's nowhere to be seen and has clearly been lured back into the store.

'You look great, going somewhere nice?' Sam smiles, looking at me strangely. I realize he has never seen me in anything other than my work clothes.

'I don't know, actually. It's a surprise.' He raises his eyebrows. 'It's a date,' I add bashfully. 'It's a long story. I'll tell you next time you come in.'

'Er, right. Well, I'll look forward to it,' Sam says, pulling his hat down over his ears and turning to look for Ella, clearly distracted by her absence.

I use this as my exit opportunity, hurrying off before I have to say goodbye to them both, slightly displaced by the strange sensation I felt at seeing them together.

I continue quickly down to Piccadilly Circus, propelled by my urge to see Joel, and am body-slammed by a riot of colour and noise. I'm pushed and shoved by the crowds who fill the streets and I jostle through determinedly. At Leicester Square there is more space but, unbelievably, even more people. The Christmas funfair is in full swing and I rush past, glancing back long enough over my shoulder to see the hundreds of happy faces illuminated by the neon lights.

I pull my coat around my body as I dash through the streets. It is a cold night; my breath frosts like cigarette smoke and I can't help but imagine myself as a young Lily in 1950s London, having

269

just finished a dancing shift at The Windmill and smoking a cigarette on her way to meet a suitor for late night drinks. It's not hard to imagine in my get-up. I've also pinned a cute cream beret to the back of my head, being especially careful not to muss up Lily's Victory Roll as I put it on. I'm so ensconced in my fantasy of 1950s London that I realize only just in time that I'm walking past the enormous Christmas tree in Trafalgar Square. The impressive twenty-metre-high Norwegian spruce stands proudly alongside Nelson's Column, framed by gushing fountains and back-lit by the warm apricot glow from the lights of the National Gallery. It looks wonderful and I can't help but stop to stare at it for a moment, my hands clasped together as I allow the scent of fresh pine needles to tickle my nose and my imagination.

Joel is waiting in front of Charing Cross station as I dash up breathlessly. He is the most casual I've ever seen him, in a thick, dark grey roll-neck that cups his chin, creating a creosote shadow across his jaw. He's also wearing jeans that are slightly too pale to be trendy, but I'll let him off. American men are famously good at wearing bad jeans. You only have to look at Tom Cruise or George Clooney to realize that. Besides, I'm not one to talk. I'm not exactly a fashion expert. Although, I guess in my current role as a 'personal shopper' that's exactly what I'm supposed to be.

'Woah.' He smiles as he takes me in appreciatively, his eyes waltzing across my body like it's a
dancefloor, before forming happy crescents as they
gaze into mine. Then he kisses me gently on the
lips. I try not to blush as I apologize for being
late.

'It's a girl's prerogative, isn't it?' he teases, and
slides his arm around my back. I inhale sharply
at his touch. It sends waves of pleasure coursing
through me so that between the warmth of him
and the chill of the December air, it feels like I'm
being electrocuted.

We begin to walk side by side. I can feel his
hand brushing accidentally against mine, as if it's
magnetically drawn to me.

Breathe, for God's sake, Evie, breathe.

'So, how was the baby-sitting?' Joel asks chat-
tily as he leads me gently down the Strand. His
hand is now resting against the curve of my back.
I try to focus and start telling him about Raffy
and Lola, only just remembering in time that
they're meant to be 'friends' children', not my
niece and nephew. He laughs in all the right places
when I tell him stories about them and even makes
endearing 'Awww' noises when I describe Lola.
He tells me he'd love to have a daughter one day.

Is he for real? A successful, sexy, interesting man
who calls when he says he will and *loves kids.*

He's now busy telling me about how much he
loves Christmas and how his family celebrate it
back home in Pennsylvania, and I'm lost in his

271

description of a traditional American Christmas. It's all eggnogg, candy canes, and cranberries and popcorn strung round the tree. I'm overwhelmed by a feeling of wanting to be there with him for the holidays.

Obviously I'm not going to admit that. I mean, I'm not a *complete* idiot. His eyes glisten fondly as he talks about his mum, dad and brothers back home, and suddenly it feels that the Strand may as well be Siberia; it's like there's no one here but us.

'You miss them, don't you?' I say.

He nods. 'We're really close. It's hard being away at this time of year. It's the first time I've ever missed Thanksgiving.'

Without thinking I envelop him in a hug. He smells musky, like cloves and spices. My head rests on his chest and I squeeze him, then release.

He looks surprised and embarrassed by my show of affection and I wonder if I've done the wrong thing.

'I feel like I'm always telling you things I shouldn't,' he says. 'It's just . . . you're such a good listener, Carly.' He smiles at me meaningfully, his eyes dark pools of intensity. 'Right,' he brightens visibly as he glances behind me and then turns me around, 'enough of me being all sentimental. Let's have us a good time!' He points at the beautiful big building we're standing in front of and gestures with his arm. 'Your Winter Wonderland awaits, ma'am,' he says with a lopsided smile as I slowly turn round.

'Come on, Carly!' he laughs. 'You trust me, don't you?'

I glance up from the handrail and look into his azure-blue eyes and shiver as I realize that, actually, I do. He nods encouragingly and I tentatively put one foot in front of the other away from the rail until I am safely in his arms.

He holds me tightly and then he murmurs, 'So, are you ready to be swept off your feet?'

Yes, I think, *I really am.*

An hour later, giggling with exhaustion and delight, feet throbbing from being on ice skates, we collapse onto the benches and put our shoes back on.

'That was brilliant!' I gasp. 'You didn't tell me how good you are at that!'

'A gentleman never boasts about his talents,' Joel laughs as he leans forward and slips his feet into his trainers, then sits back up. 'I used to play ice hockey back in Pennsylvania. It's practically a national sport.'

'Well, you're a brilliant teacher. I never thought I'd be able to stand upright, let alone go backwards! And that bit where everyone stopped and watched us as we sped around the ice was AMAZING! I felt like Cinderella!'

'Not Jane Torvill?' Joel says teasingly.

'No, not quite . . . Hey!' I pause from doing up the buckle on my shoes. 'How do you know her first name?' I prod him in the stomach. 'You said you'd never heard of Torvill and Dean.'

275

He holds his hands up. 'Oops. Busted. Sure I know who they are. I just wanted to hear you sing the Bolero for me.' He winks cheekily at me.

'I can't believe you did that!' I gasp. 'That was so mean!' I pummel my hands against his chest.

He grabs my wrists with one big capable hand and pulls me towards him and we gaze at each other, our lips hovering inches apart. 'Shall we get out of here?' he whispers, and I nod silently. 'To my hotel?' he asks, his eyebrows lifting hopefully, and I feel a shiver of longing shoot through my body. I nod, mentally making a note to ring Delilah to let her know I won't be home tonight. Then he takes me silently by my hand.

It is credit to his kissing skills that I barely notice Joel's suite at Claridge's as we tumble through the door and onto the bed, kissing each other until my lips feel numb. His hands slide down my body, over my waist and hips, lightly squeezing my bum, his fingers brushing up my spine until they reach the zip on my dress. I am excited and terrified all at once, but mainly I'm thanking God that I had the foresight to put on the only good underwear I own. It's a pretty black satin all-in-one with a balconette bra that simultaneously holds up my boobs and holds in my stomach. I bought it in Paris the weekend that Jamie dumped me. I've never had the opportunity to wear it and even though it's giving me a little bit of extra confidence I'm still petrified at the thought of unveiling my body. It has been a long, long time. Too long, I realize now as Joel's lips brush my neck gently. I have been living like some kind of spinster for the past two years.

Joel lifts me up so I am straddling his lap, and he kisses my neck. I hold my breath as he stands, lifting us both off the bed and pulls me up to a standing position so I'm leaning right against his body. He moves his hands across my shoulders and cups my face as he kisses me along my jaw and round the back of my neck until he is standing behind me. I can feel the length of his body pressed against mine and I throw my head back so it is resting on the nape of his neck. I gasp as his tongue flickers like hot, hungry flames caressing my ears and throat. He murmurs my name as he unzips my red dress and slowly slides it down my body, kissing my skin as it is exposed, before letting the dress drop to the floor. I step out of it and close my eyes as he turns me round to face him, trying to make myself invisible as he takes in my semi-naked body.

'You're delectable,' he murmurs. 'How on earth did I find you?' I smile and step towards him, tugging at his jumper as he lifts up his arms and I pull it over his body. His torso is smooth, tanned and ripped. He has pecs and a six pack. I have never seen a body like this. I actually don't believe they make men's bodies like this in England. At least, none that I've seen. I am trying my best not to gawp like some sort of desperate virgin. Which to be honest, I almost am.

Concentrate, Evie, I scold myself as I remember where I am and what I'm doing. *You have a semi-naked man standing in front of you. Do something sexy to him, for God's sake.*

Joel smiles at me expectantly and I take a tentative step closer so our bodies are touching again. I slide my arms around his neck and kiss him deeply, my tongue searching for his urgently, as I try to think about what to do next. I thread my fingers through his hair and tug it a little. *Is that sexy?* I open my eyes and try to look for clues from Joel. But his eyes are still shut. I can feel his erection pressing against my body and figure it must be time to take his trousers off. I tug at his belt clumsily and my hand accidentally brushes against his groin, which apparently comes across as lusty eagerness.

'Oh, Carly, Carly,' he groans into my ear, which sends shivers racing down my body. 'I want you so bad.'

I don't reply; I can't. I'm trying to push away the unwelcome mental image of Carly and work out what the hell she would do now. She must be much more practised at all this than I am. Would she talk dirty? I can't do that, I just can't. I'll feel like an idiot. I kiss him again to buy myself more time, then in a flash of instinct I undo his belt, pull his trousers down and drop to my knees, trying not to gasp at the sight of his muscular thighs and bulging groin clad in tight, white pants. I pull them down gently and take a deep breath. Surely *this* is one thing a girl never forgets?

Apparently not, is the answer, as Joel groans and gasps and cries out with pleasure. Just as I think he can't take any more, he pulls me up to me feet, lifts me clean off the floor and lays me gently on the bed. Then he lies beside me, tilting his body so he is propped up on one arm. His bicep bulges magnificently in my peripheral vision. I can't see his other arm – or hand – and I gasp as I suddenly realize why. It has snaked its way between my legs. He kisses me all over as his fingers work their magic and I cry out with pleasure. He pauses, looks down at me for a moment and smiles as he slides the straps of my underwear over my shoulders, deftly unhooks it as I arch my back, then peels the satin down my body, over my thighs, my calves, my painted toes and throws it across the room. I stretch my arms above my head, which simultaneously lifts my breasts and holds in my stomach. Then I watch in awe as he lowers his body on to mine and we become one.

This is it. At last.

And Oh. My. God. I've forgotten how good it feels.

WEDNESDAY 7 DECEMBER

18 Shopping Days Until Christmas

CHAPTER 21

The pale peach morning sunlight streams through the windows as the blinds are slowly opened and I blink blearily, rub my eyes and stretch, luxuriating in the feeling of the wonderfully thick, warm duvet weighing down on my body.

'Hey there, sleepyhead,' Joel murmurs as he walks over to the bed, casting a shadow over me and momentarily blocking the light so that he is back-lit by the morning sun, creating what looks like a yellow aura around his entire body. He looks angelic, Godlike, even. He lowers his face and kisses me softly on my lips. He is already dressed, I notice. Then he walks to the end of the bed where he picks up a tray that has on it a pot of coffee, fresh juice, fruit, pastries, toast and a silver platter. He lifts the platter up to reveal a delicately arranged English breakfast.

'I didn't know what you wanted to eat, so I ordered you everything,' he smiles.

I sit up in bed as he places it on my lap.

'To be honest,' I say huskily, my voice still thick with sleep and lust, 'I'd have ordered the same as last night.' I restrain myself from putting my hand over my mouth with shock at what just came out of it. Who took my personality and replaced it with a rampant sex goddess's? Is this the sort of thing Carly says to her lovers? Am I literally channelling her now? I can't help but be impressed with myself.

Joel laughs as he sits on the edge of the bed. He goes to kiss me but I hurriedly thrust a croissant into his mouth, aware that he has cleaned his teeth and I haven't. He takes a bite and then sighs as he munches on it.

'There is nothing I'd like more than to stay in bed with you all morning, but I've got an important meeting I just can't get out of. You look beautiful when you sleep,' he adds gallantly.

'Psssh,' I splutter in embarrassment, my mouth full of croissant. He kisses me and I focus on keeping my mouth firmly shut.

He shakes his head woefully and strokes my face. 'I have to go now, but you stay as long as you like and enjoy this wonderful room.' He stands up and I suddenly remember that I have a job, too.

'Er, what time is it?' I ask.

'Seven thirty,' he replies. 'Plenty of time for you to get to work by nine.'

I try not to let the panic show on my face as I nod and reply in a strangulated voice. Joel has no idea that in my real job as stockroom slave I'm meant to be at work by seven. Which means, in the words of the White Rabbit, I'm late I'm late

I'm really really late. And not only that, I've just remembered I never did get round to ringing Delilah last night. Let's just say I got . . . distracted. I feel a wave of shame as I reach for my phone and see there are three missed calls from her. Shit. I'm in big trouble.

Once Joel has gone – and I never thought I'd be pleased to see him leave – I scramble out of the gigantic bed and dart around the room, picking up garments that are scattered all over the place and hastily get dressed, cursing as I realize I'll have to do the walk of shame in the same clothes into work. I can only hope that Sharon hasn't been into the stockroom yet and so won't notice just how terribly late I am. It's the first time I've ever been late, so if she has noticed I pray she'll accept my apology and be lenient with me. I'll tell her the truth: that I slept in. Which I did; I just won't add that it was with a super-hot man.

I brush my hair furiously, then pin it up to disguise that it hasn't been washed, before grabbing Lily's handbag from where I dropped it last night and open the door. I turn back and look at the suite, overwhelmed with regret that I can't enjoy this incredible hotel room longer. Although one might argue, I enjoyed it more than I thought was physically possible last night.

I hop into the lift, nodding at the attendant as I smooth down my slightly crumpled dress and try to look like I should be there as other hotel guests get in. Again I feel grateful to Lily for her loan of the Chanel handbag. It has given me much-needed Claridge's class. The lift doors open at the ground floor and I try to step gracefully out, channelling my inner Audrey, but I freeze in front of the lift when I realize that there are several members of staff gathered in the lobby, including the doorman I saw last night and from when Joel and I came to tea. He's going to think I've become a permanent fixture.

Someone tuts and stumbles into me, and I turn round and see I've caused a domino-style traffic jam of posh people trying to exit the lift. The doorman looks over at the commotion and I hop behind the enormous John Galliano-designed art deco 'Under the Sea'-inspired Christmas tree and peer out from around its sparkling leaves and pink coral. It seems an interminably long way across the grand foyer to the bronze and gilt revolving doors, and I don't want anyone to know I'm doing the walk of shame so I wait for my moment, then make a dash for it, walking quickly with my head lowered and my designer bag clutched protectively in front of me. All I can see is the blur of gleaming black and white chequered tiles as I make my speedy dash towards the doors, too afraid to look up in case the doorman spots me. I sigh with relief as I step inside the revolving doors but to my confusion I forget to look up, somehow miss the exit and end up spat back out in the foyer with the doors swishing smugly behind me.

'It's Mr Parker's . . . friend, isn't it? Miss Taylor,

I believe?' says the doorman, who is now standing in front of me and looking very serious.

I nod, trying to hide the embarrassed flush that I know is climbing up my neck towards my cheeks. I feel like I've been stripped naked and exposed. Oh God, he's going to say something.

'Please, allow me,' he says briskly, then steps inside the door and holds his arm out.

Worse, he's *actually* going to throw me out onto the street. He probably thinks I'm a lady of the night or something. I look at him desperately but to my surprise he winks at me and proffers his arm. I thread my arm uncertainly through his and he says loudly, 'It's been a pleasure to have such an esteemed guest here, Miss Taylor. Do come again soon.' Some of the guests in the lobby look over and start whispering to each other, clearly trying to work out who I am. I widen my eyes at him and the doorman squeezes my arm.

I clear my throat. 'Well, you know Claridge's is always my favourite hotel when staying in London,' I reply, trying not to laugh and feeling like a princess as we begin to walk through the revolving doors. I get a little bit carried away and find myself waving regally at the crowd of guests now gathered in reception and I feel the doorman's body shake as he chuckles.

Once out on the street, he gracefully untwines his arm and tips his gold-brocade-trimmed hat at me.

'Thanks for that . . . James,' I say, looking at his

name badge and then smiling broadly at him. 'You saved me from certain humiliation.' I pause. 'Well, for today, at least.'

He laughs and lifts his hand to his head in a mock salute. 'Please call me Jim, ma'am. I hope to see you here again soon.'

'Thanks, Jim!' I say. I shake his hand enthusiastically, then I hitch my beautiful, classic vintage handbag over my shoulder from where it has slid down my arm, and walk proudly and gracefully down the street.

Once I'm out of sight, I forget all about my inner Audrey, throw any grace, calm or refinement to the wind, and, staggering clumsily in my heels, wave frantically at any taxi that passes, whether the For Hire lights are on or off. Finally, a cab pulls over and I hop in and slam the door.

'Hardy's, please – as fast as you can,' I say breathlessly, feeling a little thrill as I do so. I've always wanted to say that.

I sit back in my seat and gaze out of the window. The city is already bustling with cars and people, and our progress is slower than ideal. I pull out my phone, scroll to my sister's name and press the Call button. Delilah answers just as we pull up in front of Hardy's. I scramble around in my handbag for money and thrust it at the driver, including a generous tip. He deserves it for getting me here relatively quickly, despite the morning traffic. He beams at me as I slam the cab door behind me and wave at him.

'Evie?' Delilah barks. 'Where the hell are you?'

'Er, at work,' I pant as I head towards the staff entrance.

'I know THAT,' she says pointedly. 'I mean, where the hell were you last night? I was worried sick. You didn't come home, you didn't call and, most importantly, you weren't here this morning to get the kids ready for nursery.' Her voice becomes muffled and I hear her shout, despite her hand being over her phone, 'STOP THAT, LOLA!'

I hover by the staff entrance, waiting for my clearly irate sister to come back on the line and shout at me some more. I feel terrible and I know I thoroughly deserve it, but I can't help wishing she'd stop shouting long enough for me to tell her the amazing thing that happened to me last night. Twice.

'Well?' she says eventually, her voice fizzing with fury.

'Oh, Delilah, I'm so sorry. I meant to call you but I was out with Joel and we had such an amazing time, and then, well, then he invited me back to his hotel.' I lower my voice to whisper. 'He has a suite at Claridge's,' I say wondrously, knowing she'll appreciate that detail. I remember how she used to give me minute-by-minute accounts of her dates with Will. I'd listen rapturously as she divulged the glamorous places they went to, the wonderful things he said, and the incredible nights they had. I know she'll want

289

the same from me so I am expecting an excited reaction but there is only silence.

My voice falters a little. 'Anyway, you know, one thing led to another and I just totally forgot to ring you. Please don't be angry at me. I've had such an amazing time and I truly meant to ring you. I did.'

'Well, it's not good enough, Evie,' she says prissily, though her annoyance is definitely dissipating. She has a short fuse, but she never stays angry for long. I'm just not used to her wrath being directed at me. 'Besides,' she adds mellifluously, 'I was really worried about you, Evie.'

I feel a surge of guilt and so I apologize profusely again and beg her forgiveness until she relents.

An hour later I feel back to my jubilant self, especially as my lateness has apparently gone completely unnoticed by Sharon, or anyone else, for that matter. It seems that sometimes it pays to be invisible. Then the stockroom door creaks open and Jane from the lingerie department pops her head round. I pause from my job of sorting through a tangled pile of vintage diamante clasp earrings, brooches and necklaces, and look up.

'Hi, Sarah,' she says mournfully. 'Have you got time for a cup of tea?' She asks the question apologetically as if she's requesting something enormous of me. I have a lot of time for Jane. She has such a wonderful personality, she's warm and witty and has this incredibly infectious laugh.

She's larger than life, in more ways than one, with tumbling dark curls that coil down her back and this gorgeous, soft body that oozes womanhood. At least, she used to be. Recently she looks faded; less confident, more introverted.

'Come in, Jane! I've always got time for tea with you,' I say brightly as I put down the tangled necklaces and get up. 'I'm still recovering from the fact that somehow Sharon didn't notice I was over an hour late this morning. How lucky am I!'

'That is bloody lucky,' Jane says with a tight smile. 'That woman is like a meerkat: she sees everything. She's already been poking her nose around my department this morning, telling me that my displays "just aren't good enough" and "why haven't I had any customers yet, Gwen and Guy are both rushed off their feet blah blah blah . . ." I mean, it's not even eleven o'clock yet! You know,' she sighs, 'I can't help but think that if I don't do something with my department soon, I could be in trouble. But I'm used to measuring people's bust sizes, not doing big, fancy displays. Besides, there's only so much you can do with beige bras and bloomers.'

I laugh at this. It's true, the lingerie department in Hardy's is aimed at the over sixties only and is embarrassingly unsexy.

'So why were you late?' Jane asks me as she sits down, her generous body sinking gratefully into the soft sofa.

I feel myself blushing. Should I tell Jane about

Joel? It's so refreshing to be asked something about me for a change. I'm trying to work out how to say, 'I was still in bed after a night of hot sex with my lover,' without completely oversharing, when Jane lets out a deep, long sigh as she peers into the kitchen where I am busy brewing our tea.

'You haven't got any cakes, have you?' she asks hopefully. 'I need something to cheer me up.'

I pull down a pack of Chelsea buns from a shelf.

Jane's eyes brighten and then she shakes her head. 'Oh, I shouldn't. I'm trying to lose weight,' she says, looking regretfully down at her body.

A generous size eighteen, Jane has been battling with her weight for as long as I've known her but she never used to be as unhappy with it as she is now. Admittedly, she has gone up a couple of dress sizes recently, but she has the sort of shape that carries it well. She's tall, with a big bust, a small waist and long legs. Unfortunately, Jane doesn't see any of that. She just sees the extra pounds on her scales. She also thinks it's the reason why her husband has lost interest in her sexually. They've been married for five years, but she's told me that in recent months their sex life has dwindled to practically nothing. I suspect this is what she's upset about today, too.

'I just don't know what to do any more, Sarah,' she sighs, clasping and unclasping her fingers. 'Stuart just isn't interested in me at all now.' She looks up at me tearfully as I hand her a cup of tea and sit down next to her. 'We used to be inseparable; holding hands, cuddling, kissing, and our sex life has always been great. I mean *really* great.'

I try not to blush or look away as I don't want to hurt her feelings. Why do people feel the urge to tell me this stuff? Have I got 'Overshare with me' written on my forehead or something? It's baffling. Particularly as it's not like I have a habit of going round telling everyone *my* deepest, darkest secrets. Probably because no one ever gives me the chance. But even so, I don't think I'm the type.

She exhales and looks down mournfully at her body, which seems to deflate like a balloon. 'But now it's like he just doesn't want me any more.' She shakes her head as her eyes fill with tears and her fingers grasp at each other. 'I think he's going to leave me,' she says, gasping with the shock of what she's admitted to me. Her beautiful alabaster skin goes blotchy and she dabs at her eyes with a wet, crumpled tissue that she pulls out of her shirt breast pocket and that has obviously seen a lot of tears recently. I lean over to the coffee table and take a fresh tissue from a box that I always keep for situations just like this.

'What's given you that idea?' I say gently. 'Stuart always seems besotted by you.' Jane's husband comes into Hardy's quite regularly as he works round the corner as a duty manager of a hotel. He's a small, unassuming man with dark gingernut hair and freckles like cinnamon sprinkles all over his face. I have never thought him the type of man who would be bothered by his wife's weight. He seems sensitive and sweet and thoughtful. Not to mention utterly devoted to Jane. You can just see it by the way he looks at her.

'He *used* to be,' she sighs, 'but now when we go to bed he just cuddles me, turns over and goes straight to sleep. It's like he can't even bear to look at me. I even turn the lights off now before I climb in so he doesn't have to see me without my clothes on. I know I'm disgusting,' she says quietly, 'so I can only imagine what he's thinking. Perhaps I should tell him to find someone else. He's so wonderful he deserves a beautiful wife who can fit into a pair of jeans . . .'

I put my hand over Jane's as she starts sobbing. 'Do you really, honestly believe that's what he thinks?' I say, brushing her hair off her face.

She nods and gulps as she blows her nose. 'I wanted us to start trying for a baby this year,' she gasps, in between her tears. 'We talked about it months ago but since then, nothing. It'd have to be the immaculate conception, at this rate. I know it's because he doesn't want me to get pregnant as then he'll be stuck with me.' She is sobbing hopelessly now. Tears and snot are streaming down her head as she buries her face in my shoulder.

I stroke her head, trying to work out what to say. None of this sounds like the Stuart that I've seen. I can't help but wonder if it's Jane's lack of confidence and her paranoia about her body that are creating these problems between them, and not, as she imagines, her body itself.

'Tell me something,' I say quietly, cringing a little inside at my next question. 'I know this is really personal, but what happened last time you had sex?'

She clasps her tissue in her fist and holds it over her mouth. 'It was four, maybe five months ago?' she says meekly. 'We'd been out for dinner and I was feeling gross because even though I'd told myself I wouldn't, I'd had this huge piece of cheesecake for dessert. We got home and Stuart began kissing me in the hall. He'd had some wine, we both had, but he can't handle his drink as well as I can, probably because he's so much lighter. Anyway, he flicked the hall lights on and he started getting . . . well . . . a bit heated.'

She is blushing and I am trying not to. Aside from last night I'm not exactly a sex expert myself so am not entirely sure if I'm going down the right avenue here. But I have a hunch and I'm going to follow it through. I nod and she takes a deep breath to continue.

'I leaned across to the wall and flicked the lights off and started to go upstairs. Stuart followed me. I was wearing this dress that unzipped at the back and he undid it as I walked up the stairs. I was wearing my Spanx underneath and I didn't want him to see I was wearing them so as soon as I got into our bedroom I made excuses and went into our ensuite. By the time I came out twenty minutes later in my nightie and dressing gown, he was fast asleep. He just didn't want me . . .' She shakes her head again.

I grasp her hands as she begins to sob, amazed at how someone can get something so wrong. 'Can't you see, it's not that he didn't want you, he thought you didn't want *him*! He wouldn't care about you wearing support pants; he's your husband and from what I can see he's utterly infatuated by you. He just wants you to be confident, and feel sexy and loved and relaxed in your own skin, but as far as he's concerned you won't even stand in front of him in your underwear!'

Jane looks at me doubtfully, then down at her body. 'But I've changed so much recently. I've gone up two dress sizes. I mean, he has always said he loved my curves but how could he be attracted to this?' She pulls at the soft mounds of skin under her baggy shirt and even baggier trousers.

'Er, because he loves you, silly?' I laugh and punch her playfully on the arm. 'And because when he married you the most important thing was that it wasn't just him who loved your body, you did too. You know, I remember when I first met you I was blown away by how gorgeous you are.' Jane turns away and shakes her head in disbelief. 'It's true! I'm no stick-thin model myself, you know,' I say. 'I've battled with wanting to be smaller, then I start working here and see you with

296

your long, gorgeous curls and your Rubenesque body, like some glorious Sophie Dahl-alike in that perfume ad that got banned for being too erotic and I thought, if only I looked like her.'

'Really?' Jane says quietly, her startling violet eyes growing glassy with tears.

'Yep,' I smile. 'You just had this air of being completely at ease in your skin. The clothes you wore were all gorgeous jewel colours and it was like you just glittered, you know?'

'I used to feel good about myself,' Jane says, as if remembering the girl she once was. 'I was so proud of the fact that I wasn't a skinny size ten.'

'So what's changed?' I ask her, knowing that there must have been someone, or something, that did this to her.

Her eyes dim for a moment as she searches for the answer. 'Well, I guess it started when I went to my school reunion last summer,' she says slowly. 'Someone organized it on Facebook. I hadn't seen any of these people since I was seventeen and was really excited about going. But when I was there it was like my weight was the only thing they could see. Not my marriage to Stuart, or how much I loved my job, or what I was doing. Suddenly, compared to all my ex-classmates, I felt like a failure. The next day I decided to go on a diet, start working out, do everything to be like the girls from my year group who seemed so superior to me because they could all fit into skinny jeans. Obviously it didn't work,' she says, looking ruefully at me, then at the Chelsea buns. 'Can we crack those babies open now?' she pleads. 'They've been taunting me for the past ten minutes.'

I grab the packet and we sit and munch in silence together for a few minutes.

'It's ironic really,' I say thoughtfully as I swallow my final mouthful. 'You work in an underwear department but you're not confident enough to stand in front of your husband in yours.'

Jane smiles sadly. 'Well, it's not like my lingerie department is exactly inspiring. It's all body stockings and nylon nighties. My last customer was eighty-eight years old. I've been buying my underwear at Hardy's with my staff discount ever since I started working here. I don't think I own anything that isn't beige and big enough that I could set up a camp with it.' She smiles and in the twitch at the corner of her lips I can see a glimmer of the old Jane.

'I've got it!' I snap my fingers and dive into the fourth aisle, the one where I've put all the beautiful 1950s basques and suspender belts, still in their packaging.

I pop my head back round and see Jane reaching for another Chelsea bun. She looks up and she sees the beautiful, unworn vintage underwear I'm dangling from my fingers.

'Wow!' she breathes, then says ruefully, 'That'll never fit me.'

'Trust me, Jane, these were made for you,' I say. I hand her a basque, the stockings and a suspender belt. Then, as another thought occurs to me, I snap my fingers again and dive off into another aisle. 'I've got just the thing that'll give you your va-va-voom back,' I call as I delve through shelves and finally pull out what I'm looking for. I scamper over to Jane and thrust it into her arms on top of everything else. 'Go and get changed into these,' I say bossily as she looks doubtfully at her armful of goods. '*Trust me!*' I laugh.

She shrugs and stands up, shaking her head as she disappears behind some shelves. I sit drumming my fingers impatiently against the arm of the sofa as I wait to see Jane in her new incarnation.

I can barely believe my eyes when she steps out from behind the shelves and stands before me.

'B-lood-y HELL!' I gasp.

Gone is the overweight and unconfident girl and in her place stands a statuesque woman with a perfect hour-glass figure, her incredible curves dripping out of her outfit. Which just goes to show what good, well-cut underclothes can do. As well as the 1950s underwear, which has pulled in Jane's small waist, supported her bust and given her such an incredible shape, I also gave her an old Hardy's staff uniform from a box I found when I first started here. It's a classic 1940s wartime-green skirt with a white, button-down, puff-sleeved, collared shirt, which shows off Jane's impressive bust perfectly, a wide black belt that pulls in her waist, and black stockings. The skirt hugs her hips tightly and finishes just below her knees, with a small slit up the back. She turns and tilts one leg behind her to show off the sexy seam running down the back of her stockings.

'You look AMAZING!' I tell her in awe.

She beams at me. 'Where did you find this stuff?' she marvels. 'It's like it was made for girls like me. I'm never going to try and squeeze into a pair of skinny jeans again. This is *way* more fabulous.' She puts her hands on her hips and turns her torso from side to side. 'I feel sexy!' she laughs. 'What have I been doing? Poor Stu must be wondering where the hell his wife has gone,' she says. 'He hasn't seen my body for months. Come to think of it, nor have I. Do you reckon I can buy these with my staff discount?'

I'm not sure, but I'm feeling reckless. Besides, Jane is suddenly a much better advert for her department than she was before. You can just tell she's wearing great underwear.

'Sure,' I smile. 'I may have to charge you in shillings and pence, though,' I laugh.

'And I adore this uniform,' she says, fingering the lapel and the little embroidered lapel badge, which has 'Hardy's' sewn in dark green italic letters on gold cotton. 'I'm going to wear it for the rest of the day. It's not like I'm going against store policy; it's all Hardy's stock!' She claps her hands. 'I can't wait for Stuart to see me in this. In fact, I'm going to call him and tell him to pop by in his lunch hour. He's not going to believe his eyes!' She grabs my hands and squeezes them before disappearing out the door.

Alone again, I go back over to the aisle that houses all our underwear stock. Ignoring the stuff that's already on display, I dig out the garments at the very back of the shelves. Now the lingerie manager is looking so hot, I think it's about time the entire department had a makeover.

THURSDAY 8 DECEMBER

17 Shopping Days Until Christmas

CHAPTER 22

I slip out of the house quietly and get swallowed up into the morning darkness once again. I'm anxious that the month is slipping past really quickly. Usually I'd be excited that each day that passes brings Christmas closer, but this year it brings closer Hardy's potential closure, too. There seems to be so much to do, but so little time.

I push off blearily on my bike, yawning. It's so early in the morning that there are no lights on yet in any of the big Regency houses that frame the square, and as I cycle on to Regent's Park Road, not a single car passes by. It seems that the whole city is shrouded in sleepy darkness. Since starting these makeovers I feel like I'm operating in a completely different time zone from anyone else. I'm out so early that no one in the house is awake. Luckily, my cooking dinner for Delilah last night placated her enough to allow me to leave early again this morning. She knows that the job is important to me but I can see she wonders why. I don't know how to explain how much I care about it. I might not have to take international

305

conference calls, or to juggle million-pound accounts, but it's my life. In recent weeks it's become not just a job, but a home too.

Things were awkward between Delilah and me at first. We circled each other silently round the kitchen as I made dinner. Will was apparently 'working late' again. But we didn't talk about it. To be honest, I didn't know what to say to her.

I pedal furiously down the road, grunting with the exertion as I head towards the park, still thinking about our relationship. I've always hung around my big sister like a little adoring puppy, ready to do her every bidding as soon as she asked. Maybe it's because there's such a big age gap between us that the power balance is off, or maybe it's because Delilah has always seemed so much more than anything I could ever be. We're so different, *I* can barely believe we were blood related most of the time and neither can a lot of other people.

Mum would always try to back me up when people compared us. 'Evie's the quiet, creative one,' she'd say, squeezing my shoulders and telling them in detail about my latest art project, or scrapbook I was working on. But I could see their eyes glazing over.

Felix is arching his back and stretching his arms when I walk through the staff entrance. It's just gone five o'clock again, but this time, he doesn't ask why I'm early.

'Evie!' he exclaims. He looks perky this morning,

which is lucky as it was too early to pick up his usual Americano. I've been worried about him recently; the long nights alone in this poky little office seem to be grinding him down. It's no place for a lonely widower in his sixties. Today he is sporting one of his many colourful bow ties. He says Maisie always used to say he looked very smart in them. He has different colours to reflect his moods, but for the past couple of weeks he hasn't been wearing one at all.

'So,' he says, clapping his hands, 'you looking forward to tonight?'

I feel a momentary flash of confusion, then panic. Shit. It's Thursday. The drinks I organized with Sam, and that I invited Lily and Felix to, are meant to be tonight. But Delilah is going to kill me if I'm not home to baby-sit later.

'Oh! Yes! Of course! Can't wait!' I say, smiling widely, nodding to disguise my forgetfulness. Felix beams at me and adjusts his tie. He's obviously looking forward to it and I can't let him down. Delilah will understand. So what if I've had a few nights out this week? I'm just making up for lost time, right? 'Right!' I say, my mind made up. Felix raises an eyebrow. 'Er, I mean, right, must get on. Things to do, stock to unpack. Er, see you later, though, Felix!'

And I dash off, trying to push down the feeling of discomfort that is trickling through me at the thought of letting Delilah down again. I pick up my phone, then, realizing it's too early to phone,

I send a quick text instead explaining the situation. She'll see it when she wakes up and I hope she'll be fine about me having the night off.

By the time I've got to Jane's department on the first floor and flicked on the lights I have completely forgotten about Delilah, Felix and anything other than the job in hand. And it is a pretty overwhelming task, that's for sure. In front of me the department spreads out like a sea of beige stretching towards an ecru horizon. The walls are decorated with a few ageing posters of middle-aged ladies smiling suggestively in soft focus whilst wearing what appears to be underwear as armour; everything starts at their neck and stops at their knees. On the walls rails of uninspiring, oversized slips, pants and bras hang limply, as if even they think they're not worth looking at. There is *some* colour in the department, just not any shade that would be considered remotely stylish or sexy. The half a dozen or so free-standing rails, which crowd the middle of the department, are full to bursting with an endless selection of flannel nightgowns in varying shades of soft pastel, and, for a real burst of the rainbow, there are also quilted dressing gowns in quite startlingly garish colours: Cookie Monster blue, Groucho green, Elmo red and Big Bird yellow. If I close my eyes I could be on Sesame Street, not just off Regent Street. I clearly have a lot of work to do.

I am mid-makeover, doing battle with some

basques and trying to simultaneously work out if my display of feathers and pearls is too much, when I hear noise down below. I go to peer over the rail of the staircase and see some of the cleaners gathered in the middle of the handbag department, clearly having some sort of meeting.

'Hiya!' I wave down at them and Justyna looks up and then scowls as Jan Baptysta shouts his greeting.

'Morning, Evie-English-Wife! You are early, *nie*? You vork too hard.'

'Ah, you know how it is, Jan,' I yell back. 'When you have The Lord carrying you, there is no such thing as hard work!'

His laugh at our shared joke reverberates around the store. 'You are so funnys! Isn't she funnys?'

Justyna glares at him, and then at me, her monobrow lowered dangerously over her dark eyes. Oh God, that's all I need. I dash down the stairs to them on the ground floor. For some reason their workforce is at least halved this morning; only Jan, Justyna and Velna are here.

'Where is everyone?' I say, slightly puzzled as I look at Jan's serious face. 'Surely they haven't all called in sick on the same day?'

Jan shakes his head glumly. 'This is vat we vere just havingk a meeting abouts. They have been laid.'

I try not to blush. I'm not sure if I'm comfortable with Jan divulging the intimate secrets of his staff quite so publicly. I mean, we're all friends here, but even so . . .

'Offsk.' Justyna tuts, lifting her beaky nose skyward with displeasure. 'He means laid offsk.'

Ahh. That makes more sense. 'You mean they've been sacked?' I ask. Looking at all their unhappy faces I can tell that's exactly what's happened. Even Velna, who is usually so perky, has clearly been badly affected by this news. Her little pink plaits have sagged and her earphones are hanging limply around her neck.

'It isk so sad for them,' she says, her eyes brimming with tears. 'They works so hard for so long, and now this!' Justyna pats her on the shoulder maternally and then folds her arms and glares at me as if it is my fault.

'What happened?' I ask.

Jan's pitbull features look weary as he tells me how half of his staff were laid off by the cleaning company, who received a call yesterday from Rupert, telling them he could no longer afford to pay so many cleaners. 'Then my boss called me and I had to decide who stayed and who . . .' Jan's voice breaks. 'It vos very hardsk. Everyone works hardsk. But I had to choose.' Justyna strokes his arm lovingly and the thick hair on his forearm bends under her touch like grass in the wind, or maybe it's more like tree branches.

'But that's terrible!' I say. 'So Rupert didn't even tell you himself?'

'We are not vorth his times,' Justyna says bitterly.

'We vork hard here for years to make the shop nice and it is like ve are vorth nothing! You people make me sick,' she spits.

'Justyna!' Jan scolds and then continues to speak to her but in Polish. She hangs her head, clearly ashamed at being reprimanded.

'My apologiesk,' she says gruffly.

I smile at her and shake my head. 'It's fine, you're angry. I would be too. Your colleagues deserved more than that and so do you. I know how hard you have to work, even with a full team. I see it, even if no one else does.' I glance at them all, at their downcast, despondent faces. 'Listen,' I say as a thought occurs to me. I kick myself for not thinking of it before. 'I've arranged to go for some drinks tonight with some people from the store . . .' Justyna looks ready to spit at me so I finish quickly, 'None of them works on the shop floor. There's Lily from the tearoom – she's just fabulous – then there's Felix who you probably know from Security,' Jan nods vigorously, 'and a friend of mine, a delivery guy called Sam. We're going to a pub tonight. Would you all like to come? It would be so nice for us all to have a chat out of work hours. And I think you'd really like everyone.'

Jan beams at me. 'Thanksk you, Evie-English-Wife, that would be very good. We shall all come, no?'

I swear I hear Justyna growl but just then Velna sings something unrecognisable, before spinning on one foot, doing a clap, then finishing with some jazz hands. We are all looking puzzled when she announces, 'It was the winning entry for my country, Latvia. In 2002? 'I Wanna' Yes?' Justyna rolls her eyes and turns on the industrial vacuum cleaner, and we all laugh as Velna proceeds to shout-sing the rest of the song as Justyna cleans around her.

The stockroom feels dark and lonely after the last couple of hours I spent busily transforming Jane's department whilst singing British Eurovision songs with Velna, whom Jan had assigned to clean my floor. And she was delighted that I knew so many. I'd even been able to teach her a pointy-hand dance move to Michael Ball's 1992 entry, 'One Step Out of Time', which I somehow knew all the words to. Unfortunately this meant I have spent the last half-hour listening to her singing it over and over again.

Luckily as soon as I flick the lights on there is a knock at the back door.

I fling open the door and Sam grins sleepily at me. He looks even more tousled and crumpled than ever this morning. He's wearing an old, navy duffel coat with the hood flung over his head. His eyes are red-rimmed with tiredness and he still has sleep creases on his freckled cheeks. He waves a bulging Starbucks bag at me and goes and collapses on the sofa.

'Blimey,' I say, feeling my throat tighten. He

must have had a late night. Probably with Ella. 'Someone has been burning the candle at both ends. Coffee?'

He nods at the bag. 'I brought us some gingerbread lattes, fruit toast and – just to get into the Christmas spirit – some mince pies,' he smiles. 'I thought we could have a breakfast picnic!' He lifts his rucksack onto his knee, opens it and pulls out a rug, which he lays on the floor. Then he gets out two plates, some cutlery, and lays out the food on the plates and places the takeaway coffee on the rug in front of the sofa. Out of the bag also comes some plastic cups and a bottle of fresh orange juice. Then he scrambles off the couch, sits cross-legged on the rug and beckons me to join him. He pours some juice and as he's looking down and concentrating I notice his eyelashes sweep heavily over the generous curve of his cheeks. He butters our toast, adds a thick layer of jam and then takes a long sip of coffee.

'Christ, I need caffeine this morning,' he groans, smiling at me as he stifles a yawn, but then gives into it completely, accompanying it with a full stretch with his arms flung up over his head, which reveals a tiny patch of a pale but surprisingly taut stomach, his belly button (an innie) and a little thatch of hair crisscrossing its way down past the brown buckle of his belt. He looks adorable, like a 5-year-old in adult's clothing.

'Why are you so tired?' I ask, kneeling down on the rug next to him.

He rubs his eyes, then looks at me. 'I've got a confession to make.'

'You're a male gigolo and have been working nights all week?' I say teasingly, taking a bite of fruit toast.

He laughs. 'Close.'

I choke a little on my mouthful. 'What? But I was kidding! Which bit? The gigolo?'

'No, you fool.' Sam taps me playfully on the arm. 'The working nights bit. You know how I've always wanted to be a photographer? I've started assisting this really cool guy who does editorial stuff. I've helped him on a couple of night shoots, which is fantastic. But it also means I've had no sleep.'

'That's fantastic, Sam!' I say putting down my toast and wrapping my arms around my body to warm it; it's a little draughty sitting on the stock-room floor. Sam leans over and pulls a corner of the rug over my legs and I smile in thanks. 'But you never said you were planning to do something like this?'

He shrugs bashfully and his thick-knit cream cardigan, which is zipped up to his neck, tickles the curly hair at his nape. 'I didn't think I was until I did it. I mean, I didn't expect anyone to give me a chance. I don't have any training. Just because I like messing around with a camera doesn't mean it's necessarily a realistic career aspiration.'

'So what changed your mind?'

314

'You did,' he smiles, rolling his red cup between his hands to warm them.

'What? How?'

'It was when you got that promotion . . .'

'Didn't get, you mean,' I interrupt.

Sam looks at me sympathetically. 'But when we thought you had, it made me realize that you're here because you're working towards something. You love this place and want to work in this industry, even if you don't want to be in the stockroom forever. This job might not be your dream, but at least you're on your way. Whereas I'm stuck doing deliveries at my dad's company because . . . well, let's just say you made me realize that it was about time I took control of my life. I may not get anywhere with this whole photography lark, but at least I'll have tried.'

'So how did you start working with this guy?' I ask, intrigued by Sam's secret career.

'After you told me you were leaving the other day, I wrote down the names of a load of photographers whose work I admire, googled them and phoned them up and asked if they would meet me. I caught this one guy on a good day; his assistant had just moved to New York and he said to come along and meet him. We got on well and he asked me to come to one of his shoots. I've been working with him for the past three nights and he's asked me to help out next week too. There's no money in it yet, so I'll have to keep doing

315

deliveries for a while. But I've learned so much already, it's amazing! I know for sure this is what I want to do and it's all thanks to you.'

Sam is sitting up now and his eyes are gleaming. I wish I could share his excitement. But I just feel even more of a loser. The promotion-I-never-got inspired Sam to change his life, when it was meant to change mine. How ironic.

'What's wrong?' he says, his face falling when he notices my glum expression. 'Aren't you pleased for me?'

'Of COURSE I am,' I say, chastising myself mentally for letting my emotions show and being so selfish. 'I think what you've done is brilliant. I just can't help feeling sad that one day soon there'll be someone new delivering Hardy's stock, and I'll still be here, unpacking boxes . . .'

'Oh, come on,' he says, throwing an arm around me and giving me a squeeze. 'That's just not true! Someone soon is going to see how talented you are. You're wasted in this stockroom. I've seen your drawings, you know . . .' he adds slyly.

'You have?' I say, looking at him with shock. 'How?'

'Because you throw like a girl,' he laughs. I hit him and he yelps. 'But you sure don't hit like one.' He rubs his arm and I wait for him to explain himself. 'I keep having to clear away these screwed-up balls of paper before I can put my boxes down. They've been all over the place recently and I'm not afraid to say I've unrolled a few of them and seen amazing sketches of floor layouts and displays.'

I blush and look away, and he bends down to my eye level and turns my face round to his.

'They're good, Evie. You should seriously show them to someone. Your ideas for the Christmas windows are really inspired.'

Now it's my turn to be bashful. 'They're just scribbles,' I say modestly, taking a bit out of a deliciously crumbly mince pie and washing it down with some coffee.

'Well, if they're scribbles, I'd love to see the finished drawings,' he laughs. 'Honestly, Evie, you just seem to be able to capture the real essence of this place. I love the one of the shoe tree. I can see more life in your drawings than there's ever been in this store.'

'Well,' I admit quietly, 'actually I've been bringing them to life *in* the store recently.'

Sam looks at me quizzically. 'Tell me more,' he says, folding his arms and leaning back against the sofa.

I tell him about how I overheard Rupert saying Hardy's was in danger of closing and that, before then, various members of staff would be laid off. Then I tell him how I've been coming in early every morning and making over Hardy's department by department.

Sam whistles. 'You are full of surprises, you know that, Evie Taylor?' he says, and I laugh. 'So why don't you tell Rupert what you're doing?'

317

'He doesn't even know my name. Why would he believe me?'

'Why wouldn't he?' shrugs Sam. 'You'll never know unless you try.'

'Maybe not everyone is as brave as you,' I say, brushing some rogue crumbs off my lap. 'Besides, if he knew who it really is he might lay off those other members of staff and I can't risk that happening. Anyway, it suits me this way. I don't want attention and I've realized that I'm too scared to do anything else other than work in this stock-room.' I stop flicking crumbs and look up at him. 'Whereas you, you've gone for what you really want and have grabbed your dream with both hands.'

'Not quite, I haven't,' Sam says, half under his breath.

I raise my eyebrows but he doesn't elaborate. 'Anyway,' I say, wanting to shift the conversation back onto him, 'I'm really impressed by what you've done Sam, truly.' I pause then add, 'Ella must be too.'

'Ella?' Sam shrugs and takes a bite of a mince pie. 'Yes, I guess so. She's not said anything, though. It's not the sort of thing we talk about. Besides, she's happy with me doing deliveries – at least it brings in the money.'

I wonder how any girlfriend could want her partner to stay a delivery guy forever if he's not happy. Whatever happened to supporting each other's dreams? Then I think of Jamie, and remember that it didn't get me anywhere. Perhaps

318

she has got the right idea after all. Besides, it's none of my business.

'So,' I say brightly, 'now tonight can be a celebration of your new career instead of mine!'

'Tonight?' Sam says, a perplexed expression on his face.

'Our night out?' I say, clocking Sam's blank expression. 'Oh ho, now I get it,' I add playfully, 'a stockroom girl not good enough for you now you're going to be a famous photographer.'

'No! Don't be silly,' Sam says quickly. 'I just didn't realize . . . you didn't specify a day . . .'

'I didn't? Shit! Sorry, Sam!' I shake my head at my idiocy. I'm so wrapped up in these makeovers lately I seem to be forgetting everything else. 'Is tonight any good for you?' I ask hopefully, whilst thinking, please say yes, please say yes.

He nods and smiles. 'I don't have a shoot tonight . . .'

'Ooh, get you,' I tease and mimic him playfully. '"I don't have a shoot tonight."'

'Hey, stop that,' he smiles as he stretches and yawns. 'I'm too tired for sarcasm right now, but I'm planning on having an afternoon nap after my last delivery so you'd better watch out later.' He smiles at me so little dimples appear in his cheeks. 'So where are we going?'

'The Lamb in Lambs Conduit Street, Bloomsbury. Eight o'clock.'

'It's a date,' he says, then we both make a dive for the last mince pie.

'Got it!' he says, laughing and brandishing it jubilantly over his head.

I scramble over to him and clamber on his lap, reaching up to grab it from him, which I manage to do, but he tickles me and I collapse on the floor giggling as he tries to get it back. Laughing, I stuff it greedily into my mouth, half of it crumbling back out. He hovers over me for a moment, but then sits back on his haunches and puts his hands up in an admission of defeat. 'You win. I should know to never come between a girl and a snack.' He pulls me to my feet. 'Now, I reckon it's about time I got that delivery in.'

The morning passes in a blur as staff buzz in and out of the stockroom with armfuls of stock to replenish their shelves, as well as grabbing orders on their way. I can't keep up with the endless orders on the printer and I'm actually starting to think that I may need an assistant. Perhaps I'll speak to Sharon about it. I could suggest that we hire one of the cleaners who got laid off this morning. Although I can just imagine what she'll say: 'An assistant? To do your job for you? I don't think so.'

Jane pops in and grabs an armful of satin slips, lace garters and all-in-ones, and then shoots out again. She is totally working her new look, sashaying around like she was born to be a beacon for women with an hourglass-and-a-half figure. It's fab. She even brings in her husband at lunchtime who just looks at me long enough to splutter, 'Thank you,' before Jane drags him back out. By his belt.

I pop my head out of the stockroom several times during the morning to marvel at the change that is occurring within Hardy's. Word of mouth, and my little additions to the window displays, mean that customers are weaving through the store, chattering gaily with the staff and to each other, picking up various items from the shelves or simply browsing amongst the different departments. The atmosphere is lighter, the shop floor brighter, even the staff are happier. I keep seeing clusters of them huddled together, brainstorming ways to make their departments better. Those people whose departments haven't yet changed are happily pitching in with their colleagues, helping to replenish shelves, or serving customers.

If a building could sigh with happiness, I think that's what Hardy's would be doing right now. Which makes knowing what I do about its future even harder.

Because even though I am excited by the surge in custom I know that to save Hardy's we'll have to sell thousands of trilbies and bottles of perfume. A few more people stopping to browse and purchase goods from us aren't going to be enough. Hardy's doesn't need just to double, or triple its takings this month, it needs its takings to rise by at least 500 per cent. And Rupert made it quite clear that if we can't do this then the store has no hope of survival.

I close the stockroom door, the noise and bustle of the store dissipates and I'm left with silence. Now I've seen what Hardy's can become, I'm even more determined to do something to make a difference, especially as I can see how important it is to the rest of the staff.

As Hardy's is metamorphosing, so are they. And, more than anything, I've realized that my colleagues don't just rely on this place for their salaries; it goes much deeper than that. Their friends, their confidence, their self-worth all live under this roof. The truth is they need this place as much as I do.

There must be something more I can do, something I'm just not seeing? I look around my stockroom, desperately searching for answers. People love department stores at Christmas, so what is it about Hardy's that sets us apart from the rest? I can't help but think of the sad, soulless Oxford Street Christmas lights I looked at earlier in the week, and the futuristic store windows that people were flocking around, and wonder, not for the first time, where the true spirit of Christmas has gone.

What will bring the customers flooding back through the doors of Hardy's like they did in the old days?

'The Old Days!' I exclaim, and clap my hands as my brain zips through my internal map of the stockroom. I dive right down aisle number seven and skid onto my knees at the far corner where I pull out an old, battered box that is weak with

322

age and covered with dust. I trail my finger down it and leave a long track like a sled in the snow.

It is one of the two dozen or so boxes of vintage Christmas decorations I discovered when I first started working here. My hands are shaking as they tug at the box and I'm suddenly bombarded with images and ideas of what Christmas is and should be. I think of the colours: gloriously merry reds, lush greens, biscuit browns and, of course, white, powdery snow. I think of the sights and smells of Christmas, cinnamon and spices, gingerbread, eggnog, mulled wine and pine needles crunching underfoot. I think of the bare trees in Primrose Hill, covered with a light frosting of snow, I think of snowglobes, and Joel and I iceskating at Somerset House and how festive and traditional it felt. I think of all the old Christmas movies I've loved since I was a child, and which always made me want to go to New York and wander down Fifth Avenue, gazing in windows as I took my beautifully wrapped gifts for my loved ones at home. I think of the Christmas cookies my mum makes every year, and the building of the German gingerbread house, which became an annual tradition in my family and which Jonah, Noah and I fought over when we were kids because they had always eaten the perfect little sugared windows and doors and accessories by the time we went to construct it. And then Mum and I would make our own home-made frosted icing replacements that somehow made the whole thing even more authentic. Then I think of Christmas and what it means: family, love, dreams and magic and, most importantly, childhood.

I gaze back down at the box in front of me and I suddenly remember how I wondered all those months ago when I first discovered them how anyone could possibly forget about such incredibly beautiful and nostalgic things; but forget they had and – shamefully – so had I.

I open the box carefully, coughing and covering my mouth as a cloud of dust fills my nostrils, and gasp as I pull out some vintage Pifco fairy lights from the 1950s. The box itself is bright red and blue and has a picture of a little boy and a little girl gazing in wonderment at the pretty Chinese lantern-style lights hanging above their heads. I put them to one side and look back inside. There are endless tangled strings of fairy lights, some clearly from the 1980s, with gaudy plastic Cinderella carriages covering multicoloured bulbs. I ignore them and pull out a long string of lights in the shape of little candles. And there's lots more beautiful Christmas tree lights too. Some, like these, have clearly been used in the store's own displays; others, still in their boxes, were obviously leftover stock from the store.

In another big box I find lots of boxes of Batqers Harlequin miniature crepe crackers. I pull down another box and discover sets of wooden reindeer, boxes of beautiful hand-carved toy soldiers and tree decorations depicting Christmas tableaux. In one a little girl is putting a present under a tiny tree, in another a child is receiving a gift from his parents. There are lanterns and candy containers, hundreds of glass baubles still in their boxes, which, when I turn them over, state that they were made in the small German town of Lauscha and are dated 1937. There are ornamental Santa's boots and little statues of Father Christmas himself, complete with a wiry wool beard. As I gaze at them all, suddenly I know just what I have to do. It's just a case of deciding when. And how.

Because this is too big a job for me on my own.

CHAPTER 23

Later that morning, I bound out of the store into the crisp air, wrapped up in the gorgeous belted 1960s three-quarterlength dogtooth-check coat that I pulled out of The Wardrobe this morning. I'm finally tiring of my old, trusty duffel coat. It may be warm and practical, but this coat is surprisingly snug too, with the added bonus that I feel so chic in it, it actually makes me want to leave the house so I can put it on. I've had it for two years and still can't believe I've never worn it before. And the other great thing about it is that I can get away with wearing my plain black trousers and a jumper underneath and still feel like I've made an effort. Although I have to confess, I pulled on the tight, blush-coloured angora jumper this morning as it feels so warm and soft. And instead of my old black trousers I'm wearing a pair of cute, cropped cigarette pants. I took Lily's advice and rolled my hair up from my face again. She's right, it does suit me. I even tried painting my lips a dark, wintry red. But the brogues remain, albeit with a lick a polish, which has made them look surprisingly fashionable. You know, overall it's a surprisingly cool look.

I want to be sure I'm always ready for a surprise visit from Joel. I haven't seen him since our date at Somerset House, which ended at his hotel, but that doesn't mean I haven't been thinking about him. And he's called and texted me regularly since, to apologize for being so busy. He's promised we'll go out again soon. Until then, I have plenty to occupy me.

I'm feeling pretty chirpy as I leave the store and am in such deep thought about the treasures I found in the stockroom this morning that I don't see Carly coming in the opposite direction.

'Oof, sorry!' I say as I bump into her, spilling her latte down her front. She shrugs glumly as she looks at me and then brushes her shaggy fleece waistcoat, which is now dripping with milky coffee and which I'm sure is supposed to be massively stylish but actually makes her look like an Afghan hound. A coffee-soaked Afghan hound, to be precise. Her hair hangs in straggly strands over her shoulders, she is wearing what looks to be a cream crochet doily on her head and for the rest she is wearing head-to-toe black with what appear to be black Doc Marten boots, which I thought went out of fashion when Madness did. Her big Bambi eyes are smudged with black liner, which gives the appearance she's been up all night. I'm sure it's a trendy look, but it's really terrible. I have never seen her looking so unkempt or so sorrowful.

'Hey, what's up?' I ask as she finishes brushing herself down.

'Oh, you know, just work stuff,' she shrugs. 'Turns out it's not that easy being an assistant manager. Designers still hasn't sold anything, Elaine is being a total bitch about it, and Rupert has called me in for a meeting to discuss things this afternoon. And the rest of the staff keep badgering me to go and makeover their departments next. I mean, as if I haven't got enough on my plate. Don't they understand it takes time and energy to be creative?'

I nod sympathetically as she sighs and sips what's left of her coffee.

'I just don't understand why no one else can see what I see. This store needs something fresh, new and exciting,' she goes on. 'It might take some time but the customers will start to accept my vision soon. After all, it works for Rumors . . . I-I just don't understand why it isn't working here . . .' She falters a little; her unwavering confidence has clearly been knocked. 'God, listen to me,' she says, rolling her eyes. 'I sound like such a bore, banging on about work. I seriously need to have some fun. With alcohol and people and—'

I have a brilliant thought. 'Why don't you come out with me?' I suggest excitedly, thinking how fab it would be for Carly to get to know my friends. They'd love her. Everyone does. 'I'm going out tonight with some people from work. They're lovely . . .'

She's looking at me with a strange expression, her perfectly plucked eyebrows drawn together.

'Who are you going out with?' she says in a puzzled voice. 'People from the shop?'

I nod vehemently and her face falls.

'And I wasn't invited? Bloody Elaine, she's turned everyone against me.'

'Oh, she's not coming, or anyone else from the shop floor, for that matter,' I add hastily. 'Just a few of my close friends who work behind the scenes, like me. There's Sam, who does all the deliveries – you won't have met him – then there's Jan, Justyna and Velna – they're the cleaners. They're funny and sweet, but they finish really early in the morning so you wouldn't have met them either. Ooh, but you might know Felix from Security, he starts his night shift at seven . . .'

'The old bloke who looks like he should be in a Carry On film?' Carly replies, a smile crawling over her lips.

'Yes! That's him! He's great. Then there's Lily; she works downstairs in the—'

'The old dear from the tearoom?' Carly splutters as she takes another sip of coffee. 'Are you serious? Oh, Sarah, you are funny.' She holds my arm as she bends over laughing. 'You're seriously going for a big night out with a couple of pensioners, some foreign cleaners and a delivery boy who probably hasn't even got his GCSEs? Oh, wow!' she laughs grabbing my arm. 'You do know how to live life in the fast lane, don't you!'

She wipes away a tear of laughter and smiles brightly at me. 'You know what I like about you, hon? Somehow you always manage to cheer me up.'

I grit my teeth, feeling both upset and defensive. They may not be the sort of people Carly's used to hanging out with – they may not be rich or stylish or have trendy jobs – but they're real. And they treat me like a human being and not some stupid stockroom girl whose only use is to make other people feel better about themselves.

I look at Carly and it dawns on me suddenly how shallow she is. 'Fine, don't come,' I say lightly as I start walking off. 'Your loss.'

And it is her loss, I think as I leave her standing outside the store like an abandoned and bedraggled puppy. It really is.

I arrive at Lola and Raffy's nursery right on the dot of three forty-five. I managed to leave work on time today, despite it still being busy when I left. Sharon, in an out-of-character act of kindness, offered to take over from me for the rest of the afternoon. I suspect it was more to do with the fact that Rupert had decided to do a spontaneous stock-check. She and Rupert are really bonding these days. They've become quite the little team and it's rather sweet to witness. Anyway, I left them to it and then texted Delilah again to let her know I'd be picking the kids up as normal but that I needed to be back in town this evening. I still haven't heard back from her, which is unusual. But I'm sure she'll understand. She's probably just been too busy to reply.

The kids' nursery is located in a church just off Regent's Park Road. It's nestled within yet another wealthy, tree-lined square full of multi-million pound Georgian houses, overlooking Regent's Canal. The kids don't go to a church nursery because of any religious proclivities that Delilah has. I think it's more to do with the fact that her yummy mummy friends all send their children there too, and apparently it has the best Ofsted reports in the area. So in order to get Lola a place Delilah attended Mass for a few months. Sometimes it's good for me to know that my big sister feels the need to pretend to be something she's not some of the time, too, in order to fit in. Living in this ridiculously wealthy village full of the rich and famous I *always* feel like I'm in the wrong world. I look around at the shiny, expensive cars that are parked in front of the houses, the beautifully painted pastel façades, the perfectly pruned window boxes, and then I think of the type of place I'd be living in if I tried to rent somewhere on my paltry wage: a dark, dank shoebox in the outer echelons of North London. Not that I've ever looked into it. The set-up at Delilah's has always worked so well, I've never actually considered moving out on my own. But now the prospect of some privacy for me to bring friends home (and by 'friends' I mean Joel) is looking seriously appealing. Delilah's place has never felt like home. Not really.

I wave as another mum approaches the nursery just as I do. I recognize her immediately even though she is wearing the usual identikit Primrose Hill yummy mummy uniform of super-skinny jeans, black high-heeled ankle boots with scary-looking studs all over them, an expensive-looking white T-shirt, a black blazer with the sleeves rolled up to reveal the lining, and some flimsy black chiffon scarf around her neck with skulls all over it. I'm sure it's designer but I don't for the life of me know who, and besides, wearing it in this weather is utterly pointless. As are her big bug-eye sunglasses. I mean it's mid-December, for God's sake, and raining!

I put my hand up and wave. 'Hi, Sassy,' I say brightly. We've met many times; not only is she one of Delilah's good friends but I see her here at the nursery on average three times a week.

She looks at me blankly, iPhone in one hand, designer handbag and dog lead in the other, with what looks like an oversized rat attached to it. She tries to furrow her brow. Then she realizes she can't, due to the Botox she's obviously had recently. She flicks her highlighted Californian-blond hair and smiles instead, but it doesn't reach her eyes. 'Hiya . . .' she says slowly. I wait for her to remember my name. '. . . uh, uh . . .' She looks around, clearly hoping for someone to rescue her.

I clasp my hands and wait. I'm not helping

her, no way. I raise my eyebrows and smile encouragingly.

'Delilah's nanny!' She snaps her perfectly manicured fingers and looks ridiculously pleased with herself despite the fact that she hasn't *actually* remembered my name. 'I just didn't recognize you in that gorgeous coat. I think I saw it in the window of MaxMara when I was shopping on Bond Street last week, right?'

I swallow the urge to tell her I paid ten pounds for it in a charity shop on Kensington High Street.

'I have to say, I wouldn't have thought it would be *your* kind of shop,' she adds sweetly. But the put-down is loud and clear to my ears.

'Really? Why is that?' I challenge, feeling dangerously close to breaking point.

She blinks slowly and her heavily kohled eyes flicker up and down my body. 'Oh. No reason,' she says, and her laugh grates as much as her comments do. She screeches as the rat jerks on its lead and pulls her off balance. 'Monet! Bad dog! No!' She flutters her fingers and smiles. 'Bye, er, er . . .'

'EVIE!' I bellow in annoyance as she gets ungraciously dragged up the path towards the nursery entrance. 'My name is Evie! And my "designer" coat is from a charity shop!'

She glances back with what I think is a startled expression, but because of the Botox I can't be sure. She'll remember me next time.

★　★　★

Twenty minutes later I'm trudging across Primrose Hill, flanked by Lola and Raffy, who are both chattering ten to the dozen. Raffy is refusing to be carried because he wants to pat dogs. Which means we are having to stop approximately every thirty seconds as another one passes us.

'Ruff ruff dog!' he says happily to the poodle we've just passed as Lola tells me all about her day.

'We had some snacks, then we did do painting, then we did sing a bit.' She clears her throat to give me a demonstration: '"Jingle bells, la la laaaaaa". Then we had milk and biscuits, mine was yummy and I ate Raffy's too! Then I skipped and hopped and jumped and now I'm ex*hausted*, Teevee, I am.' She sits on the ground, which is both wet and muddy, and folds her arms.

'Oh, that's a shame,' I say, shaking my head sadly. 'That means you must be too tired to make some Rice Krispie cakes to have as a treat after tea . . .'

Lola scrambles up, her dark curls bouncing on the collar of her red winter coat. She jumps up and down so that her wellies make a squelching sound in the mud.

'Not too tired, Teevee, I'mnotI'mnot! Let's goooo!'

She pulls me by the hand as Raffy yells and pulls me by the other hand and, laughing, I scoop them both up under my arms and run across the hill as their squeals pierce the darkness of the winter afternoon, making it suddenly feel infinitely warmer and brighter somehow.

Two hours later and the kitchen looks like an explosion in a chocolate factory. There are chocolate handprints over the stainless-steel work surface, chocolate splashes over the floor, walls and cupboards, and Lola and Raffy look like they have simply rolled through a vat of chocolate: they are covered from head to toe in the stuff. They are now sitting happily at their table, eating their cakes, having been bribed by me to eat some organic slop for their tea beforehand. It is nearly six o'clock. Delilah should be home at any minute. I am whipping round the kitchen, Flash-wiping everything in sight and trying to make the place look respectable again. I still need to get changed and, in order to be at the pub in Bloomsbury on time to meet everyone, I need to be on a bus by seven thirty at the latest.

Ten minutes later and Raffy and Lola are in the bath in my ensuite, which is a huge treat for them. (They have their own bathroom downstairs with twin sinks and a whole Under the Sea theme going on.) I'm bathing them up here so I can multitask by getting ready at the same time. Tonight I'm going for a pretty floral tea dress with opaque tights, T-bar shoes and a little brooch that I've made into a clip and used to pin a section of hair away from my forehead. Which, thanks to Lily, is becoming my signature style. I've also got a cute

335

black swing coat, which I'm going to wear over the top and to which I've pinned another vintage brooch on the collar. I think of Lily and how proud she'd be of me as I paint my lips red.

I am admiring my reflection and trying not to get hit by flying bath toys when I hear the front door go. Delilah, at last. I glance at my watch. It's six forty-five so I'll just have time to get the kids dry and in their beds for stories and then I can dash out of the house.

I lift out Lola and then Raffy and bundle them in big, soft white towels, drying them a little before they fling them off and start tearing round my room naked.

I open my bedroom door and call down the stairs, 'DELILAH?' But there's no answer. 'LI-LA!' I shout again. Still nothing.

'Lola,' I grab her as she streaks past me, 'I have a very important job for you that only big girls can do.'

Lola tilts her head and stares at me with a very serious expression on her face. Then she puts her hands on her hips and says, 'Hit me with it, Teevee.'

I stifle a laugh. Where on earth has she got that expression from? I suck in my cheeks so she can't see me smiling.

'Can you get your pyjamas on for Auntie Teevee nicely, and then help Raffy with his, please?' I beckon Raffy over and he obediently lays on the floor so I can put his nappy on. Then I hand the pyjamas to her and she grabs them.

'Come ON, Raffy, time for PJs,' she says bossily, pulling a top over his head roughly, clearly relishing having her very own reallife doll to dress.

I step out of my bedroom, shutting the door behind me and hoping that they won't do too much destruction to my room while I'm gone. I head down two flights of stairs. Delilah's clearly gone straight down to the kitchen as she's not in her bedroom, or the lounge, study or dining room. I am about to descend to the basement when I hear a man's hushed voice. Will.

'I can't talk for long.' Pause. 'Don't be unreasonable. You know my situation, Helen.'

I sit down on the stairs and lean against the banisters, my heart racing as I strain to hear what he's saying.

'I've told you what I want,' he softens his voice, 'so what are you going to do about it?' Another pause. 'You know that's not possible. Delilah can't find out. It would destroy her. I love her, which is why I want to somehow make this work without her finding out. Surely you can understand that?' He lowers his voice and I lean further to try to catch what he's saying. 'Listen, can we meet soon? You know how much I want to . . .'

I hear the back door open and close again. I can't hear any more but I don't need to. I've heard enough.

Delilah's husband is having an affair. Now I just need to work out what the hell to do about it.

337

CHAPTER 24

I'm sitting on the bus staring out of the steamed-up windows into the darkness beyond, watching as raindrops pound against the side of the window and then run down the glass as quickly and freely as I imagine Delilah's tears would if I were to tell her what I've just overheard. Outside, the lights from the buildings and streets pulsate like a heartbeat and I hear the steady *swoosh swoosh swoosh* of the passing cars driving through puddles, their drivers gazing blankly out of their windscreens as if they've been hypnotized by their long week of hard work. Suddenly the city seems to me to be a living, breathing nocturnal animal and its dwellers are just little amoebas that live on it.

Speaking of amoebas, I can't stop thinking about Will-the-Cheating-Bastard.

After I accidentally overheard him on the phone I crept back upstairs quickly, to find Raffy, still naked, jumping up and down on my bed.

'I tried, Teevee,' Lola sighed ruefully from her sitting position on the floor where she was looking at her little brother with despair. 'But he is very very VERY naughty.'

Just like his daddy, I thought, and bundled a squealing, wriggling Raffy into my arms and into his dinosaur pyjamas, and then took them both downstairs to get their beakers of milk.

I descended the stairs trying to make as much noise as possible to ensure Will would know we were coming, which isn't exactly hard when flanked by two stampeding toddlers. I didn't want to hear any more of his conversation and I certainly didn't want the kids to either. Will was sitting on one of the bar stools in front of the enormous, brushed-granite island unit as we came into the kitchen. His iPhone and a large glass of red wine were in front of him.

That's right, drink away the guilt, I thought as he took a large glug and avoided eye contact with me.

Then Will turned and beamed as his kids ran towards him squealing with delight, and I tried not to let the disgust I felt show in my face. Will and I have never been really close, but I'd say we tolerate each other. He finds me too under-achieving and I just find him so bloody smug. There's never been anything major to dislike about him – until now. Just that he's annoyingly public-school handsome, rich and clever, and yes, he works really hard in his job, and yes, I've always thought he looks after my sister well and is a good dad. But Delilah is amazing, he's bloody lucky to have her, and sometimes I feel that he just takes that for granted. Well, judging by the call I've just overheard that's an understatement.

I am furious with him but the worst thing about it is that I just don't know what to do. Although I have to say I am happy that my dislike of him has been verified. Mum has always insinuated that I don't like him simply because he comes between me and my sister. But that's ridiculous. As if a man could ever do that. I feel a stab of guilt as I think of how I didn't really believe Delilah the other evening when she was upset about Will. I've always told myself I don't want to get involved with Delilah's marriage, but at what point do I make exceptions to that rule? Do I tell her and risk breaking up their family? Because there's also Lola and Raffy to consider. Maybe I should just keep quiet for their sake. Oh God, I just don't know.

I bite my lip feeling suddenly horribly weighed down by my knowledge. Stupid Will flapping his stupid willy around the first woman that showed any interest.

If it is the first, I think suddenly. For all I know he could've been having affairs for years. I've read articles about blokes who went to their lover's bed straight after their wife had given birth. What if Will is one of those? The thought utterly reviles me. I may not have always thought Will was good enough for my sister, but I certainly never imagined him to be a complete bastard. I feel like I don't know him at all any more. I'm so angry with him for gambling his marriage and Lola and Raffy's blissful childhoods. But I'm also angry at him for putting me in this position. Do I tell Delilah? Or do I let her find out for herself? The dilemma occupies me for the entire bus journey into town.

Thank God I have something to take my mind off it all, I think as I push open the pub doors and immediately get enveloped by the warmth and noise. I've chosen a typically old-fashioned pub for our little get-together. The Lamb is somewhere I thought Lily and Felix would feel comfortable, and it's always been one of my favourite drinking holes. Not that I really have a 'drinking hole' per se, but if I did, this is where I'd come all the time. It's a classic Victorian pub just near Russell Square, with dark wood, leather sofas, chocolate-brown walls with sepia photographs dotted around, as well as lots of period artefacts, such as the old jukebox that's tucked away in a corner. The exterior has beautiful original Victorian green tiles and a wrought-iron streetlamp hanging above the entrance. And it's the perfect place for a secret rendezvous, as the pub also still has the original snob screens – small panels of etched glass positioned at head height to conceal a drinker's identity. You can just imagine all the secret love affairs that have gone on here. This makes me wonder if perhaps I should bring Joel here, too. And then I think of Will again and my heart sinks.

I spot Felix in the corner, sitting on a banquette

in the middle of two round tables. I wave at him and push through the crowd as he looks up and smiles at me brightly. He has clearly dressed up for the occasion in a slightly too-tight-for-his-stomach striped shirt tucked into his jeans, a lightly checked blazer over the top, the look finished with a jaunty paisley scarf tied round his neck and tucked into the open collar of his shirt. I realize I have never seen him wear anything other than his dark blue security uniform before and that, if I had, I'd have known immediately that he was a widower. No wife would have let him out of the house looking like this, but I'm not going to say a word. He looks so pleased with himself.

'Hello, love!' he says, his face crinkling like crepe paper into a warm smile. 'I thought it'd be busy so I decided to come a bit early to bag us a table. Can I get you a drink?'

'Don't be silly, Felix. I'll get it,' I say, waving him back into his seat from which he is now trying to get up from.

He frowns at me as he tries to extricate himself from behind the table. 'You bloody well won't, Evie. Let me buy you a drink to make up for all those early morning Americanos you've brought me!'

'Well, when you put it like that . . . I'll have a glass of white wine, please.' I smile as Felix heaves himself around the table and makes his way towards the bar.

I sit back and look around, relishing the feeling of being out for the evening. The sad thing is I can't remember the last time I did something like this. Carly and I go out occasionally, but it's only ever me and her, and we tend to go to some swanky new bar that she's chosen and which I don't feel remotely comfortable in because they're always full of self-satisfied media types waving their hands and expensive handbags around, drinking achingly cool drinks made from fruits I've never heard of, served by unbelievably handsome bartenders who never seem to notice me waiting at the bar, desperately trying to get served. I end up sitting uncomfortably on some stool that was made for someone two stone lighter and a foot taller than me, gripping on for dear life and trying not to drink so much that I need to go to the toilet, because the bar would have undoubtedly found some new way of not making it look like a toilet but like a space-age egg, or there'll be a two-way mirror on the cubicle door so you can see the people waiting outside whilst you're trying to pee.

Which is why for tonight's get-together I've tried to choose somewhere that everyone would feel comfortable – including me. I glance over and see Felix patiently waiting to be served amongst the busy cross-section of customers. There's the pre-requisite stressed-out suits, a bunch of students, a smattering of couples having pre-dinner drinks, there's the local business people, the shop workers, and trendy executives in black-rimmed specs from the media agencies that are dotted around this area.

The table Felix has chosen for us is in a cosy and tucked away corner, which is great, as the place is heaving already. I'm just thinking how much I need a drink, when I spot a familiar figure sailing through the crowd. Lily beams at me as she approaches, and not for the first time I marvel at the grace and ease with which she appears to move through life. People part for Lily like she's Moses moving the Red Sea. She smiles graciously as she passes them, lifting one hand a little like the Queen to thank her subjects for letting her pass.

'Darling!' she breathes. 'Let me look at you!' I reluctantly stand up as Lily, on the other side of the table, gives me a quick assessment. 'You look *glorious*, Evie darling. That tea dress is just made for you! And didn't I tell you that you're a red lip kind of girl? It suits your colouring so wonderfully! I mean, suddenly your eyes are bigger and darker, your hair has more lustre, your skin is lumin*escent*. It's like looking in the mirror of my youth.' She sighs dramatically and perches on a chair, popping her handbag on her lap.

I smile shyly at her compliment. But I can't imagine I'd ever remind Lily of herself when she was young.

'Well, you look wonderful, too, Lily,' I say. And it's true. This evening she's channelling Jackie

Onassis with her usually scraped-back hair floating in soft, dark waves around her face and wearing a pearl-grey shift dress with a cardigan slung over her shoulders and an expensive-looking silk scarf tied neatly around her neck. And red lips, of course.

'I thought I'd make the effort for you, my dear. I'm sad to say I don't get out as often as I'd like these days. It's the darnedest thing about getting old. Suddenly you're up like a lark at six and ready for bed just as the evening is beginning. Besides which, people my age seem to forget they're still alive. I'm lucky if I can find someone to go for afternoon tea with me, let alone an alcoholic drink or dinner past 7 p.m. Boring, the lot of them.' She gesticulates dramatically so that a man in a suit behind her has to duck out of her way. 'I still remember the days when I used to stay out all night and not need a jot of sleep.'

She clasps her hands together and smiles at me. 'Now, I don't know about you, but I need a beverage. What would you like, darling?'

'Felix is at the bar getting me a glass of wine,' I reply, standing up and straining to see where he is. 'Let me go and get you something.'

'Oh, you'll do no such thing. I can go myself. I need to tell them just how to mix my Martini, anyway. None of these young bartenders seem to know how these days. It's a tragedy.'

I smile as Lily gets lost in the crowd and, seconds later, I spot her standing at the front of the bar being served ahead of Felix, which makes me chuckle out loud.

'Feel like sharing the joke?' a familiar voice says teasingly.

I look up and see Sam grinning shyly, his hands stuffed deep into his coat pockets. He unwraps his scarf, takes off his beanie hat and rubs his hand over his head. I am surprised to find myself wondering how it would feel to do that myself. His closely cropped hair looks almost like suede as he touches it: soft yet rough.

I swallow as he shrugs off his coat and throws it round the chair in one swift movement. There is a moment of awkward silence as we appraise each other.

'You look gorgeous,' Sam says softly.

I smile at his compliment and quickly allow my eyes to take in his appearance. He's wearing a soft oatmeal-coloured V-neck jumper, which compliments his syrupy-coloured hair as well as his caramel eyes. There's a crisp white T-shirt just peeking through underneath the jumper, and he's wearing smart, pressed black trousers. I'm surprised how much effort he's made for such an informal night out. I mean, anyone would think he was as desperate for a night out as the rest of us. But he and Ella probably go out all the time. Dinner, the theatre, nice bars, all the things couples do.

'You scrub up pretty well yourself,' I smile and then look away, embarrassed suddenly.

346

'Well, here we are,' he says, clutching the back of the chair. I notice that his knuckles have gone white.

I nod, suddenly lost for any strand of conversation, which is weird. I mean, this is Sam. My mate Sam. 'Yep, here we are,' I reply.

Sam opens his mouth to speak again and then closes it as three drinks arrive on the table in front of us, delivered by Felix.

'Here we are!' says Felix heartily as he puts down two pints and my glass of wine. Sam looks at him, then at me, then to his left as Lily slips into the seat next to him.

'Not bad,' she says as she takes a sip of her Martini. 'Not bad at all. By the next one I think he'll get it just right.'

Sam looks at Lily, then at Felix, then back at me and raises his eyebrows questioningly.

'Lily, Felix, this is Sam,' I say, making the introductions. 'He does the deliveries for Hardy's so you probably won't have met him before.'

Felix hands Sam his pint as Lily raises her glass, gives Sam a sideways glance and then winks at me approvingly.

'I took the liberty of getting you a pint of lager while I was at the bar,' Felix says. 'I saw you talking to Evie here and figured you were with us.'

'With us?' Sam questions robotically as he accepts the drink and sinks back in the banquette.

'Lily and Felix are good friends of mine who work at Hardy's,' I explain to Sam. 'Felix is our

347

security man, and Lily runs the tearoom. When you suggested having a get-together to celebrate the promotion-I-never-got, of course I wanted to invite them. Ooh, and here are the others!'

I stand up and wave as I spot Jan Baptysta and Justyna towering over the crowds. I hear Velna before I see her. And then when I see her I wonder how I could have possibly missed her. She is wearing a multicoloured roll-neck jumper with a bright pink denim skirt, cream tights and fluffy boots. She has her hair in plaits, and it appears to be dyed green.

'Hi, guys!' I say warmly as they line up in front of the table. 'Everyone, meet Jan, Justyna and Velna! They're Hardy's brilliant cleaners. 'You guys must know Felix, right? And this is Sam and Lily.'

'Yesk!' Jan nods as he takes Felix's hand and pumps it enthusiastically so that Felix's pint slops over the top of his glass. Justyna slaps Felix on the back and a little more spills out and Velna gives him a warm hug, her elbow knocking his glass again. Then they all wave at Sam and Lily.

Felix laughs and puts his glass down. 'Is that everyone?' he says.

I look around and nod, thinking of Carly, who could have been here too if she'd just given us a chance.

'Well,' Felix glances at his now half-empty pint. 'It looks like I could do with going to the bar again to get some more drinks. Ladies and gentleman, place your orders, please!'

Everyone starts grabbing chairs and chattering noisily as Felix heads off with his list of drinks. I can see from the expressions on everyone's faces that they're thrilled to be out for the evening, mixing with colleagues they have worked with for years, but not ever had the opportunity to get to know properly. Lily is listening intently whilst Velna explains just how home hair-dye works, whilst Jan interrupts to ask Lily what it is she's drinking.

'A Martini, of course, darling,' she replies. 'It's the only drink worth drinking if you like vodka, which I presume you do?' Jan nods and begins explaining the myriad differences between Polish and Russian vodka. A minute later Lily has climbed delicately onto her chair with Jan's help, snapped her fingers and got the barman's attention. She makes some hand gestures and two minutes later the same barman delivers a Vodka Martini to her, complete with a little bow. I laugh with disbelief as she slides it across the table to Jan.

'How did you do that?' I ask. 'It usually takes an hour to get served in here!'

'Years of practice, darling,' Lily drawls as everyone leans in to listen to her. 'Back in my day a bartender had your drink ready for you before you even came in, and if they didn't, all it would take was one flick of my hand and two would arrive to compensate for my wait.' She waves her hands. 'Of course, I always stuck to Dorothy Parker's rules and only drank the two.' We all look perplexed and Lily gazes around in mock horror at us. 'Have you never heard her famous saying?' We shake our heads and she tuts and begins to recite: '"I like to have Martini, two at the very most. After three I'm under the table, after four I'm under the host."'

Everyone laughs and Lily uses this as a cue to start telling one of her stories from the Good Old Days, with extra details thrown in by her new side-kick, Felix, who has returned from the bar. They appear to be in their element telling everyone about life working at the Hardy's of old.

'People used to flock there,' Felix says nostalgically to his captive audience. 'They'd chat and browse and have lunch or tea; it was a whole day's outing for them.' Lily nods in agreement.

I've heard this potted history several times before from Felix but am enjoying it as much as everyone else. I remember the first time Felix filled me in on Hardy's background. It was the January after I started, a particularly quiet month, and he was telling me how back in the sixties and seventies, the Hardy's sale used to draw a crowd as big as Harrods', and you'd see streams of people leaving the store clutching handfuls of Hardy's distinctive cream and gold carrier bags. Unable to believe it, I asked him what had gone wrong.

'People have lost sight of what Hardy's stands

for,' he replied sadly. 'I mean, Walter Hardy, senior, opened the store with the belief that he could change the way that people shopped. He wanted Hardy's to be an extension of customers' own homes. It would put public service over profit and there'd be no hard-selling or store snobbery.' He told me that under Walter's watchful eye it became London's most popular department store. So cherished was it by customers that it became a symbol of hope through two World Wars, as it somehow miraculously survived the bombing that changed the city's panorama so dramatically. As their own homes were destroyed, so Londoners flocked to Hardy's, the warm, welcoming store whose doors were always open to them.

Lily has now been handed the reins of the story by Felix, who is sipping his pint with satisfaction as she talks. 'In 1945, Walter senior retired and his son, Walter junior, took over the running of the store, promising to carry on his father's legacy. And he did for over forty years. But when he passed away his son, Sebastian, became the new owner, but he didn't share his father and grand-father's vision. Under his tenure it became a wealth- and status-obsessed store aimed at serving an élite customer, namely his Sloaney friends.' Felix pipes up that it's the reason he originally left Hardy's. He'd worked there for over thirty years but 'couldn't work for someone who didn't have the best interests of the store at heart.'

Lily pats him on the hand and continues.

'Sebastian always blamed the store's location for its drop in profits under his ownership but it was its loss of values that was the problem, not its position.'

'Surely the position can't help, though,' I pipe up. 'I mean, Hardy's may be in W1 but the street it's situated on is full of other forgotten folk, like the independent umbrella shop to the left, and the traditional cobbler's on the right, neither of whom seem to do a remarkable trade either.' I often wonder how they manage to stay afloat, with the soaring rental prices in this area. It's such a shame, as the pretty, tree-lined street has so much potential with its quaint shops with brightly coloured awnings, and little specialist cafés and delicatessens.

Felix just sniffs and says, 'We did all right for eighty years, until Sebastian came along.'

I glance across the table at Sam: he is unusually quiet and staring glumly into the distance. 'Are you OK?' I ask quietly as Lily and Felix continue to entertain the rest of the group with their stories. I stretch my hand across the table to touch Sam's. It is warm; he pulls it away slightly.

'I'm fine,' he says, then pauses and looks at me. 'I just thought . . .' He trails off and then looks down. 'It doesn't matter,' he says to the floor.

'No, Sam, what's wrong? Tell me.' I'm worried suddenly that I've done something wrong. Does Sam not like the venue? Would he have preferred the swanky bars that Carly frequents? Was he expecting more people? A bigger get-together? Better company?

He exhales and gazes at me meaningfully. 'I just thought it was going to be you and me tonight.'

I am dumbfounded. Since when did Sam and I ever talk about going out on our own together? I have no recollection of that at all. Maybe when he suggested celebrating with everyone he thought it'd just be us two as he thinks I don't have any other friends at Hardy's? I suppose I am always talking about how no one at the store knows my name. Sam is aware how the shop-floor staff all come in to tell me their woes but know nothing about my life. Maybe he thought he was doing me a favour by coming out for a drink with me. And now here I am surrounded by wonderful friends whom Sam has never even heard me talk about.

'Sorry, that was my mistake.' I smile apologetically and squeeze his hand. He slides it from my grasp and clasps his hands together under the table. Maybe he's just shy and doesn't like big groups of people he doesn't know. 'But this is a much better arrangement, surely?' I continue brightly. 'I mean, I suddenly realized after the promotion débâcle that even though Sharon and Rupert don't know I exist, and everyone who works on the shop floor thinks I'm called Sarah, there are actually *lots* of people at the store who know me pretty well and who I consider really good friends. Just like you.'

'Friends, right,' Sam says, and his Adam's apple bobs up and down as he swallows.

'Don't be nervous,' I say quietly, thinking he's overwhelmed by the unexpected group of people. I would be too. Everyone here is great and they are going to totally love you as much as I do.'

Sam glances up at me just as another pint of lager is put in front of him.

'To friends,' I say as I lift my glass and wait for him to do the same. But he just stares at his glass before taking a long sip.

An hour later and the drinks and conversation are flowing as freely as if we've all known each other for years. I can't help but wonder, as I take a trip to the bar and look back at our table, what the other pub-goers make of our disparate group. I'm sure if I was trying to guess how we're all connected I wouldn't be able to come up with anything. There's Lily, who looks like she's used to spending her evenings dining at The Ritz, chatting animatedly to Jan, who wouldn't look out of place in a beer-soaked football shirt on a match day down at the Arsenal. Velna and Felix appear to be swapping outlandish style tips and Justyna is slapping Sam on the back as he roars with laughter. Or pain; I'm not entirely sure which.

I feel a swell of pride as I look over them all. It takes a group of special people to bond so well so quickly and it makes me wonder if I have underestimated the depth of my friendship with them. Why have I been so obsessed with thinking that no one at Hardy's knows me? Felix and I have talked about everything during our early morning coffee chats, from his relationship with Maisie and their struggle to have children, to my struggle to make a mark in my family. He knows how close Delilah and I are, and that I'd love my father to be as proud of me as he is of her. He knows that I worry about my mum, who misses her children so much – too much really – and that I know when it is just she and Dad she feels really lonely. He knows that my dad works too much and that my brothers play too hard, but that I love them all and just wish I didn't feel like the runt of the litter. And Lily and Sam have always listened to me when I've needed to vent my frustrations about my job and my lack of social life.

I don't know Velna that well but she makes me laugh every single day at work, which has to count for something. And whilst I've never had long, protracted conversations with Jan, we've always been able to find common ground. And not only that, he really helps me in the store, taking a break from his cleaning to cart armfuls of stock around the departments for me early in the morning, that his presence has become invaluable to me. I don't think I'd want to work at Hardy's without any of these people. Which makes me wonder why I've been expending so much energy trying to impress people like Carly and Sharon so that they'll notice me. It suddenly occurs to me that I've also been guilty of taking the people I work with for granted.

I walk back to the table with three glasses pressed between my hands before returning to the bar to get the rest. Lily has moved on to tonic water now. As she said to us earlier after her Dorothy Parker quote: 'The most important thing about having fun is knowing when to stop, darlings.' At which point Jan had rebelliously downed his pint and slammed it on the table, which had made us all laugh.

I deliver the rest of the drinks and slide into my seat next to Sam. The conversations at the table have been split between the men on one side and the women on the other. Sam, Felix and Jan appear to be having a lively discussion about football, which I have no wish to participate in, and Lily and Justyna are talking quietly but passionately about something I can't quite hear but I'm presuming from the longing/murderous looks Justyna's throwing across the table that it's Jan.

'Are you OK?' I ask Velna, who appears to be lost in her own little world.

'Oh, YES, I'm vondervul,' she says vehemently, beaming at me brightly, which reveals the cute gap in her front teeth. 'I vos just thinking how vondervul it is to be out with such vondervul people. It's . . .' she sighs as if searching for a word to best describe how she's feeling, '. . . vonderful.'

I smile. Her command of the English language is good, if somewhat limited. 'Everyone is so vondervul here. Sam is very nice to look at, no? Oh, and Felix! How he makes me laugh!' she exclaims. 'And,' she claps her hands, 'Lily has said she will teach me some moves-of-the-dance for when I enter the Eurovision Song Contest. She is a – what is the word? – ah, yes, she is a *vondervul* woman.' Velna looks at Lily and nudges me. 'She is helping Justyna to not be so crazy-scary so Jan will fall into love with her.'

We both glance over and watch just as Lily pulls down Justyna's harsh, tight bun. It immediately makes an enormous difference. Suddenly her shoulders don't seem as large, or her forehead so big, or her stare so intense. Then Lily shows her how to flick her hair becomingly off her shoulders with one hand. We watch as Justyna replicates what Lily does, except somehow she looks more like she's violently batting off flies than trying to attract a man. Lily patiently shows her again and explains how to make the movement more fluid and femi-nine, which seems to work. Velna and I lean in to hear more of Lily's wisdom.

'Now, my dear, if you want a man to fall in love with you, you must master the art of being coy,' she is saying.

'Like a fishk?' Justyna furrows her monobrow.

'No, dear.' Lily somehow manages to refrain from laughing, despite the tell-tale twitching in her lips. 'Not like a fish, like a woman. Watch.'

And Lily looks down so that her eyelashes rest against her powdered cheeks then she looks up, flutters them in Jan's direction and looks away. Justyna stares at Lily, concentrating hard. 'Now you try it, dear,' Lily says with a wave of her hand.

Justyna looks down, then she purses her lips, looks up and stares at Jan like she wants to decapitate him. Velna sniggers and Justyna shoots a look at her that suggests she is next on her hit list.

'Not quite, dear,' Lily says kindly. 'Let's try it again. Watch me first . . .'

With one more try Justyna manages to catch Jan's eye, look coyly at him and look away so well that she doesn't notice him look longingly at her afterwards.

Velna and I applaud her and Justyna throws a begrudging smile in our direction.

The guys all look over at us at a natural lull in their conversation and talk soon turns to the store. Jan shakes his head wearily as he tells us how hard he found it this morning to get the store cleaned to the standard he'd been used to with a full team.

'It isk impossible. We cannot work like that. It isk like they have given up on the place,' he says sadly. 'If the store looks bad and not clean then the customers, they will not comes in.'

Justyna and Velna nod sadly in agreement as Lily puts her hand up.

'No offence, Jan darling,' Lily says. 'You've

always made the store look spit-spot, but it still didn't make customers come in. It wasn't until these wonderful makeovers started happening recently that Hardy's has started to sparkle again. But you're right, Jan. Cutting corners in essential departments like yours is not going to help Hardy's survive.' She sighs as she pulls her neck scarf through her fingers. 'I fear that whilst your team have been the first to suffer, it won't be long until all of us are out of jobs.' She presses her scarf to her mouth as her eyes fill with tears. 'It just makes me so sad,' she says. 'Hardy's has become my life. I'm not sure I'd want to carry on without it. I'd just be another OAP sitting around at home doing nothing. And Lily Carmichael does *not* sit around doing nothing.'

I take a deep breath. 'Well, you don't have to, Lily. Do nothing, I mean.' I say obliquely, faltering a little over my words. 'You could help. You all could, in fact.'

'What do you mean?' She dabs her eyes as Velna pats Lily's shoulder.

Felix winks and nods at me encouragingly as if he knows what I am about to say. He has a devilish sparkle in his eyes that tells me he knows more than he's letting on. I can't think how, though. I thought I'd kept my secret well. The only person I've told is Sam. I look at Felix questioningly and he clears his throat.

'I think our Evie has got something to tell us,' he says, clasping his hands together and sitting

359

back in his chair. I feel six pairs of expectant eyes looking at me. 'Isn't that right, love? She's been a busy girl over the last few days . . .'

'You know?' I say deliberately obliquely. Everyone is looking at each other in confusion.

''Course I do, love!' Felix laughs hoarsely and it turns into a cough. Lily leans over and pats him on the back. He smiles at her gratefully. 'I spend my entire shift watching security cameras – how could I not know? Besides, those makeovers have got Evie Taylor stamped all over them. Anyone who knows you could see that.'

'You?' A look of realization floods across Lily's expressive face as Velna, Justyna and Jan gape at me and then start clapping. Sam just smiles at me.

'Of course! she says. 'How could it possibly have been anyone other than dear Evie! You clever girl, darling! And clever you, Felix, for being a super-sleuth!' She pats both of us on the hand and I blush whilst Felix puffs up and nods proudly. I dip my head, embarrassed by the attention. 'I should've known it was you, darling. I mean, it's obvious. After all, you have such a flair for . . . what do they call lasting style these days?' She snaps her fingers so a flash of red polish whips through my vision. 'Vintage chic. Yes, that's it.'

'She's been doing a wonderful job, hasn't she?' Felix smiles at Lily. 'The place is looking just like the Hardy's we both knew and loved.'

'Vondervul!' echoes Velna as she grasps my hand and squeezes it. I smile at her thankfully.

Felix picks up his pint glass and addresses the group. 'I've been watching her for the past week, you know, gradually transforming each little enclave of the store in her own vision. It's magic what she does. Pure magic.'

'I've not seen the actual store makeovers themselves,' pipes up Sam, 'but I've seen her sketches of window and shop-floor displays, and they're brilliant. No wonder she's got the customers coming back to Hardy's.'

'But it's not enough,' I say sadly, draining then setting down my glass of wine on the table.

'Why not?' Jan and Justyna say in unison. She smiles shyly at him and he grins at her and scratches his shaved head.

I sigh, twirling my empty wine glass as I look at them all. 'Because I overheard Rupert telling Sharon that Hardy's takings need to rise by at least five hundred per cent to stand any chance of survival. The board have already told Rupert that if this hasn't happened by Boxing Day, the building will be sold and turned into the flagship London store for the high-end American chain Rumors. They're already in negotiations for the takeover.'

'But that's terrible!' Sam says, his eyebrows knitted together making him look older and more brooding. 'There must be something we can do?'

'I've been trying,' I say wearily. 'But I'm not sure it's enough.'

'Piffle!' Lily says, rising to her feet. 'The makeovers you've done in the store have drawn in more people in the last week than the store has had all year. The customers can't stop talking about the beautiful, nostalgic displays you've created. They're coming into my tearoom in droves and talking about why they've never been here before! It's quite astonishing.' She waggles her finger at me. 'You've started something, darling girl, you can't go giving up now.'

I smile at her and my eyes flitter around the table at all the concerned faces. 'I've got no intention of giving up, Lily. This store means too much to me, and to so many other people, to do that. But I can't do this on my own any more.'

'We'll help!' pipes up Velna, and starts singing an unrecognizable tune. We look at her blankly and she stops singing for a moment. '"Everyway That I Can",' she tells us knowledgeably and then sings the chorus. 'It vos Turkey's winning entry? In 2003.' Then she closes her eyes and carries on singing.

'Yes, whatsk can we do to help?' Justyna says loudly over Velna's voice. I think it's the first proper sentence she's ever spoken to me without baring her teeth.

'Well, I think I've thought of a way to make people sit up and take notice of Hardy's,' I say slowly. 'Not just the people who are walking by

362

and wandering in because of the makeovers on the ground floor.' I take a deep breath, feeling my confidence and passion build with every word. 'We need much more custom than that. I want to get the Regent Street shopping crowds coming to us because we're a destination store. I want the Londoners and tourists and out-of-towners that come to the West End to experience an old-fashioned shopping spectacle this Christmas that they won't find anywhere else.'

'Vondervul,' murmurs Velna as Lily claps her hands in delight.

But I haven't finished yet. Suddenly I am carried away with my vision and my enthusiastic audience, all of whom are listening intently to me. 'I want beautiful, eye-stopping, jaw-dropping, traditional-with-a-twist store windows and an enormous Christmas tree in the centre of the store by the staircase.' The words are falling out of my mouth as my mind spews out its secret vision to the only people I can trust. 'I want glittering fairy lights, and reindeer and a sleigh flying overhead. I want children to be charmed and adults awestruck. It's got to be big, beautiful, but most of all, it's got to be everything people want Christmas to be.'

My heart is racing and I'm out of breath as I finish my speech. There is a moment of silence, then Felix starts whistling through his fingers and Jan lets out a whoop. Sam stamps his feet and bangs on the table in appreciation, Justyna joins him and Lily blows kisses across the table at me. Velna starts humming Cliff Richard's Eurovision smash hit, 'Congratulations'.

'So I take it you are all with me?' I say with a smile.

'Yes!' they chant, and I laugh.

'Well, we've got a lot of work to do. Why don't we start by brainstorming some ideas?'

Felix eyes his empty glass ruefully.

'It's my turn to get the drinks in,' Sam says, standing up. 'I think we're going to need something special to help the ideas really flow.'

'I know just what we need,' Lily says, as she edges out from the table and over to Sam. 'Now then, darling boy, why don't you take my arm and escort me over?'

I smile as I watch Sam lead Lily off.

'What's she up to?' I say to Felix.

'Causing mischief, if I know Lily Carmichael!' Felix replies with a grin. 'She's always known how to draw a crowd. It's partly why I hired her all those years ago.'

I gawp at him, annoyed at myself that I've been so caught up with the makeovers and Joel that I've forgotten to ask Felix more about this. 'One of the best decisions I made, an' all,' he says. 'It was shortly after Walter Hardy, junior made me store manager. She was my first hire, actually. The tearoom had been struggling to make any money and I realized it wasn't about the tearoom, or the cakes, or the quality of the beverages, it was about who was running it. They had some pursed-lipped old dear who was good at baking but not good at selling. Lily drifted in one warm spring day in 1961, if I recall rightly. Anyway, it was shortly after she'd retired from dancing due to an injury. She loved fashion and was a regular in the Designers department. She was in her late twenties and wasn't looking for work – she was happy teaching dance at a local stage school – but she caused such a scene in the store when she came in I offered her the job anyway on the proviso she bring in her chums regularly and create a buzz about the place. And she certainly did that. She was as good with the celebrities and arty people as she was the regular Joes. Everyone loved her. Her little tearoom became the place to be seen. Of course,' he coughs a little, 'it helped that so many people wanted to see an ex-Windmill girl fully clothed and serving tea and cake. I knew that. She turned out to be as much of an attraction as the store's goods were. As were her friends.' He laughs. 'Being a bloke, I knew that men would flock here and bring their wives. In those days it was the men who held the purse strings, so if they came, their wives shopped. It was as simple as that. Takings went up the first day she started. Walter junior thought I was a genius,' he adds proudly.

He nudges me and nods his head in Lily's direction. She is now behind the bar expertly mixing Vodka Martinis to cheers from the waiting crowd of punters. The bartender carries them over to us on a tray, followed by Sam, who is making 'I am not worthy' bows as he leads Lily through the crowd.

'You are really something, Lily!' I laugh, as the bartender hands round our drinks.

'Thank you, my dear.' She curtsies gracefully and then grabs a glass off the tray and thrusts it at me. 'And so are you. A toast,' she says, taking the final glass for herself and holding it out over the table. The six of us hold up our glasses to hers and Lily smiles round at us all. 'To Evie, Hardy's very own Secret Elf. Long may her good work continue.' I blush as everyone clinks their glasses together.

'To Evie!' they echo.

'Evie?' Velna pipes up and I turn to face her. 'Why do all the other staff at Hardy's call you Sarah? It is not your name, no?'

'No, it's not,' I smile, and she purses her lips and pulls them to one side of her face.

'So why do they say Sarah the stockroom girl?' she asks, scratching her head, clearly quite confused.

'Do you know, Velna, I really don't know,' I reply, and I look around the table at Sam, Felix, Lily, and realize that these are my real friends; the ones who matter. The ones who have always known me – and like me for who I am.

'And to us!' says Felix, continuing the toast by holding his glass aloft again, 'Evie's specially chosen helpers.' He pauses as a wide grin spreads over his face. 'To Evie's Christmas Elves!' he exclaims.

'Evie's Elves!' echoes everyone. I feel my eyes fill with happy tears as they all cheer. It may be a cold December night outside but I'm flooded with the warmth of the comradeship that has flowed throughout this evening.

FRIDAY 9 DECEMBER

16 Shopping Days Until Christmas

CHAPTER 25

It's a busy morning in the stockroom. I'm not sure if it is the legacy of Lily's lethal cocktails but I'm struggling to keep up. The printer is spewing out tickets like they're going out of fashion, and my well-practised regime of collecting several required items and sending them up in groups to the necessary floors in the dumb waiter lift I have in the stockroom, and that I'm meant to use in busy situations like this, is somehow failing me. So far I have sent some talcum powders up to Designers, a handbag to Haberdashery and a couple of corsets down to Menswear. I only realized when Guy flounced in, sporting one of the corsets over his three-piece suit and asking me if I was trying to hint that he'd put on weight.

I shake my head and exhale slowly as I fight another wave of nausea. For someone in their twenties I am pathetically unpractised in the art of drinking on an empty stomach or staying out late. I staggered through the front door last night just before midnight. The house was in complete darkness and, after making myself some toast, I was about to tiptoe upstairs and collapse into bed when my phone beeped. I pulled it out of my bag and saw with a jolt of pleasure and then of guilt that I had three new texts, all from Joel. I'd been so caught up in my night with the gang that I hadn't even thought about him, let alone checked my phone. I also had a missed call and a message from Delilah but I ignored them and opened the texts from Joel instead.

'Hey there beautiful ice-skating queen, when can I see u again? Jx'

The next one had been sent fifteen minutes later.

'I miss you.'

Then the last one, which he'd just sent.

'I'm in my big hotel bed and it feels very empty without you. Want to come and join me? Jxxx'

I looked at the toast in my hand, my handbag, which was on the floor, and my front door keys, which were lying on top of the island unit, and made a quick assessment. If I got a cab on Regent's Park Road I could be with Joel in ten minutes.

In a flash I ran upstairs, grabbed a dress, some fresh underwear and tights, a toothbrush and make-up (I wasn't about to do the walk of shame again), chucked it all in my bag, scribbled a note for Delilah and dashed back out of the front door.

I was being spontaneous and it felt amazing.

To be honest, what happened when I got to Joel's hotel had felt pretty amazing too. And after that. And again in the morning when we woke up and lazily reached for each other under the covers, our gentle, tentative morning kisses quickly turning into something deliciously passionate. This time I managed to extricate myself from his glorious hotel bed at the same time as Joel, we showered together, got dressed and then wandered into town with our arms wrapped around each other for warmth, chatting animatedly as we walked through the gloriously quiet streets, trying not to slip on the icy pavements and delighting at the sight of an almost completely empty Regent Street.

Joel was due at a breakfast meeting at the Sanderson Hotel and I made an excuse and said that I had a big order of clothes to pull together for a customer. He took me in his arms and kissed me outside the store as the clock struck 7 a.m., we said goodbye and I floated in through the staff entrance. Luckily Felix had the morning off so he wasn't there to grill me. Dave, the day security guard, just nodded as I walked past and I actually felt relieved to be ignored. I didn't want anyone seeing me with Joel in case it somehow got back to Carly. She still talks about 'Mr Eye Contact Guy' like he's going to walk into the store any minute and sweep her off her feet.

And it's not like I can tell her he sort of already has.

I put down the armful of silk scarves that I'm sorting into colour, size and style on the accessories shelf as I feel a fresh wave of nausea overcome me. I glance at my watch. Noon. I've somehow missed my tea break and now it's time for lunch. I stand up, groaning a little as my head spins, holding on to the shelves for support for a second as another flurry of orders comes through on the printer. I grab the items and put them in the dumbwaiter, this time double- and then triple-checking that they're all correct. Then I reach for the phone, punch in the office number and wait for Sharon to answer.

'Hello,' she sings gaily, and I can't help but immediately wonder if Rupert is in the office with her. An image of the two of them together, like Joel and I were last night, fills my head and then I feel another wave of nausea that isn't related to my big night out.

'Hi, Sharon,' I say. 'It's Evie here.'

'Who?' she replies quickly. I mentally kick myself at my mistake.

'I mean, Sarah.' There's a long pause as she tries to work out who it is. 'From the stockroom,' I add wearily.

'Oh, yes. I know,' she says defensively. 'What can I do for you?'

'I've missed my break but the shop is really busy and there's lots of orders coming through on the printer,' I explain brightly. 'Could you send someone in to cover me so I can get some lunch?'

'But you've never had anyone cover you on your breaks before,' Sharon says sharply. 'What makes you think I have the spare staff now?'

'I-I just didn't want to leave the stockroom whilst there are so many orders coming through,' I explain.

'That's very sensible,' Sharon says pointedly.

'B-but I really do need a break.'

'Don't we all, dear,' she laughs.

I feel uncharacteristic anger rising through my body. I've worked so hard for so long, and for what? Not even a little bit of respect. Well, I've had enough, I'm not being treated like this any more.

'Sharon,' I say evenly, 'I have been here since seven this morning. In my contract I am entitled to a half an hour break every four hours. Not only that, I have been doing unpaid overtime for the past week.' And the rest, I feel like adding. 'The shop-floor staff all have people to cover them when they go for a break and I think I deserve to be treated the same.' I pause and take a deep breath. 'I am happy to put a call through to Mr Hardy to explain the situation if I have to. Unless he's there with you now?'

I hear Sharon's sharp intake of breath. 'Fine. I'll send someone down who's not busy immediately.'

'Thank you,' I say, and put the phone down, feeling a small swell of triumph as I do so.

Ten minutes later the stockroom door creaks open and Carly storms in, her face clouded with annoyance.

'Oh, Carly!' I say brightly, pulling my bag onto

my shoulder. 'Have you come for a chat? Now's not a great time, I'm afraid. I'm about to go for a break and I'm just waiting for someone to come in to cover me. Sharon agreed we needed someone to oversee things here while I'm gone. It's great it's so busy this morning, isn't it?'

I smile warmly but Carly doesn't answer. She just folds her arms and stares miserably around the stockroom.

'They should be here any minute. I'm dying for some fresh air and a cup of Lily's tea.'

'Just go then,' she mutters moodily.

I'm confused. 'But I have to wait for—'

'They're here, all right?' she says testily. 'I'm here. Sharon sent me to cover you. She said that even people in management positions have to get their hands dirty sometimes,' she looks around the stockroom and grimaces, 'and she said I may as well start now. God, I'm so depressed! How dare she stick me in this hellhole, away from the action!'

I feel myself bristle. Hellhole? I am as offended as if she'd dissed my own home. It's obviously good enough for her when she wants to come down and talk about herself for hours, but it's not good enough for her to work in?

'I'm sorry you feel like that,' I say evenly. 'I like it. Although I guess I have to, working here for eight hours every single day.'

'I suppose some people are more cut out for this kind of work than others,' Carly says, inspecting her fingernails.

I clench my jaw. 'Well, I'll only be half an hour. Do you need me to explain anything about how everything works?'

'It's hardly rocket science, is it?' she scoffs. 'No, I'll be fine. Go have your break. Ooh, and can you bring me a cup of tea on the way back?'

I open my mouth to point out that she could just make one herself, and then close it again. She has already settled herself down on the sofa, pulled out a magazine from her handbag and is flicking through it as if she has already forgotten I am there. I turn and walk swiftly out of the stockroom, trying not to let my annoyance show.

I stride purposefully through the beauty department towards the grand central staircase, feeling my mood lighten as I go. Gwen and Jenny are proffering perfumes, taking Iris's soaps from the display and handing them to smiling customers.

Suddenly I spot a familiar figure sashaying towards me. It's Jane, working her new look like she's a supermodel. She's even wearing the little black netted hat I gave her as an added extra accessory and which she'd said she'd never wear as she didn't want people staring at her. Now, both staff and customers (men and women) all turn and stare admiringly as she glides past them. It's like looking at a different woman. I wave but she doesn't see me.

'If Sharon asks, I'm just off to get a quick sandwich,' she says to Becky, who is helping out in the beauty department again. 'It's so busy up there I don't have time to take a lunch break so I've just left Elaine covering while I'm gone. I'll only be ten minutes,' she calls over her shoulder. I grin to myself as I walk down the stairs. Who'd have thought that there was such a siren hidden underneath all those tent-like clothes Jane used to wear?

As I reach the bottom of the stairs I see that Rupert is in Menswear doing his daily rounds. He is chatting to Guy, his rotund, weather-beaten face even brighter than usual as he throws his arms around animatedly. I walk a little closer to see if I can hear what he's saying.

'What you've done in this department is remarkable, Guy, just remarkable!' Rupert is exclaiming. I feel a glow of pleasure at the deflected compliment. Even if I do say so myself, it looks like an entirely different place from how it was a week ago. It's buzzing with customers; the displays are bright and interesting and stylish. I even heard on the store's grapevine that a pop star and his stylist came in yesterday and bought three entire looks off the mannequins, apparently for some new video he's shooting. Guy had been most excited. Apparently this guy is set to be the next big thing on the music scene. Everyone in the store was talking about it.

I fire off a quick picture text to Sam to show him the bustling department. He kept saying at the pub how gutted he was he hadn't had a chance to see any of the makeovers for himself. I've promised to give him a tour when he next does a delivery, but until then, I've been sending him updates.

'Oh, thanks, Rupe. It is rather fabulous, isn't it?' Guy says with his usual lack of modesty. 'It was a lot of hard work but it seems to have paid off.'

'It certainly has,' Rupert says, patting Guy on the back. 'I just wish I knew how you'd done it.'

'Oh,' Guy says, waving his hand, 'it's just a natural creative flair, you know? You could call it a gift, I guess.'

I smile to myself. A gift. That's it. It was my Christmas gift to Rupert – and Guy.

'You must have had some help, though,' presses Rupert. 'I mean, looking around the place it feels like someone with a real knowledge of vintage fashion must have had a hand in it. Someone who works as a stylist every day, you know, someone like Carly? I mean, she's our in-store style expert.'

'Oh, um, well, of course she helped,' stutters Guy, clearly struggling to retain some glory without risking Carly's wrath. He has no idea who did the makeover either, so it could have been her. 'Has she said anything?'

Rupert shakes his head. 'I think she's too modest.'

'Well,' Guy says, drawing himself up and pulling on one of his braces, 'I couldn't have done it without her, obviously. We, er, we make a great team. Her style, my vision, we're irreplaceable!'

'If you carry on selling like you are you certainly will be, Guy,' laughs Rupert. 'I can't wait to show the Board your department's figures. Keep up the good work!' And he moves off, making notes on his clipboard as he passes me at the bottom of the stairs.

'Hello, Mr Hardy,' I say shyly, but he's so busy scribbling he doesn't seem to hear me.

Lily's tearoom is full of customers as I walk in, cups are clinking, the cake stands are empty and Lily is happily purveying her territory from behind the counter.

'Evie darling! I wondered where you'd got to this morning. I thought maybe you hadn't made it to work after last night!'

'I made it all right,' I say with a grimace. 'I just haven't been able to escape till now, it's been so busy.'

Suddenly I wish I'd followed Lily's lead when it came to stopping at two drinks. She had a sip from her third when we did the toast but then refused to have any more. So, obviously I drank it for her. Now she looks as fresh as ever, whereas I feel like something that Rupert would feed to his animals at his farm.

'I know, fabulous isn't it?' Lily exclaims, her blue eyes glittering like a sun-kissed ocean. 'Although I have to say I could do with some help in here. My legs aren't what they used to be and I've been rushed off them this morning. Luckily, I called Iris and she said she'll come in and help me.'

I spot Iris, serving tea and tiny triangle-cut sandwiches to a couple sitting in the corner. She has a retro-print 1970s apron on over her mustard polo neck, cream chinos and a big floppy fedora.

'I bet she's a wonderful assistant,' I smile.

'She is,' Lily says. 'We've got a great system going. I have to say, it's rather lovely having her here, not to mention all the customers. Last night made me realize just how lonely I've become, spending all day in this empty tearoom and then going back to my little flat. It's just not how Lily Carmichael was meant to live. I'm a people person, darling. Always was, always will be!' She pauses and clasps my hands in hers. 'You know, I had such fun last night. And I'm so happy Sam suggested we meet every week. It'll give me something to look forward to. You have no idea how lonely I've been ...'

'Oh, I think I do,' I murmur before meeting her gaze. 'You're not the only one who hasn't had much of a social life until now, you know,' I say with a wry smile.

'But that's all changing, right?' she says, raising a thin, pencilled eyebrow. 'Is that nice young Sam the fella you've been courting?'

I feel a blush rise to my cheeks. 'Sam? No, he's just a friend.'

Her smile fades a little. 'Oh, I see. But I wonder if he does ...?' I frown at her as I try to work out what she means. She leans in closer. 'If I'm not much mistaken, Sam is sweet on you, my girl,' she says, tapping my arm with her hand.

I'm about to deny this when Iris dashes over, gives me a squeeze and delivers an order to Lily. 'Two teas, one scone, one Chelsea bun and a plate of roast beef and horseradish sandwiches, please, dear, and make it quick!'

'Coming up, Iris darling!' Lily takes Iris's scribbled piece of paper and then turns to me. 'Do you fancy making the teas for me?' And she throws an apron at me.

'Do I have much choice?' I reply.

She shakes her head. 'Nope. You will get lunch on the house, though. Now come on, no time for chatting!'

By the time I've helped Lily and Iris through the lunchtime rush, had my sandwich and weaved my way back through the busy store, it's been well over half an hour since I left the stockroom. Carly isn't happy and when I look at the stockroom, nor am I.

'What on earth's happened here?' I ask as I look around at the bombsite that used to be my haven.

'It was busy,' snaps Carly from where she's sitting in the middle of an aisle, surrounded by overflowing boxes. 'You weren't here. I did the best I could. You could have left me some instructions; I thought you'd only be gone ten minutes.'

'Sharon asked you to cover me for my lunch break, which is always half an hour,' I say evenly as I bend down and start scooping up the stock to tidy it away. Seeing my neat stockroom look like this is making me feel even more nauseous than I did before lunch. I stand up. 'And I did offer to tell you where everything was but you told me you didn't need me to.'

'Well, you should have told me anyway,' Carly says petulantly.

'All the aisles are clearly marked for the relevant department, and each section in the aisle is marked alphabetically with the relevant groups of items. *And* I left out the annotated map for you. Like you said yourself, Carly, it's not rocket science.'

'Oh, well, you're back now,' she says brightly. 'I guess I should go and see what's going on with my staff on the shop floor. Who knows what they'll be up to without their manager around.'

'Aren't you going to help me clear up this mess?'

'Oh, no, I've got far more important things to do. Besides, you're the expert here. See you, honey!'

And Carly swoops out of the stockroom without a backward glance, leaving me surrounded by her chaos.

CHAPTER 26

'She is driving me mad!'

'Who does she think she is?'

'That promotion has gone straight to her head!'

'Rupert's an idiot if he doesn't see it . . .'

'. . . She didn't do the makeovers, no way!'

'She doesn't know what she's doing!'

It's 5 p.m. and I've finally managed to leave for the day. The store has quietened down with just a few straggling customers wandering through the ground floor. A group of staff is clustered by the perfume counter, talking about Carly. They don't notice me quietly joining them at the back.

'I just can't stand the way she speaks to me,' says Elaine. 'She's a complete nightmare to work with. And she hasn't got a clue what she's doing.'

There is a murmur of agreement.

'I don't think that's fair,' says Paula from Personal Shopping, valiantly defending her old colleague. 'She was a brilliant personal stylist. Tamsin and I miss her up there – as do all the customers.'

'Well, you can have her back then,' grumbles

Elaine. 'It'll get her out of my hair. Anyway, unlike pretty much every other department in this bloody place, Designers is quieter now than before the makeover. That's why I don't believe she's responsible for the others.'

'So who is?' pipes up Becky. 'And by the way, if it's any of you lot can I request my department be the next on the list? I've become a glorified beauty assistant because my department is still so quiet.'

'You're a very good beauty assistant, though,' says Jenny, kindly.

'Thanks, Jen,' Becky sighs. 'I just think I need to prove that I can do my job. Rupert was sniffing around today and he didn't seem very pleased. He and Sharon kept muttering together, but that woman's voice is so loud I could hear what they were saying. According to them if I don't get my act together, I'll be out of a job before the New Year.'

I take a sharp breath and vow to make over Becky's department next.

'Don't you worry,' says Susan from Haberdashery, and Bernie nods in agreement. 'We'll stick up for you. You're a very good saleswoman, you just need some help with merchandising.'

'I know,' Becky wails. 'I just don't know how to make a load of brown and black handbags look nice.' Everyone nods sympathetically.

'I just wish we knew who was doing the makeovers,' says Gwen.

'Do you think it's Sharon?' Paula says. 'She's the most experienced.'

'Nah, she's as bemused as the rest of us,' says Tamsin.

'What about Rupert?' Becky suggests.

Everyone laughs. 'He wouldn't have a clue,' Tamsin scoffs. 'Numbers and farm animals are his things, not visual merchandising.'

'Guy?'

'No.'

'How about Jane?'

There is a pause, everyone looks around, but Jane is nowhere to be seen. I actually saw her leaving hand in hand with Stuart about five minutes before. They were off for some romantic pre-dinner drinks. Jane told me that they're dating like some new couple, not an old married one. She seems utterly blissful.

'Could be,' says Elaine thoughtfully. 'Have you seen how fab she looks all of a sudden? Like some 1950s siren! Maybe she's into all this old-fashioned stuff and has been secretly doing the makeovers.'

There is nodding and quiet deliberation whilst more names are thrown up for discussion. Every name, in fact, except for mine.

It don't know whether to be relieved or offended.

I slip away as they continue to deliberate who Hardy's Secret Elf is.

The street is flooded with bright orange light from the old Victorian streetlamps outside the store. And suddenly the screen on my phone is flooded with light too.

'Joel!' I answer immediately, unable to hide the pleasure in my voice.

'Hey, gorgeous,' he drawls. 'I've missed you today. How's work been?'

'Oh, you know, same old same old,' I reply obliquely, hoping he won't expect any more details.

It's one thing to pretend to be someone I'm not, but I'm trying to make things as uncomplicated as possible. As much as I'm relishing my time with Joel, I know that it can't go on forever. Either he will discover that I'm just a lowly stockroom girl and will never want to see me again, or he won't find that out, things will go on being as wonderful as they are, and then he will want to get closer to me than I can let him. You know, meet my family and friends, introduce me to his, and obviously that can never happen. Ultimately it's a no-win situation but I'm trying not to let that thought cast a shadow over everything, because for the time being I want to wallow in this imaginary world where I am a girl like Carly with a gorgeous man and a fabulous job. I know it can't last, but the prospect of going back to my old life, to the old me just yet, doesn't bear thinking about. So all I can do is block out any thoughts of what will happen when Joel finds out who I really am and focus on the here and now.

Joel and me, together, alone. With no one else

around who could spoil it. Is that too much to ask?

'I hear you,' Joel laughs, his voice as rich and warm as a cup of Java coffee. 'Sometimes work just feels like one long groundhog day. I have to say, right now, I wish that I could just pack up and go back to Willow Grove and work in the store.'

I gulp as my heart plummets. 'You're not going to, though, are you?' I say quietly.

'No,' he sighs. 'Too much business here. But it won't be long. My flight is booked for Boxing Day.'

A silence falls between us.

'That's little more than two weeks away,' I say at last.

'I know,' he murmurs, 'that's why I want to make the most of every moment with you.'

I feel a flood of joy and then despair as it occurs to me what this really is. I'm just a holiday romance, a convenient distraction while Joel's in London. He's settled for me because I'm at his disposal; he can use me for now and then get rid of me when he's done here. Just like Jamie did.

'You could come back with me,' he says hopefully, and suddenly I feel ashamed. Have I got him all wrong?

'That's crazy,' I say, immediately dismissing the idea as I imagine he hoped I would. Wrong again.

'Why?' he laughs. 'What's so crazy about visiting

388

your boyfriend over the festive season and meeting his family?'

Boyfriend.

'Boyfriend,' I say aloud, disguising my joy with a gentle tease in my voice. 'Is that what you are?'

'I hope so,' Joel replies. 'I know it's not been very long . . .'

'You're right, it hasn't,' I say softly. 'And you live in a different country, and I . . .'

And I'm not who you think I am.

'I know all that, but we can work it out. I really like you, Carly.'

'And I-I like you, too,' I reply at last.

'Well, at least that's settled!' he laughs. 'As I was saying, I just want to spend as much time with my *girlfriend* as possible. So, can I see you tomorrow? I know it's short notice for a Saturday night and a girl like you has probably got lots of offers . . .'

I can't help but smile through the tears that are forming in my eyes. If only he knew. I want to see him so badly but I promised ages ago that I'd baby-sit for Delilah as she's going out with her girlfriends. But, I'm so tempted to see Joel. After all, there's only just over two weeks left till Christmas and I have to make the most of these precious moments before he goes back to Pennsylvania and I never see him again. But Delilah, the kids . . . I've barely been there all week. And I promised. I can't go back on my promise.

'I can't. I'm baby-sitting,' I reply remorsefully.

'I could keep you company?' he offers, with a sexy tease to his voice.

'Oh, you don't want to do that,' I say quickly, knowing I can't bring him back to Delilah's house in case I slip up and he realizes I live there. 'Not on a Saturday night. Let me see if I can get out of it. I'm sure my sis— I mean, my *friend* won't mind. Let me just call her and I'll call you right back.'

I dial Delilah's number and she picks up immediately.

'Evie?' she says. 'Are you OK?' She sounds strange.

'I'm fine, I've just been really busy at work,' I reply, feeling guilty for neglecting her.

'But you didn't come back at all last night,' she points out.

'Oh, that.' I feel myself blushing. 'I went to see Joel. I left you a note.'

'I saw it,' Delilah says, the disapproval apparent in her voice. 'I just hope you know what you're doing, Evie.'

'I do!' I reply defensively. 'He really likes me, Lila, honestly he does.'

'Of course he does,' she says softly. 'How could he not? Just be careful, that's all I'm saying. I know how vulnerable you are.'

I swallow, trying hard not to cry as I think of how she nursed me through my last break-up, a break-up that until I met Joel still felt terribly raw.

And now I think of what I overheard Will saying and how vulnerable my big sister is, while she is busy worrying about me. I feel a stab of guilt at what I'm hiding from her.

'I know, Lila, but you needn't worry. Joel's a really nice guy, honestly. I think you'd like him,' I add shyly, suddenly imagining him reclining on one of her Eames chairs after a cosy dinner party. Just like one of the family.

She doesn't reply. I try to gauge if this is a good moment to ask for more time off. 'Actually, Delilah, I was just calling to ask you something.'

'I hope it's not another night off,' she says curtly.

That'll be no, then.

'Erm, it was actually,' I say tentatively, then can't help blurting out, 'Joel wants to see me tomorrow and I really want to so please say I can, Lila, pleeeease.' I hear the begging tone in my voice and suddenly see how ridiculous this is. I'm twenty-eight years old and I feel like a child asking her mother for permission to go round her friend's house on a Saturday night. Shouldn't a woman of my age have more freedom? I realize I'm holding my breath, waiting for my sister to answer.

'What? No! I'm meant to be going out with the girls, Evie. And after the week I've had I really need to let off some steam.'

'But Joel's—'

'Joel's seen more of you this week than I have!' Delilah shoots back. 'Anyway, you were with him last night!'

391

'I know, I know, but—' I begin, hoping that Delilah will change her mind. She knows how much I've needed this – and how long I've waited for it

'No buts, Evie,' Delilah says firmly. 'I need you home tomorrow tonight.' And she puts down the phone before I can respond.

I press redial to Joel's mobile miserably.

'Hey,' he answers warmly. 'So do we have a date?'

'Um, I'm really sorry, Joel,' I say, trying to stop my voice from cracking. 'I can't tomorrow. I, um, I have to baby-sit.' It's not that I'm upset that I can't see Joel, but more that Delilah put down the phone on me. She's never done that. Ever.

'Oh, that sucks,' he says distractedly. 'Are you sure I can't join you?'

'No!' I exclaim, then realize how bad that must sound. 'It's just, er, my friend isn't keen on people she doesn't know coming over when the kids are in bed, you know, just in case they wake up and get scared that a stranger is in the house.'

'OK, I can understand that,' he says reasonably. Then adds: 'How about Sunday? You're not working then, are you?'

'I'm not,' I smile, thinking of my rare one day off a week from both the store and the kids – and feeling happier just at the thought of seeing him.

'Great! Let's do something fun. You said you live in Clapham, right? I'll come and pick you up.'

'No!' I exclaim. Oh shit. Oh, I'm such an idiot. Why didn't I foresee this happening? If he picks me up from there, he'll find out who I really am. I laugh forcibly. 'I mean no you don't have to pick me up. We can meet somewhere else . . . like the, uh, tube station?' I add somewhat desperately.

'Fine . . .' Joel says quietly. There's a long pause before he speaks again. 'Listen, Carly, I'm kinda getting the feeling that you're blowing hot and cold on me. Is there anything you're not telling me? I mean, I'd love to see where you live and meet your friends, but if it's too soon or if I'm crowding you or coming on too strong, then just tell me . . .'

'No!' I almost shout. I have to think of something else to say other than no. But here it is again. 'No,' I say again. 'Look, Joel,' I try to elaborate but don't know how to without telling him the truth, 'it's not that you're crowding me, I promise, it's just . . .' I'm scrabbling around for words, desperately trying to think of a way to convince him that everything is OK. '. . . You know what?' I say at last, beaten by my lack of imagination. 'I'd really love for you to see where I live . . .'

'Great!' he replies enthusiastically. 'So shall I pick you up at yours then?'

'Yes! Lovely!' I say in a strangulated voice. 'Shall we say, er, 8.30 a.m? Nice and bright and early! We could er, go for breakfast or something?'

'O . . . K,' Joel replies. 'I can do early. What's your address again?'

'Um, it's, er, Venn Street,' I say, trying to remember Carly's address.

'Oh, yeah,' he drawls, 'I remember. Number thirty-four, isn't it?'

'Yes,' I squeak.

'Great. I'll be there!' And Joel rings off.

I put my phone back in my bag and rub my forehead wearily. I now just have to hope that Carly has one of her usual big Saturday nights out and won't be getting up till past lunchtime. I know she's not usually an early riser at weekends, which is why I suggested to Joel that he come round so early. If I can just get him to meet me outside the flat, time it so I can just pretend to shut and lock the front door, I can somehow steer him away for breakfast without Carly seeing us, or having to show him inside the flat. It's a crazy, desperate plan . . . but if I'm lucky it might just work.

SUNDAY 11 DECEMBER

14 Shopping Days Until Christmas

CHAPTER 27

My Saturday night spent baby-sitting for a sleeping Lola and Raffy was interminably long and uncomfortable, mainly because I couldn't concentrate on anything, so consumed was I with worry for Delilah who, since our phone conversation the day before, kept making snide comments in my direction via her dialogue with the kids. It was all, 'Isn't Auntie Teevee looking pretty these days, Lola? She's got a new boyfriend. That's why we hardly see her any more.' She was being unfair but I couldn't say anything as I knew her mood was blacker than black because of Will's absence all day (at a weekend work meeting on the golf course, apparently). But even when she left the house to go on her night out, the icy atmosphere remained. I went to bed at ten o'clock, feeling increasingly like I was living in a place I didn't belong. That's why I'm so thankful that it's finally Sunday and I can relax and be myself for the day. Well, kind of.

The tube shudders to a stop at Clapham Common station at just gone 8 a.m., and I pick up my bag

397

and bound out of my empty carriage. On the platform, a handful of miserable, tired-looking people stare blankly into the distance as I walk past them, the unfortunate few for whom Sunday is a working day just like any other. I smile sympathetically at them as I pass, but they don't seem to see me, or if they do, they choose to ignore me. One of the downsides of working in retail is that weekends are no longer your own but I've always been lucky enough to have Sundays off.

I exit the station shivering and clutching my A-Z. It's a bright but cold morning and Clapham High Street is devoid of life, save for a few stragglers from the night before. I cross the street, past Starbucks and the newsagent's, and take an immediate left into Venn Street, past some cute bars and restaurants and a little cinema. It's a nice but not particularly salubrious street, which surprises me. The houses are all unremarkable Victorian terraces, not at all where I imagined Carly living. I'd always seen her in some swanky modern riverside flat with a private gym and roof terrace. But this is all very . . . ordinary.

I walk down the street, squinting to look at the numbers on each of the doors before coming to a halt in front of number 34. I glance at my watch: eight fifteen. Joel won't be here for at least another fifteen minutes. He might even be late. Oh God, please don't be late, I think, staring at Carly's flat. All the blinds are closed, which is a good sign. Hopefully my calculations were right and she'll be in bed most of the morning recovering from a big night out.

I sit on the wall by the front gate and wait, feeling sick with anticipation and nerves, not just because I'm seeing Joel, but because of my deception. I mean, who does this? Who goes to these kinds of lengths to pretend to a guy they're someone they're not in order to date them? If anyone had asked me a month ago if this is what I'd be doing then I'd have told them they were mad. But then again, these days I really don't recognize much about myself.

I spot Joel approaching round the corner and I jump off the wall and run up to the front door, fiddling with my keys and looking around furtively. He is walking slowly, distinctive white earphones plugged in his ears with the wires leading down to his pockets, which his hands are thrust into, his head bobbing to the tune playing on his iPod, and as I watch him, I suddenly remember why I'm going to all this trouble. I'm doing it because Joel is gorgeous and interesting and funny, and he would never be interested in a girl like me otherwise. This is the only way I can get a taste of what life is like for girls like Carly; beautiful girls with great jobs and their own flat and lots of friends. A life I can only dream of – or at best, pretend to have.

I am still fumbling with my own house keys, pretending to use them to lock Carly's front door when, to my horror, the front door swings open and Carly herself appears before me. Her chestnut hair is scraped back into a pony tail, she has a black baseball cap on, and gym clothes and trainers. Understandably she looks somewhat surprised and confused to see me. So much so that she appears to be struggling to work out who the hell I am.

'Who the hell are y . . . ?' she begins, peering at me from under the shadow of her baseball cap. 'Sarah?' she finishes incredulously, looking me up and down. In her defence I guess I do look more dressed up than normal. Today I have chosen a cute 1960s orange dress with contrasting white collar, sleeves and pockets. I curled my hair and pulled it back into a ponytail so it's really bouncy, and I'm wearing black tights, my black brogues and a cropped black jacket, with a thick white scarf wrapped around my neck. It's kind of quirky but I'm hoping it says 'relaxed but stylish Sunday attire, perfect for a day spent sightseeing and snogging a gorgeous American'. Either that or it just says 'overdressed'.

I wave and smile slightly desperately. 'Hiya, Carly! Er, can I come in?'

'Sure. I didn't recognize you all dressed up like that. Hey,' she winks, 'have you been out all night?'

I glance back over my shoulder and see that Joel is approaching the curve in the road and if he looks up in the next five seconds he's bound to see me on Carly's doorstep, talking to her, and then I am going to have some serious explaining to do.

'It's complicated!' I squeak, pushing past Carly and into her hallway without being invited. Thankfully she shuts the door behind me quickly.

'Are you OK, Sarah? You seem really out of sorts,' she says, clasping my arm in concern. 'What are you doing here anyway? I was just on my way out for a run.' She laughs somewhat forcefully and holds her forehead. 'I've found it's, you know, the best way to cure a hangover. I, er, had a really big night out last night too at this great new club on the King's Road. I was out with all my girlfriends and we had this completely crazy night. You'll never guess what happened. We, er . . .' She pauses and bites her thumb-nail. 'Sorry, do you want a cup of tea?'

'That would be great!' I say, edging into lounge and away from the front door.

I take a moment to glance around. The room has got a blue sofa and an old, stained white armchair covered with a throw. There is a parquet floor with an old, cappuccino-coloured rug on the floor, which I recognize as being from Ikea. In fact, it all looks entirely furnished by Ikea. White church candles and magazines are scattered on the tea-ringed coffee table. There is a single plate with some leftover pasta and a half-empty glass of wine on the table and a TV guide open tellingly at Saturday night's pages.

'You know,' Carly calls, poking her head round

from the galley kitchen just off the lounge, 'I didn't know you knew where I lived.' She glances at the plate and then back at me. 'Oh,' she blusters. 'That was the dinner I ate before I went out on my *crrrazy* night last night!' She comes in and scoops up the plate and the wine glass, then scurries back out again.

I hear the kettle boiling and water being poured into two cups. I use the opportunity to open the blinds and peer out at the street. Joel has paused in front of Carly's front gate, his back to the flat, fumbling with his earphones, which he is stuffing into his pockets. He smooths back his hair and turns round, and I quickly close the blind just as Carly comes into the room holding two cups of steaming tea.

I hear footsteps on the pathway and panic. Joel is about to knock on the door.

'Sugar!' I shout, thrusting my cup back at her. 'I need sugar, please!' Carly looks at me strangely but takes the cup and walks back into the kitchen. She pauses mid-walk as there's a knock at the door, and turns back to me in the lounge.

'Who can that be? I'm not expecting anyone.'

'Oh, er, it must be the religious nuts I saw earlier when I was waiting for you,' I say, thinking quickly. 'They've been knocking on doors all down the street. Don't worry! I'll get rid of them for you!'

She disappears into the kitchen and I dive into the hallway and open the front door breathlessly.

'Joel!' I whisper, and smile at him. He leans forward to kiss me but I push him away with my hand. He looks confused.

'Not here,' I hiss. 'Er, the neighbours might see.' I tap my finger against my nose. 'They're nosy, verrrry nosy.'

'R-ight,' he says, a hint of a smile forming on his lips. 'Can I come in then?'

'No!' I say, squeezing the front door shut against my head. 'I can't let you in. The place is in a real state and, er, I'm embarrassed! Yep, that's right. I'm ashamed.'

'You don't have to be . . .'

'I do! It's really awful. Listen, give me fifteen minutes and I'll be right out. I'll meet you at the little café at the bottom of the road. You can see my place another time.' And I slam the door in front of Joel before he has a chance to protest. I lean back against it, breathing heavily before dashing back into the lounge just as Carly re-enters with our tea.

'Who was it?' she asks.

'Oh, you know,' I roll my eyes, 'just those Bible nuts, like I said. I told them we're not interested.'

'Thanks, Sarah,' she says handing me my tea. 'Now, is everything all ri—'

I take a sip of tea and glance over my shoulder at the window. 'Shi-SUGAR!' I shout again, thrusting my cup back at Carly. 'I need another sugar!'

Carly looks at me and shakes her head as if I am mad, but takes the cup and walks back to the kitchen just as Joel passes by the lounge window. This time I follow her into the small galley kitchen. Dirty plates and cups line the surfaces and Carly is trying to stack them quickly into the sink. Her flat isn't at all like she described. She always made it sound so perfect and stylish; a real haven. But it looks like she and her best friend live in very messy, rented digs. I glance at the old, white fridge that is covered with Post-it notes of scrawled messages like 'Carly, don't touch my milk!', 'Pay the leccy bill!' and 'Anna's food on the left, do not touch!' I furrow my brow as I look at them. I thought Carly shared with her best friend. She has always talked about how well they get on. But this Anna girl, whoever she is, doesn't sound at all like a friend. A friend would share everything, surely? As much as Delilah and I aren't getting on right now, she would never leave me messages like that. It's just disrespectful. Then again, maybe I have an unrealistically romantic vision of what flatshares are like. I've never had one, after all.

Or maybe, a voice inside my head says, *Carly has painted an unrealistic vision of her flatshare.* I am beginning to think, having seen her home, that Carly's life isn't as fabulous as she's made out. I suspect that the pasta, wine and TV guide was her actual Saturday night, not the crazy night out clubbing she was telling me about.

I glance at her as she stirs my tea, wondering if Carly hasn't been 100 per cent honest with me either.

Half an hour later I manage to escape Carly's flat. She didn't seem to want me to leave. She started interrogating me about what had caused me to end up at her flat early on a Sunday morning. I just invented some work crisis, which meant she quickly lost interest and moved on to telling me all about her fabulous weekend, and what she is planning to do for Christmas. But right now I wouldn't be surprised if Carly is actually going to be home alone for most of it. Her perfect life just doesn't ring true any more.

I push open the café door and immediately spot Joel, sitting in the middle of the room, nursing a coffee and reading the Sunday papers.

'Joel,' I say, standing in front of him. He doesn't look up. I pull out a chair and sit down. 'I'm so sorry about that. I'm a bit OCD when it comes to tidiness; my sister calls me OCD-Evie, actually,' I babble and Joel frowns.

'Why?'

'Why what?'

'Why does she call you OCD-Evie? That's not your name,' Joel points out.

My heart actually properly stops beating for a moment and I think I might just throw up.

'Oh, pff,' I say, waving my hand dismissively, 'you know, it's just a stupid pet name. She thinks

405

it's funny. *Obviously*, it's not. Sisters, eh, who'd have 'em?'

Joel smiles weakly and takes a sip of his espresso.

'Do you want a coffee?' he asks politely, all intimacy gone between us.

I gulp, thinking about the fact that Carly may soon leave her flat to go to the gym and I stand up again. 'No, thanks,' I say with a big, fake smile. 'Shall we just go? I've had a good idea for what we can do today.'

I walk towards the door eagerly and open it, glancing out covertly first to check that Carly isn't jogging down the street.

Joel looks up at me, frowns and shrugs as he drains the rest of his coffee.

'OK, you're the boss,' he says, and he throws some money on the table and walks past me, his hands plunged into his pockets, eyes averted.

You could literally drive a bus between us, I think as we wait at the bus stop for the double-decker that will take us to Waterloo. Joel is standing two feet away from me, staring ahead, his hands still in his pockets as if to ensure that they don't roam anywhere near mine. I don't blame him, though. For one thing, it is very cold, and for the other I've been acting so strangely this morning I'm clearly going to have to work really hard to build up his trust again. He hasn't accepted my excuses in the same way that Carly did. It's as if he knows me better than that.

We hop on the bus and Joel takes the seat in front of me.

'So where are we going then?' he says, turning round to face me without much enthusiasm. I swallow, desperate to win back his affection. I hate him being so distant from me. Not when we've shared so much already.

'Um, well, I thought you probably haven't had a chance to see much of London and I figured there was one brilliant way to do it. Especially on a day like today.' I glance out of the window just as a burst of bright sunshine beams through. I delve into my handbag and pull out two tickets and present them shyly. 'We're going on the London Eye!'

His face breaks into a welcome smile and he takes the tickets and looks at them.

'For real? I've wanted to do that since I got here!'

I exhale in relief. 'Oh, I'm so glad,' I say, beaming back at him. 'I thought maybe you'd done the whole tourist thing here already. After all, you are American,' I add playfully, slightly nervous about teasing him when he is clearly so confused by my behaviour. There is a moment of silence and I wonder if my gamble has backfired.

'Will I be able to see Li-*che*-ster Square?' Joel drawls loudly, deliberately using the wrong pronunciation so that the other passengers on the bus overhear him and roll their eyes. 'What about Bucking*ham* Palace?' he adds. Then his eyes crinkle and he laughs loudly. I join him, mostly out of relief that the Joel I know and, well, like a lot, is back with me. For now.

The queue for the London Eye is long, winding back and forth along the Southbank. The traditional German-style Christmas market is just opening; there are little log cabins dotted along the river's edge, selling all sorts of festive goodies, including hot cider. After the morning I've had, I'm tempted to buy one, but acknowledge it's a little early. We grab a couple of lattes instead and join the end of the queue, chatting animatedly about our week. Joel seems to have thawed considerably and is back to his friendly self, but he has still made no effort to kiss me or even hold my hand. I try not to worry as I stand next to him and focus on being myself.

Joel takes a sip of his coffee and wraps his other arm around his body. It is bitterly cold and the only thing saving us from frostbite is the bright sunshine. I'm sure we'd both be warmer if we were snuggled closer together, but clearly I've messed up that opportunity for today. And Joel looks so cosy, too. He always looks great in his suits (not to mention out of them) but I'm really loving his off-duty casual look: soft, cashmere jumper and big, navy military-style coat thrown over the top. There is a shadow of stubble over his chin, and his lips and his cheeks are flushed with the cold. He's wearing dark jeans with big leather boots and a red and brown scarf looped around his neck. He's even wearing a cute red skater-style beanie hat pulled over his ears. It would look ridiculous on anyone else other than him. Or Sam, come to think of it.

'So how's business at Hardy's?' he enquires, folding his arms and leaning towards me intently. I love the interest he always shows in my job. For so many years I was working at crappy jobs, following Jamie around whilst he pursued his career as a chef, that I could never imagine what it'd be like to do something that people were actually interested in. And since I've been working at Hardy's no one has been impressed by my stockroom status. Quite understandably, really. But Joel? He loves to hear all about Hardy's and seems genuinely interested in what's happening at the store.

I tell him about the makeovers and he nods thoughtfully.

'It does seem to be making a difference, doesn't it?' he replies, staring into the distance. 'And no one knows who's doing it?' I shake my head. He leans in a little closer to me so his lips are deliciously close to mine and for a moment, I honestly think I might faint. 'Not even you?'

'I don't know what you mean,' I reply defensively.

He laughs and puts his arm round me and draws me in to him. He smells of cinnamon and musk and, God, just of *man*, really. I glance at his hand, which is squeezing my arm. His fingernails are filed to perfection and seem to shimmer with health, and I fleetingly wonder if he has regular manicures. It wouldn't surprise me. He puts his head on my neck so that his mouth is right by my ear and I pray that my knicker elastic is strong enough not to ping right off and my knickers fall on the floor there and then.

'Sometimes you're too modest. Everyone thinks it's you. Rupert always talks about how good you are at your job.'

'He does?' I'm overcome with pleasure, then realize that Joel is talking about Carly. 'What does he say?' I ask, slightly less enthusiastically.

'Just how visionary you are, and that he loves your ideas for the future of Hardy's. He thinks you're a great personal shopper, obviously, but that you have great management potential too and he's convinced that together you and he can turn the store's fortunes around.'

'Wow,' I say, thinking that Rupert couldn't be more wrong. Carly's vision is entirely misplaced and none of the staff is responding well to her so called 'management skills'. 'That's nice. How do you know Rupert, again?'

'Oh, we go way back,' Joel says. 'We did our MBAs at Harvard Business School together.'

'Clever and cute,' I say without thinking.

'Me or Rupert?' grins Joel.

'Oh God, not Rupert,' I say a little too vehemently. 'Shit, that didn't come out right. I mean . . .'

410

Joel laughs. 'It's OK, you don't have to explain. Rupert's a good guy. And so passionate about his family business. That was part of the reason we hit it off. We each have a family legacy we wanted to save.'

'How is Parker's doing?' I ask, realizing that I haven't asked Joel much about his own store.

'Oh, you know,' he sighs. 'Pretty goddamn awful, given that it's meant to be the busiest shopping month of the year. It's like the whole town has forgotten that we exist. And now they're building this big new shopping mall, which is sure to be the final nail in Parker's coffin. I just wish I knew what to do. Parker's could do with a makeover like Hardy's.'

'So what's stopping you?' I say.

Joel furrows his brow. 'What do you mean?'

'Giving the place a makeover. It seems to be working for Hardy's, why couldn't it work for Parker's, too?'

Joel looks uncertain. 'It's just not my area of expertise,' he says, shaking his head defeatedly. 'I'm a money man through and through. I can balance books, look at costs, do business plans and think of financial ways to improve the store, but the whole aesthetic thing? I'm just not good at that.'

'So find someone who is,' I shrug. 'Or at the very least take some inspiration from Hardy's. You said that it reminds you a lot of Parker's, right?'

Joel nods. 'Yeah, I mean, obviously we don't have

the whole traditional British thing going on and we haven't been around for quite as long as Hardy's has, but it's an old-fashioned family store in a gorgeous old building and in a prime location . . .'

'So harness some of Hardy's ideas but adapt them to suit your American clientele,' I say. 'The whole focus of Hardy's makeovers has . . .' I pause, '. . . *seems* to have been a retrospective. Instead of competing with the brand-new stores like Rumors, with all their high-concept contemporary displays, whoever has been doing these makeovers seems to have been looking back, making the old stock relevant again and giving customers something different; something nostalgic and traditional that no other London store is offering. It's what people seem to want.' I pause as I think about Carly and her love of contemporary fashion and then add hurriedly, 'I mean, it's totally not my thing, *obviously*, but there's no reason why you couldn't do similar.'

Joel studies me as a slow grin crawls across his lips. 'Clever *and* cute,' he says, and then he leans forward and kisses me lightly on my lips, his mouth lingering for longer than I expect until I feel the warmth of his tongue meet mine and we are kissing like love-struck teenagers, our hands curled round each other's necks, fingers stroking each other's hair. And then suddenly we are at the front of the queue and we step into the big glass pod with our arms wrapped round each other, leaning

412

against the hand rail as we look out, ready to be lifted high in the air and over London Town. And as the people pile in and we begin to move up, up, up, I realize that once again, it is snowing and being in this pod with Joel is like being in my very own snow globe.

'I wonder if we can see Hardy's,' I mutter, more to myself than to Joel.

'I think you care about that place more than you let on,' he says, moving behind me and leaning the weight of his body against my back, curling his arms around my stomach as we look over the city.

'Yes,' I reply, without thinking, 'I guess I do.'

'You know, sometimes I feel like I'm dating two different people,' Joel says, and I feel myself stiffen in his arms. 'One minute you're this visionary, ambitious, powerhouse of a girl and the next, I see flashes of this soft, romantic side. It's like you have a love/hate relationship with Hardy's. So come on, tell me what you love about the place,' he murmurs softly.

And perhaps because up here, suspended like this over the city I love, with Joel's arms around me, miles away from Carly and my family and people's expectations of me, I somehow believe that anything is possible. Or maybe it's because from up here, the big, expansive, vibrant city – which seems to have swallowed me whole ever since I moved here, making me invisible to everyone – suddenly looks like it's constructed out of matches and I, for once, am a dominating presence looming over it like a puppet-master, pulling the strings of the people below and utterly in control of my destiny. But all I know is that for once I want to be totally 100 per cent truthful with Joel. And so I tell him about Hardy's and how much I love it, without revealing anything else about me or my real role at the store. I realize with a growing frustration that *this* is the person I want Joel to fall in love with: the simple stockroom girl whose colleagues barely acknowledge her presence, who lives with her sister and is a glorified babysitter, and who desperately wants her life to change, but who has also come to recognize that she doesn't want to be someone she's not in order for that to happen.

As we make our descent to the ground I feel overwhelmed with sadness. Yes, I'm having a wonderful time with Joel, and for once I feel like I'm in an old black-and-white movie rather than obsessively watching them, and Joel is my Cary Grant and Errol Flynn and Jimmy Stewart all wrapped up in one gorgeous gift. But the truth is this gift wasn't meant for me. It was meant for Carly. And the parcel Joel has received may have glossy packaging, but inside it's pretty disappointing.

The pod slows almost to a stop and Joel turns me round and kisses me again, but this time I pull back. I can't look at him. I know that if I do, I will cry and I don't want to let that happen.

'I'm sorry but I have to go,' I gasp and, as the doors open, I run out into the bitterly cold air, feeling it whip against my exposed skin, as if it is punishing me for not being myself.

I pause for a moment as I work out which way to go. I literally have no idea. I run blindly down the Southbank, staggering into stall-holders trying to sell me their Christmas wares, the sound of Joel's voice calling out Carly's name carried to my ears by the cruel wind.

CHAPTER 28

I trudge miserably up the path that leads to the top of Primrose Hill, leaning into the wind and trying to ignore the couples that are filing past me, chatting animatedly whilst wrapped in each other's arms. It seems everyone in the world has someone to share their Sunday afternoon with; more to the point, someone with whom they can really be themselves. I glance up and shiver as I look at the bare trees stretching their aged branches into the bleak, monochrome sky that is groaning with thick grey clouds.

My phone bleeps and I pull it out of my pocket wearily. It is the fifth text I've had from Joel in half an hour. I put the phone back in my pocket and keep walking. I don't really know what possessed me to run away from him like that earlier; all I know is that I couldn't handle being near him and not being myself for one more second.

Now I'm mired in regret and wish I'd stayed. I don't want to go home and I don't want to be here alone. But I walk on up the hill anyway, feet digging in the mud and slush until I reach the top and, by some stroke of luck, manage to find a free bench to sit on. I lean back, cross my legs and lift my shoulders around my neck to stop the wind whistling down my coat as I gaze at London sprawled majestically across the horizon. Then I wipe away a stray tear with the sleeve of my coat. It is so beautiful up here, but right now it feels like a place I don't belong. Perhaps I should just give up and go back home to Norfolk, accept that my fate is a quiet, country life with no handsome men in the picture and no high-flying jobs in fashion.

I sniff miserably at the thought just as a figure passes in front of me and then sits next to me. I glance at my park compatriot wondering who else is alone on a day like this. He looks sad, like he is missing having someone with him too. I focus my eyes through the blur . . .

'Sam?' I say in delight.

'Evie!' he gasps as he turns towards me. 'I had no idea that was you huddled up there. What are you doing here?'

'I live here, remember?' I say, laughing through my quickly evaporating tears. 'More to the point, what are *you* doing here?'

There is a pause. 'Um, well, it's funny you should ask actually,' Sam begins uncertainly, studying my face as if searching for some sort of sign. 'It's a long story and one that I've kind of been wanting to tell you for a while . . .'

'OUCH!' I yell as a ball suddenly whacks me

against my leg and two snotty-nosed little boys come running up to grab it, before careering down the hill, kicking the ball and letting out peals of laughter.

'Bloody kids,' I shout as I rub my calf. I turn to Sam. 'That really hurt! Why can't their parents stop them from attacking unsuspecting people who are just trying to sit in peace and enjoy the view on a Sunday afternoon?' I pause. Sam looks horrified by my outburst. 'Oh God!' I wail. 'I sound like Scrooge!' I shake my head as he laughs. 'But honestly, sometimes I wonder why people bother having kids at all if they can't look after them. I mean, it's not a part-time job; it takes time and effort, and you need to dedicate all your energy to it. I just wish more parents would realize that. Then maybe there wouldn't be so many frustrated children running about, and so many unhappy families, come to think about it . . .'

I'm ranting but I'm no longer aiming my anger at the two 8-year-olds who have inadvertently caused severe muscle damage to my leg. Instead I am thinking about Delilah and Will, who seem willing to dump their kids on me at any given opportunity in order for them to be able to pursue their careers. It just doesn't seem right.

'Oh,' says Sam, shifting uneasily on the seat, probably trying to edge away from the madwoman sitting next to him.

'Sorry, Sam.' I reach my hand across to his knee. 'I have some pent-up frustration I haven't quite dealt with. I didn't mean to take it out on you. Now, what was this long story you were about to tell me?'

Sam examines his fingernails and then looks away. 'Oh, it was nothing.' There is a pause and then he stands up and stretches out his hand towards mine. 'Fancy grabbing a drink? I need to be someplace warm before I lose some really essential body parts to frostbite.'

'You're on.' I grab his hand, laughing as he pulls me to my feet.

Giggling and still grasping each other's hands, Sam and I run down the hill, past children and dogs and grandparents, and groups of friends and couples, towards the sparkling lights of the high street. We burst through the doors of the Queen's Head pub, which sits on the corner of Regent's Park Road and at the epicentre of Primrose Hill's little high street and I grab a spare table in the corner, right by the roaring fire, while Sam goes to the bar to order drinks. I watch him for a moment as he stands next to a group of lads all discussing football. Sam looks at me and rolls his eyes and I smile and fake a yawn in their direction.

Moments later he brings over two glasses of mulled wine, pulls out a stool and sits in front of me. The table is small so our knees our touching and I try to shift them away but there's no room, so I relax and allow our legs to press softly together. He pushes the glass of steaming, ruby-coloured liquid across the table and I clasp my hands around it, sighing with pleasure as the scent of cinnamon, mixed spices, apple and wine waft up to my nostrils.

'Mmm,' we say in unison, and there is a moment of mutual contentment.

'So why were you sitting up there alone, looking so miserable?' he asks gently, sitting forward on his stool, fixing his eyes on me intently.

I shift a little in my seat as the space between us lessens and I feel a rush of intimacy that I didn't expect.

'New boyfriend trouble?' he says, averting his gaze as he takes a sip of mulled wine.

'I guess so,' I admit reluctantly.

Sam nods and I take a deep breath and blurt out everything that I've been feeling. I can't tell Sam I'm pretending to be Carly, that's way too embarrassing to admit, so instead I focus on the worry that I'm trying to be something I'm not to impress Joel because I feel like he is out of my league. Sam listens quietly to everything I tell him, sipping on his mulled wine and nodding every so often to encourage me to continue. When I've poured out my heart to him he puts his elbows on the table and rests his head in one of his hands and looks straight at me.

'It's tricky, Evie. It sounds like you really like this guy and he is clearly totally enamoured of you.' He pauses. 'And who could blame him?' I feel myself blushing as Sam continues, 'The truth is I'm no expert on relationships – in fact I'm probably the last person you should ask; I'm a bloke, after all – but if I had to give it a shot all I'd say is that I know without question that to truly fit with another person you have to tell them everything about yourself, no matter how hard that may be. We each have a past but in order to have a future with someone you have to be able to reveal every single layer of yourself.'

I suddenly notice that Sam is no longer looking at me or even directing his words to me any more. Instead, he looks down and mutters, 'It's the only way,' then drains his glass and stands up. 'Are you ready for another one?' he asks, but heads to the bar without waiting for me to answer, leaving me to ponder his words.

'You know, Sam,' I say when he places another glass of mulled wine in front of me, 'you're right. I always thought that in order for someone to want to be with me, I'd have to show them a different version of myself. Take my ex, Jamie. Even though I thought I was being myself, I put my life on hold for him just so he could follow his dream. I wanted to be close to him but I lost sight of my own ambition and where my life was going, and became his shadow. No wonder he ended up with no respect for me. What an idiot I was.' I shake my head as I take a long sip of the warming wine.

'I can understand why you did that,' Sam says quietly. 'Sometimes even the most mundane job is more pleasurable if there's someone there you like.'

'So what's your history?' I ask, interested suddenly in Sam's life before I met him. 'Have you left a trail of broken hearts in your wake? Are you a womanizer, a commitment-phobe, a new man or a serial monogamist?'

'Are they my only options?' Sam laughs. 'Not all blokes fit into such stereotypes, you know.'

'Really?' I reply drily, thoroughly unconvinced.

'OK, fair enough, most do, but some of us have a more, let's say, chequered history.'

'*Really*?' I repeat, leaning forward over the table, suddenly intrigued.

'Oh God,' Sam almost chokes on his drink as he clocks my expression, 'now you think I'm some sort of Lothario! I can see it in your face!'

I laugh and shake my head. 'No, I don't, I just think there's something more to you than meets the eye. I can't quite put my finger on it,' I say, narrowing my eyes as if trying to study him more closely than I ever have. 'You seem experienced . . .' Sam raises his eyebrow and I suddenly realize how that sounds. 'N-no,' I stammer, 'I don't mean like *that*, or um, then again you know, maybe you are, I don't know. What I mean is, how could I know that?' I take a deep breath, suddenly struggling to articulate myself. 'Anyway, that isn't my point. What I *mean* is, you seem experienced in love, like you've had something wonderful, but it also seems like you've also been badly hurt.'

Sam tilts his head to one side. 'Carry on, Mystic Meg, you're doing pretty well,' he says wryly.

'Well . . .' I pause as I try and sum up what I've seen in him . . . 'it's kind of like you've known the best that love has to offer, something really simple and pure, but that it has also been cruelly snatched away from you when you least expected it. Yep, that's it, I think,' I finish jubilantly.

Then I look at Sam's face. He seems overcome with fatigue and sadness, like all the life and laughter have been drained from him, and I realize that, without meaning to, I have touched a terribly raw nerve.

'Oh, Sam, I'm sorry, I didn't mean to—'

'No, it's fine, Evie, honestly,' he says, his voice thick with emotion. 'I guess you just hit me where it hurts. The truth is I do love someone deeply – I have for years now – but because of situations beyond my control I can't be with that . . . person as much as I'd like, and it kills me. And then on top of that I feel the same as you: that because of this person, I can't really be myself with the other people – person – I care about.' He sighs as he struggles to explain his situation. 'I don't know . . . it's kind of complicated.'

'I'm sorry, Sam,' I say, stretching my hand across the table and placing it over his. He clasps it as if he is drawing strength from my grasp. 'What a pair we are, huh?'

He looks at me, his soft brown eyes melting my heart a little as I suddenly see how much he's been hurt. I want more than anything to help to mend him, to make him feel like he has a chance at love, but as the air between us grows thick with intent, I suddenly panic as I see his lips reaching across the table for mine. I can't do this. There's Joel. And Ella. I pull back suddenly and he slumps down in his seat.

'Let's not make our lives any more complicated than they already are, eh?' I rasp, a sudden searing pain in my throat constricting my words.

Sam nods, answering without looking at me. 'I'm sorry, Evie. I don't know what came over me. It's just the wine and the fire and the . . .' He waves his arm round the pub, which is glowing with life, love and festivity, the Christmas tree in the corner sparkling merrily, snow now falling softly outside the window. 'It won't happen again,' he mumbles.

'I know,' I say as we push out our stools and silently put on our coats before heading out into the bleak midwinter.

We hug awkwardly and then turn and go our separate ways.

I pause for a moment on the now-empty street and glance back at Sam, who is trudging up the foggy, snow-capped hill, softly illuminated by the frail yellow glow of the Victorian streetlamps, and I feel a pang of regret as I wonder just what would have happened if I'd let him kiss me. I cross the street and head for Chalcot Square, secure – but not necessarily happy – in the knowledge that now, I'll never know.

MONDAY 12 DECEMBER

13 Shopping Days Until Christmas

CHAPTER 29

Despite it being Monday, and even though I'm feeling particularly weary after my emotional day yesterday, I'm still at the staff entrance at 6.30 a.m. Well, there's no time to waste. I don't even have time to chat to Felix today again, but I'm a bit thrown when I arrive and discover he's not in his office. For the two years I've worked here he's always been at his desk when I've walked in. Maybe he's not very well. I miss his cheerful face and I suddenly realize that without his seeing me it could be hours before anyone even knows I'm here.

I wander out into the still-dark store and sigh as I try to summon up the energy to makeover another whole department on my own in the space of two hours.

Just then, the lights click on and, as if by magic, Felix, Lily, Sam, Jan Baptysta, Justyna and Velna appear. I gasp and laugh as Lily steps forward and waves gaily at me. She is wearing black cropped trousers with flat pumps, a black top and a scarf wrapped around her head, like Norma Desmond. She most certainly looks ready for her close-up.

'Morning, Evie!' she trills. 'We hope you don't mind, but after our session on Thursday night we decided you could do with a hand – well, a few hands actually – for the next makeover. We figured you'd start today. So, just tell us what you want us to do; we're all here ready to help!'

'Really?' I exclaim, feeling choked as I look around at everyone, but avoiding Sam's gaze. I turn to the cleaners. 'Are you sure you guys can spare the time? I know you're short-staffed as it is. I didn't expect you all to start today.'

Jan smiles benevolently. 'Aaaah but Eve-English-Wi . . .' he glances at Justyna and trails off with a cough. 'We *want* to start today. We gotsk here extra early so we could help with the department makesover. Sam and Lily helped us. They are very good at cleaning, *nie*?'

I gape at Lily. 'You've been cleaning?'

'Oh, yes, dear,' she says, patting her headscarf. 'I am a woman of many talents. Now, let's stop dawdling and let the makeover magic begin! So which department are we working on today?'

I am speechless with gratitude. I don't know how to thank them so I just smile broadly at them all.

'Come on,' Lily nags. 'We don't have all day.' She's right.

'Handbags,' I say decisively. 'I overheard Becky saying that Rupert has been disappointed with her department's performance. I've got a couple of ideas but feel free to add any of your own as we go. Now, Lily,' I turn to her, 'do you think you could oversee everyone's work?'

She nods and throws a deep, graceful curtsy in my direction.

'Oh, and, Felix . . .' He grins widely and unfolds his arms. '. . . I know you can't really leave your security office, and besides, you need to warn us in case any staff happen to come in early, but perhaps you could review our efforts and ring me if you have any suggestions? I know you used to be a dab hand yourself at merchandising.'

Felix swings back on his heels and nods. 'Well, Walter Hardy, junior did tell me I had a gift,' he says proudly, and he heads off in the direction of the staff entrance.

'Sam and Jan Baptysta,' I turn to them and they simultaneously salute me and then look at each other and burst out laughing, 'you need to be in charge of the carpentry work. Jan, did you bring your tools in, like I asked you to at the pub?' He nods vigorously. 'It's just I've had this idea of fixing these big frames against the walls and then hanging the vintage handbags inside to make them look like art. But you're going to have to build the structures first.' Sam looks panicked but Jan just nods. 'Do you reckon that's something you could do?'

'Of coursk!' Jan replies, throwing his arm round Sam's shoulder and squeezing him so that Sam squeaks a little. 'We make a good team, no? And I am Polish! We are very good with our handsk!'

Sam extricates himself from Jan's grip and rubs his shoulder, grimacing a little. 'And, Evie,' he says, touching me lightly on the arm. I pull it away, driven by a subconscious reflex. Sam blushes. 'I, er, I had an idea, too. I, well, I just thought I could maybe take some reportage photos of the makeover in progress? You know, but without revealing who anyone is. Then I could take them to the local newspapers. It might create the buzz we need to get some more customers into the store. What do you think?'

'That's GENIUS!' I exclaim, and resist the urge to hug him. A few days ago I wouldn't have felt weird about it, but now? There's this strange awkwardness between us. Like what happened yesterday has tainted our friendship. I clear my throat and try to speak as businesslike as possible. 'Can you do it without making it obvious who we are, though? I don't want any of the staff – or, more importantly, Rupert – to get suspicious. He needs to believe all of his staff are invaluable to him and he absolutely can't know who has really been doing the makeovers.'

Sam nods and pushes his hands into his jeans pockets. 'I can shoot you guys in shadow so you just look like silhouettes. All I have to do is use some clever backlighting. Leave it with me.'

I nod and throw a small smile of thanks in his direction before quickly moving on.

'Velna and Justyna, do you guys want to come with me to the stockroom to get the extra merchandise we need? I need some help carrying the stuff.'

'Oh, Evie? I've thought of something that could help you with that,' Sam pipes up again. 'I've left two of my trolleys from the van outside the delivery entrance. You can load all the stuff you need on those, which will save you going back and forth.'

'Great! Thanks, Sam,' I say, feeling a flood of excitement as I look at all the bright, eager faces surrounding me. 'Right then, guys, let's get to work!'

Everyone scatters to their various positions. Lily starts dismantling the current department's display whilst Jan and Sam head to the stockroom with us, wrapping up in their coats and scarves as they're going to build the structures outside the delivery entrance. Jan appears to have brought an entire building kit, including a jigsaw and all sorts of other DIY paraphernalia.

By the time the girls and I get back to the shop floor with the stock, Lily has cleared the department and is mopping her brow.

'You be careful, Lily. I don't want you working too hard,' I say, patting her shoulder. 'You sit down now and just tell us what looks best.'

I turn to Velna and Justyna, who are standing behind me. 'I'm going to start with the displays for the vintage evenings bags,' I explain. I burrow around in the boxes on the delivery cart until I find what I'm looking for. 'Ah, yes, here they are!'

I pull out an old 1950s cake stand, which comes with a beautiful glass domed lid. There are at least a dozen more inside the box.

'What are we doing with those?' Justyna barks.

'I had this idea that we could place each of these on the white blocks that mannequins usually stand on,' I explain breathlessly as I pull out half a dozen more. 'We can build the blocks to different heights and then put a cake stand on the top of each one with a gorgeous evening bag inside and the glass over the top so that they look as untouchable as the crown jewels in the Tower of London. I want customers to think these bags are so desirable that they have to be encased in glass.'

'Bravo!' cheers Lily, from where she is perched with perfect posture on the end of the trolley. 'What a wonderful idea!' She rubs her index finger around her lips thoughtfully. 'Perhaps we could accessorize each bag in its glass dome with some accoutrements, like some pearls or a beautiful costume ring or a headpiece.' She sighs. 'We used to wear such wonderful headpieces in the fifties. When I was at the Windmill . . .'

I clap my hands, as much with delight as to prevent Lily from going off on a tangent. I love her stories but we simply don't have the time for them this morning.

'That's brilliant, Lily! Velna, can you run back to the stockroom, find the accessories aisle, which is the third on your left. On the fifth shelf up you'll find pill box hats, cage veils and headpieces – can you bring me a peacock-feathered fascinator and a couple of netted hats? Then go down to the third shelf. On the far right-hand side you'll find lots of strings of pearls. There should be one with a beautiful silver butterfly clasp, but bring me a couple of extra strings as well. Oh, and then right down on the shelf above the floor is a box of costume rings. Just bring that entire box. Oh, and brooches!' I clap my hands again. 'They're on the second shelf. Can you bring a box of those too? I think there's two or three boxes to choose from. I'll let you decide which one. But a mother-of-pearl one with a cameo head would be lovely.'

Velna dashes off.

'Right, Justyna, can you help me with the blocks? They're pretty heavy so we'll probably have to do them together.'

'Nie, do not be sillysk!' She puts her hand in front of my face and then strides over to the unused blocks, which are stacked against a wall on the ground floor. She lifts one easily, heaves it on to her shoulder and strides back before dropping it on the floor in front of me. Then she's off again.

Lily's eyes widen. 'That girl is superhuman,' she whispers, and I stifle a giggle as Justyna deftly delivers another block at my feet.

'I am helping, *nie*?' she shouts over her shoulder as she sets off again.

'You're incredible!' I shout back, and Justyna turns with her hands on her hips and grins toothily at me before heaving up another heavy block.

433

'Right, Lily, let's start choosing the evening bags.' We delve into the boxes on the trolley and 'ooh' and 'aah' over the ones we pull out.

'We must have this silk purse,' Lily sighs. 'Just look at the oriental print on the front and the delicate silver chain. This must be from the 1930s; my mother had one just like it.'

'And what about this?' I pull out a glittering box clutch with a chunky gold clasp. 'This would look wonderful with a pair of ex-display gold T-bar dancing shoes I have in the stockroom. They're too faded to sell, but will set this bag off perfectly. What do you think, Lily?'

'I think if they're the ones I'm thinking of, I wore a pair just like them at the Windmill,' she replies wistfully. 'Such happy memories.'

'I bet you were an incredible dancer,' I say.

'Oh, I was,' she says without a hint of modesty. 'Not that people saw us as that. The nudity got in the way of the art a little. Though it was very liberating.'

'Wow.' I shake my head and sit back on my heels as I pull out and examine another clutch before rejecting it. 'You were so brave. I just can't imagine being that exposed in front of so many people.'

'Ah, it was a breeze,' Lily replies with a wave of her hand. 'I was proud of my body and proud of my dancing, and when you're proud of what you do, you don't mind how exposed you are. It's only when people are ashamed of themselves or have low self-esteem that they hide themselves away.

They don't believe that they deserve to be noticed.' She throws a sideways glance at me and I finger a bronze sequined bag with avid concentration, doing my best to avoid her gaze. 'And you do, you know,' she says softly, lifting my chin with her finger. 'You so deserve to be noticed and given all the attention that you give to so many other people. You just need to believe it, Evie.'

I feel the tears begin to fall silently down my face and I let them, unable to pretend any more that I want anything other than to be noticed and respected and loved for who I am, not for who I'm pretending to be.

'Just be yourself,' Lily says, squeezing my wrist before drawing me into her embrace. 'And be proud of it. The biggest gift you can give yourself in life is your own acceptance of who you are.'

'But,' I say, wiping away my tears as I rest my head on her shoulder, 'who I am doesn't make a difference to anyone. I'm invisible.'

'Not to me, you're not, or Felix or Sam, or your family . . .'

'I'm not so sure,' I sigh.

'Well, I am,' Lily says. 'You're a beautiful, kind, loving girl, and anyone would be proud to have you as a friend, or a daughter, or sister. I know I am. Come on, darling, don't lose confidence now. You've come so far.'

'What do you mean?' I say, sniffing a little as I pick up another clutch.

'Well, look at you, darling!' Lily opens her arms.

'You've got rid of the plain clothes you used to wear and have found your own individual style, which you're wearing with confidence.'

I look down at the emerald-green pussybow blouse I put on this morning with some high-waisted black trousers and a cute little pair of silver heels I bought ages ago but have never worn.

'You've come out of hiding from unpacking boxes in that little stockroom of yours and are making a difference to this store. You're a great leader and are showing such creative flair. You know you're good at what you're doing and it shows. I can see your passion – we all can. It's remarkable.'

I blush as I look at Lily doubtfully. 'Really? But it all seems so . . . inconsequential.'

'Inconsequential?' she scoffs. 'Is that what you call saving jobs, helping bring people together, giving people hope and direction and inspiration, and doing all that without anyone knowing it's you? I hardly think that's inconsequential. Have some self-belief, my darling. It's the only thing I've ever had and I can honestly say it's the only thing worth having. Not money or some fancy job title, or a boyfriend.' I swallow as I think of Joel. 'None of that matters if you don't believe in your-self. Now, are we going to makeover this dreary old handbag hovel, or what?' And Lily puts one hand on her knee and takes my hand as she stands up, giving it a gentle squeeze before she starts flying around the department, holding up bags against

436

walls and calling out as I watch her in amazement. I could learn a lot from this lady, I think to myself as I set to work. Then I look down at my outfit and smile.

Maybe I already have.

Two hours later we are grouped together in a semicircle, staring at the new-look handbag department.

'It looks bloody good,' Sam says as he whips around, taking pictures of the department. 'These frames are great, Jan! And these handbags look amazing hung inside, Evie!'

It's true, they do. From the big, brass hooks I found in a box in the stockroom, I've hung a selection of old and new handbags inside the three gigantic wall frames that Jan built and that reach from the floor all the way up to the first-floor mezzanine. Lily and I spray-painted the frames gold before we hung the leather bags inside. Suddenly the dull leather of the bags, which have always been clumped together and thrown on top of each other in big trays, now look like bags you want – no, that you *have* – to own. The leather is soft and expensive, the craftsmanship incredible. Hardy's stock may be considered old-fashioned by some, but it has always been beautifully made. We've just got out of the habit of displaying it all to its full potential.

The cake stands have also worked beautifully. With Lily's help, we handpicked the best bags and the most gorgeous vintage accessories to show them off. And Felix piped up with another idea, too. He phoned from his office to suggest we place a couple of old-fashioned hat stands in the department to hang some of the beautiful millinery, the hats and fascinators that we have in Hardy's. He said that the trilbies had proved such a bestseller in Men's that we should do something similar to get customers wanting to go to our hat department, and that a few vintage hats on the hat stand on the ground floor would entice them upstairs to see more. It's a great idea and it really pulls the department together. But more than anything it's a good way to get customers moving throughout the entire store.

And finally, at Becky's tillpoint, we have put a couple of vintage designer handbags, which had been gathering dust in the stockroom, in the glass case underneath, which used to be empty. There's a mustard YSL satchel with a gold clasp, and a soft, small bronze 1980s Bottega Veneta shoulder bag with its distinctive Italian leather weave. And as the pièce de résistance, Lily has added her black quilted Chanel bag she lent me for my date.

'That bag has seen a lot of wonderful parties over the years,' Lily said as she handed it to me and I placed it inside the counter. 'I don't want to sell it because I want to make sure it goes to the right home, but for now it'll help make the other handbags look even more desirable and get customers really looking at our bags.'

'I've got some great shots of the store,' Sam says, smiling at me as he continues clicking. 'I'll go straight to a few local newspaper offices and see if I can get the picture editors to take a look at them.' He glances at his watch. 'With luck, someone will want to run it as a story in one of this week's editions.'

'Oh my gosh, it's eight o'clock!' I gasp, peering at his watch. 'Sharon will be here any minute. Everyone, we need to make ourselves invisible! Thank you so much for all your hard work, guys. It's the best makeover yet and I couldn't have done this without you!'

Everyone scatters and I head to the stockroom just as my mobile rings. I answer it immediately when I see who it is.

'Evie darling? I know you're at work but can you talk? It's just me, Mum.' I smile and murmur a hello back. My mum always manages to forget that technology is advanced enough that mobiles have a caller display so you don't need to explain who it is every time you call. 'Oh, it's so good to hear your voice!' Mum sighs, immediately making me feel guilty for not calling her recently. We usually speak most days, but since Joel, and everything that's been happening at the store, I have been neglecting her somewhat.

'Sorry, Mum, things have just been pretty hectic recently.'

'I know, I know, you live this wonderfully busy life in the big city and don't have time for your little old mum any more,' Mum says with a laugh.

'Old? Hardly, Mum. You're the most youthful, glamorous-looking not-quite-sixty-something I know.'

'Why, thank you, Evie darling, but believe it or not I wasn't calling to get a morale boost.' She pauses. 'I'm actually on the train to London! I got bored at home as your father is in town on one of his business trips; he's been staying in the flat in Hampstead since last Wednesday. He was meant to come home on Saturday but apparently he and his lawyer friends decided to have some spontaneous boozy early Christmas work dinner so he decided to stay the whole weekend. Anyway, I woke up this morning and thought, why don't I come into town to do some Christmas shopping? And then go and see you at work? Wouldn't that be lovely? You can tell me everything that's been happening with you.' She pauses again. 'And Delilah.'

I roll my eyes as I realize that my mum doesn't want some cosy little chat. She wants to check up on her brood.

'OK,' I sigh. 'Why don't I meet you in Lily's tearoom at twelve? We can have lunch there.'

'Lovely, darling! See you then!' And she rings off.

At twelve sharp I walk into Lily's to find my mum already sitting at a table in the corner, bag on her lap, looking as glamorous as always in a red shift dress with black opaque tights, black high heels and a chiffon scarf wound around her neck. Her big black tote is perched neatly on her lap and she is looking around anxiously, clearly waiting for me to arrive.

'Evie!' She stands up and embraces me warmly, pulling my head into her neck and giving me a squeeze. 'I've missed you so much! Look at you!' She pulls back, her mouth dropping open as she assesses my outfit. 'Where's my tomboy in the hoodie and baggy jeans gone?'

I blush as I remember that Mum hasn't seen any of my ensembles from The Wardrobe before. 'I just fancied a change,' I mutter as I glance down at my outfit.

'You look beautiful,' she gushes. 'That green top really brings out the colour of your eyes. You look just like your sister. Speaking of which . . .'

But Lily glides over before she can say any more.

'Grace Samson? Is that really you?' Lily gasps. 'Well, I never!'

'Lily!' exclaims my mum, embracing Lily warmly. 'You haven't changed a bit!'

'What are you doing here?' Lily asks.

Mum smiles at me before turning back to Lily. 'Oh, you know, just catching up with my daughter . . .'

'You!' Lily says, smacking me on my arm. 'You never told me Grace Samson was your mother! Well, if I'd known that . . .'

441

'I didn't think . . .' I begin as my mum and Lily exclaim over one another. 'I didn't think you'd remember her.' This isn't entirely true. But I can't admit that for once in my life I wanted to be able to be someone other than Delilah's sister, or Charles and Grace Taylor's daughter. I knew it'd come up sometime – just like it did with Felix – but my family have overshadowed me my whole life. With Lily I could just be me, Evie Taylor, no expectations. I've wanted to keep it like that for as long as possible.

'Charming,' they both say in unison, and begin laughing.

'No, I mean . . . oh, never mind,' I grumble as Lily pulls up a chair and begins shooting questions at Mum. But I'm compelled to listen as they reminisce about their old days at Hardy's.

I gaze at Mum, who looks so bright and happy as she talks about her old life, and for the first time, I wonder why she gave it all up. It seems as if it made her so happy. She is laughing as Lily reminds her of the clients who fawned over her, the celebrities who requested her hairstyling services and the endless parties that she'd get invited to.

'You know, Lily,' I interrupt, 'she's never told me any of this.'

'You never asked, darling,' Mum replies, and I glance at her as she looks down at her handbag. 'The problem with being a wife and mum,' she says to Lily, 'is that once you become those things, people don't see you as anything else. It's kind of like you're invisible and everyone – including you – forgets about the life you had before.'

Lily nods sagely. 'It's why I never did the whole baby thing,' she says. 'You lavish all that time, love and attention on them for years, and do they appreciate it?'

'Do they hell!' Mum laughs.

'I am here, you know,' I mumble in protest, but for the first time I feel like I'm really listening to my mum. She gave up everything for us and we have never acknowledged that. Not Dad, not I, nor Delilah, nor the boys. I feel a wave of shame as I consider how wrapped up in my own life I've always been. All this time I thought that no one could ever understand what it's like to feel so invisible when it turns out my mum has been feeling that way for way longer than I have.

Ten minutes later, after much chatter and laughter and reminiscing, Lily sidles off to serve some more customers and to make our sandwiches. I turn to Mum and grab her hand.

'Mum, I'm really sorry if we haven't appreciated you enough.'

'Oh, don't be silly, darling, it's fine,' Mum smiles, and for the first time I see that she looks a little sad. 'I love being a mum and a wife. It's just sometimes I miss being me, you know?' I nod and squeeze her hand. 'Being here has just reminded me of that, I guess.'

She looks around and shakes her head. 'I can't believe I haven't come to see you here before, Evie! I always thought it would be too hard. From what you told me, the place was falling apart and I couldn't face seeing darling old Hardy's like that. But it all looks incredible!' she exclaims. 'The beauty department is to die for,' she says excitedly. 'I spent half an hour in there choosing gifts for people.' She holds up an embossed Hardy's carrier bag. 'I bought these beautiful soaps for my friends, which I just know they'll love. I actually remember this brand from back when I worked here. Every woman I met who shopped here swore it was the best age-defying treatment you could ever use. I've never been able to find these anywhere since. I can't believe you still stock them! And they're so much cheaper than all that new-fangled Creme de la Mer stuff that everyone spends a fortune on! Ooh, and I bought your father one of those trilbies on display in the window. He'll look so suave in it!' I smile as my mother continues: 'And for Delilah I bought this beautiful vintage evening clutch bag for when she goes on dates with Will.'

She looks at me as she takes a small bite of her sandwich, which Lily delivered before dashing off to serve more customers. She places the sandwich carefully back on the plate and rests her elbows on the table as I brace myself for the grilling.

'I'm worried about Delilah, you know, Evie,' she sighs.

I nod, secretly wishing that for once we could just have lunch and talk about each other. I want to hear more of Mum's stories about her days at Hardy's and I suddenly have this desperate urge to tell her all about the makeovers I've been doing in the store.

'I want to know if you've noticed anything different about her? You two are so close and you more than anyone would know if anything was wrong.' She sighs loudly. 'Sometimes I feel so isolated, stuck away in Norfolk away from you all. And none of you tells me anything . . .'

'That's because there isn't anything to tell,' I reply unconvincingly, wanting to protect Delilah's privacy. I know she'll tell Mum when she's ready. 'If there was, you'd already know.'

Mum studies my face and I look away, afraid she'll see right through me. 'Come on, Evie, I'm not a fool. I know my daughters and I know when something's wrong. What's been going on?'

I shrug, twiddling my pretty china tea cup around on its saucer. I'm used to Mum's inter-rogations but I'm finding it hard not to crack under the pressure this time. I want to tell her what I know about Will, am desperate, in fact, to share my burden, but I just don't think it's fair if I do. What if I'm wrong? And what if Delilah knows, but she and Will have decided to work things out? Mum knowing will only complicate matters. 'What's Delilah told you?'

'Nothing!' Mum exclaims, throwing her hands

up in the air. 'That's why it's so frustrating. I feel like I'm being left out of the loop. Delilah hasn't been herself for a long time,' she adds. 'Ever since she had Raffy. And it's getting worse, not better. I don't think she's been at work for the past few days . . .'

'What?' I reply, shocked. Delilah has never missed a day's work apart from when she gave birth. But even then she was back on her BlackBerry, responding to emails the very next day. 'That can't be right. She's a workaholic. Nothing would keep her away from the office. It's her life.'

'I know, darling, and that's what worries me. Evie, have you stopped to wonder whether Delilah is happy?'

I shrug again, not wanting to reveal anything. 'What do you want me to do, Mum?'

'Talk to your sister,' Mum pleads as she cups my face with her hands and gazes at me intently. 'Find out how she's feeling, listen to her. Be the loving little sister that you've always been to her.'

Used to be, I think. And suddenly I feel really sad.

TUESDAY 13 DECEMBER

12 Shopping Days Until Christmas

CHAPTER 30

'Morning, everyone.' Rupert looks around the stockroom. Our Monday morning meeting was postponed yesterday due to the amount of replenishment all the staff had to do after our busiest ever weekend. Carly and I are squashed together on the sofa with Guy and Becky, and the rest of the staff are standing in a semicircle around Rupert and Sharon, waiting patiently for the good, or bad, news. Everyone is silent as Rupert flicks through the pages of reports on the clipboard he is holding and Sharon looks blankly ahead.

I glance over at my Advent calender, which I now have pinned above the sink. This morning I opened the number 13 door – unlucky for some – and was rewarded with a piece of chocolate money. I just hope that with just twelve working days left till Hardy's deadline, it is a sign that our dire financial situation has been turned around. But looking at Rupert and Sharon, I have this terrible feeling in my gut that it hasn't.

Next to me, Carly is whispering to Guy and giggling, but the rest of us are hushed. Only the sound of the wall-clock, ticking like a timebomb, penetrates through the silence. I glance at Jane from Lingerie and she smiles warily at me, holding her crossed fingers up, red fingernails flashing like flags of hope. She is wearing her retro Hardy's uniform again and has pinned her hair up so it shows off her long, elegant neck.

Everyone is focused on Rupert now, desperate to hear whether everyone's hard work has paid off. Even Guy shushes Carly as Rupert clears his throat to begin to speak.

He begins slightly nervously, his clipped voice struggling to fill the cavernous room. 'Thank you all for coming.' He pauses and for the first time since he walked into the room his flushed, ruddy cheeks lift into a smile. 'Firstly, I just want to say how much I appreciate all your hard work. Hardy's has had an unprecedented weekend, with some departments, especially Lingerie, making an exceptional turnaround on previous weekly figures.'

Jane blushes proudly as everyone turns to look at her.

'Menswear and Beauty have continued to exceed expectations too, and I must also congratulate Becky for the wonderful transformation of Handbags. For the first time in years, our leather goods were flying off the shelves and there were a lot of very happy-looking women browsing through that department at the weekend. Becky coped admirably with the increase in trade and it was wonderful to see Gwen and Jenny helping her out when she needed it.' Rupert drops his clipboard to his side for one moment as he takes his eyes off the all-important figures and looks around the room.

'Over the past two weeks you have all amazed me with your dedication to this store and with the respect you've shown to the loyal customers we've had for years, as well as the new ones that have been streaming through the doors. This place is important to me because it is part of my family heritage, but it has been hugely overwhelming to see just how much it means to you, too. I feel blessed to have you all and hope that we will be working together for a long time to come.'

He swallows and when he speaks again his voice is stronger and more confident. 'For the first time in many, many years, Hardy's is starting to feel like the store that my great-grandfather had visualized, a place that was to be a centre for community spirit, that would be aimed at the masses and put public service over profit, which we have done for many years now, more by force than choice.'

There is a ripple of laughter at that and Rupert flushes with pleasure before continuing.

'But despite the threat of closure and the unexpected but welcome influx of new customers and revenue recently, I have witnessed only the best of Hardy's customer service and for that I am truly thankful.'

He glances at Sharon and smiles fondly, and she practically swoons in response before remembering where she is and gathering herself together.

'I understand from Sharon that over the weekend Jane helped many grateful women find underwear that made them feel infinitely better about themselves and she has become the perfect ambassador for her department.'

There is a round of applause and cheers, and Jane blushes prettily, winking at me and mouthing 'thank you' as she does so, which fills me with happiness.

'And in *most* of my other departments . . .' Rupert quickly glances at Carly and then back at his clipboard again, '. . . I see my staff being helpful without being overbearing, treating our customers with the respect they deserve. It is truly wonderful to see, and I want to thank you deeply on behalf of myself and my family for all your hard work.'

Applause breaks out again as Rupert smiles at us all proudly. He is transformed from the bumbling man who was more used to sheep than staff. He is so much more confident and is now leading us with a gentle authority that is impossible not to respect. The staff – not just Sharon – are all looking at him adoringly and it is clear he has us all in the palm of his hands.

'I also want to talk about the incredible makeovers that have been happening in the store.' He looks around at us all, and Carly shifts into an upright position on the sofa and beams at him whilst I try to sink further into my seat. 'I have my suspicions as to who is working such magic in the store.' I see him sneak a shy, sideways glance at Sharon before he touches her arm gently. 'Sharon here has been a tireless campaigner for maintaining the integrity of the store and whoever's vision it has been to enrich the store's display with all these vintage treasures has truly proven themselves to be a creative genius.' His voice swells as he continues to speak. 'Somehow this person has managed to make Hardy's take a step back in time, whilst simultaneously propelling it into the future. It really is quite remarkable. I just wish that someone would step forward and take the credit.' Rupert pauses and raises his thick eyebrows hopefully. Carly coughs loudly, which causes Rupert and a few other staff members to look in her direction, but other than that, there is only a rustling of clothes and shuffling of feet as everyone looks at each other, trying to see if anyone will own up.

Carly leans in towards me. 'Do you reckon it's time to own up?' she whispers furtively.

I feel my heart pounding as I turn sharply to look at her. How does she know? 'After all, it *could* have been either one of us,' she adds wickedly. 'No one would ever know, especially as no one seems to want to take the credit anyway . . .' My heart returns to its normal pace. She doesn't know. Thank God.

'Well, then,' Rupert sighs, 'it seems we have our

very own Secret Santa. And if I can't thank the person – or people – responsible personally, I'd like to assume that you all have a hand in it, with the help of a truly wonderful manager.' He touches Sharon's shoulder gently, and she looks like she might just faint with pleasure. Her ironing board body seems to go limp, she leans into Rupert for support and he places an arm around her.

'But, folks,' he continues, 'I'm afraid it isn't all good news. Whilst Hardy's has seen an incredible turnaround in the last two weeks, we're not out of the woods yet. In fact, we are still very much in the thick of it. Hardy's has been trading at a desperately low level for a long time now and the Board have had enough. The offer from Rumors is still on the table and the only way they will consider turning it down is if we prove that we can compete with the other department stores over the holiday period. That means we need customers to be flooding through our doors every day in the week before Christmas. We also need every department to be performing as well as the ones that have been successfully made over.'

He pauses and looks at the sales figures on his clipboard. 'Unfortunately,' he says, his voice taking on a more serious tone, 'Designers had another very unsatisfactory weekend, with only one sale on Saturday – a tartan taffeta gown that Lady Fontescue had pre-ordered for her annual Hogmanay celebration. But when she came to collect it, it was found to be on a sale rack. She was not amused.'

'I wasn't to know that ugly bit of tat had actually been chosen by someone,' Carly grumbles defensively. 'I was trying to show some initiative in creating some revenue out of the crappy old stock we keep clinging on to so I can make room for some more fab new designers.'

Rupert purses his lips and there is a murmur of disapproval and discontent from the rest of the room.

'That "crappy old stock" has been selling pretty well in my department recently,' pipes up Jane bravely.

'Mine too,' says Gwen. 'Our customers can't get enough of those lavender soaps. I've heard some of them swear it's better than Crème de la Mer!'

'And I've lost count of the number of trilbies I've sold since they've been out on display,' Guy adds.

Carly scowls at him and sinks back in her seat.

'I think the point I'm trying to make, everyone, is that *all* the departments need to be dramatically increasing their sales,' Rupert says pointedly. 'We need to be actively competing with similar-sized stores, like Fenwicks. We've proved that Hardy's has the chance of a future, but now we need to blow the Board away with sales figures that they won't be able to ignore. If we can prove that we can more than compete with anything that Rumors could do on this site, then we could, by some miracle, stop the buy-out.' He presses his fingers to his lips in a prayer position before he speaks again. Clearly he's not convinced by the statement. 'These are going to be the most important twelve days of Hardy's one-hundred-year history. I need everyone to pull together, which means helping those in the most underperforming departments, like Designers—'

'That would be good, Rupe,' Carly interrupts flippantly. 'I mean, my ideas are working, I just need some support from certain members of staff,' she says, and throws Elaine a meaningful look.

'That's not fair,' Elaine exclaims, scowling at Carly. '*She's* the one who doesn't have a clue what she's doing. She doesn't understand what our customers want. She just flounces around acting all high and mighty and not actually doing anything to improve the department. It looks like a bloody art gallery in there, and those designers she's chosen just aren't ri—'

'Oh, and you'd know all about that, wouldn't you?' snaps back Carly. 'I mean, look at you; you're not exactly the best advert for the designers department. You wouldn't know couture if it came and draped itself all over you.'

'That's exactly the point!' Elaine shouts. 'Nor would our customers! *Hardy's* version of Designers should be wearable classics, investment pieces that will attract all ages into the store. We could have the occasional new designer, sure, but they have to be ones that fit in with the style of customer.

456

We're never going to sell edgy fashion or couture, and you're more of an idiot than I already thought if you think we can!'

'Don't call me an idiot,' Carly snarls, jumping up to her feet and launching herself at Elaine.

Guy and I quickly pull her back as Rupert starts flapping and the rest of the staff squeal and clap in the excitement of a possible bitch-fight.

'Well, no one else has made such a mess of their department, have they?' shouts Elaine as Sharon physically restrains her.

'Oh, *really?*' yells back Carly. 'Well, my ideas are working in the rest of the store, aren't they?'

A sudden silence descends over the room and everyone looks at each other uncertainly and then back at Carly. Guy and I drop our hands and step away from her.

I'm shocked. Even though she threatened to take the credit for the makeovers I didn't think she actually would. Part of me admires her for being so fearless. She knows that no one knows just who is making all the changes, and she also knows that Rupert really believes in her so it won't be beyond the realms of possibility that she'd be the one doing it; it's why he promoted her, after all. But with one glance around the room I can see that none of the staff believes her. They are all looking at Carly with disgust and outrage, including Sharon. But Carly keeps a brave face, her chin lifted proudly, her arms folded defiantly. I should be upset that she has stolen my thunder, but the truth is, what she's just done is no worse than what I've done to her over the past two weeks. Just like me, Carly is now pretending to be something she's not. Clearly, we have more in common that I ever thought.

'Ladies, I think that's enough, don't you?' Sharon says coldly. 'This is not the way to behave in a staff meeting.' She claps her hands and everyone visibly stands to attention. 'Now, everyone, there's work to do. This is an important week for Hardy's and, as Rupert says, we all need to be working together as a team.' She shoots a frosty glance at Carly. 'Off you go.'

As everyone files out, Carly sinks back down on the sofa and sits staring at her shoes. I don't know what to say to her so I busy myself tidying the stockroom, which looks like a disaster zone after such a hectic day yesterday. I get so involved in my tidying process, revelling in the feeling of bringing order and calm back to the chaos with every single item that I put back on a shelf, that I forget she's even there.

'Sarah,' she says quietly, and I peer around the shelves to see her looking disconsolately at me. 'Can I talk to you?'

I try not to sigh. I really want to tidy the stockroom before the store opens as it's so important that we have a good day. I can't help but wish she'd just go and sort her own department out. After all, didn't she hear what Sharon and Rupert just said?

I look at my watch. 'OK, Carly, but I don't have long. There's a lot to do.'

'Thanks, you're a real pal. I just don't know what to do any more, you know?' she says, swiping a long, bronze-coloured strand of hair out of her eyes, which I'm surprised to see are glistening with tears. 'I mean, two weeks ago I was on top of the world, I had this promotion and another great job offer on the table from Rumors, I was out having fun all the time, and so what if I didn't have a boyfriend? I was dating all the time, which was good, as it meant I didn't have to spend much time at home with my horrible flatmate—'

'I thought you were best friends?' I interrupt.

Carly shakes her head and shrinks a little. 'I had to find a new flatmate after my best friend moved out,' she says quietly.

'Why did she do that?'

'Because she got this boyfriend and all of a sudden she wanted to do the whole "playing house" thing. I mean, we used to have so much fun and it didn't matter to me that I was always single. We'd just hang out together. But now she's always staying in with her boyfriend, or saving up for things for their flat, and this new girl I'm living with treats me like I'm invisible. I thought we'd hang out loads but she's either working late, or she stays in her room and only communicates with me through shitty Post-it note messages. Now I have no one to go out with. Blokes never seem to want to do anything more than date me until we have sex, then they dump me. And now everyone at work hates me too. And Rumors haven't called me back since my second interview.'

She starts to cry and I sit next to her and put my arm around her somewhat awkwardly. 'You're my only friend, Sarah. I honestly don't know what I'd do without you. I'm so sorry for being like this, I don't recognize myself any more. It's like someone came and stole my former life and left me with this crappy one where everyone ignores me and I spend most of my time on my own. I just wish things could be back to normal. I never really wanted this bloody promotion. I liked being a personal shopper – I was good at that. I knew what looked good on people and how to make them feel better about themselves. I just wish someone would make *me* feel better.'

As she puts her head on my shoulder and sobs, I do my best to comfort her, simultaneously feeling like the worst person in the whole wide world because the truth is *I'm* the one who has stolen her life.

I don't feel any better when Rupert and Sharon come into the stockroom about an hour after she's gone. Once again, I'm squirrelled away at the back and they don't see me. Sharon doesn't even think to call out my name and I know Rupert wouldn't as I'm not sure he even knows I exist. Instead they start discussing the events of the morning meeting.

★   ★   ★

460

'I don't know, Rupe,' Sharon says softly, sounding more gentle and feminine than I've ever heard her. 'I'm just not sure that Carly has really got what it takes to be a manager.'

Rupert sighs. 'I know, and I had such high hopes for her, too. But she's clearly alienating the staff and I can't afford for that to happen, no matter how talented she may be at visually merchandising the store.'

'*If* she is that talented,' Sharon says barbedly.

'Do you have anything to tell me, Sharon?' Rupert says. 'I mean, I totally understand why you don't want to admit that it's you who has been doing these wonderful makeovers. I know that you want me to think it could be any one of the staff, but honestly, you can tell me. I promise it won't affect anyone's jobs; we're past that now. Well, perhaps with one exception.'

'Oh, Rupert,' Sharon gushes, 'I'm so flattered you think it might be me, but don't you think I would have told you what I was doing? I tell you everything, after all. No,' she sighs, 'I may be a good manager but I can't take credit for the secret makeovers. And I don't think Carly can either,' she adds.

'Really? But why would she lie?' Rupert asks. 'Isn't that a dangerous game to play?'

'More like a desperate one,' Sharon points out. 'The poor girl has had a terrible couple of weeks. It's clear she's out of her depth and isn't right for the role. I agree she was a wonderful personal

461

shopper, but her talents just don't seem to translate into management.'

'So what do I do?' Rupert asks. 'I can't demote her back into personal shopping. That department was overstaffed anyway, and even with the new customers, there still isn't enough demand for it. The service my great-grandfather wanted for Hardy's was that every customer would feel like they had an assistant's undivided attention for as long as they want, helping them with every single part of the Hardy's shopping experience. As far as I'm concerned that *is* personal shopping. It isn't a department, it's the *raison d'être* of the whole store.' He gazes wistfully into the distance. 'My dream, if Hardy's survives, is to have a higher staff-per-customer ratio than any other store. We'll incorporate American retail standards but maintain the British reserve of not being too, you know, "in your face".'

I stifle a snigger as Rupert uses that uncharacteristically 'street' phrase, but I find myself becoming serious when I hear him speak again.

'I don't know, Sharon, Carly is causing such discontent in the store, if she doesn't dramatically turn around her department – or at the very least her attitude – I'm going to have to look at demoting her immediately, with a view to letting her go. After all, maybe she's better suited to a more modern store than this anyway? I mean, Elaine had a point when she was talking about the type of designers we should be stocking here

462

at Hardy's. She may not be as glamorous as Carly, and she can be a bit lazy, but she knows her stuff, that girl, and she's been really helping out in other departments. She's actually turned out to be a good team player.'

'Well, you should do what you think best for the store: you're the boss, after all,' Sharon replies before adding shyly, 'and a wonderful one you are, too.'

'Why, thank you, Sharon.' I don't need to see Rupert to know he has turned a deep shade of red. 'There is something else I wanted to talk to you about, Sharon, something more um, personal.' He coughs nervously. 'Would you . . . you know . . . by any chance be free to, well, actually, I mean to go for dinner at some point with me? More specifically I mean tonight, er . . . maybe?'

'Rupert, I'd be delighted,' breathes Sharon. And they walk out of the stockroom, the door slamming shut behind them.

I sink down against the shelves and put my head in my hands, rubbing my forehead with exhaustion and concern. Poor Carly, she has no idea she's about to lose her job and I honestly don't know how she'll cope. The poor girl is at her lowest ebb and I understand just how that feels. In fact, right now Carly seems to have inherited my bad luck and I feel like it's all my fault. I mean, the universe has to send it somewhere, right? And ever since I wished for my life to change, it has – but at the same time Carly's has changed too, for the worse.

Just then my mobile rings and I feel a complicated flash of lust and panic as I see Joel's name appear on my screen. I haven't spoken to him other than to text to apologize for running off on Sunday. He said he'd call, but part of me didn't expect him to. And his call is reminding me that this should be for Carly. *She* should be dating some gorgeous American man right now who would lift her confidence and make her feel wonderful, which would make her better at her job and happier at work. I know the power that the attention of a man like Joel can wield. It's why it's proving so hard to let him go.

I stare at the phone and watch as it switches to voicemail, vowing to phone him back later. The only way I can deal with the guilt of what I've done is to save Carly's job and to make people think that Carly *is* the one doing all the makeovers. Even though Carly has already had a go at making over Designers, I know I have to redo it in a way that will really impress Rupert and Sharon, as well as regain Carly's respect from the rest of the staff. And it will also stop me from feeling so guilty about Joel. Because I have to see him again. I just have to.

CHAPTER 31

'Hello, it's me,' I murmur from where I'm crouched in a far corner of the stockroom, surrounded by a forest of beautiful garments encased in shimmering plastic. I've spent the afternoon cherry-picking Carly's best stock purchases in preparation for her department's makeover. No one can deny the girl knows her fashion, I think, as I run my fingers over a beautiful, nude silk-chiffon draped column dress – then I glance at a tiny black leather chain-embellished minidress that's on top of my discarded pile and make a face – she just doesn't know Hardy's customers. I prop my phone against my ear and luxuriate in the low hum of Joel's voice as he murmurs softly down the line.

'Well, hey there, stranger,' he says softly. 'I've been wondering if you might call me back. I wasn't sure you would after you ran out on me on Sunday.'

'I'm so sorry,' I mutter, ashamed.

'So what was the deal with that?' Joel asks, the tension now apparent in his voice.

'I-I just freaked out a little,' I reply in what could be the Understatement of the Century. 'I was having such a good time and I just thought about the fact you'd be going home soon, and I just felt that things were moving too fast . . .'

'But I've said you could always come with me,' he interjects, snowballing me slightly. 'So why don't you?'

'What?'

'Come home and meet my family. They'd adore you. You'd love the holidays in the States. And even though we'd miss Christmas Day, all the decorations would still be up . . .'

A flood of glorious images rushes into my mind: popcorn and cranberries on string, snowy sidewalks, pumpkin pie oozing with spices, eggnog laced with rum, red-and-white-striped candy canes, big department stores draped with sumptuous decorations and gorgeously gift-wrapped presents.

'I-I couldn't,' I stammer.

'Why not?'

But I'm barely listening. He wants me to MEET HIS FAMILY? At CHRISTMAS? And, oh God, I want to, so badly. Each year since Jamie and I split up I've sat around the dinner table with my parents, Delilah and Will, and Jonah and Noah's ever-changing carousel of girlfriends, and had to deal with the ribbing from them that there I was, single, again, dealing with hilarious gifts like a book called *How to Find Career Success* from my dad, Nigella's *How to Be a Domestic Goddess* from my mum, truly hilarious blow-up boyfriend dolls from my brothers (no, really), and a beautiful piece of designer clothing from my sister that is always so small I could never squeeze into it in a million years. I'd give anything to spend this year with Joel. To run away from everything and everyone. I suddenly find myself caught up in a fantasy where I move to Pennsylvania so we can run his family store together and live happily ever after. I visualize our farewell party, complete with bunting and cupcakes and 'The Star Spangled Banner' playing in the background. I can even imagine Raffy and Lola's wails as they cling to my legs and yell, 'Don't leave us, Teevee, we love you, take us with you!' whilst I cover their heads with kisses. But that would mean him knowing who I really am. He's attracted to a version of me that doesn't really exist. He would drop me like a shot if he knew the truth.

Or would he?

The more I get to know Joel, the more I think maybe, just maybe, he might have come to love me. Evie. I mean, like me, he loves his family, he wants to settle down and, judging by how hung up he was on his ex, he's a one-woman kind of guy. And he's loyal to his friends – just look how he's helping out Rupert with Hardy's finances. If I'd just told him the truth in the first place then I wouldn't be in this predicament. Perhaps now I would be using my savings to book a plane ticket and would be preparing for the Christmas of my dreams. If only I'd had the confidence just to be myself.

I realize that Joel is waiting for an explanation.

'I-I couldn't . . . leave my family,' I reply. 'My sister, well, she's having marriage problems and she needs me.'

'You don't talk about her much,' he says. 'Are you close?'

'Yes,' I reply without thinking. And then I think about how long it's been since we had a proper conversation that didn't involve frostiness and recriminations. 'Well, we were,' I say sadly before adding: 'It's complicated.'

'Sounds it,' Joel laughs, and I can't help wishing that he'd ask me more. But he doesn't. 'So listen, it's funny you called. Guess where I am?' He pauses for a nanosecond. 'Hardy's!' he announces jubilantly.

'W-where?' I manage to stutter.

'Actually I'm in the designers department!' he says proudly. 'I decided if Mohammed wouldn't come to the mountain . . .'

My stomach lurches. Oh God. Not again. Why does he keep doing this to me?

'Right!' I say brightly. 'Great! I'll be right there.' I glance at the dresses around me and grab an armful. 'I'm, er, just picking up some stuff from, er . . . Personal Shopping. See you in a minute!'

I chuck my phone on the floor and stagger down the central aisle of the stockroom towards the door, carrying the beautiful, expensive gowns. I have to get up there and find Carly. Then I have to distract Joel and . . . then . . . then, well, I honestly don't know what I'll do then. I'll have to think on my feet.

I run up the stairs, panting heavily as I weave my way between bewildered-looking customers, trying to stop the dresses from getting tangled between my legs whilst simultaneously wishing that I was wearing my trusty loafers and not the stacked 1970s wedges I picked up from Spitalfields last week.

'Argh!' I cry as I stumble over the last step and topple to the floor, one hand held aloft like the Statue of Liberty. A pair of well-shined shoes appears in my eye-line and I glance up to see an amused-looking Joel standing over me. My eyes are immediately drawn to a certain part of his anatomy.

'. . . knows no bounds,' Joel chuckles as he helps me to my feet.

'What?' I say, dragging my eyes away from his groin as I glance at the crumpled dresses I'm lying on in dismay. I'll have to get the steamer on them later.

'I said,' he repeats, 'your enthusiasm to see me knows no bounds.'

'Oh, yes, right, ha ha, very funny. Ow.'

'Bruised ego?' Joel says, slipping his arm around my waist and pulling me gently to my feet.

'No, bruised knees,' I reply, rubbing them whilst furtively scanning the department to see where Carly is. I spot her mooching around by the till. She appears to be pouncing desperately on passing customers, who are waving her away like an annoying fly. I can see she is trying too hard.

'Er, shall we go downstairs?' I hiss, trying to lead Joel round in a circle and over to the stairs that I've just run up.

'Why don't you show me this department instead?' Joel says, turning me back around. 'I guess this is where you do all the styling for your high-end customers.'

Carly is now ensconced in a magazine at the till. I have to get her out of here.

'Of course!' I say enthusiastically. 'Er, I just need to chat to my, um, staff first. Work before pleasure, you know! You wait here.'

I drag Joel to a far corner of the department and stand him directly behind a long grey slashed dress splattered with red. Carly has hung it from the ceiling, making it look like a prop from some sort of macabre murder scene. I dash over to her, glancing back to see Joel's feet peeking out from underneath the dress and stifling a nervous laugh.

'Er, Carly,' I say and she glances up at me with sad, doleful eyes. Her cheeks are blotchy and it looks like she's been crying. 'Hey, are you OK?' I ask, touching her gently on the arm.

She nods and goes to speak, but then her eyes start filling up with tears.

'Oh, don't cry,' I say, alarmed, 'not here. Come on, let's get you back to the stockroom. You look like you could do with a cup of tea.'

'But what about the department?' she protests tearfully.

'Don't worry, I'll sort it out. Give me five minutes and I'll meet you down there,' I say, and push her towards the stairs. She turns and slopes despondently off and I wait for a moment before darting over to where Joel is still standing patiently waiting for me. He looks up from his iPhone and smiles, his eyes shining with pleasure.

'Hi, you,' he says, and slides his phone into his pocket.

'Hi. Um, Joel, I appear to have a bit of a staff problem,' I say pulling a face. 'You know how it is. I really need to sort some stuff out. Sorry, you've caught me at a bad time. I could meet you later, though?'

'Sure,' Joel shrugs. 'I guess I did kinda come unannounced and I can't just expect you to drop everything. I know how important you are to this place. Actually, I'm due to meet Rupert anyway, so why don't you come and find me when you're done and maybe we can have lunch?' He leans forward and kisses me on the lips, which makes me want to leap into his arms and beg him to take me away from all this. Instead, I smile bashfully as I pull back, then quickly, unable to stop myself, I lean forward and give him a long, lingering kiss before I dash off, frantically looking for Elaine to see if she can cover the department for half an hour.

I eventually find Elaine in Haberdashery, helping Bernie and Susan, who appear to be working on their very own department makeover.

'Elaine,' I pant breathlessly, 'I'm so glad I found you. Can you cover Designers for a bit? I, er, I need Carly with me in the stockroom.'

'Go on, dearie,' Bernie says in her lilting Irish voice as Susan beams brightly at us. 'We've got it from here, sure we do. The buttons are going to go over here, and the vintage fabric is going to be displayed under this bunting that Susan's made.' Susan picks up an armful of fabric flags and holds them up: lots of perfectly sewn triangles of beautiful vintage fabric, some patchwork, others showcasing some of the gorgeous fabrics they sell in the department; pale mint and white polka dots, lilac and blue gingham and gorgeous Cath Kidston-style floral designs.

'What a great idea!' I exclaim, and Susan's pale, powdered cheeks go a little pink as Bernie nudges her proudly. 'And these buttons are amazing!' I pounce on the box of shiny old buttons and rifle through them.

'Ahhh, yes, Susan here had the idea of going and searching in the stockroom for all the other old buttons and fabrics that we knew had been kept, well, ever since we've worked here, which is what, Susan? Forty years now?'

'Forty-one, so it is,' Susan corrects proudly.

'We've decided to give it a "Make Do and Mend" theme. It's very trendy these days, apparently. We're even thinking of setting up a craft corner right here in the department, doing different demonstrations each week and inviting customers to come and learn a new skill, like quilting, or lace-making or crocheting. Susan and I can do them all, you know.'

I clap my hands. 'That sounds wonderful,' I say, feeling a swell of pride that these two stalwarts of the old-school Hardy's have taken the store's redesign to their hearts and are using their own expertise to update their department in a way that I never could. 'It's looking better already.'

'Ahh, sure, we couldn't have done it without Elaine. She's been telling us just what the youngsters like these days and giving us ideas.'

'I've loved it,' Elaine says happily. Then her tone darkens. 'And I'm not going back to Designers if Carly is still there. I can't work with that girl a minute longer.'

'She won't be,' I say. 'Please, Elaine? Just for half an hour or so?'

'OK, seeing as it's you,' Elaine says begrudgingly.

I smile gratefully and dash off.

I'm alarmed to find Carly slumped on the sofa in the stockroom, lights switched off and sobbing into a cushion. I rush over and flick the Christmas tree lights on, then perch on the end of the sofa and stroke her hair soothingly.

473

'Hey now, it can't be that bad,' I say, trying to shake the guilty feeling that I am to blame for her misery.

'Can't it?' She sniffs and turns her face to look at me. She looks terrible. 'No one will speak to me, no one!' she blubs despairingly as I put my arm around her. 'I'm trying to do my job as b-best I can but no one will let me. Elaine won't work with me in Designers, and when I try to go to other departments to help them remerchandise they just tell me they want to wait for the Secret Elf to come and do it. I-I'm meant to be the assistant manager! How am I supposed to impress Rupert if no one will let me do my job?'

'He knows how hard you work and how valuable you are to this place,' I say soothingly, feeling my stomach twinge with guilt when I think what I heard him say about her this morning.

'Do y-you think so?' Carly asks desperately. 'I'm not so sure. And Sh-Sharon i-is always hovering around just waiting for me to make some terrible mistake so she can tell him to sack me. He always listens to her and she's got it in for me now, just like the rest of them. Oh GOD, I hate it here, Sarah, I hate it!' And she bursts into fresh tears.

'Shhh, no you don't,' I say, cradling her head as she sobs into my shoulder. 'There's just a lot of changes going on right now and you need to adapt to them, that's all.'

'I just want it to go back to how it was before,' she cries. 'When I was popular and people listened

474

to me. I just feel like everything's changed, and I don't know why. Maybe I should just leave . . . not that I have any other job to go to.'

'Carly, listen to me. You're an amazing girl and a great personal shopper, and most stores would love to employ a girl like you,' I say, desperately wanting to boost her confidence. I feel like I've stolen it, along with her man. 'You're talented, stylish, and you know exactly what looks good on people. Hardy's is changing but it doesn't mean that you're not good at your job. You are. The staff are just used to you being one of them, and now you're not. And if you make them feel inferior to you, it's going to upset them.'

'I didn't *want* to do that!' Carly protests. 'But Sharon told me when she and Rupert gave me the promotion that if I was going to be a manager I had to distance myself from the team. So that's what I did.'

'Let's face it,' I say gently, nudging her a little to try to extract a laugh, 'Sharon isn't exactly the most popular person in Hardy's either, is she?' Carly sniffs. 'Which means you have to make a choice. Do you want to be popular or be respected?'

Carly lifts her head off my shoulder, which is now damp from her tears. 'Can't I be both?' she whimpers.

'No,' I say firmly, 'you can't. And to be honest, Carly, some of us don't have the choice of either.'

'Don't be silly,' Carly says, wiping her nose with

her sleeve. 'Everyone loves you. And Sharon is always banging on about how the stockroom has been a changed place since you arrived.'

'Well, I can't have made that much of an impression. After all,' I mutter without thinking, 'no one even remembers my name.' I stand up hurriedly and turn away as I realize what I've said.

'What do you mean?' Carly sits up and looks at me, her eyebrows knitted together and frown lines on her usually smooth forehead, but despite this, the blotchiness and the red, running nose, she still looks annoyingly beautiful. 'Of course we know your name. Everyone knows Sarah the Stockroom girl!'

'But that's just it,' I say in frustration. 'You don't! No one does. Not really.' Carly looks blankly at me and I realize I've said too much. I take a deep breath and let my arms drop to my sides as I summon up a small smile. 'Ignore me, Carly, it's fine. I'm just . . . a little tense at the moment.'

'*You're* a little tense,' Carly says peevishly. 'Try being me.'

You have no idea.

'Listen,' I say tightly, 'why don't you stay here for a bit? I'm going for a break now and I've got someone covering Designers. Put some fresh make-up on, get yourself together, then go back upstairs. And remember, everyone will come round to your new job if you treat them with the same respect that you want them to give to you.'

And I walk out, leaving Carly looking like a

476

dishevelled angel, slumped forlornly under the Christmas tree.

I scan the store as I walk through each department, trying to find Joel. It's 11 a.m., which is when Rupert usually does his rounds of the store, so I'm presuming that Joel will still be with Rupert somewhere. It doesn't take me long to find them in Menswear.

I hover on the stairs, look down and immediately see Rupert and Joel standing next to each other like the Odd Couple. They are watching on the sidelines, deep in discussion, whilst Guy works his magic on the customers. I watch for a few minutes and it soon becomes clear that the conversation is tenser than I imagined. Rupert's face is going increasingly red and he looks upset; he keeps shaking his head and looking up at Hardy's beautiful, domed roof despairingly. Joel isn't faring much better. He is clearly struggling to explain something and I can't help but wonder what. Lip-reading never was my strong point. I watch as Joel rubs his forehead and then gestures wildly, sweeping his arms around the store as if trying to show Rupert something. Then Rupert clenches his fists, says something and storms off.

I walk slowly down the stairs and approach Joel, who is staring at his feet and rocking back and forth, his hands buried deep into his pockets, his brow furrowed. I don't want to approach him now

477

he's had a disagreement with Rupert but I have no choice. I have to get him out of the store before Carly leaves the stockroom.

'Joel? Is everything OK?' I ask gently.

Joel focuses on me and smiles distractedly. 'Hey, Carly, sorry, I was miles away. Just thinking how much I hate my job sometimes.'

'Don't we all?' I say, then add drily. 'It's why we call them "jobs" and not "barrels of laughs".' Joel chuckles, despite himself. 'So what's up?' I ask, trying not to display too much interest in what he was talking to Rupert about, but nonetheless completely intrigued.

'Oh, it's just business,' he sighs. 'You wouldn't understand.'

'Try me,' I say, pushing aside my disgruntlement at his patronizing answer. I'm surprised and a bit discomfited that he suddenly reminds me of my dad.

He's looking at me as if sizing up my ability to comprehend the situation when Guy approaches us.

'Well, hellloooo, handsome,' he drawls as he looks Joel up and down. 'And what brings such a stylish customer to Hardy's? Usually my customers leave my department looking like you, but they sure as hell don't come in like that. I have some beautiful tailored suits that would look divine on your . . . body.' He drops his eyes. 'Obviously I'd have to take some measurements first.' He turns to me. 'You don't mind if I steal him for a minute, do you, Sarah darling?'

I glance at Joel in panic as Guy says my name and Joel raises his eyebrow enquiringly at me and I shrug, as if to say, 'I don't know what he's talking about.'

Guy is still talking at us. 'By the way, you look ravishing today too, darling. I'm *loving* the retro look you've been sporting recently,' he gushes. 'Now, enough of this chit-chatting, I've got a hunk to dress!' And he drags Joel off by the elbow as Joel looks back at me helplessly and holds his fingers to his ear in an 'I'll call you' mime.

I watch them go and try not to panic about Joel being let loose in the store without me – not to mention what the hell Guy will say to him. The only good thing is that Guy will have him for at least an hour so hopefully Carly won't bump into him. I resolve to call him after that time to try to save him from Guy. I can't help but wonder what Joel said to Rupert that made him so angry. One thing I know: if he's upset Rupert, and Rupert is trying desperately to save the store, then whatever it is, it can't be good.

I'm deep in thought and barely notice the throng of customers around me until I bump right into one. Apologizing profusely, I look up and stare in abject alarm into a familiar face: my dad's. He never comes into see me at work. I can't help but wonder why he's here now.

'Darling.' His voice resonates against my body like a gong as he pulls me into a gigantic bear hug in the middle of the store. I gaze up at his warm, smiling face, slightly freaked out but pleased by his surprise visit.

'What are you doing here, Dad?' I ask, trying to sound businesslike on my turf. But it's quite hard when you're having your hair ruffled. I don't want to draw attention to the fact that he's here; the last thing I want is to bump into Joel and have to do the awkward introductions. I mean, imagine.

Glancing around, I pull at my dad's arm and try to lead him towards the stockroom where we can hide away. Unfortunately, unlike me, my dad doesn't exactly know how to fade into the background.

'Can't a man come and see his daughter when he's in town?' he says, throwing a hand over my shoulder and squeezing the breath out of me.

''Course,' I wheeze. 'You've just never done it before.'

'Well, maybe it's time I started,' he laughs jovially and then lowers his voice a little. 'How about I take you out somewhere nice, you know, Claridge's or somewhere? As a treat.' My mind flits inappropriately to Joel and our night in his suite, and I blush.

'I can't, Dad, I'm working. But I can have a quick tea break. We can go to the stockroom?' I suggest hopefully. 'I can show you what I've done in there!'

Dad's top lip curls a little.

'Nonsense, darling, let me at least treat you. How about the tearoom your mother and I used to go to? Do you remember how you used to come with us on our anniversary every year?'

I smile fondly as I think back to those happy days and I slip my arm through Dad's, finding comfort in the familiarity of his presence. Yes, he can be a bit stuck up and terribly overbearing sometimes, but I love him. And he's reminded me just why I love Hardy's so much, too. It's part of the fabric of our family history. I know he and Mum will understand why I want to try to save it.

'Hang on.' I stop mid-step as a thought occurs to me. 'Your anniversary is the twelfth of December. Wasn't that yesterday, Dad?' I'm thinking of poor Mum alone in Norfolk for the past few days whilst Dad works in London.

Dad looks understandably alarmed. 'Oh, shit, I've really messed up,' he says, pulling out his BlackBerry and glancing at the date. 'I'd better call Sally and see if she remembered.'

I purse my lips. Sally is Dad's long-suffering PA.

He grins and winks at me as he ends his call. 'She remembered to send flowers!'

'That doesn't excuse you, though, Dad,' I scold. 'Make sure you make it up to Mum.'

'Of course I will, darling,' Dad laughs, holding his hands up. 'Haven't I always treated her like a queen?'

I smile, placated, and squeeze his arm as we start walking companionably, chatting about our weeks as I look around anxiously for signs of Joel and try to hurry Dad along. He tells me how he has been spending a lot of time in London because of a big broker deal he's been working on.

'You must get lonely in that flat all on your own,' I say. 'You should come for dinner at Delilah's sometimes, we're just down the road, remember.'

'Thank you, darling,' he replies, 'but I've been so busy I've just been going back to the flat to sleep. That's why your mother hasn't come this time. I feel bad that she's at home on her own, but work is just too busy to spend any time with her.' He glances at me and smiles sadly. Poor Dad, I think. I bet he's really lonely. I hate thinking of him going back to an empty flat every night. Especially as I know how much he needs Mum. She's like his right arm.

'Well, maybe I could come and stay with you for a couple of nights?' I offer. 'Make you dinner or something?'

He doesn't answer and I realize it's because he's popped on one of the trilbies from Menswear and is admiring his handsome reflection in the mirror.

'Hurry up, Dad,' I chide. 'I've only got twenty minutes or so. I can't leave the stockroom for too long.'

'Why?' he replies, popping the hat back on the shelf. 'It's not like the place is ever busy.'

I look at him in astonishment. My dad is a clever man, but he is oblivious to anything that doesn't directly revolve around him. Are the throngs of people currently weaving their way around him completely invisible or has he just been blinded by his own reflection? I sigh as I step into the tearoom and embrace Lily warmly as she rushes over to greet me.

'Well, I never . . .' Dad says as he looks at Lily closely.

'Charles Taylor,' Lily says, holding her hand out before smiling and bobbing charmingly at my father. There is an uncomfortable pause as he takes her hand and she hastily prompts: 'Lily Carmichael.'

'Of course!' laughs my father jovially as I cringe at his inability to remember people's names. 'Lily! How could I forget?' I shake my head. Lily is nearly eighty years old and has managed to conjure up his name from the depths of her ailing memory, but yet he hasn't recalled hers, and nor is he embarrassed by this fact. My father is used to being remembered by everyone. It makes me so mad. Maybe that's why I've always endeavoured to remember everyone I meet, carefully memorizing their name and a fact about them so that I would never ever put them in the position that he's just put Lily in. It makes people think he's aloof although once they got to know him they'd see he wasn't. He's just a bit . . . wrapped up in himself.

'Well, well, well,' he says, and then looks around the tearoom until he spots a spare table to sit at and stares at it pointedly. I make an apologetic face at Lily as she hastily ushers us over, and she squeezes my hand before I sit down.

'What can I get you?' she asks politely, and Dad gives her his order without even asking her how she's been. Lily scribbles down our order and then glides silently off, sylphlike as ever.

'That was a bit rude, Dad,' I say, and he looks at me blankly.

'What?' he asks innocently, and I roll my eyes. 'Well,' he smiles, and sits back in his chair, stretching out his long legs, so anyone wanting to get past would have to step over them. 'It's nice to see you here in your . . . little job,' he says with a smile. 'Although,' he leans forward, 'I'm amazed you still have one. I mean, this place is just so past it now, isn't it? A bit like the staff,' he whispers, and then smiles at Lily, who has just arrived with our pot of tea.

'I can't believe you've just said that,' I shoot back after she's gone.

'Well, Evie, it's sad but true,' Dad replies with a smile. 'It just doesn't make good business sense to keep this place as it is. Sebastian Hardy must know it.'

'Well, Sebastian Hardy isn't in charge any more; his son Rupert is. And unlike his father, he has some family loyalty and sense of history . . .'

'Aaah, but loyalty doesn't make money, darling!' he laughs.

I grasp my tea cup for support and to stop me tearing my hair out with frustration. I don't know

484

why I bother, but I feel the need to defend Hardy's to my father.

'Hardy's can't close and it won't,' I say firmly, putting my tea cup back on its saucer. 'It's a store with history and a heart. Londoners love it and so do the staff. We all think that, with a proper chance, this place can be great again. We're already busier than we've been for years, the departments have been updated and we're taking way more money than before . . .'

'More of nothing isn't a lot, though, is it, darling?' Dad responds smoothly. That comment hurt, mostly because he's right. 'I'm sorry, love,' he continues more softly. 'You can try and convince me all you like but you're a romantic, just like your mother. And romance doesn't get you anywhere in this life.'

'But surely you must have some emotional connection to this place?' I say. 'It's part of the reason I love it here so much. I mean, you and Mum fell in love under this roof!' I hope that by reminding him of what Hardy's has brought him – a loving wife, a wonderful family – it'll help Dad see how important this place is to so many other people, too.

He leans over and squeezes my hand. 'Of course it's important, darling. But life moves on. You can't live with memories forever and history can't buy you a retirement plan. So if you're still working here out of some misguided sense of romance about my and your mother's relationship, well, then I . . .' He is distracted by his bleeping phone and doesn't finish his sentence.

'Well then what?' I ask impatiently and he looks up at me blankly as if he's already forgotten our conversation, already ensconced in sending a text, a small smile hovering over his face.

'Well, then what?' I repeat impatiently, and Dad looks up.

'Er? What were we talking about? Oh, yes, your misplaced sense of romance when it comes to business. What I was going to say was if that's the case then maybe the stockroom is the best place for you.' Dad smiles at me widely, clearly unaware he has just mortally offended me. 'Not everything in life can be some big ideal, Eve darling, and you'd do well to remember that. And so would your mother.' He drains his cup and puts it back down on the saucer with a loud clatter, so that everyone in the tearoom turns to look at us, including Lily. Then he stands up and throws on his coat.

'Right, gotta go,' he says, kissing me on the forehead as he wraps his cashmere scarf around his neck and puts his leather gloves on. 'We must do this again sometime.'

I turn my head, fold my arms and stare sullenly into the distance as he strides off.

Seconds later, I feel a warm hand rest delicately on my shoulder and I look up to see Lily gazing sympathetically down at me. She pulls a chair up and perches on it.

'I'm so sorry about him, Lily,' I say, my eyes filling with tears suddenly.

She waves her hand. 'Shush now, you don't have to apologize. Parents are always a bit embarrassing.'

'A bit?' I shake my head.

'Well, dear, if it's any consolation, you're nothing like him.'

I smile tearfully. 'I'm just so fed up of his views. Just because I don't have a fancy house like Delilah, a rich husband or work in some high-powered job, he looks down on my job, my relationships, everything. And he's not the only one . . .'

'What do you mean?' Lily says.

I sigh as I think about Carly and all the other staff who pour out their troubles to me. 'Half the people here still don't know me, or know what I can do. Carly even took the glory for the makeovers. No one would ever suspect me. They think I'm worthless except as a sounding board to their problems.'

'So maybe it's time you told them,' Lily says simply.

'What do you mean?' I twist the rim of my tea cup so that the brown liquid left at the bottom swooshes around like a whirlpool.

'Who you are, what you do.' She stands up. 'Unless, that is, you actually prefer being invisible? Maybe you think that's all you deserve? Perhaps you'd rather slink through life without anyone bothering you. After all, it's much easier, isn't it?' Lily tilts her head and strokes my arm. 'Hmm?'

I shrug and stare at the leaves of tea.

'Or is it?' she adds and with a final squeeze of my arm, she walks off.

WEDNESDAY 14 DECEMBER

11 Shopping Days Until Christmas

CHAPTER 32

'Hi, Felix,' I say glumly as I walk through the staff entrance. I am feeling distinctly Wednesday-ish and uncharacteristically unChristmassy, despite the glorious spectacle of lights and decorations that greeted me as I cycled into town this morning. Even the prospect of transforming Carly's department is not making me feel better. Everything feels like such an effort and I'm not sure I have the energy any more. Designers is way out of my league. I know nothing about designer clothes, and if Carly can't make it work then how the hell can I? But without it I know Hardy's cannot compete. One designer outfit sale could match the entire takings of some of the smaller departments.

'Evie!' Felix bounds up to me and thrusts a latte into my hands as I smile weakly at him. 'I took the liberty of getting you a coffee first. I've been thinking up ideas for Designers all night and wanted to show some things to you,' he says excitedly, his sharp blue eyes glittering like icicles.

I trudge after Felix reluctantly. It's so sweet of him to get excited but I'm really not in the mood

491

today. I just want to get on with it. I can't fake enthusiasm for some ideas that I'll never use from an old man who hasn't worked on the shop floor in thirty-odd years and who considers pattern clashing bow-ties to be fashionable. I feel mean and dispirited, and I don't want my mood to rub off on Felix, but right now I wish I could go back to doing this all on my own.

'Now,' he says, spreading out a large, rolled-up piece of paper over his desk and tugging on my arm to draw me in closer. 'I've sketched out my ideas. I haven't done this for a while so I may be a little rusty . . .'

'What do you mean, you haven't done this for a while?'

'Oh, myself and Walter junior did a rather successful store makeover back in 1974, which I had a great deal of creative input in,' Felix says proudly. 'Of course, things were different back then but you inspired me to revisit some of my own ideas all those years ago. After all, if they worked then, they could still work now. With a special Evie twist, of course!' he adds with a wink. 'I don't pretend to understand modern fashion, oh, no, or know how to marry old and new together to make something fresh and, er, funky? Is that right?' I laugh at Felix's expression and he joins in. 'Hey, I can be down with the kids too, you know, love. I know all the street talk.'

'That's more than I do, Felix,' I say, feeling brighter. I suddenly find myself compelled to look closer at the drawings. 'These are really good, Felix!' I'm unable to hide the surprise in my voice. 'I love what you've done with the till area. It looks really glamorous and, oh – what are those, over where the changing rooms are?'

'They're vintage screens,' Felix says. 'I know we've got some in the store somewhere and I thought we could do something like this with them.' He pulls out a new issue of *Living etc* magazine and shows me a reader's glamorous bedroom. I raise my eyebrow at him.

'What?' he says defensively. 'I like a bit of home decoration, you know. Maisie always said I was a DIY mastermind. I just thought instead of covering the screens with fabric, which would be expensive and time-consuming, we could just quickly wallpaper them and then put them in different spots in the department. We could drape nice clothes over them as if customers have been getting changed behind them. But – and this is my pièce de résistance – we could turn the changing rooms into a sort of VIP closet, where the most elegant designer dresses and shoes are displayed. I reckon it'd bring a real sense of luxury to the department. It could be like that walk-in closet in that programme you women always bang on about, you know, the one with the women who all like shoes and sex and talk about them all the time – especially that blonde one who looks like a drag queen.'

'You mean *Sex and the City*?' I say, mouth agape.

'My Maisie used to love that show. Not that I ever watched it, of course,' he adds gruffly, clearing his throat. 'The clothes that Carrie Bagshott woman wore were way too crazy, and the way that Mr Huge messed her around? No sensible woman would ever stand for that. My Maisie never would, that's for sure . . .'

I gape in wonder at Felix as I look from him to his sketches and then back again. Will my friends never cease to amaze me? These ideas are wonderful, way better than anything I came up with last night. I was too busy thinking about Joel, then Carly, then worrying about Delilah, who I could hear crying in her room again because Will wasn't home. Then I drifted off to sleep with just my dad's comment reverberating in my head. I ended up throwing away most of my drawings when I woke up, vowing to wing it when I came in. But now Felix has reignited my imagination and I know that, with his help, this makeover could be amazing.

I throw my arms around him. 'Felix, these are brilliant ideas! But do you think we can really get all this done this morning?'

''Course we can, darling. I've already got Jan Baptysta started on knocking the changing rooms through into a single walk-in room. I hope you don't mind?' he adds bashfully. 'But I knew you'd like that idea. Every store and girl should have one!' he adds in a faux camp voice.

I laugh again and drag him out of his office.

'Come on then, we'd better work fast so you're not missed in security!'

'Aah, sod security,' Felix chuckles. 'Most of the time I just nap, anyway. In three years I've never seen anyone come here when the store is shut. To be honest, before you started all this, they barely came when the bloody place was open!'

We walk into the store laughing companionably, suddenly able to find humour at Hardy's sad situation. Maybe it's because we finally have a glimmer of hope.

We're just greeting the rest of the gang, who are all hard at work, when Sam bursts in.

'Evie!' he gasps. 'I was hoping you'd already be here. I had to come by so I could show you these!' He is holding armfuls of prints, which he now thrusts at me. 'I've cancelled my other deliveries this morning so I can take these to the local news-papers. What do you think?'

I flick through the scenes that Sam captured from our makeover the other morning, until I feel a crowd of people around me. Felix, Lily, Jan Baptysta and the rest of the gang are all 'oohing' and 'aahing' over my shoulder.

'What do you think?' Sam repeats more urgently. 'I hope I've captured the spirit of the makeover sessions without revealing who anyone is. 'I thought these –' he points at a series of six shots of us transforming the handbag department, 'would make a great reportage sequence – and this –' he pulls out a photo that shows me with my back to the camera and in complete darkness against the brightness of the store, with blurry figures rushing around me – 'is a great central action shot.'

'They're—' I begin.

'VONDERVUL!' yells Velna.

'Beautifully shot, Sam,' says Lily, leaning over to have a look.

'Bloody brilliant,' Felix adds proudly.

'I second all of those things,' I smile at Sam, feeling the excitement and hope building. 'Do you really think the papers will run them, though?'

'I don't see why not,' Sam shrugs, running his fingers through his already ruffled hair. 'I mean, local papers love inspiring community stories like this, and it's got the right balance of drama, what with the threat of Hardy's closure. And then there's the Christmas angle, with you lot acting like the store's little Secret Elves. But we'll see. Wish me luck, guys!' he says, taking back the pictures and holding up his crossed figures.

'Good luck!' I spontaneously embrace Sam and I feel unwelcome shivers of longing as his hands rest gently on the base of my back.

Everyone cheers and Jan Baptysta wolf whistles and I pull away, suddenly embarrassed and confused. Sam is just my friend, he always has been. There's never been anything more between us. My mind races back through our relationship and pictures like mental flashcards appear before me: Sam and I talking about our lifelong dreams over our early morning breakfasts; the funny texts he sends whilst doing his other deliveries, which help to get me through another lonely day in the stockroom; the way my heart always lifts when I see his smiling face as I open the delivery doors. The searing image of him walking down the road with another girl; that same stab of jealousy when I met Ella. Him leaning in to kiss me in the pub in Primrose Hill . . .

Oh God. I gulp and take another step back from him, suddenly unable to look him in the eye for fear he will see exactly what's going through my head.

'I'll be off then,' Sam smiles bashfully to the still-cheering crowd. And I nod quickly, turn away and lose myself in the makeover, trying not to look at him as he disappears out of the store.

Later that afternoon, I wheel my bike across Primrose Hill as Lola and Raffy scramble alongside me, squealing and jumping and stopping to examine sticks and stones and anything they can to make the journey go at their pace. I let them because I'm in no hurry to get home myself. I can't stop thinking about Sam and Joel, and feel like I need this walk to clear my head. I don't understand why I've started having these feelings for Sam when someone as wonderful and gorgeous and exciting as Joel has come along. He's everything I never dared to dream about in a man. The sort of guy I always thought wouldn't look twice at a girl like me. But he has, he is, and he's made it clear that he doesn't just see this as a holiday romance. So why am I risking happiness by thinking about someone else? Someone who has been nothing more than a friend for the past two years. Could my feelings for Sam have lain dormant for so long just because I was too scared to get close to anyone after Jamie? Has being with Joel given me the confidence to admit it to myself? Or is it just that I haven't seen enough of Joel because I've been throwing myself wholeheartedly into the makeovers? Am I scared that Joel, who I really like, will hurt me and so I suddenly find myself attracted to someone safe, someone I know, who is my friend?

Oh *God*, I am so confused.

Lola slips her mittened hand into mine and smiles up at me.

'Whass wrong, Teevee?' she says as she trudges alongside me. 'You look sad.'

I haul her up into my arms and kiss her cold red cheeks. 'Not sad, Lola. I'm just thinking.'

'Hmm,' she says, tapping her lips with her finger. 'I can do that too.'

I laugh and squeeze her tightly, suddenly feeling thankful that I could get away early enough today to pick them up from nursery. I've really missed them this past week and I'm hoping that today will in some way make up for my absence. Lola starts wriggling and I slide her back down to the ground and watch as she runs off with her brother.

They're so close in age I hope they'll be best friends as they grow up. They'll need each other more than they know.

I had such a wonderful morning, working on the makeover with everyone, chatting and laughing and then working in companionable silence when we realized just what we had to do and in how little time, that it made me think about how much I miss my sister's company. For the past week we've barely seen each other. It's like we're slowly drifting apart. I'm still carrying the weight of Will's infidelity around with me and wondering what the hell to do about it, and even though in the past couple of weeks I've been happier than I've ever been, at the same time I can't help but feel bad that the people I'm closest to seem to be falling apart. So I'm simply pretending it isn't happening, wrapping myself up in my own world, which, for once, feels magical and inspiring, yet deep down I can't help feeling that something – or someone – is missing.

Once upon a time I would have known every single thought that my sister was having, I'd be at home to listen to her talk about her worries at work, her fears that she doesn't spend enough time with the kids, that Will is too stressed, that the mortgage is too big, that Mum and Dad are too far away, that they're too tired to have any fun, that she doesn't spend enough time with me. She'd talk and I'd listen. That was the deal.

But I haven't listened for a long time and I realize

that whilst sometimes I felt frustrated that it always seemed to be a one-way conversation, I *liked* feeling useful. I enjoyed listening to her problems and that I was always able to make her feel better in a way that no one else could – not even her husband. My sister, my idol, needed *me*. I could always rationalize her worries until they became barely a blip on her life's landscape, and then I'd make her laugh. Our relationship worked like that.

But now I'm seeing Joel, and I'm passionate about my job and actually think I'm finally getting somewhere with my life, it feels like I'm losing my sister as a result. Is that the price I have to pay? Does our relationship only work when we play the role of sorted older sister and scatty, searching younger sibling? I used to resent her for not helping me in the same way as I helped her, but now I'm realizing that she *did* help me. I just didn't appreciate it. She gave me a home and helped rebuild my confidence after Jamie dumped me. I would never have moved to London, taken my job or even accepted a date with Joel without her. Even if the latter wasn't exactly done in the most straightforward of ways. By inviting me to live with her she put her own family's happiness on the line. I'm sure Will would prefer it if I wasn't there. Maybe *I'm* part of the reason that their marriage is under pressure. Has he had affairs so that he could spend less time at home with us? Why didn't I ever notice the impact that could have on her marriage before?

I open the front door, usher Lola and Raffy inside and am about to take off their coats when I hear someone slamming round the house. A suitcase gets thrown from the second floor down to the top of the stairs in front of us, and I hastily grab Lola and Raffy by the shoulders and turn them round.

'Hey, guys!' I shout. 'Hands up who wants to go get cupcakes from the Primrose Hill Bakery!' I'm speaking unnecessarily loudly, to ensure that whoever is upstairs – I'm presuming it's Delilah – can hear me.

'YAY!' squeals Lola, hopping around in a circle.

'Yayyayayayayayayayayay,' echoes Raffy, to infinity, it seems.

'OK, LET'S GO!' I shout, more to Delilah than to them, and open the door and walk back out into the bleak winter's afternoon, thankful for the kid's favourite cosy café just round the corner that is always full of delicious cakes and a friendly welcome. Seconds later my phone bleeps.

'Thanks. I love you lil sis. D x'

That night, I lie in bed with a pillow over my head as I listen to Will and Delilah shouting at each other, hoping that because it's so late, the kids will be in too much of a deep sleep to hear. They may live in a gorgeous house, in a picture-perfect area of London, but the words and accusations coming out of their mouths are as ugly as anything you'd hear on *EastEnders*. I press the pillow down further, trying

501

to drown out the sound of Delilah's screaming and Will's bewildered, defensive arguments.

He tells her he's not always out because he's having an affair, he just has to work late. Then he adds that she's mad to think he would ever cheat on her and I feel my stomach churn at his blatant lies.

You're never here, she says.

Nor are you, he counters.

You're obsessed with work, she screams.

Only because you're obsessed with this ridiculously lavish lifestyle, he yells.

You never see the kids

The kids never see you . . .

Back and forth, round and round, going nowhere other than down. This family is sinking, I think. And it's all my fault. I know because I hear Will say it: 'She's always here,' he says despairingly. And I know he means me. And he's right.

My phone, which I am clutching to my chest, buzzes and glows under the covers. I press the Call Accept button and smile despite myself as I hear Joel's voice.

'I'M GOING OUT,' Will shouts at the same time as Joel says hello.

The door slams and I shiver as I hear the sound of Delilah's sobs echo despairingly around the house. But I don't get up and go to her, like I should. I can't. Joel's here and he's making me feel better and I need that right now. And besides, I can't face her. It's all my fault that this is happening. I should just stay up here, tucked away in my turret, make myself invisible beneath my covers, lose myself in the sound of Joel's gentle chat. I'll be there to comfort her and pick up the pieces later. Once I've finished this phone call.

When Joel says goodnight I put the phone on my bedside table and get out of bed. I quietly climb down the stairs, shivering as the cold grips my skin, and gently push open the door. Delilah is curled in a tight heap on the bed, the duvet a dishevelled ball thrown on to the floor, her sad, staring eyes wet with tears. Next to her lies a framed picture of her and Will on their wedding day. I move it out of the way, turning it face down on her bedside table. Then I shake the duvet out and pull it over her, tucking it in around her neck. She mutters something and I stroke her hair to soothe her. Then I climb into bed beside her and lie there with my hand on top of hers, hoping that my presence will bring her some comfort. She grasps it tightly and I realize that she needs me more than she's ever let on. A heavy silence pervades the house and soon Delilah's breathing becomes deeper and slower and her hand goes limp next to mine. I try to drift off into sleep myself but find I can't. I'm unbearably uncomfortable, despite the warmth of my pyjamas and the softness of the duvet, and I realize as I toss and turn for the first time in my life, I'm feeling what it's like to be in Delilah's skin. I lie awake for a long time.

THURSDAY 15 DECEMBER

10 Shopping Days Until Christmas

CHAPTER 33

I jump as I hear a loud banging at the delivery door and put down the old Hardy's Christmas decorations I've been sorting through, cleaning the dust and dirt off them and putting the best ones in piles according to which department I can imagine them in. There are only nine days left till Christmas Eve and our festive makeover is long overdue. It's my secret weapon, the thing I am hoping will bring customers streaming back through the doors. I'm just waiting for the right moment to do it.

I pick my way through the boxes and head over to the back of the stockroom, yawning loudly. I came to work at my normal time this morning as there was no department makeover due. I want to see what the customer reaction to the new-look designers department is before starting on another. I'm still not 100 per cent sure we got it right. The staff all seemed to love it yesterday – apart from Carly, who seemed a little disgruntled – but she soon cheered up when everyone started telling her how great it looked. Even Elaine managed to look happy. I left work just as the lunchtime rush was starting and so have no idea whether they sold anything.

I bend down and empty another box of vintage decorations. Hundreds of miniature painted wooden shoe decorations fall out. I line them up, according size and colour. They are perfectly crafted as if they have been made by the Shoemaker's Elves in the famous Brothers Grimm story. I smile as I think about how those tiny artisans secretly made the carpenter's shoes each night, working hard to turn the single pieces of leather into beautiful footwear and saving the poor, old Shoemaker's business in the process. It was one of my favourite stories when I was little. Now I know why.

I crouch down on the floor and study the beautiful handmade decorations and think about how much we've achieved over the last couple of weeks.

I know my life has changed as much as Hardy's appearance, and sometimes I wonder if it has always been for the best. There have been times recently when I really haven't recognized, or really liked, myself very much. And actually it's nice just to feel like me again this morning.

The old me, that is, the one who got up and helped Delilah with the kids, threw on some clothes and meandered into work, not caring what she looked like and not feeling responsible for the fate of a store and all its workers. Today has been a day to be normal. I've felt invisible again and actually, I'm enjoying it.

I resolved when I woke up this morning that I'd go back to helping with the kids. Delilah was already up with them when I came down. Will hadn't come back last night – or if he had, he'd slept on the couch – so we worked together to give the kids breakfast and get them ready for nursery. I gave her a hug as I left, but her response was limp and she felt weak in my arms, like she'd been drained of everything. For the first time Delilah seems broken, and I don't know how to put her back together again. I wish I could do for her what I've done to some of my co-workers, who seem to be coming to work with renewed energy and excitement every day. Jane is a changed woman, Gwen is a brilliant saleswoman (her commission levels are second to none, which must be doing wonders for her debts), even Sharon has become softer. But suddenly those small successes don't feel so good because I've neglected my sister in the process; and maybe, just maybe, she's the one who needed my help the most.

I feel a wave of guilt and try to bat that idea away by thinking about Felix: the person who's surprised me the most throughout all of this. We sat and talked in his office for half an hour this morning, just like the old days. I've realized that *this* is the real Felix: a sparky, creative, get-up-and-go guy with lots of energy and a positive outlook. For the two years that I've known him I've seen him as an old man, defeated by the world. Every morning he'd be slumped in his chair doing

Sudoku puzzles, passing the long hours until he went home to an empty house. I knew our chats were once the highlight of his day, but now he has so much more.

Today he was talking about where Evie's Elves should go for our next makeover meeting tonight. And Jan Baptysta has promised to go round to his house at the weekend and help him with lots of odd jobs; things that Felix hasn't felt able to do since Maisie died. They've even planning to get a curry and watch a film together. Felix says he hasn't had the confidence to socialize much since Maisie died; he worried he'd end up being maudlin and would bring people down. But now, he's like a new man.

There's another loud banging and I realize that I've totally forgotten there was someone there. I smooth down my hair and flick it off my shoulders before I open the doors, gasping as a blast of cold air hits me and trying not to look at Sam as I usher him in.

'I was beginning to think you'd slept in,' he mumbles. 'But I, er, I've got something I really want to show you.' He stamps his feet on the mat and throws his coat on the sofa as I close the doors behind him, covertly glancing over at him while his back is turned. His presence immediately brightens the stockroom, partly because he's wearing a garish orange, blue and red checked shirt, which makes him look a bit like he should be felling trees.

He doesn't wait to sit down or for me to offer him a cup of tea; he doesn't even bring in the stack of boxes that he's transferred from his van to outside the delivery doors, instead he just pulls a couple of papers out from his bag and thrusts them at me. 'Look at page three of the *Ham and High!*' he says, stabbing his finger at the paper and jiggling on the spot as I try to turn the pages. 'And look – we've got half a page in the *Islington Gazette* too!'

Unable to wait for me, he opens the papers and spreads them on the floor. I squeal and drop to my knees as I look at the headlines, pictures and copy.

'HARDY'S REINVENTED!' shouts the Islington Gazette, and Sam's photograph of the madeover beauty department sits proudly underneath.

'CAN SECRET SANTAS SAVE THIS STORE?' queries the *Ham and High* with three reportage-style pictures of Evie's Elves in silhouette as we transform the handbag department.

'And that's not all,' Sam says proudly, sitting back on his knees as he pulls more newspapers out of his bag. 'Most of the locals have covered it, some in more prominent places than the others. And . . .' he pauses and pulls out a paper from the bottom of the pile, grinning widely as he thrusts it into my hands, '. . . it must have been a quiet day in Fulham – we made the front page!'

I clasp my hand over my mouth to stop myself

511

screaming as I take the copy of the *Fulham and Hammersmith Chronicle*.

'CAN HARDY'S HELPERS TURN STORE FROM GROTTY TO GROTTO?' the headline yells.

'Oh my God, Sam, you did it!' I gasp, shaking my head in disbelief.

Sam flicks his hand dismissively but his eyes shine with pleasure. '*We* did it. This has been team-work. I don't know if it's enough, Evie, but it's a start. Who knows how many new customers you'll get today!'

I throw my arms around Sam and squeeze him tightly. I feel like I could hug him forever. He smells fresh and Alpiney, and for a moment I close my eyes and imagine being locked away in a snowy log cabin with him. I feel his breath on my neck grow heavy and I pull away, conscious suddenly of our closeness.

'I can't wait to show the others, Sam. They're going to be thrilled. You can bring all the papers to our meeting tonight.'

'Ah,' Sam says, pulling himself to his feet and looking awkward all of a sudden. 'I wanted to talk to you about that. I'm afraid I'm not going to be able to make it this time.'

'What?' I say, dismayed. 'Why? We only have two more before Christmas and we need everyone's ideas and input. Plus the gang will want you there . . . you need to show them all your hard work.'

512

Sam shrugs and thrusts his hands in his jeans but doesn't answer.

'Is it a date you really can't change?' I ask finally.

Sam looks embarrassed. 'I guess you could say that,' he replies quietly. 'It's Ella. She's got this thing on – a work Christmas party – so I have to—'

'Go.' I finish his sentence for him. 'Of course you do.' I swallow the lump that has inexplicably appeared in my throat and nod silently before turning away. 'Well, that's fair enough,' I say, clearing my throat. 'But I, I mean, *we'll* miss you.'

'I'll call you if any more papers run the story,' Sam says softly, and I nod, busying myself once more with untangling faded paper chains and brightly coloured Chinese lanterns.

The stockroom door swings open just as Sam is about to leave and Carly walks in.

'Well, *hello*,' she says coquettishly as she spots Sam. 'What, I mean, who do we have here?' She sashays over confidently, looking more like herself than she has for days. Her hair is bouncy and lustrous and fans over her short, black wool polo-neck dress, which is perfectly moulded to her body and falls just below her bottom. She is wearing thick, black opaque tights and perilously high heels.

She's back. And, I have a feeling that so is Designers. So why don't I feel happy?

'Carly, this is Sam; Sam, this is Carly,' I say evenly, unable to look at Sam.

She holds out her hand and flutters her eyelashes, biting her bottom lip seductively before saying, 'I'm *very* pleased to meet you, Sam.'

Sam smiles and shakes her hand gently, looking, I'm pleased to note, ever so slightly disconcerted by her obvious flirting. She is still holding his hand and I feel the need to intervene for some reason.

'Sam was just going, weren't you, Sam?' And he looks at me gratefully before dropping Carly's hand, bobbing his head at us both, picking up his bag and then hurrying out the back door.

'So who was *that*, you dark horse!' she exclaims, still looking at the door that Sam has disappeared out of. 'I can't believe you've been keeping him to yourself!'

'Oh, he's just a friend,' I say evenly.

'Really?' she says. 'Well, that is interesting. I mean, if he's *just* your friend then maybe I—'

'He's the delivery guy,' I add quickly.

Her interest visibly wanes, as I knew it would. 'He's a white van man? What a waste! Oh, well, never mind . . .'

She settles herself down on the sofa and I set about making her tea.

'You're in early this morning,' I remark, glancing at the clock. It's just before eight. I have never seen Carly walk through Hardy's doors before nine o'clock.

'Oh, it's part of the New Me,' she grins. 'After the *amazing* day Designers had yesterday I've decided to do everything I can to make the department work. I mean, the place looks amazing! Have you seen it? Customers were clamouring to get into the VIP Closet and the dresses were flying off the rails. The till didn't stop ringing all day! Even Lady Fontescue came in and bought herself a—'

'Vintage Ossie Clark dress,' I say, thinking of the gorgeous black evening dress I'd chosen just for her and which I knew would make a welcome change from her usual taffeta.

'How do you know?' she asks, looking confused.

'Oh, I, er, bumped into her when I was leaving the shop yesterday. She was full of praise for you, actually,' I say, hoping the compliment will distract Carly from my slip-up. And it does.

She smiles knowingly and examines her nails. 'Well, yes, I was on rather good form yesterday. And so was Elaine, to be fair. The customers seem to like her and she knows the stock well. And I told her that, too.'

'You did?'

She nods and smiles. 'I figured I'd take you up on your suggestion of a new management tact. It worked, I think. She was civil to me all day.'

'That's great!'

'Hey,' Carly says, glancing down at the newspapers, which are still lying on the floor, 'what are these?' She crouches down daintily, revealing the full length of her model legs and making me feel rather short and stumpy in what I thought was a flattering but practical vintage slate-grey shift dress, black tights and patent high-heeled pumps.

'Oh, Sam brought them in. He saw them on the local news-stands this morning when he was doing his deliveries and thought someone here might be interested in them. Don't know who, though,' I finish dismissively, turning away from Carly so she doesn't see my face burn bright red.

She reads out the *Fulham and Hammersmith Chronicle*'s story, which has run the Hardy's story on the front cover. 'Wow, this is good!' she exclaims. 'Can I take it and show Rupert? It might help to put me back in his good books.' She scoops all the papers up before I have a chance to answer and staggers to her feet, smiling at me. 'You know, your pep talk really helped me yesterday, hon, and because of you I've resolved to be a new person from now on. I'm going to work hard, be nice to everyone and prove that I'm worthy of my promotion . . .' She trails off and then continues with a harder, more determined tone, ' . . so that whoever it is who is trying to steal my job knows that they've got a battle on their hands.'

'Steal your job?' I repeat, feeling a flash of panic.

She nods grimly, her lips tightened into a thin line. 'Yep. I've realized that I'm being sabotaged. Someone here wants my job and isn't going to rest until they've got it. And I've got a theory that it's this so-called Secret Santa.' She stabs the front page of the newspaper with her finger. 'So I'm going to find out who "Hardy's Helper" is once and for all,' she says grimly. 'Then I'm going to expose them so that everyone can see their true colours. After all, it's not some great act of kindness, is it? No one is that selfless. They *must* have some motive, it's just a case of finding out what it is.' Then she winks at me and whips round to face the door. 'Just call me Sherlock Carly!'

I smile uncertainly and she opens the door.

'See you, hon, and remember to keep your eyes peeled for me. At least I know you're on my side.'

And she winks at me before sweeping out of the stockroom.

CHAPTER 34

I walk out the stockroom for my break, desperate to find out what's happening in Designers. But I don't have time to get there. The store is abuzz with more people and noise and chatter than there's ever been. Classic Christmas songs are being played on a loop and new, young customers are browsing through the store, women in chic camel winter coats, carrying designer handbags and chatting loudly about the 'gorgeous old store', men in sharp, trendy outfits desperately trying to escape their girlfriends and get down to Menswear.

'I can't believe I've never been here before!' a girl wearing a beautifully cut cream peacoat, mohair hat and gorgeous vintage 1970s brown leather knee-length boots exclaims in disbelief.

'It's a real hidden gem, isn't it?' her friend says, picking up a gold 1930s powder compact and looking at the price. 'My sister would *love* this,' she says before waving it at Gwen and asking her to keep it at the till for her whilst she continues shopping. 'It's like finding your own secret grotto. I could spend hours in here just looking at

518

everything. It's such a bugger I've got to get back to work. Shall we come back tonight?'

The girl and her friend walk off arm in arm to the perfume counter, pointing and exclaiming loudly as they weave through the busy store. I continue through the ground-floor departments, listening to customers, spotting the old ones I recognize and savouring seeing so many new people here. Sam's plan for getting us press has clearly worked. So much so that there actually seems to be more customers than staff. In fact, I can't seem to see *any* of the staff. I glance around, confused by the absence of Hardy's helpers. There's a large queue waiting at a till point in handbags, but no one's there. And the customers are clearly getting impatient. Sharon will go mad if she sees this queue.

'SERVICE!' shouts one particularly grumpy-looking man, wearing a well-cut suit and a dark scowl. I whip my head round to try to find Becky or Gwen, or anyone, actually, but I can't see them so I instinctively dash to the till and smile warmly at the first customer in the queue who is slumped over the counter, chin in hands, only standing up when she sees me.

'About bloody time,' someone grumbles behind her.

'I'm so sorry to keep you waiting,' I say loudly so the whole queue can hear. My voice is quivering. I haven't done this for two years; not since my training week when I was made to do an hour on the till in every department. I stare at the old-fashioned till

519

and am relieved to see it's exactly the same as I remember it. I silently thank Rupert for not bringing in any swanky new computer systems and start shakily ringing the customers items through, not stopping until I've served every last customer. Just as I'm packing the final lot of goods into a cream and gold Hardy's bag I hear the sound of disconcerted chatting by the stairs. I dash through the departments, skidding to a halt when I see Gwen and the gang huddled together in a group, pointing and whispering at another group of people a few feet away.

'What's going on?' I ask Carly, who emerges from the centre of the group.

'It's the guy from Rumors again,' she says, two worry lines appearing in between her eyebrows. 'He's here. And this time I think he means business.' She nods in the direction of a group of men who have their backs to us and I turn to look at them with panic bubbling in my belly. 'They've all just come out of Rupert's office on the first floor,' she whispers. 'Jane saw them. She says the guy from Rumors shook hands with Rupert's father and then Rupert and the rest of the directors before coming down here. They've been looking around the store for the past fifteen minutes and we've been following them to see if we can work out what's going on. It doesn't look good,' she adds gravely.

So that's where everyone has been.

I creep round to peer over at the group of suits,

who are all still in deep discussion. They are standing in a semicircle, with their backs to us but just then, Sebastian Hardy points in our direction and we all scatter as they turn round. I spend a minute carefully examining a perfume bottle before plucking up the courage to turn round again. There's six of them in total. Rupert, Sebastian, three other men from Hardy's board of directors and . . .

I strain to make sure my eyes aren't deceiving me. Is that . . . Joel?

I squint at him and watch as he holds court with all the other men, feeling relief and lust flood through my body. Carly's got it wrong, Joel isn't from Rumors, he's helping Rupert with our finances! I scuttle over to Carly, who is hovering near them, trying to eavesdrop. She has put on a scarf and a pair of dark glasses and frankly looks about as incognito as Victoria Beckham on the school run.

'Don't worry,' I hiss, 'that guy isn't who you think it is . . .'

'It isn't?' she says, and then adds in some relief, 'Oh, no, you're right.' She peers over her dark glasses. 'Hang on, but isn't that . . . ? Oh my God, I don't believe it! It's Mr Eye Contact Guy!' she squeals.

The group of men all look up and I clasp my hand over her mouth and drag her away before they see us. But Joel seems to look right at me before going back to his conversation.

'Mr Eye Contact Guy!' she mouths again and

points at Joel, hopping up and down on the spot. 'He's the hottie I saw a couple of weeks ago, but it turns out he's trying to take over Hardy's!' she whispers dramatically, gesturing wildly at the other staff.

'Calm down,' I say sternly. 'He's not trying to take us over, he's *helping* us. He's one of Rupert's friends. I guess you could call him Hardy's unofficial finance director.'

'No,' she says firmly. 'Rupert has been doing all the accounts and he's never mentioned any friend helping him.'

'He hasn't?' I say, feeling a claw of fear grip me. 'Not even to give him advice?'

'Nope, definitely not. It's his area of expertise. He's been up most nights trying to number crunch as a way to stop the company who is trying to buy the site; trying to stop the hot Eye Contact Guy, as it turns out.'

'But Joel and he are best friends from way back. Are you sure Rupert hasn't asked him to help with Hardy's finances?'

Carly narrows her eyes at me as everyone starts muttering. 'I'm sure. Since I've been assistant manager I've been to several finance meetings and I would have remembered if *he'd* been there.' She nods in Joel's direction and then fans her face. 'Anyway, how do you know his name?'

'Um . . .'

'They're coming over!' whispers Becky, which saves me from any explanation.

We all stand as still as statues as the men file past and head towards the stairs. Then Carly and I tiptoe a bit closer to see if we can hear any more of their conversation.

'Well, Joel,' Sebastian Hardy booms loudly, 'it's been a pleasure doing business with you, my man. I'm sure you'll help Rumors make this place great again in a way that my son couldn't quite manage, eh, Rupe? Joel always was more savvy than you, though, wasn't he?' And Sebastian slaps his red-faced son on his back and roars with laughter as all of the staff look on, utterly aghast.

'See?' Carly hisses, but I have staggered backwards away from her, away from them and, most importantly, away from Joel, who is now laughing.

I look over again and see him for what feels like the first time: tall, proud, handsome but also smug and self-satisfied. His brash American accent disgusts me and his perfectly tailored suit and sleek looks are suddenly too good to be true.

He's been trying to buy Hardy's all along. He lied to me, he lied to Rupert and now Hardy's is going to be turned into some fancy, high-end, soulless establishment and all because of him.

I watch with increasing anger as a self-satisfied Joel shakes hands with Sebastian and then poor Rupert, who smiles limply as his so-called old friend pumps his arm and grins widely back at him, totally insensitive to his feelings, the bastard. Acrid bile rises unexpectedly in my throat and I realize that I have to get away from Joel and away from all of his lies. I can't believe I fell for them. I'm such an idiot.

I stumble backwards and in my haste to get away I knock over a display of beauty products, which makes everyone look at me. For a moment, Joel stares at me and then starts to make his way over. I have to get away. Tripping on my heels, I turn and break into a run. I dash over to the front doors, pushing past customers in my desperation to leave Hardy's and my terrible mistake behind me. Carly calls my name but I ignore her. Then Joel calls Carly's name and she turns round but I don't even care. What the hell does it matter now anyway? I'm not Sarah and I'm certainly not Carly. In fact, I'm not exactly sure *who* I am any more, but then again I don't know who Joel is either.

I cross the street and run past the newsagent's opposite. Brian is putting out the *Evening Standard* sandwich board as usual, announcing the day's headlines. He shouts over to me but I run past blindly, unable to say hello back or stop for a chat like I usually do. I can't breathe. I feel like I'm drowning. Hordes of people surround me and I think I might suffocate in the claustrophobia and loneliness that comes from living in this city. It's not my home. I shouldn't be here. I don't belong. I never have and I never will. I'm just a silly country girl who thought she could have a big city life.

He was just using me all along, I think as I sprint down the street, the cold air biting at my cheeks and burning my eyes. He never wanted me, he just wanted Hardy's. I was just a convenient spy for him, telling him all about the store and what the place needed to make it work. I feel a wave of nausea as I realize what I've done. In trying to help Hardy's, I have ultimately helped to destroy it.

I trip on my heels again and, with tears streaming down my face, I pull off my stupid high shoes that made me feel taller, prettier, more confident – more like Carly – and I drop them behind me on the pavement, before running in my stockinged feet down the road. I won't be needing those shoes any more.

And then it starts to snow.

CHAPTER 35

The pub is busy. All around me my friends are chattering excitedly about our next makeover but I'm unable to join them. I am sinking in an alcoholic gloom, trying to find the words to tell them what I saw today and admit that their impending job losses are all my fault.

'What's wrong, Evie darling?' Lily says, stretching her hand over the table to mine. Everyone stops talking and turns to look at me. 'You're not your usual self tonight. Is there something bothering you? I mean, it can't be the store. The makeovers have been a wonderful success and the newspaper coverage, well, who would've ever believed it?'

'It is VONDERVUL!' Velna says, raising her glass and hiccuping slightly.

'We should make a toast,' says Felix, rising to his feet.

'We must wait for Sam first,' Lily says, looking around the pub for him. 'Where is he anyway?' she asks as she sips her Martini.

'He's not coming,' I say dully. 'He had a prior . . . engagement.'

'Ohhh, noooo!' Velna looks like she might cry and her pink hair has gone all limp. Even Justyna looks disappointed, or maybe angry. It's hard to tell as all her expressions look the same. But then I notice Jan Baptysta take her hand and her mono-brow seems miraculously to separate, her mouth lifts, and is that . . . ? No, it can't be, hang on, I'm sure it's a . . . smile? If I didn't feel so shit about the world, it would actually make me feel warm and fuzzy inside.

I'm glad that everyone else feels that our group isn't complete without Sam. He gets on so well with everyone and is so darn positive all the time. I wish he was here now. He'd know what to say about what happened today.

'Well, it doesn't matter,' Lily says, patting my hand. 'We'll see him tomorrow morning for the next makeover. Is he taking more pictures? What do you want to do next? Felix has had some more brilliant ideas, you know.' She glances fondly over at him. Felix waves his hand dismissively and blushes.

'There aren't going to be any more makeovers,' I say dully, taking a large glug from my gin and tonic. Everyone starts talking at once.

'What?'

'Why?'

'Has Hardy's been saved?'

'Get the champagne in!'

'Shhhh! She's trying to say something! We've done it, haven't we, Evie! Haven't we?' Lily presses.

527

I put down my glass and look at all their hopeful, eager faces and feel like I could cry. I don't know how to tell them that all their hard work has been for nothing.

'Evie?' Lily says, brushing away a stray tear from my cheek. 'Darling, what's wrong?'

'I'm sorry,' I sniff. 'It's just that *you're* wrong.' I look up at them all. 'There aren't going to be any more makeovers because there isn't going to be any more Hardy's. I found out today that Rumors have bought us out. All our efforts have been wasted. It's over. I'm just sorry that I dragged you all into my stupid plan. I should have known it would never have worked. I'm so sorry.'

There is silence for a moment as we all sit staring at the table whilst the festive crowds in the pub chat and laugh. It feels like we're stuck motionless on the ground whilst the rest of the world whips madly on a merry-go-round before us.

Felix speaks first. 'You have nothing to be sorry for, Evie.' He clears his throat and holds his fist up to his mouth, and I see that he is emotional himself. 'I've had the happiest two weeks working with you all. Doing this has brought me to life again. I just wish that it could have done the same for the store. But no one else had the courage to try, and so you should be proud, Evie, not sorry. We may not have our jobs any more, but I for one feel I have made some wonderful lifelong friends. And that's been worth any amount of hard work.'

'Hear hear!' claps Lily, dabbing her eyes with

her Chanel-monogrammed scarf. 'As some Frenchman once said: "There are some defeats more triumphant than victories." We did our best for Hardy's, and whilst we didn't manage to save the old place, what we did was make a difference to a lot of people. You have to remember that, Evie darling.'

Just then the pub door swings open and a gush of cold air blasts in as a familiar figure appears, holding a bundle of newspapers.

'Sam?' I say, standing up as he approaches our table quickly. He's clearly been running: his face is flushed and there are little beads of sweat on his forehead. He pulls off his hat and rubs his head.

'Sorry I'm late,' he grins round the table at us all, and I'm sure I see Velna swoon.

'What are you doing here?' I ask. 'I thought you couldn't make it tonight?'

'I rearranged th . . . things, didn't want to hah miss a me . . . meeting,' he pants. 'Besides, I couldn't wait to show you guys this!' He thumps down a pile of *Evening Standards* on the table and everyone grapples for a copy, their hands obscuring the front cover. I finally manage to grab one and have to steady myself by holding on to the table when I read the front page.

'We made the front page?' I gasp, looking up at Sam with utter disbelief.

'We sure did!' Sam says proudly, his brown eyes shining. 'Our story is the spoiler on every newspaper sandwich board across the city!' I put my hand to my mouth as I have a flashback to Brian yelling at me as he put out his sandwich board this afternoon. He didn't just want a chat, he was obviously trying to tell me Hardy's had made the news.

'CAN SECRET SANTAS SAVE THIS DEPARTMENT STORE?' yells the *Standard*'s headline, and there's another of Sam's photos underneath followed by an in-depth article about the gradual reinvention of Hardy's. I can hardly believe it. But my surprise and delight is dulled by my knowledge of what went on today. If only this had happened a few days ago.

'That's great,' I say, the initial excitement draining from my body as I think about how close we may have come. It makes it all the harder to accept that our fight is over.

Everyone else nods at Sam and then glumly puts their papers back on the table and picks up their drinks.

'Hey? What's up?' Sam says, looking around at our faces. 'Don't you see what this sort of coverage means? Customers! More than Hardy's can prob-ably handle! And that's not the only good news . . .' He waits for our reaction. But there's nothing. We sip our drinks uncomfortably. 'Come on, guys!' he rallies. 'Can't you look more excited? This is what we've been aiming for! In fact,' he adds, his mouth twisting upwards into a smile, 'it's more than we've been aiming for . . .'

I can't let him go on any more. He needs to know the truth.

'It's brilliant news, Sam, really, it is,' I say. 'But it's too late. It's all too late.'

Sam sinks down onto an empty seat and stares at me. 'What do you mean?'

'I overheard Rupert and Sebastian and the other board members talking to the guy from Rumors. The sale was agreed this afternoon.'

'But I thought we had till Boxing Day?' Sam says, furrowing his brow.

I shrug defeatedly. 'Looks like they changed their minds.'

'But that doesn't make any sense!' Sam says, shaking his head. 'They haven't given us a fair chance and, besides, that was before any of them saw this!' He holds up the paper and we smile sadly at him. He puts it back down on the table and looks at us all despairingly. 'Come on, guys, are we really going to give up just because the board of directors have? These sorts of deals take ages to finalize! We might still be able to claw Hardy's back from an impending sale! After all, no one has stopped us so far! So who's in?'

I see Lily lift her chin determinedly and glance at Felix, who is straightening his tie and rolling his shoulders back as if preparing for some OAP-style fisticuffs. Jan Baptysta is cracking his knuckles. As is Justyna. Velna has started humming 'Waterloo', Abba's 1974 Eurovision-winning entry loudly, which I presume means she too is up for a fight.

531

I glance at Sam and he raises his eyebrows questioningly at me. I pause and look at everyone. 'So are we all with Sam?' I say at last, and there is a chorus of approval from the group. Sam nods and smiles at me as Felix disappears to get Sam a celebratory drink. Minutes later he plops a pint down in front of him. Sam takes a sip and immediately takes charge of the meeting.

'Can I tell you the even better news now you're all feeling a bit more positive?' Sam smiles as he picks up the *Evening Standard* again. 'On my way here I had a call from someone at the *Metro*. They've seen the *Evening Standard*'s coverage and are running something in their morning paper, too . . .'

'That's great news!' I exclaim. 'That'll reach all the commuters in the morning who didn't get the *Evening Standard* tonight!'

'But that's not all,' Sam grins. 'The editor from the *Metro* told me that the *Daily Mail*, who own the *Metro*, have agreed to run it in their paper, too, in a couple of days' time! Forget local papers, we're going national!'

Lily whoops and claps her hands and everyone joins in.

'Oh my God, that's incredible Sam!' I gasp. 'How the hell did you manage that?'

Sam shrugs modestly. 'I've been told I can be quite charming when I want to be,' he says with a wry wink. 'There is a catch, though: the *Mail* need a new angle. They don't want to regurgitate

532

coverage of the same story and the same makeovers. We need to do something big, something brilliant that will get the whole country talking . . . and then shopping at Hardy's! But the question is, what?'

Everyone immediately looks at me. I pause for a moment to gather my thoughts. 'I guess it's time to bring out the Christmas Big Guns,' I say at last, thinking of the reams of vintage decorations I've been sorting through in the stockroom and the ideas we've been working on since the last meeting. We've been waiting for the right moment to give Hardy's the Christmas makeover it really needs. And there isn't going to be a better moment than this. I clear my throat and stand up, feeling like a sergeant major rounding up his troops.

'We need to turn the store into a winter wonderland so that Sam can take the picture to the *Mail*'s offices. Which means, we need to do the makeover to end all makeovers. Tonight.' I look at my watch and drain my glass. It's nearly nine o'clock. That gives us eleven hours. 'So who's coming back to the store with me?'

There is no reply and for a moment I think I've gone too far. Then my ears are filled with the sound of chairs scraping as everyone stands up and pulls on their coats, chattering excitably. Sam takes my arm gently and we all pour noisily out of the pub and into the cold – but no longer bleak – midwinter.

CHAPTER 36

The store is eerily dark when we pile in through the staff entrance. A layer of snow has settled on the pavements outside and taken the temperature down to Arctic levels. Everyone is shivering and looking blankly around us. All of a sudden the store feels really big and our group feels really small. I'm paralysed with fear that I don't actually really know what I'm doing. It doesn't help that everyone is looking at me expectantly, waiting for me to tell them where to start. Justyna coughs loudly and for a moment I am reminded of the sound of an air-raid siren. It is just the trigger I need.

I close my eyes for a moment and try to imagine the Hardy's I want to see; the one that it used to be back in the post-war glory days when country had gone through hell and heartache and Hardy's survived to tell the tale. I imagine well-dressed women strolling through the halls arm in arm with their lovers, mothers, children and best friends. I imagine Nat King Cole's velvety voice crooning from the speakers, singing about chestnuts roasting and Jack Frost nipping. I can visualize thick garlands of greenery draped around the atrium with mistletoe and holly twined around it, gloriously coloured home-made vintage paper chains hung round the doors, twinkling fairy lights wrapped around pillars and doorways. Crepe-paper crackers and nativity scenes, the hand-carved wooden shoes I unpacked yesterday . . . and, of course, the most important thing of all, the Hardy's Christmas tree, back standing proudly by the grand central staircase.

'Jan?' I say briskly. 'I have a job for you. It requires you somehow finding and purchasing a very big Christmas tree. Tonight.'

'He can take my van!' Sam offers, and within minutes Jan has disappeared on his mission.

'Right, everyone,' I clap my hands and look at them all. 'Are you ready?'

The next four hours pass in a haze of hard work and high spirits. Boxes of decorations are unpacked and hung, assembly lines are created to get all the decorations moving from the stockroom to the shop floor, songs are sung, jokes are made and Sam takes photographs of us all working. Hour by hour the empty boxes and mess that surrounds us gradually starts to look like the winter wonderland I have in my head. The tiny shoe decorations have been cleverly stacked by Lily on a Perspex stand, which Sam has built in the shape of a Christmas tree and wrapped with strands of mistletoe. We're going to put it in one

535

of the windows illuminated with some pretty fairy lights and then recreate the Tree of Shoes idea in the shoe department using the gorgeous vintage Hardy's ex-display evening shoes.

Felix has come up with a brilliant idea of putting vintage beauty products, like the gold lipstick holders and pretty compacts, into actual snow globes in a display in one of the windows.

Inside the store I've laid a path of letters to Santa that leads to a grotto on the fourth floor. Felix has promised to dress up as Santa and hand out gifts in the days leading up to Christmas. These letters have been painstakingly handwritten and popped into faded old airmail envelopes by Velna and then tied into little bundles with string. Lily has been sitting wrapping boxes in brown paper and then decorating them with ribbons of gold, green and red for the past two hours. She has a ballet dancer's eye for detail and each one is beautifully finished. And Velna and I have spray-painted gold over one hundred Conference pears, which I plan to thread on string with some cranberries and holly and then drape over the door arches of each department.

And this is all without Hardy's secret weapon; the store's original decorations that used to deck the place; the ones that look and smell and feel like Christmases past. A row of painted toy soldiers line the windows, like marching marionettes. Little Santas and snowmen and faded felt-covered reindeer join them. As well as entire snow-capped villages and little painted elves, there are old Santas' boots that were once filled with candies, and miniature vintage bottlebrush snow-covered Christmas trees. Vintage glass jars have been filled with old satin-sheen and glass baubles that have lost their hooks and can't be used on our tree. All of them make you dream of snow and stockings, Santa and carol singing. Looking around me I am suddenly filled with the real spirit of Christmas. And for the first time since yesterday I've even forgotten all about Joel and what a pig he turned out to be.

Well, almost.

By 1 a.m. we're all flagging. Lily has just handed out a round of hot chocolate when a grinning Jan Baptysta comes in with four burly Polish men all dragging an enormous Norwegian pine, and we all applaud as they lay it on the floor.

'I had to callsk in some reinforcements,' explains Jan. 'Everybody say hello to Alesky, Viktor and Konrad. They havsk been working on a Christmas tree farm in Essex and opened up late so I could come and choossk one!'

'It's HUGE!' I squeal, clapping my hands excitedly like a seal. 'Are we going to be able to put it up ourselves?'

'*Nie* problem, Evie, leave it to us. We haves more reinforcements comings. However, we would be verys grateful for some of that chocolate drink, OK?'

'Coming right up, Jan!' Lily says, and scuttles off to her tearoom.

Jan's arrival is just the lift we all need. The next three hours pass quickly as the tree is hauled into place by the burly Polish men. Then all we have to do is decorate it, which is a feat involving ladders and assembly lines. It is nearly 5 a.m. by the time we finish, all collapsing on the floor in a tired but happy huddle as we sit and survey our work.

It's clear to us as we gaze in awed silence that Hardy's is a store transformed. Gone is the sad, faded, lifeless shop it used to be, and in it's place is a joyful, glittering wonderland of bygone Christmases.

'It looks beautiful,' breathes Lily tearfully. 'It reminds me of the good old days,' and everyone murmurs their agreement.

'Fingers crossed everyone else thinks so, too,' I say, and silence descends as we consider the terrible alternative.

'Of course they will!' Sam responds – Mr Positive, as ever – and I smile at him gratefully.

'Thank you, everyone,' I say, feeling my throat constrict with emotion. 'You've been amazing. Now go and get some rest. I can do the remainder of the clearing up here.'

Everyone is so exhausted that they don't even argue; they just throw on their coats and file out of the store. Everyone except Sam, who starts sweeping the rogue pine needles off the floor.

'You too, Sam,' I say. 'Honestly, I just need to take all these boxes back to the stockroom and sort a few things out.'

'Don't be silly, I'm not leaving you now,' Sam says gruffly, putting down the broom and scooping up an armful of empty boxes. 'Race you back to the stockroom. Last one there has to make the tea!'

FRIDAY 16 DECEMBER

9 Shopping Days Until Christmas

CHAPTER 37

I open my eyes and rub them, shivering a little despite the blanket that has been thrown carefully over my body. My cheek is wet, presumably because of the pool of dribble that has escaped from my mouth whilst I was sleeping, and my eyes are sticky from falling asleep with my contacts in. Sam helped me tidy up and put away all the boxes and then we sat on the sofa, talking about our lives and drinking tea until dawn broke. Or until I fell asleep, I'm not sure which. I vaguely remember leaning my head against Sam's shoulder just as he said he had to go and start his deliveries. He must have waited until I was asleep and then put this blanket over me. Part of me can't help but wish that he'd stayed. But Sam's just a friend. He's with Ella, and besides, I still haven't spoken to Joel and found out what the hell he has been doing.

Part of me wants to put off confronting him; I don't need to know that he was using me and that he never liked me at all. As much as things were complicated when I was trying to be Carly, it also felt like life was finally going my way. And the attention I got from Joel was a big part of that. If it really was all just an act, then I'm back to square one. Back to being me: invisible, forgettable, me. But then again, maybe it's better that way. Everything is back to its natural order.

I yawn and throw the blanket over the arm of the sofa, smacking my lips and trying to work out if I can substitute gum for toothpaste and if a strong coffee will overpower my morning breath or just enable it. I splash water on my face from the sink and pull my hair back into a ponytail, wrapping a thick strand tightly around the elastic band to make it look more finished. My days of letting myself go have gone, even when I've been up all night and have only the prospect of a long day in the stock-room to look forward to. Not for Joel; not for anyone else other than me. The tea dress I wore to the pub last night has managed to stay remarkably fresh and crease-free, and with a lick of lipstick, a swipe of deodorant and squirt of Chanel No. 5 from my handbag, I'm just about ready to face the morning. Or at the very least, get through it.

'Oh my God!' shouts Carly as she suddenly bounds through the stockroom door, making me jump. 'You have to come here, now!' and she runs over, grabs me by the arm and drags me out into the shop floor.

'LOOK!' she gasps, turning in a circle as she takes in the store's Christmas makeover.

'Wow!' I breathe in what I hope is a believably surprised manner.

Carly eyes me suspiciously. 'How come you didn't notice it yourself when you came in this morning?'

'Er, I came in through the delivery doors. Anyway,' I shoot back, 'what are you doing here so early. It's way before your clocking-on time.'

'You know what they say,' Carly says flippantly, 'the early bird catches the worm and all that. Actually, I was hoping to catch the Secret Santa but it looks like they've been and gone already. I'm going to have to be more cunning.'

She narrows her eyes thoughtfully and I start to walk back towards the stockroom. I really don't want to get into this conversation with her again.

'Hey, don't go!' Carly calls, 'I still haven't shown you this . . .'

I turn round and see Carly holding up a copy of the *Metro*, open at page 3 and with 'Hardy's Christmas Miracle' as a headline.

'It looks like Hardy's is still getting more positive press despite the takeover,' she says, and I grab it excitedly from her and scan through it.

'It's good, isn't it?' she says, looking over my shoulder. 'Maybe Hardy's won't be sold after all? I mean, Rupert is bound to use this in our defence.'

I look up at her curiously. 'I thought you wanted Rumors to take Hardy's over? You said you'd much prefer to work for a more modern store that was cooler, more fashion forward . . .'

Carly shrugs and brushes her hands over the

vintage silk blouse she's wearing today. Weirdly, it looks like something I'd wear. 'A girl can be wrong. I mean, there's plenty of stores like that in London, but there's not one like Hardy's, is there? I realize now how short-sighted I was being. Besides, Rupert has been good to me. I've made friends here . . . I've lost a few too, but I'm hoping I can get them back.' She gives my arm a squeeze. 'Your advice really helped me, you know,' she says softly. 'I always knew you were a great listener, but you're really worth listening to as well, you know.'

I swallow back a gulp and smile gratefully at Carly as my phone buzzes in my hand. 'Home' flashes up on the screen and I mouth, 'Got to take this,' to Carly and head back to the stockroom.

'Hello?'

'Evie?' says a barely recognizable voice. 'Where are you?' The phone sounds muffled, like the person is holding their hand over it.

'Delilah? Is that you?'

'Yes,' she sobs, and her voice sounds muffled again. 'Where are you?' she repeats.

'I'm at work. Are you OK?'

'Noooo!' she wails desperately, her voice taking on a manic tone. 'Will didn't come home last night, nor did you, I tried calling Mum but she didn't answer. I don't know what to do . . . my marriage, it's over. I know it.' She is crying inconsolably now.

'Hey, shhhh,' I say, feeling my stomach constrict with concern.

Delilah sounds on the edge. I know I need to go to her, but I don't know how I can get away. Sharon is taking a dim view of sick days in this week before Christmas and I honestly think that leaving here now could cost me my job. But what about my sister?

'Listen, Delilah, stay calm. I'm sure there's some explanation for Will not coming home. Where are the kids?'

'They're at nursery,' she sniffs.

'OK, I'm going to try and get away as soon as I can. I'll meet you at home, all right? Are you going to be OK till then?'

Delilah doesn't answer.

'Delilah,' I press urgently, 'I said will you be OK till then?'

'I don't know,' she replies quietly, 'I just don't know,' and she rings off.

I immediately call Mum on her mobile.

'Hello, Grace Taylor speaking, how may I help you?' Mum's prim voice answers as if she is an office receptionist.

'Mum, it's me,' I say quickly.

'Darl—'

'It's Delilah, Mum,' I interrupt. 'She's in a bad way. I'm really worried about her.' And I relay our conversation.

'Oh, my poor girl,' Mum moans. 'I was so worried something like this would happen. Will told me they haven't seen her all week at work. He's really worried about her. He said he was

547

going to talk to you but maybe he hasn't had a chance to—'

'Mum,' I interrupt. I can't bear her portrayal of Will as the perfect, concerned husband any longer. 'There's something you should know. Will's been having an affair. Delilah suspects something but I overheard him on the phone. Oh, Mum, what are we going to do?'

Mum makes soothing noises and tells me not to worry. But I can't help it. I've abandoned my sister in her time of need. I've been so preoccupied. For the past few weeks I've listened to everyone in the store, I've thrown the rest of my energy into saving Hardy's but I haven't once stopped to listen to my own sister when she was crying out to me for help.

'Oh God, she sounded awful,' I sob, and Mum consoles me, but I can tell she's struggling to hold it together too.

'I'm going back home now,' I say determinedly through my tears.

'But you're at work, darling,' Mum says. 'I'll go. I'll just throw my stuff in a bag, hop on a train and I'll be there in three hours.'

'Do that anyway, Mum,' I say, 'but in the meantime I'm going straight home. Sod the store and my job. Delilah needs me.'

And I put down the phone, aware that for the first time in a long while I'm doing the right thing.

CHAPTER 38

I unlock the front door and step gingerly inside, still smarting from the scolding Sharon gave me for leaving work on one of the busiest shopping days of the year. But I don't care. My sister needs me. I've neglected her too often over the past few weeks. The house is unusually quiet. The kids are still at nursery, which would account for the peace, but Delilah should be here somewhere.

'Lila?' I call tentatively as I walk through the echoing hallway, my voice bouncing off the tiled floor. Arty monochrome portraits of Will, Delilah and the kids, looking like the perfect family, smile at me from the walls disconcertingly. I open the lounge door and peer into the imposing room. A rather forlorn, minimalist silver Christmas tree, which perfectly matches the room's elegant dove-grey colour scheme, stands in front of the bay window. Lola's antique grey and white speckled rocking horse has been pushed to one side to make room for it. A quick glance tells me Delilah isn't here. I try the office and playroom, then go downstairs to the usually spick-and-span kitchen. But today it is strewn with empty wine bottles, dirty

549

glasses, plates, food, milk, mugs . . . and pills. I gasp when I see there are packets of paracetamol strewn over the island unit and with panic rising I examine the boxes. They're all empty.

I feel my stomach lurch with fear as I turn and run up the stairs, taking them two at a time, my heart pounding as fast as my running feet as I open and shut doors on different floors, desperately searching for Delilah.

'Lila!' I scream. 'LILA!' I throw open her bedroom door. It is dark and reeks of stale air and alcohol. The bedclothes are crumpled, there are clothes all over the floor and a body is slumped over it in the foetal position. Delilah's body.

'Oh my God,' I cry, and I throw myself towards her, pulling her limp frame onto her back so I can see her face. I am crying now, sobbing with fear as I look for any signs of life. 'Delilah? Delilah, please speak to me.' I press my hand to her face and her eyelids flutter open.

'Evie?' she says hoarsely. 'What time is it?'

'Oh, thank God, Lila, you're all right,' I sob into her chest as she begins to move herself slowly up into a sitting position, pulling me up with her.

'Ohhhh,' she groans, 'my head.'

'How many did you take?' I ask, shaking her. 'Tell me! I need to know so I can tell the ambulance crew.' I throw myself over the bed, scrambling towards the bedside table where I pick up the landline phone. She groans again and rubs her head. 'Tell me how many!' I shout back at her.

'How many what?' Lila says groggily.

I stab 999 on the phone, already imagining the worst: that my sister has caused irreparable brain damage from taking an overdose.

'Pills, Lila, Pills! Tell me how many pills you've taken!'

'None,' she groans. 'I couldn't find any downstairs. The packets from the medicine cupboard were all empty. Bloody Will never throws things away. And I've still got this terrible headache. Probably from all the wine,' she adds bleakly. 'I opened some first thing this morning after I dropped the kids off,' she says shamefully.

I put down the phone and slump onto the bed with relief. 'Oh, Lila, you scared me. I thought you'd taken an overdose.' And I begin to cry.

'I'm sorry,' she says tearfully, 'I didn't mean to scare you. I'd never do that. The kids need me . . .'

'I need you too,' I say, throwing my arms around her. 'I'm so sorry, Lila, I've been awful.'

'No, you haven't. You just haven't been around, but I don't blame you for that. Things have been pretty horrid here. They still are, in fact,' she says somberly. She wriggles out of my embrace and leans across the bed, then throws a brown envelope in front of me. I look at her quizzically before opening it. She leans back on the pillows and stares at the ceiling as I flick through the damning evidence that proves Will has been having an affair. There are six grainy, black-and-white photos of him with an attractive woman. The photos seem to be from two different occasions, as they are both wearing different outfits. In one they are sitting outside a cafe and another in a pub. In both they are leaning intimately into each other, deep in conversation. In another Will appears to be handing the woman a bundle of money. I'm about to speak when Lila passes me something else. It is a bank statement.

'Will has been taking large sums of money from our account,' she says her voice suddenly without emotion. She points at the pictures. 'He's either paying a prostitute or keeping his mistress happy with cash gifts. In either case, he's a disgusting, cheating bastard and I want him out of my house tonight.'

'Oh, Lila . . .' I begin, but words seem meaningless. I can't imagine how she feels. 'How did you get these?' I wave the photos and she looks down.

'I hired a private detective. I just needed the proof that would ensure the kids and I would be able to stay in the house and I could have a speedy divorce and custody of the children without some horrible court case. He can't defend himself against these.'

I grasp her hand. I can't believe that it's all come to this so soon: acrimony and alimony. Poor Delilah. And the poor children.

'I'm going to confront him tonight,' she continues firmly, sitting up on the bed, wincing as her hand floats up to her forehead. She looks pale and gaunt, but determined. 'Tell him to pack his bags and go.'

'Not whilst the children are here,' I plead. 'They don't need to be a part of this, Delilah.'

She shrugs. 'Maybe it's better that they know what a scumbag their father is now rather than later. Saves a lot of pain all round.'

'You don't mean that,' I say quietly. 'Will is still a good father—'

'Is he?' she snaps. 'He's never here, Evie, he barely knows them!' She shakes her head and looks down. 'He hasn't just cheated on me with this . . . whore,' she stabs the photo of the smiling blonde in disgust, 'he's cheated on Raffy and Lola too. All those late nights when he could have been home, giving them their baths, telling them their bedtime stories and he was more concerned with . . . her . . .' She scrambles off the bed suddenly and into the ensuite and I hear her retching uncontrollably. 'I'm sorry,' she groans, 'I can't believe this is really happening. I know we haven't been happy, but I never thought . . . I never thought . . .'

She is sick again and I follow her into the bathroom and hold back her dull, unwashed hair.

'I know, I know,' I say soothingly, and pull the chain as she starts to cry over the lavatory. 'No one did.' I push back my memory of overhearing Will on the phone, yet another guilt trip to add to my list. If I had told her myself it wouldn't have been such a shock to her. But to have to go through this, and all on her own . . . I think of the grainy photos scattered on Delilah and Will's marital bed and feel sick myself. 'Look, Lila, I know this has all been a shock to you and everything, but the kids are so young, you need to protect them from all this. It isn't fair to involve them.'

Delilah stops crying and I can tell she's listening.

'Mum's coming up on the train right now,' I add, gently pulling her back into a sitting position. Delilah looks as young and helpless as her three-year-old daughter. 'Why don't we ask her to take the children back to the flat in Hampstead for the night? You know how much she'd love that. And so would Lola and Raffy. That way you can have it out with Will without worrying about them.' Delilah doesn't say anything, she just nods and I know that she realizes what I've suggested makes sense.

'Is Mum really coming here?' Delilah says plaintively. 'What about Dad?'

'She said she was coming as soon as I called her. Dad's in London anyway – I saw him the other day – so, yes, maybe he'll come over, too.'

Delilah nods again and I know she's thinking that Mum and Dad will make everything all right. Just like they always do.

At three o'clock I collect the kids from nursery and walk them slowly back across Primrose Hill, explaining carefully about their impending trip to their grandparents' for the night.

'GRANDMADAD! YAAAAY!' yells Raffy as he scrambles across the grass, stick in hand, his welly boots and scarf flying behind him. He waves it and shouts, 'ABRADABBA!' like it's a wand, and I can't help but wish I had one of those right now.

'Can we make cakes and have tea and play dressing-up and do puzzles and watch TV and paint and do cartwheels?' Lola asks. She stops suddenly and pulls a face. 'I need a wee wee. Now,' she adds, lifting up her coat and dress and squatting on the ground.

'Can you wait until we get home, Lola?' I plead as she grapples with her tights. She looks up at me, screws up her nose as if considering my request and she shrugs.

''K,' she says. 'I'll just squeeeeeeeze. But you have to carry me.' I sigh and pick her up, and she grins at me and kisses me on the nose. 'Love you, Teevee,' she says, and all of a sudden I want to cry.

'I love you too, Lola,' I manage to say, wishing fervently that I could stop her little world from falling apart.

Maybe I could have done, once upon a time. I used to be good at fixing things for people. But now it's too late.

By the time we get home, I can sense that there has been a change of atmosphere in the house. I glance at the coat hooks by the front door and am alarmed to see Will's expensive Dunhill coat hanging there. I hear the sound of raised voices

555

upstairs and quickly bundle the children into the playroom, shutting the door loudly behind me so that Delilah and Will hear that we've arrived. Then I quickly put CBeebies on and turn the volume up to loud.

'We can watch *TV*?' Lola says in wonderment. 'In the *afternoon*?' She clambers onto the huge, squishy sofa before I change my mind, having clearly forgotten all about her bladder.

'WOW!' Raffy says in wonderment as the Chuggington trains appear on the screen and he scrambles up next to his sister.

'Chugging TON!' I sing loudly, as Delilah's faint screams reach my ears, 'Chugga-chugga-chugga-chugga . . .'

'CHUG-GINTON!' join in Lola and Raffy merrily, and I perch next to them, putting my arms around them and squeezing them both as we all sing together, feeling a bit like Maria in *The Sound of Music*, singing 'My Favourite Things' to the Von Trapp children to drown out the noise of the storm outside.

Just then I hear a sharp knock at the front door and I glance at the kids, who don't seem to have noticed anything. I slip out of the playroom, shutting the door behind me again. Everything seems to have gone quiet upstairs for the moment, which is just as worrying as the screaming and shouting. I rub my face wearily and walk over to the front door.

'Mum!' I cry as I see my mother standing on

the doorstep, her eyes fixed to the ground, her overnight case perched carefully beside her. 'Thank goodness you're here!' I fall into her arms and wait for the warmth of her embrace. But it doesn't come. Her arms remain limply by her side and I can feel her body shaking. I pull back and she looks up at me, her usually bright eyes now glassy and dull.

'Can I come in?' she says quietly, and I step to one side. 'I can't stay at the flat. Your father has been having an affair, you see,' she adds shakily but alarmingly matter-of-factly, slipping off her coat and hanging it up on the hook. My mother is like me, tidy even in the face of adversity.

I throw my hand up to my mouth and stare at her in horror.

'What? How?'

'Where are the children?' she says, ignoring my question. 'I'd like to see them. And how is Delilah?'

I hear a creak on the stairs and see Delilah's feet descending, her body and face still obscured.

'Evie, I need to tell you something important,' she calls down as she descends, with Will following closely behind her. Her face is grave. 'Will hasn't been having an affair, Evie, it was Dad . . .' She stops in the middle of the stairs and suddenly sees me holding on to Mum, who now has tears streaming down her face. Horrified, Delilah tumbles down the rest of the stairs and pulls us both into her arms and begins to cry too. Eventually she looks at me over Mum's shoulder and shakes her head. Delilah is still swathed in her dressing gown and she still looks deathly pale, but there is hope in her expression now, and strength, which she seems to be absorbing from our frail, broken mother.

The stairs creak again and Will appears at the bottom, looking grim-faced and apologetic.

'Ladies,' he says softly, his expression concerned as he takes in the sight of his wife and mother-in-law, 'I'm going to put the kettle on. It looks like we could all do with a strong cup of tea.'

'Will?' I question as he walks past me. 'What's happened?'

'Tea first,' he says gently, and walks down to the basement where I hear him flick the kettle on.

Mum's hand shakes slightly as she picks up her cup and gazes at us all. We're sitting around the big oak dining table, trying to make sense of the drama. The kids are still happily ensconced watching CBeebies upstairs, and Will is explaining to us what he's known for the past month.

'Jonah, Noah and I overheard your father several times on the phone to her,' Will explains apologetically. 'At first we thought we'd made some sort of mistake, but he was getting more and more careless at family gatherings. He'd take calls in front of us and it was clear that whoever he was talking to, well, they had nothing to do with work.' A blush spreads across Will's cheeks and he looks away from Mum.

I can't even begin to imagine what he heard. I feel sick at the thought of my dad, the man I trusted the most in the world, doing something like this. It's like he's cheated on all of us. I stifle a sob, aware that I have to try to be strong for Mum. She is staring blankly at the table, lost in her thoughts, impervious to Will's explanations.

'The boys wanted to tell you sooner,' Will continues quietly, 'but then we thought perhaps we could make him see sense; make him see what he was risking. Grace, if it's any consolation, we all think he's a fool,' Will adds gruffly.

Mum looks out of the window.

'So how did you get involved?' I ask defensively, still concerned by the unexplained pictures of Will with another woman. If he thinks he's getting out of it that easily, he can think again.

'We all sat down with him that last Sunday afternoon and told him he had to end it, that if he didn't we'd tell you girls. He begged us not to, said it would destroy you all. But he didn't say he'd stop. He said that every man had a mistress and that we were fools to think that we'd go through a marriage without one. He said that we'd be responsible for tearing the family apart if we said anything.' Will is struggling to hide the disgust from his voice.

I glance at Mum, but she is still staring into the distance.

'So when reasoning with him didn't work, Jonah, Noah and I decided to take matters into our own hands. We took the woman's name and number from Charles's phone and I sent a text arranging to meet her. I said I was a friend of Charles and that I had a business proposition for her. We thought that if we offered to pay her to stop seeing your dad that would be the end of it, Charles would realize we were serious and he'd stop his mid-life crisis nonsense before it destroyed his whole family.'

Will looks down at his mug and shakes his head before reaching across to stroke Delilah's hands. Suddenly I realize what the pictures were that Delilah's private investigator took: Will trying to pay off Dad's secret lover.

'I just didn't realize that it would come so close to destroying mine. I'm sorry, Grace,' he adds. 'I shouldn't have got involved. I was just trying to protect you all . . .'

I cover my mouth with my hand. It's so wrong. Not Dad. They were supposed to be the perfect couple. The ones who made it. Thirty-five years of devotion from Mum and he does this?

'Will went down to Norfolk last night looking for Dad,' Delilah adds. 'That's where he was. He wanted to tell him himself that his mistress had accepted the pay-off and the affair was over. But Dad wasn't there.'

Mum smiles wanly. 'No, and now I know why. She must have gone straight back to the flat after taking your money, Will.' She sobs and muffles it with her handkerchief, not wanting to lose control in front of us. Her quiet strength makes my heart hurt.

Will nods solemnly. 'When I turned up at your house and realized that Grace was alone and Charles was in London I thought that might be the case. I had to pretend to Grace that I had come on business. I didn't want her to know what had happened. I foolishly hoped I could make it all go away. But I just made things worse.'

I see Delilah squeeze his hand and Will looks at her with such tenderness it makes me want to cry even more.

'Where did you go after you left the house?' Mum asks Will. 'It was too late to get a train back . . .'

'I stayed in a hotel next to the train station and went straight into work from there this morning. I left early today so I could come and see Delilah and explain everything. I had no idea what she thought . . . what you all . . . well. I've never been unfaithful to your daughter, Grace. Never have, never will.'

Mum looks at Delilah and Will. 'You're a good man and a good son-in-law, Will. Delilah is lucky to have you. I hope she knows that.'

Delilah bows her head and grips Will's hand even more tightly.

'The truth is I've suspected Charles has been having an affair for some time. I just haven't had the courage to confront him,' Mum says quietly.

'Ignorance is bliss, I guess. And then when Evie told me about Will . . .'

I look at Will apologetically and he nods his head as if to say, 'It's all right.'

'. . . it just made me realize what any sane woman should do if they found out their husband was cheating on them. Of course, I didn't know for sure that he was, so I felt safe in the knowledge that I mightn't actually have to do anything at all. And then . . .' She pauses, draws breath and continues bravely. 'Then I walked into the flat. And they were there. Together. In bed.' She dabs her lips with her handkerchief and puts it carefully down on the table, flattening it with her hand. She pauses and dabs her eyes again. 'I've been such a fool.'

I throw my arms around her and shake my head defiantly. 'No you haven't, Mum. You couldn't have known, no one could. God, I hate him for this!'

'Don't say that,' Mum says dully. 'He's still your father.'

I scoff and Delilah shoots me a warning look to say, 'Not now.'

'So what are you going to do, Mum?' she asks. 'You can stay here if you like – for as long as you want, right, Will?'

'Of course,' he nods, and I feel such relief that Will wasn't the villain in all of this after all. I don't mind admitting that I've got him wrong. I've got a lot of people wrong recently. Maybe Mum was right: maybe I was jealous of him coming between me and Delilah.

'That's very kind of you but there's no need,' Mum says calmly. The initial shock has passed and she seems to be growing stronger and more assured in front of my eyes. Then again, maybe it's just the effect of the large brandy Will has poured for her. 'I've already taken your father's keys to the flat and after I'd kicked him . . . and *her* . . . out I had the lock changed by a locksmith. I've already decided I'm going to move permanently to London. I hate being stuck so far away from you all. It was never my choice to live in Norfolk, and I don't want to go back to the house on my own.' She pauses. 'Not now.'

'Oh, Mum,' Delilah cries, standing up and running around the table. 'I'm so proud of you. You know we'll all do anything we can to help, won't we?'

I nod and cling on to Delilah and Mum.

Will stands up too. 'I'll go and see to the children.' He hovers for a moment, then comes over and kisses Mum and Delilah on their foreheads and squeezes my arm. 'You Taylor women are pretty incredible; I've always thought so,' he says, and walks out the room, which sets us all off into a fresh bout of tears.

'He's a good man, Delilah,' Mum says, patting her hand. 'Do you promise me that you'll get some counselling and work out your problems together?'

Delilah nods and buries her face in Mum's shoulder, and I stroke her hair.

'I don't deserve him,' comes Delilah's muffled voice.

'Yes you do,' Mum says sternly, pulling her face up and looking intently at us both. 'Girls, listen to me, I may have made mistakes in my marriage – no,' she holds up her hand to stop us from protesting, 'I have, trust me, I *know* I have. Just promise me one thing?'

We nod, still gripping on to her tightly.

'I want you to promise that you'll never change who you are for a man.'

Suddenly I find it hard to look my mum in the eye, but she is gazing wistfully out of the window anyway.

'I had my own life and a career before I met Charles, but I gave it all up for him. I changed who I was to fit in with the image of a wife and mother that he had, and in the process I lost myself. I always thought I'd have a career *and* kids but . . .' She strokes a strand of hair from her face and gathers herself, smiling back at us lovingly.' Of course, I ended up with my four wonderful children so I don't regret it. I just don't want either of you girls to make the same mistakes. Know who you are and believe in yourself fully, because no matter who you share it with, this is your life and you only have one chance. Now,' she says, cupping our faces and kissing each of us on the cheeks, 'I'd like to see my gorgeous grandchildren.'

Delilah nods and lifts herself off Mum's shoulder, and I stand up.

'You know,' I say, 'I think I'm going to go for a walk, if that's OK?'

Suddenly I feel like I have an awful lot to think about.

CHAPTER 39

I walk up the hill slowly. It's dark and the paths are slippery with the glistening evening frost that has already settled. The cold and surprisingly strong wind is whipping my hair into a tail spin and I feel as if I might just take off. I stop for a moment, swaying on my feet and look back down the hill at the rows of perfect houses that surround it and that are emitting a warm saffron glow. Suddenly they appear to be more like bleak statues than homes. It's like I can suddenly see through the outward perfection to what is underneath and it isn't as attractive as I've always thought.

I plunge my hands deep into my pockets and continue the climb. Despite the shocking bombshell about my father, everything suddenly feels clearer somehow and I am left, not with the cotton wool of confusion I've had about my life for the last few weeks, but just with my mum's words whirling about in my head as if blown by the wind. *Promise me you'll never change who you are for a man.*

Her words circle around again and again as I

climb, making me rewind the past three weeks of my life since I met Joel. What have I done apart from completely change for him? I turned myself into someone I thought he wanted and, in the process, became someone I didn't like any more. Self-obsessed, vain, impatient, I stopped listening to the people I really cared about because I became so focused on changing *my* life. Oh, I wrapped it up in a pretty parcel, convincing myself that I was helping others by changing Hardy's and making it a better place to work for everyone and saving their jobs in the process. But if I'm honest, it wasn't exactly an entirely selfless act. After all, I was doing what I've always dreamed of: being on the shop floor, being creative, making a difference. And in doing so I neglected my family. And all because of a man.

The wind whistles in my ears as I trudge further up the hill. It seems to be calling me. '*Ev-ie Ev-ie*,' it moans as if reminding me who I am again. Not Carly and not Sarah. Poor Mum, if only she'd realized just what she was worth before she married Dad. Perhaps then she could have had her own identity *and* a happy marriage. As it is she's spent the last thirty-five-odd years fading into obscurity behind the childrearing, cooking, baking, crafting and homemaking.

'*Ev-ie Ev-iee . . .*'

Suddenly I realize that it isn't the wind calling my name, but a figure standing at the top of the hill, waving at me. I squint and quicken my pace,

567

breathless with exertion and cold as I reach the top, unable to believe that the person I most need to see is right here. I bend over to catch my breath, then stand up.

'Sam!' I exclaim, taking in his watering eyes and wind-ruffled hair. 'Fancy seeing you here again.'

'I thought you'd never hear me,' Sam smiles. 'You looked completely lost in thought.'

'I was,' I reply gazing down at the twinkling lights of London across the horizon. 'It's been a crazy day.' I plunge my frostbitten fingers deep into my duffel coat and bite my bottom lip, then begin to talk, the words falling out of my mouth. 'I thought my sister had taken an overdose because her husband was cheating on her.' Sam's jaw drops in alarm and I hurriedly add, 'It's OK, she hadn't and he wasn't.' I take another deep breath. 'But then we found out my dad has been cheating on my mum. God knows how long for.'

Sam doesn't say anything. He just puts his arm around my shoulder and pulls me close. I turn and nestle into the warmth of his body, thankful for his support. He feels so steady, safe, reliable, like nothing bad could ever happen when I'm around him. I look up and see him staring down at me with a worried expression.

'Do you want to talk about it?' he murmurs softly.

'Do you know what? I don't think I do,' I say, wiping away a stray tear. 'I actually want to forget all about it.' I look up at him and a crazy, reckless thought suddenly occurs to me. 'Have you got any idea how?' I tilt my lips up towards his. I don't know what has come over me, but suddenly all I want is to feel the warmth of Sam's mouth on mine and for him to take me away from the last few hours of my life. I know he has the power to do that, I can feel it. I don't know why I've never noticed it before.

But he turns his face away and I am overcome with embarrassment. I'm an idiot. I've turned him down once already, I still haven't sorted out everything with Joel and I've just told him about my messed-up family. Ella's probably following behind him and will appear over the hill at any second.

'Sorry,' I mumble, and pull away.

'Don't be,' he says, kissing me on the forehead like a parent would their child. 'Listen, are you free tonight?' he asks, rubbing my arms to warm me up. 'There's one last makeover we need to do. Meet me at Hardy's at nine. And dress in your best!' He steps away from me and looks awkwardly over his shoulder. 'I've got to go, but I'll see you later, yeah?' And he walks away, pausing to wave and smile at me before disappearing over the top of the hill like he was never here at all.

CHAPTER 40

The once-sleepy store looms proudly out of the darkness as I approach just before 9 p.m. I was worried about coming tonight but Delilah insisted I go. I left her and Will working everything through with Mum, and Delilah said she owed me lots of nights out for all the help I've given her over the last two years. It doesn't make me feel any better for abandoning her for the past few weeks, but Delilah told me that she's not my responsibility, and nor are her kids. She practically pushed me out of the door.

I stand for a moment and look at my charge, because that's what Hardy's has become to me. It seems to be standing taller somehow, like it has woken up from a deep sleep and is ready to face the world. Long red curtains have been pulled across the store windows ready for the big reveal tomorrow. They make Hardy's look like she is dressed up for a Christmas party in a gorgeously glamorous old-fashioned gown. After seeing the final Christmas makeover this morning Rupert has even had the foresight himself to put some make-up on the old girl. When I left the store earlier today Jan Baptysta and his laid-off cleaners were working flat out, painting the big window frames on the ground floor a modern Farrow and Ball green hue to enhance the old, traditional sandstone brick above it. Rupert has even commissioned a new sign to be made by the oldest signmakers in London so that it reads 'Hardy's' once again. Now the black iron letters shine proudly against the pale green background and underneath, in smaller black letters, is painted the words Est. 1910. The sandstone bricks have been cleaned too, and as I gaze upon her now I acknowledge that Hardy's looks how I feel: fully made-up and ready for her big moment.

I smooth my hands over my dress, feeling inexplicably nervous. Sam said to dress up, but I'm not sure I should have chosen this, the 1950s sage-green chiffon dress from The Wardrobe. God, how long ago it seems now since I tried it on in front of my sister. I can hardly believe I'm wearing it for real. I just hope I haven't gone too far. I don't know where to meet Sam or what we're doing, I just have to hope that he won't think I look crazy. But I wanted to make the effort. I pat my chignon awkwardly and pull a few more tendrils of hair down around my face to create a more relaxed look. Just as I'm beginning to wonder if Sam has forgotten all about me the staff entrance swings open and a grinning Felix, dressed in a full rig of black tie and dinner jacket, grins and then bows at me before ushering me in.

'Felix!' I exclaim, pretending to be surprised but a bit disappointed that he's here. Sam will have assumed that seeing all my friends will cheer me up, which ordinarily, it would. But tonight? I can't help but feel a little sad – and foolish. When I was getting ready, part of me hoped it would be just me and Sam. And not just because I'm not really in the right state of mind for a big group get-together.

'Evie, you look bleedin' gorgeous!' Felix says, before correcting himself.

'Ah-hem,' he clears his throat and stands to attention. 'What I mean is, ma'am – your table awaits!' He bows as I walk through the door. I have to cover my mouth to stop myself from giggling. He looks so unlike Felix in this get-up. His stubble has been shaved, his messy hair slicked down with a side parting and his toned-down, tasteful attire is most out of character. He winks at me before proffering his arm. 'M'lady?' he says with a small smile.

'Why thank you, sir,' I reply, curtsying and taking his arm.

We walk down the corridor past the staff board and I fleetingly glance at the passport picture of me that had my name, Eve Taylor, angrily scrawled in black ink over the top. I think back to that day when I so wanted the staff at Hardy's just to *see* me and wonder why I didn't realize that so many already did; the ones who are most important to me, anyway. I squeeze Felix's arm and he grins at me, before tugging at his bow tie.

'Bloody thing,' he says, clearly forgetting his

572

'posh' voice. 'Don't know why I wear 'em. Maisie always said they made me look all trussed up like a turkey.'

'Here,' I say, turning Felix round to face me and pulling at his tie to undo it so it hangs around his neck. I open his top button and then pull the tie so it lies evenly against his white shirt. 'That looks very suave; artfully dishevelled I think you'd call it,' I say. 'Much more you.'

Felix grins gratefully and we walk into the store. All the store's main lights are off, and just the magical glow of the gigantic Christmas tree by the grand central staircase guides us through the ground floor. We slowly descend the staircase. I can't run my hand down the banister as I usually would because we twined them with holly and ivy during the makeover. At the corner of each stair, different sized red church candles have been lit and they flicker warmly, helping to guide us down to the basement where yet more candles lead us to Lily's tearoom.

'What's going on?' I whisper to Felix as we walk slowly down our candlelit path. 'Are we having a Christmas party?'

'Kind of,' he says, leading me into the doorway.

I gasp as I look around me. Lily's tearoom has been transformed into an old-fashioned, festive dream. The little room is full of fragrant tealights flickering gaily in vintage tea cups that have scented the air with pomegranate and spices. All the tables have been pushed into the corners of the room, apart from a single table for two, which has been placed in a hand-crafted and painted sleigh in the centre of the room. A canopy of fairy lights is draped from the ceiling above so in the darkness of the room the table/sleigh appears to be swooping through the stars in the night sky. Against the back wall, half a dozen small fir trees have been placed and covered with white fake snow, giving a magical Narnia effect. I can only imagine that these are Jan's doing. The table inside the sleigh is covered in a dark red table cloth, with Lily's mismatched vintage crockery in reds and greens set upon it. There is a centrepiece of candles on a vintage cake stand with gold-leafed pears, cranberries and a scattering of holly and chestnuts around them. Rat Pack Christmas music is playing softly in the background.

Felix leads me over to the table that is laid for two and helps me to step inside the sleigh. I smile shyly and feel my heart soar as Sam stands up and bows at me before helping me off with my jacket and gesturing for me to sit down. A big, soft cashmere rug has been placed on my seat and Felix drapes it gently over my knees to keep me warm. We discovered when we did the all-night Christmas makeover, Hardy's can get pretty chilly at night. Once I'm settled I glance up and look at Sam. He is wearing a dinner jacket and his hair is slicked back so he looks just like a movie star from one of Lily's photographs.

Felix pours from a bottle of champagne into two

crystal glasses and then heads off to the counter, where Lily and Iris stand waving manically at him, dressed all in black, with white pinnies on.

'Hold your horses, Lil,' I hear him say to her. 'Starters can wait. Just give 'em a chance to have a chat first. Come on . . .' And they all scuttle off, muttering to each other.

I shake my head as I look around me and then back at a smiling, bashful Sam.

'I can't believe you've done all this!' I say in awed delight. 'It's just beautiful.'

'Well,' he says, averting his eyes and playing with his cutlery, 'I thought you needed cheering up and Hardy's seemed the best place to do it. You're not the only one with a talent for makeovers, you know,' he adds with a laugh.

'So I can see!' I smile and stare at him, rather than the room because I want to take in properly his handsome, groomed appearance. Gone is the dishevelled delivery boy, with his ruffled face and puppy-fat cheeks and penchant for unironed clothes, and in his place is, well, a man. A cool, suave, proper grown-up-looking man with cheek-bones illuminated by the shadow of burnt-umber stubble and dark, slick hair. He looks gorgeous. I can't work out if he's always looked like this and I've just never looked at him properly or if he's done something drastically different. Whatever it is, I like it.

'You look very handsome,' I say shyly as Dean Martin croons softly in the background.

'And you . . .' he shakes his head as he gazes at me, '. . . you look truly divine, Evie.'

I blush and look away.

'Look—' we say in unison.

'You first,' Sam begins.

'No, you first, I insist.'

He clears his throat behind his fist and looks at me nervously. I clasp my hands together, which are sweating most unattractively under the table. He clears his throat again. 'I just wanted to say first of all that, well, actually I've wanted to do this . . . you know, go on a date, for a very, very long time. Since I met you, if I'm being totally honest. But it never seemed . . . well, let's just say there always seems to be others standing in our way.' I look up at him and see the regret flicker over his face in the candle-light. Ella, I think. 'And then when Joel came along . . .' he continues, '. . . well, I guess what I'm trying to say is that I know things are complicated right now and it's still not the right time. I just want you to know that I don't expect anything from tonight, I just wanted to have a nice meal with my favourite girl and enjoy your company properly. As friends. So let's just be normal and chat like we always do – no weirdness, OK? And no expect-ations. Just being here with you is enough for me. He lifts his glass and smiles at me tenderly. 'To what might have been.'

I nod, feeling choked at his speech, but I raise my glass, feeling more relaxed all of a sudden. I take a sip of champagne, which helps even more.

'But you'd better give the memo to them.' I nod at Felix, Lily and Iris, who are all nudging each other and giggling like schoolchildren as they approach us carrying two plates between the three of them.

Sam laughs and shakes his head. 'I knew they'd be trouble. They'll be gone after the main courses. I've promised Lily a Martini on me if she helped out tonight. Not that she can cook, mind. Felix and Iris have been in charge of that. But she helped me decorate this place.'

'It looks incredible,' I say. 'It's like Christmas has come early.'

'Or, hopefully, just in time,' Sam says, raising his glass again.

'To Hardy's,' I say clinking my glass with his.

'Let's hope she gets her Christmas miracle,' Sam adds as the Three Stooges deliver our starters.

'Sir, modom,' Felix says as he places our plates in front of us. 'Your salmon and spinach roulade, lovingly prepared by me.' He steps away and puts his hands behind his back, rocking a little on his heels. 'Maisie used to say it was my speciality,' he adds proudly.

'It looks wonderful, Felix,' I say, glancing dubiously down at the pale pink, cream and green spinach and smoked salmon dish served on a bed of limp-looking greens, and feeling my mouth twitch and my stomach lurch a little.

'Go on then, taste it!' Felix prompts eagerly, peering over us closely.

'Oh, Felix, let them be,' Lily chastises, pulling him back. 'Here you go, darlings,' she coos as she places a basket in the middle of the table and Iris pops down some olives with a wink. 'Here's some pumpernickel bread. I didn't bake it myself, obviously. It's from Selfridges Food Hall. Now we'll be off. Call us if you need us!' And Lily and Iris back off gracefully, each dragging a reluctant Felix by the arm as they retreat.

Sam and I look down at our starters, then back at each other and laugh.

'It's a retro roulade,' I whisper.

'I know,' Sam hisses back. 'I'm just worried he actually made it in the 1980s and just got it out of the freezer for tonight. You're lucky, though, we nearly got prawn cocktail until I asked for something more "modern".'

'Bless him,' I say, wiping away a tear of laughter, 'we shouldn't judge until we taste it. It might be delicious.'

Sam looks at me and then his plate doubtfully.

'OK, well, I'm going in,' I say dramatically, lifting my knife and fork and taking a deep breath. 'Are you with me, or not?'

'Um . . . not?' Sam says, making a face at his plate.

'He's still looking, you know,' I say, waving my fork and smiling at Felix.

'Oh God,' Sam sighs. 'I should've known this was a bad idea. I should've just ordered takeaway. After three, OK? One, two . . .'

'Three!' I swipe at the roulade with my knife, stab it with my fork, look at it for a moment, then pop it in my mouth. I look over but Sam is still staring at his.

'Hey, cheat!' I say with my mouth full of cream cheese, spinach and salmon. 'You know,' I say thoughtfully, 'this is actually pretty nice.' I adopt a *Masterchef* tone of voice. 'Creamy, smooth cheese with the sharpness of lemon, then there's the crunch of the leaves with the saltiness of the salmon. Oh and the festive, earthy tang of nutmeg.'

'Really?' says Sam, taking a mouthful himself and then immediately grabs his glass and washes it down with a large gulp of champagne. 'Liar!' he hisses, and then waves at Felix, who's still hovering in the corner, and calls out to him through gritted teeth: 'Mmm, it's delicious, Felix!'

'Come on, eat up!' I laugh as I smear some on Lily's posh bread. 'Don't be such a wimp.'

Our starters over, our main courses of beef Wellington have been delivered accompanied by lots of leading comments from Lily, who stood by our table looking at us maternally and occasionally patting my hair as if she's a proud mum. Eventually she retreats and Sam and I are left to continue chatting.

'It's been a crazy few weeks, hasn't it?' Sam says, slicing through his pastry.

I nod, thinking of all that has happened. Joel, Delilah and Will, the store's makeover, my own.

Even being here now with Sam is something I would have never imagined three weeks ago. 'It certainly has,' I sigh and then start giggling.

'What's so funny?' Sam says, slightly perturbed. 'Have I got gravy round my mouth? Or on my shirt?'

I shake my head and find I can't stop laughing.

'Then what?' he presses desperately. 'Come on, Evie, you're making me paranoid.'

I put my knife and fork down and wipe away a tear. 'I was just thinking about how weird all this is. I mean, we're usually stuck together in that dusty stockroom, sorting through boxes, me all forlorn and depressed about my job and you looking like you just rolled out of bed to do all your dad's deliveries and wishing you were doing anything else . . .'

'I'm not a morning person,' grumbles Sam defensively.

'Nor am I!' I reply, and this makes me laugh even harder. 'And now here we are, all done up to the nines, having a fancy dinner in the dead of night whilst the store is shut, after secretly making the whole place over. I mean, it's crazy!'

'It certainly is,' Sam says with a wide grin. 'But it's good-crazy. I've had the best time since we all started working on this place. You've really helped me go for my photography dream, Evie. I honestly can't thank you enough. And having my pictures printed in the papers, well, it's been amazing. Not just because it's helped Hardy's, but because I know it's going to help me too. I never thought anything like this would happen. I'd kind of resigned myself to the fact that I'd be doing deliveries forever . . .'

'But why?' I ask. He is always so open, yet there is so much I don't know about him. 'You're young and you always seem so positive, what made you give up so easily?'

Sam shrugs, and I sense he's uncomfortable. He looks up at me and goes to say something but then seems to reconsider. 'Just . . . circumstances. After dropping out of uni before I'd finished my degree, I had to get a job quickly, which didn't leave me many options. My dad kindly offered me a job and I decided to take it. He always wanted me to go into the family business and part of me felt like maybe I was accepting the inevitable. After all, my dad's done all right. He's worked hard to build a business that could support his family . . .' Sam clears his throat and takes a sip of wine. 'I guess I just thought maybe I should do the same? Be responsible. Be a man.'

'But you're only in your twenties. You don't have to be responsible yet . . .' I point out.

Sam looks down at his plate and goes silent. It takes him a few minutes of pushing food around to speak again. 'I guess not, but that's not how you always feel is it?' He looks up at me. 'I mean, take you. You have responsibilities too . . . your sister's kids for a start . . .'

Now it's my turn to look down at my plate. 'I

guess so, and I suppose sometimes I have resented it. It's not what a single twenty-eight-year-old should be doing after all, is it? Staying in every night, cooking tea and watching CBeebies. But then again, I do really enjoy being with them. And it's not like I've ever been the sort of person who wants to go out clubbing every night. I guess I've always been a home girl at heart.'

Sam leans forward and rests his elbows on the table, listening closely to me. It feels nice. I'm not used to talking about myself.

'I think I was happy to look after them for so long because I wanted to be close to Delilah and be part of her life. I've always looked up to her so much but because of the age gap we never really had the chance to live together for long. She'd moved away to go to university by the time I was twelve and before that she was always out with her friends. I always felt like I wanted to be near her . . .' I pause for a moment as a thought occurs to me, '. . . to bask in the reflected glow of her life as it's always seemed so much better than mine. Hers has always seemed so smooth-sailing whereas I've always felt like I'm scrabbling around, trying to find order and beauty and calm out of what feels like chaos. Nothing's ever felt easy. I didn't really have any natural talent – apart from being creative – but my dad always told me that wasn't enough and that left me feeling bereft. I just didn't know which direction my life was meant to take, or have the confidence to make choices on my own, so I dutifully followed other people's lives, hoping they'd lead me down the right path. Like my ex, Jamie.'

Sam nods and I know he understands.

'When that all fell apart I quickly moved on to my sister. By living with her I hoped that her life and the ease with which she's always seemed to live it would rub off on me. And in some respects it did. I was happy and positive for the first time in my life. I loved being at Hardy's even if it wasn't my dream job and I loved being at home with her and the kids. But over time, the realization that I was living in her shadow and that no one in the city seemed to be able to see me, or appreciate anything about me, began to dawn on me. I was seeing Delilah less and less, and at work I didn't have much contact with anyone either. Except you, of course,' I add shyly.

Sam smiles. 'But it's not like that any more,' he says gently. 'You've made such a difference to this place and to so many people's lives. I mean, just look at how much Felix and Lily love you. We all do,' he adds, and our eyes lock for a moment. Sam coughs again. 'I'm sure that once Rupert knows who's been doing these makeovers you'll see the last of that stockroom, too.'

'But he can never find out,' I say seriously. 'You know that, right? I mean, if he did, lots of people's jobs could be in danger again and I can't let that happen.'

'But you deserve to be recognized for what

you've done!' Sam protests. 'Don't you want everyone to know the real Evie Taylor? Show them what you can really do?'

I shrug noncommittally. 'I did, I guess, but funnily enough it's not such a big deal to me any more. Doing all this has made me realize that I'm suited to the stockroom. And as for everyone knowing the real me, well,' I look at him through my lowered eyelashes, 'I think the most important people already do. And that's enough for me.'

'Wow.' Sam sits back in his chair and shakes his head. 'You're something, you know that? I'm not sure I'd be so accepting of my fate.'

'So says the sulky delivery boy,' I laugh, throwing my napkin at him. 'If you want people to know who you really are, why don't you tell your dad you're leaving the business and put all your energy into becoming a photographer? Go on, I dare you!'

Sam raises an eyebrow at me. 'Did you just dare me?' he says, throwing down his own napkin on the table.

I lift my chin and meet his eyes with a steely gaze. 'I most certainly did.'

'Well, that's annoying, because now I'm going to have to take you up on that dare. What if I double-dare you?' he shoots back.

'I'm not a gambling kind of girl,' I reply sweetly.

'Oh, you're good, Taylor, too good, damnit.'

We are in fits of relaxed laughter by the time Lily delivers our Arctic rolls.

'We're off,' she says, glancing behind her at Felix.

584

'So we'll be leaving you young lovebirds to it.' And she kisses us both and then departs in a cloud of sweet-smelling perfume as we collapse into even more giggles after she's gone.

'Young lovebirds!' I chuckle. 'Subtlety never was her strong point!'

'And if she thinks we're young lovebirds, what does that make her and Felix?' Sam splutters. 'The old lovebirds?'

I stop laughing. 'You don't think they're . . . do you?' I gasp.

Sam's mouths lilts into a smile. 'Haven't you seen how Felix looks at Lily? He's utterly besotted.'

I smack my hand against my forehead. 'How could I have missed it! It's so obvious now you say that.'

I think of Felix and his more frequent visits to Lily's tearoom over the past week or so. I thought it was because he and Lily were bonding over the store's makeovers, coming up with ideas after he'd finished his night shift, but it seems that there was something more to it. And now I think of it, they're the perfect match. Once again I realize I've been so wrapped up in what's been happening in my life recently I've stopped noticing everything.

'Oh, I *do* hope they get together!' I exclaim. 'Do you think there's anything we can do to help things along a bit?'

Sam smiles and peers out into the store where Felix and Lily disappeared into a few minutes ago.

'I'm not sure we need to,' he smiles, and he beckons me to follow him as he stands up, creeps over to the entrance of the tearoom and peeks through the doorway. I huddle behind him, holding on to his arms as I sneak a peek too and have to stop myself from crying out with pleasure when I see Felix and Lily, quietly waltzing in the middle of the candlelit menswear department to the music that's been playing in our tearoom all evening.

Just then the opening strains of Nat King Cole's most famous song, 'Unforgettable', begin to play.

As Nat croons, Felix and Lily gaze at each other as they twirl around the shop floor.

I squeal with excitement.

'Shhh,' Sam hushes me, and puts one hand over my mouth and the other round my waist. 'Isn't that just the most adorable thing you've ever seen?'

Just then Felix swishes Lily round in a circle and lifts her effortlessly off the ground.

'Wow, Felix's quite the mover!' I whisper. 'He looks like he's in his element.'

'She's been giving him private lessons, apparently,' Sam whispers, and I coo with delight as he twirls her around again.

'I reckon they could teach our generation a thing or two about the art of romance,' Sam says, and then he turns and leads me gently back into the tearoom to give them some privacy.

He stands opposite me with his arms outstretched. Suddenly from feeling wonderfully relaxed and comfortable I feel awkward and anxious and all legs and arms. I can't look at Sam because I don't know how I feel. I know he said he just wants to be friends but I'm not so sure I can do it like this.

When I finally bring myself to look up at him I burst out laughing. 'What the hell are you doing, Sam?' I splutter.

'What does it look like I'm doing?' he replies incredulously. 'I'm dancing!'

'Is that what you call it?' I laugh. Sam's got his hands in the air, rave-style, his face is a picture of concentration and he appears to be in the middle of the 'big box little box' dance move. 'Forget Felix's old-fashioned moves, this is how I've attracted every woman I've ever gone out with,' he grins. 'It never fails. Come on, try it!'

I look at him for a moment, then shrug and join in with him, giggling helplessly when I think about what we look like.

Sam stops suddenly and puts his hands on my shoulders and I do the same to him, and we morph seamlessly into doing the classic school disco side-step slow dance whilst trying to maintain straight faces. It doesn't work. We collapse into each other's arms, tears of laughter streaming down our faces just as the song enters its final chorus, at which point our laughter subsides and we hold on to each other and sway softly in time to the music. I close my eyes and rest my head on Sam's shoulder and he rests his hands gently on my back, and for a moment, I forget where I am and what I'm doing, and all I know is that suddenly, just like Nat King Cole says, it seems that someone I really like, finally thinks I'm unforgettable too.'

'Evie,' Sam mutters hoarsely, his voice thick with intent in my ear. 'There's something I need to tell you, something really important.'

'Shhh,' I say, my lips brushing the curve of his neck by accident. 'Let's not spoil the moment. It's just perfect.'

'I know,' Sam answers, and pulls away from me. 'That's why I need to tell you this.' I look up at him in confusion and he rubs his head sorrow-fully. 'Evie, I do really like you but you know there's someone else. Her name's—'

'Ella. I know.' I pull away from him. Deep down I'd hoped it was all over with her.

'No, no, that's over . . .'

I feel a tidal wave of joy wash over me.

'I'm talking about Sophie, she's—'

I extricate myself from him arms. 'God, how many women are there, Sam?' I exclaim in horror. 'You know what, don't answer that. I don't want to know the graphic details. You really had me fooled, you know that?' I snatch my jacket off my chair and throw it round my shoulders, but it gets all tangled up and instead I screw it up into a ball in my arms. Then I push past him and run blindly towards the door, feeling a complete fool for about the millionth time in my life.

'I thought you were different, Sam. I really

thought you were different,' I say without turning round.

'Evie, wait!' Sam calls desperately.

But I don't hear any more. I run back through the store, up the stairs and towards the staff exit, wanting Hardy's to swallow me up and spit me out back in my bed, where I can forget all about tonight and just fade into the background.

Because no matter what Nat King Cole just tried to make me believe, I know that I'll never be unforgettable.

MONDAY 19 DECEMBER

6 Shopping Days Until Christmas

CHAPTER 41

I open the delivery door reluctantly. I can barely bring myself to look at Sam after what happened on Friday night. And he clearly feels the same as he has his back to me and is busily unpacking the usual Monday morning delivery from the van. Instead of holding the door open for him, I prop it open and disappear down an aisle so I can get back to sorting out my already ridiculously tidy shelves.

'That's everything, Evie,' I hear him say at last, and I move a few items around needlessly before wiping my hands on my pencil skirt, smoothing my pin-curled hair and pulling the neck bow on my emerald-green satin blouse and emerging into the stockroom. 'I just need you to sign this.' He holds out a clipboard in front of me and puts his other hand in the pocket of his battered jeans. He looks tired, I think, like he hasn't had much sleep. Well, ditto.

I reach out and take the clipboard and am surprised to find a newspaper on it, not a delivery report. It's today's *Daily Mail*.

'What's this?' I query, looking up at him.

'We're in there,' he says gruffly, nodding at me to open it. 'Page seven.'

I turn the pages quickly until I come to our story. 'Bloody hell, Sam, this is incredible!' In my excitement I forget about what happened between us. But only for a moment. 'Um, I mean, this is great,' I finish flippantly. 'Let's hope it's not too late,' I add coolly, and give him back his clipboard without looking at him.

'Evie . . .' he pleads, stepping towards me with his arms outstretched. 'About the other night. Just hear me out, won't you?'

I put my hand up to stop him coming any closer. I don't trust myself not to just melt into his embrace and I refuse to make an idiot of myself again. I've done that quite enough for one lifetime.

'It's fine, Sam, honestly,' I say firmly, whilst staring at the floor. 'You made your situation quite clear.' It really needs cleaning. I must get the mop out later. There's no point in Hardy's exterior looking gleaming and new if the stockroom looks a mess. 'Let's just forget all about the other night, shall we? I mean, it's for the best. I'm still with Joel, anyway . . .'

'But I was under the impression that was all over?' Sam says looking confused.

'No, no,' I say defensively. 'There's just been a bit of a misunderstanding. We're going to meet up to talk about it.'

This much is true. Joel called me this morning and asked what's been going on. I told him I'd seen him talking to Rupert and Joel told me he could explain everything. Funny how men keep saying that to me. Even my dad phoned this morning trying to say the same thing. I didn't let him, either.

'I'm sure we'll work it out,' I add, sticking my chin out and folding my arms. This bit is a lie. I don't believe Joel and I'm pretty sure it won't work out. Apart from the fact that I'm not sure I want it to, how can I ever trust him again?

Sam sighs and stares at me for what feels like an uncomfortably long amount of time. 'Well, if that's what you want,' he says finally.

'It is, Sam, it is,' I reply. 'Friends?' I say, offering my outstretched hand in a formal gesture.

Sam stares at me for a moment, his gaze burning my face like the sun. Then he turns and walks out the delivery door. I drop my outstretched hand sadly and get on with unpacking today's boxes, wondering how, for someone so tidy, I have the capacity to mess things up quite so monumentally.

'Sarah? Sa-rah! Where are yooooou? I need you to listen to this!'

I've managed to have a couple of precious hours on my own, sorting through my thoughts and putting them into the relevant boxes marked in my head as I robotically unpack Hardy's new stock delivery. Carly's voice is an unwelcome reminder of everything that is wrong with my life. I feel an uncharacteristic surge of annoyance at her presence in my haven. It's *her* fault that I've ruined my chances with Sam and neglected my sister. If I hadn't wanted to be like her, if I hadn't tried so hard to change myself, then maybe none of this would have happened. Sam and I would still be friends, my sister and I wouldn't have to rebuild our relationship and I would have been there for Mum to help her face the mess that Dad has put our family through. I tug at the bow on my blouse in frustration as I look down at myself in my stupid 'Wardrobe' clothes. I must look ridiculous, all dressed up like some retro throwback just to unpack a load of boxes. Tomorrow I am going to go back to being plain old Sarah. I mean Evie. Maybe I'll even get used to wearing those horrible black trousers and plain white shirts again.

I just can't face Carly this morning so I crouch in the aisle, and peek through the shelves as she looks around for me.

'Sa-RAH!' she calls again, heading straight for my aisle. Knowing I am about to be discovered anyway I scramble to my feet, feeling my stomach surge with anger.

'For God's sake!' I shout, pulling down from the shelves stock that I've only just put away. 'WHAT?'

Carly's bemused face appears round the shelves and then the rest of her, and she looks at me in astonishment. She is back to her beautiful best, in tight, black cropped jeans and a 1940s-esque creamy pale floral chiffon shirt with a black blazer with pointed, statement shoulders over the top.

Black high heels and red lips complete the look, with her hair pulled into a high ponytail with an Elvis-style quiff sprayed into place at the front.

'Are you OK?' she asks in concern.

'No I'm bloody NOT!' I exclaim wildly. 'I'm sick of this place and sick of people treating me like shit!'

'Hey, Sarah, it's OK' she says, walking slowly towards me, trying to calm me down but she only makes things worse.

'It's not OK, don't you SEE? GOD, that's not even my name, Carly! I'm Evie, Evie Taylor!' I shout.

Carly looks at me in complete astonishment and then edges away a little as I stomp around the stockroom putting away the stock that I've just pulled down in a fit of rebellion. Even in this state I am unable to deal with having mess around me.

'What do you mean, that's not your name?' she asks slowly.

I sigh, the anger draining from my body like air from a balloon. 'Sarah was the name of the girl who worked in here *before* me,' I explain.

I look at Carly for a moment and then shake my head, knowing that I can't begin to make her understand. I walk to the stockroom door and turn round to face her as I put my hand on the handle.

'Don't you get it, Carly? Everyone has always been so wrapped up in their own lives and problems in this bloody place that no one has ever noticed that I'm an entirely different person! Not even you . . .' I trail off and look her in the eye. 'And you're meant to be my best friend here.'

Then I open the door and walk out, slamming it shut behind me.

The store is quiet and dark, despite it being 9 a.m. on the last Monday before Christmas. Everyone should be here by now, preparing to open up. I'm trying to work out where everyone is when the store's lights are flicked on and I look around in astonishment as I see every single member of staff lined up in front of Hardy's Christmas tree. Lily and Felix are standing at the front of the line next to all the cleaners, Jane, Barbara, Guy, Becky from Handbags, Gwen and Jenny the Beauty girls, the Haberdashery sisters – everyone, in fact. Even Sam is standing meekly amongst them.

Felix steps forward and clears his throat. His cheeks are all flushed with colour and his blue eyes are bright and animated. He looks the best I've ever seen him: at least ten years younger and the grey, world-weary pallor has been replaced with excitement and enthusiasm.

'We are gathered here today,' he begins, then Lily nudges him gently. He shakes his head and clears his throat again. 'What I meant to say is, dear Evie, we've all been waiting for you this morning as we wanted to tell you in person how much we've appreciated everything you've done for us and the store. We hope you don't mind, but

Lily and I . . .' he pauses and slips his hand into hers, '. . . we thought it was time that all the staff knew just who was behind these wonderful makeovers. Everyone was desperate to know who the Secret Elf was who'd worked so hard to save their jobs. But when Lily and I started talking about our Evie, they got very confused. They couldn't understand who this girl was that we were raving about. They said, "But there's no one called Evie here," and Lily and I said, "Yes, yes, there is," and when we explained all your wonderful qualities; like your ability to listen and advise without ever expecting anyone to ask about you, how you make people feel better about themselves simply by showing an interest, how you remember important dates of everyone's lives – birthdays, anniversaries – how you notice and compliment when someone has a new haircut or is wearing a new item of clothing. And most of all how you listen to people's problems without ever telling a soul. And that's when everyone started thinking and talking at once.' Felix smiles at me and then over at Jane. 'First of all Jane here explained how you helped her find her, ahem, how do I put it? Her va-va-voom, which she says has saved her marriage.' Felix glances at Jane and she steps forward and does a little shimmy as a ripple of laughter fills the room. 'Then everyone else started explaining how much you'd helped them trans-form their lives over the past two years that you've worked here. Hell, Evie, you're even partly responsible for a baby . . .' Jenny from Beauty steps forward and waves at me with one hand, whilst rubbing a newly sprouting belly with the other. The IVF must've worked!' I put my hand up to my mouth as I feel my eyes fill with tears.

Felix is still talking as Jenny steps back into line.

'But then they said to Lily and me, "But she's just the stockroom girl . . ."'

Lily steps forward and continues the story. 'So we said, but have you ever thought to ask her name? Or did you just think because she was tucked away in the stockroom that it didn't matter? Did you listen to her problems, ask about her weekend, notice if she was happy or upset, ask her anything about herself at all? Or did you just presume that she was just there to be a sponge for your problems? Did you think because she worked behind the scenes that she didn't really matter, she wasn't a proper member of staff and therefore didn't really give her a second thought?'

The staff shuffle around uncomfortably and gaze at me apologetically.

Felix cuts in again. 'And then we said, and all the time she's been working hard to save your jobs and stop the roof from caving in over your heads.'

Everyone drops their head and I feel a wave of shame. I don't want them to feel bad . . .

'It's fine,' I say, stepping forward shyly. 'Really, it is. I kind of enjoyed being anonymous . . .'

'Well then, you're mad,' Guy pipes up. 'A girl

600

with your talents *should* stand out. None of us could have done what you have for this store. Or what you've done for us,' he adds gratefully. 'Thank you for saving our jobs Sar— I mean . . . Evie.' He pauses and studies me for a moment. 'Your real name suits you, you know. It's kind of timeless. And timely . . .'

'Christmas Evie!' someone shouts, and everyone laughs and starts cheering my new nickname.

'Christmas Evie! Christmas Evie!'

I laugh as I realize I have a whole new nickname to get used to.

Just then the stockroom door opens and Carly tumbles through it. She stops and stares at everyone calling my name and cheering and then looks at me. And then she looks around the store.

'Y-you?' she stutters. 'You did all this? But when – how, why?' She looks at all the staff. 'And you all knew? You were all in on this? I should've guessed!'

She turns back to me. 'It's *your* fault everyone hated me! You pretended you were helping me but – but . . .' She staggers backwards. 'And in there – you were all high and mighty about the fact that I didn't know your real name. What else have you been hiding, huh?'

I lower my head, I can't tell her the rest. I know I should but I just can't.

'Well,' she spits, 'thanks for leaving me out of the party. Now I'm going to see what Rupert has to say about this . . .' She turns and goes to stalk off but Lily steps forward and grabs hold of her arm.

'You'll do no such thing, young lady,' she says coldly. 'You owe your job to this girl. Without these makeovers you'd have been let go a long time ago. And so would most of us. Now show some respect to the rest of the staff who've worked hard to accept the changes in this store. We all need our jobs, even if you don't, and if it hasn't escaped your notice, it's nearly opening time.' She claps her hands and raises her voice. 'It's the last shopping week before Christmas, people, and we have to take a fortune. Hardy's future depends on it!'

There are cheers and Lily silences everyone with her hand. 'Now, Felix and I have come up with a plan to really draw the crowds in but it requires *everyone's* help . . .'

I look at Lily quizzically and she makes an apologetic face.

'Sorry, Evie darling, we probably should've told you about our idea earlier.' She turns back to Carly. 'Now, dear, you're either with us, or against us. So instead of running off to tell Rupert who's been doing the makeovers, how about you help us with the final push, hmm?'

Carly doesn't answer; she just stares defiantly at me, then Lily, and then the rest of Hardy's workforce as we wait anxiously for her response, knowing that her decision could make or break us all.

CHAPTER 42

An hour later and I am outside the store, on Lily's orders. She can be very bossy when she wants to be. I'm wrapped up snugly to fight the chill but I barely need my layers as I'm feeling so warmed by the sight of the crowds of people who are gathered outside. There are literally hundreds of people here waiting for Hardy's to open this morning. I can hardly believe it. The store has been decked with sparkling lights and greenery all around the outside of the door and windows. This must have been Jan's doing – I hadn't even thought of decorating the outside. There is a wonderful atmosphere as we all wait expectantly for the windows to be revealed and the store's front doors to open.

A group of carol singers have gathered here by the front door and are singing a rousing version of 'O Come All Ye Faithful'. Even the roasted chestnut guy from Oxford Street has spotted a selling opportunity and set up his barrow on the pavement outside, and the sweet, nutty aroma is currently weaving its festive scent around us.

I would feel utterly overjoyed with the events

of the last half an hour and all this incredible Christmas spirit were it not for the copy of the newspaper that I am clutching in my hand. I've only just had time to read it since Sam handed it to me this morning. Alongside the wonderful story about all of Hardy's secret makeovers to stop its imminent takeover by a big American retail conglomerate, there is a picture and a small profile of Joel, who is accredited as being the CFO of Rumors, the company who will be taking over Hardy's site. It is all the confirmation I need that Joel was lying to me all along. I have no desire to see him or listen to his excuses any more. It's over. I glance at his picture again and feel a fresh wave of disappointment.

'That's a terrible shot of me,' a voice murmurs in my ear.

I turn round and am shocked to see Joel himself, in the flesh, looking as devastatingly handsome as always. He smiles at me and I immediately turn my back on him and face Hardy's.

'Hey, won't you just talk to me – or at least let me explain . . . ?' Joel pleads. He puts his hand on my shoulder and I shrug it off.

'What's to explain?' I say sharply. 'You lied to me. Now, if you don't mind, something's happening.'

As the hands on Hardy's clock reach ten o'clock the crowd's noise dissipates to a quiet, excited murmur and I am surprised to see Rupert appearing out of the front door, locking it carefully behind him again. He puts his hands up and

I see that they are shaking a little. I crane my neck and rise up on tiptoe so I can see better, but all I can think about is Joel's breath on my neck behind me.

'Welcome to Hardy's grand reopening . . .' Rupert announces nervously.

'I thought you knew I was working for Rumors,' Joel mutters in my ear, and I can't help but turn round to contradict him.

'How? You never said. In fact, you implied you were *friends* with Rupert. I thought you were on our side! If I'd known you were trying to close Hardy's all this time I'd—'

'You'd what?' Joel says, gazing intently at me.

'I'd never have gone out with you.'

'But,' he says, 'you said you thought Rumors was the future of retail. I thought you welcomed the takeover.'

I feel a flash of guilt but ignore it. He's the one at fault here. Not me. 'It's a future that I certainly don't want to be a part of,' I reply primly and turn back round. 'Now please, Joel, I'm trying to listen to Rupert.'

Rupert has relaxed into his role as store Master of Ceremonies and he now has the crowd in the palm of his hand.

'My family has been overwhelmed by the support you've shown the store and we want to thank all the customers for your loyalty over the years,' he says, his voice ringing out proudly over the crowd's noise. 'There have been big changes afoot at Hardy's, many that I didn't know about, thanks to the Secret Elves who have been working hard to save the store . . .' The crowd cheers and Rupert beams brightly.

'I don't understand.' Joel is still talking to me, even though I'm trying to ignore him and focus on Rupert. 'You always said that Rumors was your kind of store, that Hardy's was outdated and—'

'Well,' I interrupt sharply before he repeats any more of my ridiculous 'Carly' comments, 'maybe I haven't been entirely honest with you either.'

Joel looks confused. 'What do you mean, Carly? I don't understand.'

'I'm not Carly, that's the point, OK?' I sigh wearily, tired of having to explain myself again.

Joel looks at me like I've just sprouted another head.

'Joel, the truth is my name isn't Carly. Never was. And I'm not Hardy's personal shopper-turned-assistant manager, I'm just the stockroom girl.' He looks astonished and I hold out my hand. 'I'm Evie, pleased to meet you.' I bob a curtsy and feel an inappropriate tornado of laughter whirl up inside me and out. 'Wooh, I feel better now I've told you that!' I laugh nervously.

Someone in front of me turns round and shushes me. I look down, embarrassed, and then back at Joel, who is standing with his arms folded, thick dark eyebrows raised and knotted, waiting for me to continue. I sigh and take a deep breath.

'The first time we met, you confused me for

someone else, someone pretty and appealing and fun and talented, and so I just went along with it. Carly is a good friend of mine and I've always wanted to be like her. She dates hot men, like you, and I guess I thought, why not? Why not pretend to be her? It won't *hurt* anyone. Besides, I never thought you'd actually call . . .'

Joel clenches his jaw and I see it flex under his stubble. I shake my head and force myself to concentrate on what I'm trying to tell him. 'I was just so sick of having this shitty job that no one cared about, wearing horrible clothes, being so . . . forgettable. No one could *ever* accuse Carly of being that, so I thought I'd channel her. Dress a bit like her, talk like her, share her opinions, *be* her, just for a while. But then I started to like you, and it was so much harder than I thought, and you seemed so genuine and real, and I wanted what we had to be real too . . . but it never was. It never was,' I repeat sadly, shaking my head. When Joel doesn't reply I continue resolutely, 'But none of that matters now because I know that you weren't being real either. You pretended to be this sweet, caring guy who loved family-run stores when in actual fact all you wanted to do was destroy a store that you professed to be so much like your own. You care about money and power and that's all. No wonder your own store is failing. You've got no heart. Which means neither has Parker's. Not like this place,' I finish proudly, just in time to hear Rupert close his speech.

607

'. . . I have been surprised many times over the past few weeks at what my Secret Elves have achieved. And I've been told that today they have one more surprise up their sleeves for us. I don't know what it is and, to be honest, I'm not sure if it's going to be enough to save my great-grandfather's fine, fine store.' Rupert stops, choked all of a sudden, and I will him to continue. 'But what I do know is that these staff, these wonderful people who I am lucky enough to have working for me, have proved that business isn't all about money, and shops aren't all about material goods. I've realized that Hardy's is a community in itself, a home from home, a place to meet and talk and browse. It's been my family's home for a hundred years and I hope that Londoners will agree that it's been your home too. My great-grandfather wanted this to be a place for you to come and feel warmly welcomed every single day, whether you purchase anything or not. We lost our way for a few years,' there is a ripple of agreement from the gathered crowd, 'but I believe the store has rediscovered its core, traditional values. And I don't think there's another department store in this city that can compete with us.' He raises his voice as he reaches the climax of his speech. 'If you believe in family and hope and friendship and good old-fashioned values, then Hardy's is the store for you.'

Cheers erupt from the crowd and Rupert looks surprised, then utterly overcome. His cheeks go pink, he swipes his hand across his watery eyes and I see Sharon, who has been standing proudly by his side the entire time, grasp his hand and squeeze it. Rupert looks at her gratefully and she steps forward, patting her hair and smiling at everyone.

'So without further ado we'd like to unveil Hardy's last surprise.' She steps over to the window and knocks sharply on it. One by one, window by window, the lustrous red curtains are pulled open slowly like stage curtains. The carol singers start humming a beautifully heartfelt version of 'White Christmas'and suddenly I forget all about Joel and our conversation, and I smile and squeal and laugh and start applauding loudly along with the rest of the crowd at the wonderful sight that fills my eyes.

In the windows Lily and Felix have staged wonderful Windmill-esque-inspired tableaux vivants,with all of Hardy's staff standing motion-less in the window – except, thankfully, they're fully clothed in Hardy's vintage staff uniforms. Jane must have shown Lily where I pulled hers from in the stockroom, and found the men's ones, too: wonderful wartime green shirts with matching trousers.

In each window they've staged different Christmas scenes to match a classic decade: from the 1930s, '40s, '50s and '60s. In the first Bernie and Susan, the Haberdashery sisters, are perched on armchairs handing each other Christmas presents with festive-coloured green and red balls of yarn at their feet and beautiful Christmas vintage fabric bunting draped round the 1930s-styled living room and on the Christmas tree. I glance over to the next window along at Carly, who is standing in there next to Iris. She looks at me and winks. Both women are wearing original wartime Land Girl uniforms. They are frozen mid-march, except Iris's leg keeps wobbling so she has to put it on the floor. They both have one hand raised to their foreheads in a salute and the cardboard cutout of the WI women who made the lavender soaps has been placed cleverly behind them so it looks like they're leading a march. British flags are hung all around them and the window has been filled with fake snow. On the other side of the store, Jane, Becky and the Beauty girls are dressed in decadent 1950s fashion, wearing jewel-coloured, figure-hugging gowns, clutching vintage cocktail glasses at a Christmas dance. And in the central, main window there is a brick chimney breast complete with a fake, roaring fire. There is glass of whisky and a plate of biscuits placed carefully on the mantelpiece, with vintage Christmas cards hung on string all around. Felix, Lily, Sam, Jan Baptysta, Velna and Justyna are all standing either side of a chimney breast and, hilariously, they are all wearing green elf costumes, complete with curly shoes, tights and little hats. Lily and Felix are also holding up a sign that says: 'We're Hardy's Christmas Elves'.

I can't help laughing at the sight of my wonderful friends and then, along with the hundreds of people who are gathered out here on this frosty, December morning six days before Christmas, we all burst into rapturous applause.

'It's pretty impressive, huh?' Joel says softly.

I'd forgotten all about him. Almost. I nod but don't reply.

'You know, uh . . . Evie, is it? I never asked out the wrong girl.'

'Yes you did,' I say without turning round. 'I was wearing the same top as Carly that day, you'd seen her earlier in the store and she told me she was sure you were going to ask her out. Half an hour later I bumped into you outside the personal shopping department and . . . well, it was an easy mistake to make.'

'That's not how I remember it,' Joel replies. I turn round and look at him questioningly. 'The week before I met you I had come into the store to meet Rupert. I saw you then, dashing around the place with armfuls of stock.' He looks into the distance. 'You reminded me of my ex-girlfriend actually. It was quite uncanny.' I feel my stomach tighten slightly but Joel continues, 'I wondered who you were and wanted to talk to you but even though I came in every day I didn't see you again. But I couldn't stop thinking about you. I mean, there was just something about you that I couldn't forget . . .'

I shake my head in disbelief and try to turn away but Joel grasps hold of my arms.

'It's true, you have to believe me. I even asked some members of staff about you. I described you exactly, the length and colour of your hair, your cute outfit of trousers and white shirt, right down to your skin tone.'

'Like ET?' I reply, thinking about my brothers' nickname for me, and Joel looks at me strangely. 'In the film,' I mutter. 'When he's all pale and ill.'

'No,' he shakes his head emphatically. 'Like a perfect blanket of snow.' I swipe my hand across my eyes; the cold is obviously making them water or something. 'I was so happy when I bumped into you that day in Menswear, even though you did look different to how I remembered, more polished and stylish somehow . . .'

I think back to the structured, sparkly Florence Gainsbourg top and smile ruefully to myself. I look at Joel and then back at the store windows. Part of me feels overwhelmed by what Joel has just told me. It was me he wanted all along, not Carly, but the truth is nothing has changed. Not really.

'Thank you, Joel,' I say politely. 'I appreciate you telling me all this but the truth is our relationship couldn't ever have gone anywhere. You want Hardy's to close and I care about this place too much to be with someone who wants that.' I smile and go to turn away. 'It's been fun getting to know—'

'NO!' Joel shakes his head in frustration and grabs my arm to turn me round. 'That's just it! I

612

don't want Hardy's to close! I never have done. I just didn't feel like I could ever tell you what I was trying to do for the place because you kept saying how much you loved Rumors!'

I look at him in disbelief and Joel exhales slowly so his breath weaves towards me like cigarette smoke. He loosens his grip on my arm and brushes his other hand over his mouth and chin, and his stubble crackles like scrunched-up wrapping paper as he tries to explain.

'The truth is I *was* briefed to look into buying out Hardy's site to be Rumors' flagship London store. That's why I was sent over here initially.' I fold my arms and stare at him, and he quickly adds: 'But then Rupert showed me round the store, and the more I visited the place, the more I fell in love with it. It reminded me so much of Parker's but I also realized that Hardy's couldn't carry on as it was. Just like my store, it was stuck in a time warp, but Rupert and I couldn't work out what we could do and we were resigned to the fact that I'd just have to do my job and buy the site for Rumors.' He pauses. 'Then the makeovers started happening.' He looks at me meaningfully. 'They were so inspired it gave me an idea of how I could save the store without upsetting the company I work for. I didn't tell Rupert as he was under so much pressure from his father to sell up, as the family has got into huge amounts of debt. They were going to lose their ancestral home in Gloucestershire and

Sebastian Hardy saw selling the store as the only way to stop that. Poor Rupert was torn: lose his beloved home farm or lose his great-grandfather's store. So I set about trying to persuade my company that Hardy's could be big again. I told my company that in the run-up to Christmas the store could see a massive turnaround. But we needed to give it a chance. They agreed to wait and I told Rupert he had until the 26th of December to force the profits up, and that if he failed the store would close. I gave him completely unrealistic sales targets, knowing that he wouldn't be able to reach them, but hoping I knew him well enough to know that he'd have a damn good go. I didn't tell him that if the profits *did* see even a small increase, and if he could prove that over time he could better them, I'd negotiated with my company that, instead of just buying the site for their flagship store, they would invest in Hardy's to give it the finance that it needed to reinvent itself. It would be owned by my company – thereby saving Rupert's ancestral home – but the store would keep its name, the staff would keep their jobs and Rupert would keep his place on the board as CEO to help maintain Hardy's core values and keep the family name going.'

I know my mouth has dropped open unattractively but I can't close it.

Joel smiles at me and takes a step closer. 'My bosses needed some convincing, but they have been so pleased with all the press attention that has come with its makeover and they've grown to love that Hardy's is exactly like the traditional British stores we Americans always hope to find over here: small, traditional, homely and welcoming, with core values that can still hold true today. That is what makes Hardy's different and I know it's what will make it successful again. Particularly now it's found its unique identity.' He grabs my hands and pulls me close to him and suddenly the crowd melts away. 'What I'm saying is, Carly – I mean, Evie – 'Hardy's *isn't* going to close. Not now.'

I gasp and throw my arms around Joel, sobbing with relief and joy at what he has just told me. 'Oh my God, Joel, thank you, thank you so much,' I sniff, and pull back to look at him apologetically. 'You saved Hardy's.'

He shrugs modestly. 'No, the Secret Elves did that. I just wish I could have told you all this earlier.' He pauses and takes my hand, stroking it softly with his thumb. 'We messed up a bit, didn't we?' he says, and I nod sadly. 'Do you think we can try again?' he says, studying my face before cupping it and tilting it towards his with his other hand. Then he reaches into his pocket and pulls out an unmistakable duck-egg-blue box, offering it to me. I fleetingly think of my first window display for Menswear, the man in the trilby proffering the Tiffany's box, and wonder if this is what they mean by life imitating art.

'I came here today because I wanted to give you

this,' Joel murmurs. 'I bought it the day I called you from Selfridges and have been carrying it around ever since. I was already crazy about you then.'

I look at Joel in utter disbelief as I take the Tiffany's box and, with shaking fingers, I slowly open it. Inside is a beautiful, glittering platinum, white enamel and diamond ice skater charm. I blink and look into Joel's smoulderingly intense eyes, and for a moment I think that maybe we can make this work. I mean, this, him, well, it's all perfect. It's what any girl would want. The romantic declarations, the expensive gifts . . .

'I hoped it would remind you of our first date and convince you to come home with me to Pennsylvania. Carl— I mean, Evie,' he laughs in embarrassment. 'Please say we can try again.'

I look down at the charm and a misty frost descends over my eyes. I think about the past few weeks, the wonderful times I've had with Joel, the breathtaking dates, the dinners, afternoon teas and nights in fancy hotels. Maybe a girl like me *can* end up with a guy like Joel. But then I shake my head and, as if in a snow globe, a crazy chaos of confused emotions whirl into a frenzy again, and a different picture – and person – pops into my head.

'Come with me, Evie,' he pleads, stroking his thumb across my jaw. I close my eyes and open them again.

'I . . . I,' I mumble as the snow clouds part in

my head and I realize that for the first time in my life, I actually know exactly what I want. Sam. I may not be able to have him, but I know now that Joel isn't the guy for me. This, all of this, it's too much. Tiffany's. Claridge's. America. I'm just Evie, the stockroom girl. And you know what? I'm proud of that.

I hand him back the box and smile through my tears. 'I'm sorry, Joel, it's beautiful but I can't accept this. I think, despite what you say, you want me to be someone I'm not. If not Carly, then maybe your ex.' I look up through my eyelashes and Joel shakes his head. But his eyes reveal more. I know that he isn't seeing me standing here now, he's seeing the lost love, the girl he left behind in Pennsylvania. I'm just an illusion to him, as invisible to him as to almost everyone else. Suddenly a thought occurs to me.

'What was your ex-girlfriend's name?' I ask him gently. 'Joel?'

He looks away and puts his hands in his pockets. A gentle breeze blows through his hair and lifts it slightly. 'Carleen – Carly,' he says, and the name is almost lost in the gust of air.

I nod and squeeze his arm. It all makes sense now.

Suddenly the crowd starts chanting my name. '*EV-IE EV-IE EV-IE . . .*'

Joel looks at me and smiles sorrowfully. 'It wasn't just about her, you know, you have to believe me. You really are wonderful. They all know it too.'

And he gently turns me round to face the store. In the main window, Lily, Felix and the gang are now holding up a big, hand-written sign that says, 'Where's our Christmas Evie?' and I cover my mouth with my gloved hand to stifle a half-cry half-laugh. Joel gives me a gentle little push. 'I think they want you . . . Evie,' he says.

I turn to smile at him. 'I'm sorry things didn't work out,' I say.

'It's OK,' Joel sighs. 'I think I can see where your heart really lies. And mine, too.'

I throw my arms round him and squeeze with all my might. 'Good luck, Joel,' I whisper, then turn and push my way through the jostling crowd and slip inside the store.

As I walk into the beauty department all of Hardy's workforce turn from their frozen positions inside the store's windows and gesture towards me with their hands. I laugh and clamber up into the window, and they all start cheering and applauding. I take my place in the middle of the elves, and Lily and Felix come and kiss me on each cheek and lift my hands up in the air.

Outside flashbulbs pop and the crowd continues to chant my name. I wave shyly, feeling utterly overcome by it all. Only Sam, who is standing next to me remains silent. He stares straight ahead, his kind, handsome face utterly impassive. I turn and look out the window too, and I see Joel standing in the centre of the crowd, looking like some suave movie star. He lifts his hand and waves at me and then I look at Sam again whose lips remain in a thin, tight line.

'Is that him?' he says quietly. 'Is that the guy?'

'Yes,' I reply, and then there is a beat before I speak again. 'The guy who made me realize where I want to be and who I want to be with.' I look back out at the crowd, but Joel has disappeared. 'You,' I whisper softly.

Sam turns away and I worry that I've gone too far, said too much. I see Felix smile at Sam encouragingly as he hands him a small, plain brown box that has been decorated with a garland of threaded cranberries. I look up at Sam quizzically as he passes it silently to me and I open it.

'It's handmade,' Sam says shyly as I lift out the snow globe. 'By Jan. He carved the figures himself. And the building. I asked him to make it when we did the window display.'

'It's beautiful,' I gasp. 'I had no idea he was so talented.' I look up at him. 'It's perfect.'

'I think all these people would say the same of you,' Sam says with a smile, beckoning to the staff, and to Rupert and Sharon, who are standing in front of the window and applauding me. I swallow back another tear and take a closer look at the snow globe. Inside is a perfect replica of Hardy's facade. And in front of it are two figures, kissing. One has long brown hair, indistinguishable to most but if you were to just look closely . . .

'I don't have a girlfriend, you know,' Sam murmurs, and he turns me to face him. 'There is someone . . . but . . . I just didn't explain myself very well . . .' He looks at me with his soft brown eyes. He pauses and I shake the snow globe in front of us both so that tiny flecks of white soar up and then fall softly around the kissing couple. 'It's only ever been you, Evie,' Sam says, and then he is tilting me in his arms and I'm laughing and his lips are on mine and he is kissing me in front of the crowd outside, in front of my friends in here and in front of the most important person of all: Hardy's.

THE END. OR ALMOST . . .

SUNDAY 1 JANUARY

357 Shopping Days Until Christmas

EPILOGUE

'Teeveeee, teeeeveeee!' Lola and Raffy are tugging at my coat sleeves, desperate to get to the top of the hill so they can try out their brand-new sledge.

Primrose Hill is awash with people dressed in big coats and an array of brightly coloured scarves and hats, braving the elements on this snow-capped New Year's Day. Children are sledging down the hill, screaming with delight, parents are nursing coffees (and hangovers) and desperately trying to get the fresh air to revive them, as am I.

Last night was wonderful, the best New Year's Eve *ever*. Rupert threw a party for all of Hardy's staff at the store: those who work on the shop floor and behind the scenes, as well as Hardy's most loyal customers. Everyone brought food and drink, and we all sat on long trestle tables wearing Union Jack hats, eating proper old-fashioned food: quiches, coleslaw and cold meats, jelly and ice cream. It was like being at a street party. We played 1940s tea-dance music, and Iris and Felix lead the dancing like complete pros, with Lily giving lessons to those who needed it. At midnight we all stood in a circle as the snow fell outside, tearfully singing 'Auld Lang Syne'. After all, Hardy's was an acquaintance none of us wanted to forget – and the good news from Head Office was, after our incredible sales performance in the week leading up to Christmas, now we'd never have to.

Mum came with me last night and we had an absolute ball. She's been surprisingly good since her discovery of Dad's affair and he has begged her to come back. He told her he couldn't live without her, but do you know what? Mum seems to think she can. And good on her, I say. She loves being in London; she's been looking after Lola and Raffy in the afternoons now that I'm too busy with the store and she adores being able to see her kids and grandchildren regularly, as well as being independent for the first time in her life. She's even talked about getting herself a job. Delilah has said she'd employ her as a part-time nanny, which I think Mum was considering, until Rupert offered Mum a job out of the blue last night. Apparently, with the financial boost the store has been given by the US company, and our most successful Christmas sales in Hardy's history, Rupert's decided he wants to reopen the salon on the top floor. It's been closed for the past fifteen years, but now he wants someone to manage it. When I told him about Mum he came over and quickly decided she would be 'perfect' for the role. Mum was a bit overwhelmed and told him she hadn't styled hair for years, but Rupert said he wanted her to be in charge of employing staff, working on the reception and being 'the face' of Hardy's salon. To be honest, he couldn't have chosen better. I mean, if he thinks I'm creative and organized, he hasn't seen anything yet: Grace Taylor is a force to be reckoned with.

Mum was absolutely thrilled. She said she couldn't think of anything that would make her happier than being back at Hardy's. I even said, 'What about being back with Dad?' and she laughed and said, 'We'll see,' before downing her glass of champagne.

Delilah's a bit gutted as Mum would have been the perfect nanny to replace me, but she understands that, more than anything, Mum needs her own life now, and it's not like Delilah won't have plenty of time to find another one. After what happened that day at Delilah's house – God was it only a couple of weeks or so ago? – when I found her in such a state in the bedroom, Mum, Will and I forced her to go to the doctor's again and tell him exactly how she's been feeling and he has signed her off work for three months with depression. Delilah and Will are starting marriage counselling next week and Will has decided he's going to resign from his job in the City to start his own business so he can be more flexible with his work and see more of Delilah and the kids. This whole Mum and Dad thing seems to have really pulled them together and it's brilliant to see them back to their best. They even managed to throw a memorable Christmas for us all. Delilah was in her element, being able to do it at her home for the very first time. Jonah and Noah came over and even Mum seemed to love the fact that she was off duty for the first time in thirty-odd years.

Only Dad wasn't there. None of us was quite ready to wish him season's greetings. It's going to take some time to forget his behaviour, but knowing my family, I'm sure we'll get there. We Taylors are a forgiving bunch.

'C'mon, Teevee, c'MON!' Lola says as she stumbles up the snow-covered hill again, ready and raring for ride number two.

'OK, race you, Lola!' I say, wiping my snow-covered bottom and grabbing Raffy and scooping him under my arm as Lola and I run squealing towards the top of the hill. I wanted to spend today with them because I'm moving into my own place next week. It's only a cheap little unfurnished studio flat down the road in the far-less-glamorous Kentish Town but I'm so excited because it's going to be *mine*. And knowing that I can finally afford it on my new salary is amazing. Because I guess that's the big news. Since I was unveiled as the creative brains behind Hardy's Secret Elves, Rupert (who, by the way, very much knows my name now) told me I was wasted in the stockroom and that he wanted me to be the store's creative director! He said that whilst he is happiest dealing with the financial side of things, and Sharon is great at managing the staff, they needed someone with my creative vision to oversee the store's brand; which means styling and continuing to develop its overall 'look' as well as sourcing products for the store from small local businesses. Because after the success of the WI soaps (they were Hardy's Christmas bestseller), Rupert wants Hardy's USP to be that we sell items that other department stores don't. I even get a budget to travel around the UK to find new, and old, products. Obviously vintage is to be a key selling point, but he also wants new products on the proviso that everything we sell in the store is made and manufactured in Britain. It's a brilliant idea, so traditionally British and so very Hardy's.

Oh, and Carly has a new job too! She was called into Rupert's office after me and told that her role as assistant manager wasn't working out but that he wanted Carly to be the store's in-house personal shopping training manager. He said that her flair for understanding customers' individual style needs and responding to them was a rare talent, and it was one he wanted her to share with every single Hardy's staff member so that they can all give our customers a uniquely personal service. It's the perfect job for her and she seems really happy.

Even Felix's efforts didn't go unnoticed. He's back on the shop floor where he belongs as a part-time duty manager. The customers love him, as do the staff. Especially one in particular.

Speaking of which, Lily's tearoom is making a killing. She's got some staff now to do all the running around so all she has to do is focus on being a hostess – and she's the best there is. Everyone thinks so. Since going on breakfast TV to talk about Hardy's makeovers she's become quite the local celebrity and really draws the crowds. She's even writing a book about Hardy's one-hundred-year history.

I'm panting as we reach the top of the hill again and I drop Raffy down on his feet as I wave towards the two smiling people who have appeared at the top of the hill, holding hands.

'SAM!' I shout, waving and feeling my heart pound out of my chest. I am unbelievably nervous about this meeting. I mean, it's complicated. But then again, life always is, isn't it?

'SAAAAM!' echo Raffy and Lola gleefully, running behind me. They've become very fond of Sam over the past couple of weeks and are as anxious to meet his mystery guest as I am.

'HELLLOOO!' shouts back Sam as an adorable little 5-year-old girl wearing a bright red coat and cream woolly hat, with a thatch of curly strawberry-blond hair exploding from beneath it, comes tearing over the hill and skids to a halt in front of Lola and Raffy. She is crumpled and cute, and has the same endearing, instantly likeable manner as her dad. She looks a lot like her mum too, Sam's ex, Ella. They split up a couple of years after Sophie was born but have tried to remain friends for her sake. That's why I saw them at Hamleys together that time. They were buying Sophie's Christmas presents as they don't want her to be spoiled by getting competitive gifts from them both, like other kids whose parents have split up. And Sam was meant to be looking after Sophie the night of our last pub get-together so that Ella could go to her Christmas party. It's really admirable how they've put aside their differences for her. It's so grown up of them, and yet they were both only in their early twenties when they had her.

I glance down and see her looking up at me quizzically.

'Hi, my name's Sophie and I'm five and a quarter and . . .' She pauses and then grins toothily at Raffy and Lola, who have been subdued by this confident little girl, before smiling at her dad.

Sam wanders slowly towards us, grinning proudly. He kisses me on the lips and slips his hand into mine before putting his other hand on Sophie's shoulder.

'I see you've met my Soph, then,' he says, and I nod and squeeze his hand.

'She's just like you,' I smile and look at them both, not quite believing that this is happening. I've been wanting to meet Sophie ever since Sam explained that the other girl in his life wasn't his girlfriend, but his daughter. Sam decided he wanted to spend as much time with his little girl as possible before she started school, which is why he chose to stick with doing deliveries and not pursue his photography ambitions until now. I've got bags of respect for him. He's given up so much to be the best dad he can be. It's kind of made me fall in love with him even more, if that were possible.

'Sophie, sweetie, this is Evie. The one I've told you all about,' and he nudges her gently.

Sophie looks at her dad, then up at me inquisitively, squinting a little as the sun bursts through the powdery clouds. She is silent for a moment but then she smiles broadly and slips her hand into my free one, the one that Sam isn't holding.

'WOW!' she says, gazing up at me wondrously. '*You're* Christmas Evie? Can you help me meet Santa next year?'

And as we stand holding hands at the top of the hill that's bathed in the bright, fresh light of the New Year morning, I suddenly feel sure that I'll never be unforgettable again.

Not to anyone who matters anyway.